The Chemistry of Us
Drop of Poison Book One

Cadyn James

Tropes

Enemies-to-Lovers
Forced Proximity
Morally Gray Hero
Badass Heroine
Power Struggles & Control Dynamics
Cat-and-Mouse Tension
Dark Romantic Suspense
Undercover Operations & Espionage
Antihero Vibes
Slow-Burn Destruction
Psychological Warfare & Manipulation
Obsession & Toxic Attraction
Brutal, Gripping Action Scenes
Possessive / Protective Hero in Denial
Woman on the Run / Secret Identity
Touch Him and Die
Mutual Destruction
Wound Tending as Foreplay
He Knows Before She Does
Forced Team-Up / Reluctant Allies
Dangerous Chemistry (Literally & Figuratively)
Weaponized Sexuality
Breaking the Unbreakable
The Hunter Becomes the Hunted
The One Person You Can't Lie To
Dominance Games Masquerading as Romance
He Tells Her What She's Feeling Before She Admits It
Loyalty vs. Morality

Trigger Warnings

Violence & Graphic Action
Torture & Intense Psychological Manipulation
Dubious Morality & Power Imbalances
Sexual Content & Explicit Scenes
PTSD & Past Trauma
BDSM Elements
Toxic Relationships & Manipulation
Mentions of Murder & Assassinations
Betrayal & Backstabbing
Death & Threats of Death
Drug Use & Poisoning
Survival Sex & Weaponized Intimacy
Voyeurism & Surveillance Themes
Emotional / Psychological Breakdown
Moral Corruption & Justified Violence
Compromised Consent & Psychological Warfare
Revenge as Motivation
Chronic Hyper-Vigilance & Paranoia
Use of Pain as Control
Threats of Sexual Violence
Forced Compliance / Coerced Actions
Self-Destructive Behavior
Manipulative Relationships
Mild Dub-Con Undertones
Abduction / Captivity Elements
Use of Chemicals/Drugs for Control
Interrogation & Psychological Torture
Bodily Autonomy Issues
Stockholm Syndrome / Trauma Bonding Themes
Betrayal from Trusted Allies

Chapter 1
Neva

The scent of Elmer's glue and spilled juice clung to my skin as I watched my students leave.

"Bye, Ms. de Witte. See you on Fursday!" Jaime Winston yelled as he raced out of the room to his waiting mother's arms. His bright blue eyes almost consumed his entire face. Matched with the freckles that dotted every inch of free space across his cheeks, he was one of the cutest kids I'd ever met.

"Bye, Jamie. Be good. And remember, it's TH-ursday, not Fursday." I waved him off as his mom gripped his hand before they turned to leave the fenced area of the elite private elementary school.

The rest of the kindergartners ran around like hyped up psychos as they smashed art projects full of cotton balls and popsicle sticks into their bags and raced from the room like it had caught on fire. Waving goodbye to each of them, I smiled at the waiting parents and siblings through the open door.

Another teacher in-service day made for a short week for my students.

They're not your students, Lark; keep your shit together, I mentally reminded myself. My fingers twitched around the door handle as I struggled to breathe around the hole in my belly for a moment. Then I shook it off with a wave of anger sweeping away the pain. This wasn't a life for me. The soft, the easy. I brightened my smile and continued to wave.

"Ms. de Witte," a low, familiar voice said from behind me.

Turning, I felt my belly jump before I got myself back under control. "Mr. Jorgenssen." Sticking out my hand, I waited for him to take it.

He studied me for long moments, just like he always did. As if he didn't quite trust the new kindergarten teacher for his beloved Ada. But when he slid his palm across mine, I felt that sense of grief from seconds ago slide into triumph. "How did she do today?"

Pulling my hand back, I put my expression into grimmer lines. "She had a couple bad spots, but she made it through like the little champ she is. Only one incident that necessitated going to the nurse."

The barely perceptible lines at the corners of his eyes crinkled as his lips pursed for a fraction of a second. The blond hair and bright blue eyes matched his daughter's, but that's where all similarity ended. Ada wasn't a psychopath like her father. No, she was a little girl who felt everything strongly. Too strongly, really.

"Another nosebleed?" he asked.

I nodded, my long dark hair sliding down my back. "Yes. She couldn't get it stopped, so I sent her to Nurse Maddy. She came back within about twenty minutes."

"Poppy!" The girl herself danced across the room, throwing herself at her dad's long legs.

Bending down, he picked her up and held her in his arms. Pushing his nose into her blonde hair, he whispered something in her ear. She giggled and nodded. "Yes, but it didn't get on my dress. See?" She pushed his head back and proudly displayed the front of her immaculate blue dress.

"I don't care about the dress, baby. Just that you had another nosebleed." He looked at me, his blue eyes flashing midnight.

I gave him a sad smile. "You'll get it figured out and we'll keep doing our best while she's here, Mr. Jorgenson. With the marvels of modern medicine, rarely anything goes unanswered for too long."

2

Ada shifted and smiled at me. "Bye, Ms. de Witte. Thanks for your help today." She blew me a kiss and laid her head on her dad's shoulder, then petted a hand down his chest as if she could tell how upset he was.

Mr. Oskar Jorgenssen dipped his chin in my direction. "We'll see you on Thursday, Ms. de Witte."

I smiled and nodded. "I'll definitely be here." Waiting for them to leave, I let the door close and then locked it. Walking around the room, I put tiny chairs up on little desks, tossed the toys back in their bins, tidied up the markers and art supplies.

Quashing the yearning that bubbled up inside me with each task, I had a blank mind and a hard heart by the time I finished. This life wasn't real. Just like all my others, it was nothing but a means to an end. Now if I could just force myself to remember that.

My smartwatch buzzed on my wrist. Looking down, I blew out a breath at the message. Just like that, I was smashed face first back into reality. Like being plunged into the Arctic Sea naked, I was awake, alert, and aware.

And more than ready to shrug this disaster of a day off my shoulders.

**

Exactly seventy-six minutes later, I walked into a small hipster café off West Ninth Street. It smelled like burnt espresso and overpriced ambition with a whiny soundtrack to give that push of emotive hipster I hated with every fiber of my being. Of course, this is where he demanded I meet him. It fit him to the fucking core.

Smiling at the hostess, I nodded and pointed near the back where my party already waited.

"Have a great night," she offered as I walked by her.

"You, too." There was no way in hell this was going to be a great night. Not unless I could get out of here in the next twenty-four minutes. And considering who I was meeting, that didn't seem likely.

Two tables from being at the very back of the restaurant, my handler waited. Dreads on such a pale man just didn't make sense to me. But it wasn't my head, and it wasn't my hair, so in the end, it really didn't matter. He didn't bother to stand up as I approached. Hell, he barely even acknowledged my presence. With barely a flick of his index finger, he indicated I should sit down.

3

Biting back the anger that rested on the tip of my tongue, I simply did as ordered. Sliding into the chair, I tucked my feet under my seat and scooted forward. I knew what I looked like, had no illusions of what others saw. When coupled with my handler, we definitely fit in with this quirky group of angsty twenty- and thirty-somethings.

I sat in silence, allowing it to bloom like one of my pretty flowers. He'd called me here, he could start talking. I enjoyed the quiet too much to invite his voice into my ears. Really, I just needed this entire job done as soon as humanly possible.

Gods, please let it be over soon.

"You didn't check in," Brantley eventually said, not bothering to look up from his menu.

I waited him out. Let him stew in his own juices of inferiority. He would know, without a doubt, who was actually in charge. This fucker didn't have the balls, the power, or the confidence to do anything but bitch and moan.

When he finally raised his head to glare at me, I gave him a smile, nodded. "No, I didn't. This isn't my first job, Brantley. Hell, this isn't even my tenth. I don't actually need a babysitter." I folded my hands in my lap, struggling to keep the derision out of my voice. The fact he thought he was the senior agent in this fucked up little duo made me want to splash something fatal in his drink.

He really looked at me as he slapped the laminated paper down on the table in front of him. "You really think you're in charge here, Lark? That's cute." His upper lip curled in disdain and condescension. "Just do your damn job and check in like the good little asset you are. No one likes a liability."

His brown eyes went cold as frozen dog shit on a January morning. "You'll check in when I say you check in, Larkspur. Not the other way around. I refuse to fuck up my career because you don't know how to play by the rules. You say this isn't your first assignment, then prove it. But keep fucking with me, and I can make it your last."

Smiling, I gave a flirtatious laugh and curled my hair behind my ear. "Oh, Brantley. You have no idea what you're saying, you silly goose." My green eyes held his death in their depths; he just didn't know how to read the signs.

He seemed to remember that we were supposed to be playing a loving couple instead of handler and asset. Putting his hand across the table, he wiggled his fingers at me.

"But, pumpkin, I really do. Just say you'll do it my way from now on. You'll like it better, I promise you."

Sincerity rang through his tone, and even knowing he hated me to his core, I couldn't tell if he was actually lying or not. It really sounded like he loved me and just wanted me to follow his lead.

Psychopath, thy name is Brantley.

Sliding my palm over his, I gripped his palm when he tried to jerk it back. Facing the back wall as I was, I didn't have to worry about everyone else seeing my face as I let the cover drop. "I'll check in when I have something to say." I pressed my fingers into his flesh and felt his skin go damp. "Do you ever wonder how I've survived this long in my line of work?"

His brow furrowed, confusion on his face. "What the hell are you talking about?"

I smiled prettily, walking my nails from his palm up to his more vulnerable wrist. "Handlers like you come and go. You sweep in, try to take all the credit, wash back out to shore to move on." I caught a vein under one of the points of my nails. "Me, though, Brantley?" I leaned forward as if to whisper sweet nothings in his ear. "I survive. I'm still here, and honey pie, you've got nothing I haven't already beat and put in my scrapbook."

He flinched, the muscles around his eyes crinkling even as his pupils went to pinpricks. His arm trembled under my grip. As I watched, he tried to shake it off, to ignore the warning, to reestablish his dominance. "You think you're untouchable, too valuable to lose. I have the power to pull you off this mission. Make it so you're never out in the field again."

I tipped my head to the side, a pitying smile stretched over my mouth. "And what do you think that looks like, Brantley? Pulling me out, wasting all the resources I represent to both our agencies, letting the people we're after just slip through your fingers?" I let another stretch of silence fill the space between us, leaning in just enough to allow him to hear my next words. "You and I both know you don't have that kind of power."

Sliding a tune of joy into my tone, I eased back and added, "Here's how things are going to continue on this assignment. Pay attention this time, I don't think you were focusing when I said this just a moment ago: I'll check in when I have something to say. Keep trying to put me on a leash, and I'll show you how I earned my nickname." As I

5

pulled my hand from his, I scraped one of my sharp nails over the center of his palm.

I sat back and crossed my legs. With no small amount of joy, I watched as sweat beaded on his upper lip. "How does that sound, lover?"

He nodded and ripped his hand from the table and hurriedly wiped it on the fabric napkin, as if that would have saved him had I chosen to do something. His smile wobbled at the edges, but the pink dusting his cheeks told me the real story. "Careful, Lark. You're playing a dangerous game."

My laugh was all smoke and satin sheets. "You have no idea what kind of game this truly is. Because I don't play. I win. Don't get in my way on this, Brantley. I will end you before I let them out of my grasp again." Making a show of looking at my watch, I felt true excitement zip through me for the first time since getting this asshole's text.

Getting up, I leaned over the table and brushed my lips over his cheek. "I'm sorry, babe. But I've got to run. Order me something and we'll eat it at home on the couch. I'll even let you pick the movie this time." I watched the muscles of his jaw clench as I moved back.

"You're an uppity bitch for someone who doesn't know how expendable she really is." His whispered words only sounded petulant and whiny.

I titled my head, raised my brows. "Expendable?" I smiled down at him for a long moment, that throbbing silence giving my words extra weight. "And yet, here I am." I smiled wider as his throat bobbed around a hard swallow. "And there you are."

Spinning on my heel, I turned and winded my way back through the growing crowd. I felt his gaze stab me in the back with every step I took further away from him.

As I pushed through the door and back onto the street, I smiled for real. I would have just enough time to get a cab back to my place, change, and make it to the club. The one no one could know about. Praying that I would find a good partner, I hurried forward and hailed one of the seemingly omnipresent yellow cars.

**

Almost there.
So close.
Keep going.

6

Another moan filtered from my mouth as the guy between my legs thrust for home. Maybe this time I would actually get off.

"So fucking good, baby. Yeah, just like that." His pace picked up and his thrusts lost all rhythm. A low groan flowed between his lips as he slammed into me one more time and stayed there, his head tossed back on his shoulders, his grimace glinting under the low lights of the private room I'd reserved.

And just like that, my budding orgasm dissolved. Again. Struggling to keep the grimace off my face, I wrapped my arms around the guy as he crashed down against me. "That was amazing. Thank you." I pressed a kiss into his sweaty hair, the scent of a hard-working man the slightest balm to my grieving body.

He shuddered as he struggled to get his breathing back under control. After a long moment, he mumbled into my shoulder, "That was awesome." On shaky arms, he hoisted himself up so he could look down at me. "What did you say your name was again?"

"Ambrielle." No reason for him to figure out the real me. I wouldn't be seeking him out again.

His crooked smile no longer even made my lady bits twitch. "I'm Gabe."

As if I didn't know everything about this guy already. I wasn't stupid enough to ask just anyone to be my partner, no matter what club I was in.

Now I just needed him to leave so I could finish myself off. Or he could stay and watch the show, but I doubted he had anything left in his proverbial tank. Although to be honest, I wasn't sure shoving the knowledge down his throat that he hadn't satisfied me would be a great impression at the club especially since it was only my second time to be here.

Smiling a little as he dragged his softening cock out of my depths, I nodded. "I remember." And I'll be putting an X next to your name, I added mentally.

Getting up and off me, he held his hand down as if to help me get up. Chagrin twisted my lips as I let him pull me upright. Too bad he couldn't have helped me get off. Oh well, it wasn't his fault, I guess.

"You're new here, right?" he asked as he stepped back and found his club gear.

Nodding, I went to the far side of the room and gathered a blanket. Did he remember nothing of our negotiations? That kind of thing could get him killed in my world. Clinging to my polite voice like a lifeline, I answered the same question for the second time tonight. "Yeah. This is only my second time at Subterra."

I'd gone through all the other clubs in the city and the requirements to get into this one had been brutal. It was also my last chance to find some kind of safe haven during my off-hours, so here I was. Another lost orgasm and terrible personal interaction.

What is said about people doing, saying, or being anything to get their way wasn't wrong. I could count myself in that number as well. In fact, I could probably be the president of that particular club. There wasn't anything I wouldn't do to make sure I achieved my desired outcome.

He zipped up and came over to me. "That was fucking amazing. So the next time I'm here, I'll look for you." He pecked a chaste kiss on my cheek and walked for the door. When he pushed it open, I heard him say, "Oh, sorry, man. Didn't see you there. Room's occupied. You'll have to wait." Then the door closed behind him.

Rushing over, I locked the handle. I didn't need some rando perving on me while I finally caught that orgasm Gabe had failed to give me. Walking to the far side of the room where the toys I'd brought were set up, I grabbed a thrusting dildo, a clit sucker, some nipple clamps, and a gag.

Toys in hand, I felt the breath back up in my lungs as my belly twisted. I mean…I'd brought exactly what I knew would work for me. But he didn't touch a single one. Was it that hard for men to figure me out? Was I too uptight? Prudish? Or did my body just not work like everyone else's? Maybe I had some kind of defect that prevented me from achieving orgasm by someone else.

Sighing and pushing the thoughts away again, I laid back on the table. Since I'd made Gabe suit up, I needed a bit of the lube that came standard in every room. Putting some on the dildo, I slid it up inside my still needy pussy. When that was where I wanted it, I put the nipple clamps on and tightened them down. Finally ready for the finale, I lay back, stuffed the gag between my lips, and settled the clit sucker into place.

I turned on the dildo and the clit sucker and immediately my body jolted back into high gear. Knowing from experience that I couldn't want it too much, I let the toys work me over. I had the room for the entire night, so I didn't have to worry about anyone else needing to get in here, no matter what Gabe thought.

It took some time. More time than it should have, but not overly long. At least not to my estimation. But eventually I got there. That edge tightened my body, danced over my nerves, and slid down my spine straight into my pussy. My back arched as that first orgasm ripped through me with all the subtlety of a Mack truck. The gag stifled my screams, restricting my breathing in the best way possible.

As my body adjusted to the rush, I kept the toys running inside and on me. With my free hand, I tightened the nipple clamps a little, adding to the sensation rocking over and through my body. Soon enough, the next orgasm washed over me. It was calmer, but lasted longer. And it was exactly what my body needed as it relaxed into the calm once more.

Mental fantasies raced by in my mind's eye. All the things I had tried, all the things still on my sexual bucket list. It would have been fine if they had been solo fantasies. But no, my fantasies always included someone else. Some nameless, faceless man.

Because the universe knew it wasn't any of the men I'd partnered up with over the last twenty years. Two decades of being sexually active and not a single one of the boyfriends, situationships, service tops, long-term relationships, or supposed masters in the BDSM lifestyle I'd been with had been able to rock my body as well as I could on my own. They certainly didn't have what it took to quiet my mind, that was for damned sure.

Tears burned at the back of my eyes.

But I had to push those thoughts away, too. Push them far away and into the deepest parts of me or I would never get rid of the itching ache inside my body and mind. That only came with the blessed silence of multiple orgasms. And I needed that silence more than usual. Especially after the day I'd just endured.

So I shoved those thoughts aside as well. Nothing but sexy thoughts for the rest of the night. Clearing my mind, I sank back into my body, realizing that my third orgasm had died a swift death with my mental meandering.

Gritting my teeth, I began the familiar count to thirty-four. I had no idea why that number was magical, but it was *my* number. And I wasn't stupid enough to screw up what I knew worked for me.

When my mind flipped over to the unicorn number, I felt my body smooth out and relax against the table and the toys. Sensations washed over me as I allowed my mind to float from feeling to feeling. Our bodies truly were fantastic machines. Most of my training involved how to kill those machines, but the opposite side of that coin presented lovely knowledge when applied correctly.

Orgasm number three rushed up and bitch slapped me, carting Four and Five in her wake. My thighs shook and the soles of my feet began to burn. But that itchy ache still lived inside me like a dragon in a cave hoarding the precious treasure. The treasure I was determined to claim as my own, even if only for tonight.

Struggling to breathe through my nose, I gripped the gag between my teeth a little harder. A bright spark of pain slicing through my jaw told me I needed to keep an eye on that. A busted tooth wasn't on my to-do list. I certainly didn't have time to deal with it during the week.

With a quick twist, I tightened the nipple clamps again, this time tightening them so much that it made my back arch. Now we were getting somewhere. It was time to overwhelm my body. Steal the dragon's treasure and claim my blessed silence.

Hitting the button on the clit sucker to Steal My Soul level, I bumped up the power of the dildo as well. That vague flutter deep inside told me I was on the verge of something great.

Sucking in as deep breaths as I could, I settled my body and waited for Six to show up. He was elusive, content to stalk me from afar. Never getting close enough to capture, but always leaving me with a vague peek of victory. As I waited in patient anticipation, I found myself searching the ceiling idly.

The owners of Subterra had left most of the rooms in this section of the club as their original industrial spaces, just blocked off into private rooms. The exposed rafters held some intriguing hooks, ropes, chains, and furniture that could be lowered and lifted, depending on what the occupants wanted. It really was the best sex club I'd ever been in, so the high requirements for even probationary membership were understandable.

As Six continued to flirt with my nerve endings, I realized there was a small red light near the ceiling, tucked back into the puzzle of trusses. I narrowed my gaze on it.

Carbon monoxide and smoke alarms had static red lights, right?

But some instinct told me it wasn't an alarm. No, I could almost feel the eyes on me. Like a physical caress, as if whoever sat on the other end of that steady crimson bulb watched me. Studied me.

I stared at that little light, a myriad of emotions filtering through me. Curiosity?...no, that wasn't quite right. It was something though. Honestly, it felt like some kind of pull, some kind of ruthless urgency.

I stared at it just as I felt Six's pre-workout kick in.

Fucking golden chain and jasmine.

It was *need*.

The realization blared through my mind even as I jolted, my body stiffening as I fought to get free of the toys I'd put into play. Fuck. I had to get out of here. I had to let management know that some perv had put up cameras without telling anyone.

I should move. I should stop. I should...do...something.

I didn't.

Instead of continuing to fight against my body's need to exert control, my legs splayed open. My breath rushed out of my nose as my body relaxed completely against the contrary commands of my mind. I stared directly at that little red dot as my world got wrecked by Six.

The dildo slid out of my pussy as I squirted all over the table, my breathing backing up behind the gag. The clit sucker relentlessly attacked my body and shoved me into Seven's arms. My nipples felt like they could cut glass, they were so tight and hard.

Holy bleeding heart. No, no, no. NO! This couldn't be happening. It wasn't happening. This was nothing more than the toys doing their jobs, my mind finally getting into the fucking groove and letting the toys do what toys did.

But some part of me—some part I refused to acknowledge—knew that it was the eyes on me that shook my body like I was nothing more than a bag of bones. It was knowing that someone sat on the other end of that camera and watched me.

It took long moments for me to remember I could throw the clit sucker across the room. Even longer for me to rip the gag from my mouth so I could get real oxygen into my starved body. And longer still for me to pull the clamps off my nipples. That hurt like a fucking bitch and brought tears to my eyes as the blood surged back into the peaks while my nerves fired at an almost constant rate.

But the silence I'd been chasing finally arrived. That sacred quiet filled my mind and suffused my body with white static. The last thing I remembered before the dark took me was that the little red light near the ceiling seemed to…blink?

Or maybe I just imagined it with my now satiated, blessedly quiet mind. Maybe.

Almost as if whoever manned it said, "Good girl."

I fell into the all-encompassing peace and calm with a smile.

Chapter 2
Rome

"Fuck, sweetheart. Relax, take your time," I murmured to the woman on the screen. She fought and seemingly argued with herself to get some relief. The thinnest veneer of anger danced over her skin as if she fought some inner battle even while she lay splayed out on that table like a shrine to goddesses of old.

She was chasing orgasms, but she held her body under almost militant control. There were precious few times when she allowed her body the chance to simply exist. I only noticed them because they were so at odds with the expression on her face.

I knew exactly what to look for in a target. The hesitation, the nonverbal communication leakage, the way the body betrays itself mere instants before the mind locks down all control. And she—this woman, this mystery—was no different.

Unable to look away from her, I saw a single hip roll that had my breath backing up in my throat, her brows smoothing out as her toes curled, and her neck arching back as if waiting for a man to bend down and catch it in his mouth. My mouth watered at the idea of giving her that scrape of teeth even as I saw her fingers curl up as if she reached for something, someone.

I could have sworn she was calling for me with her body. The way she stared directly into the camera on the ceiling. If I didn't know there was no possibility for it, I would have been hard pressed to say she wasn't enticing me directly. But I did know the truth and so I sat there stewing in my own desire.

"Good girl." A smile stretched my mouth as I watched the woman finally sink down onto the table under her as if it were a thick luxurious bed in a posh hotel instead of four inches of foam and a faux leather covering in a renovated warehouse. Her long dark hair splayed out under her head like a matted halo. Her chest rose and fell in a smooth rhythm, indicating deep sleep.

I didn't realize she planned to stay in the room when I'd all but crashed into the guy exiting it in the hallway on my way to my office. We'd been dealing with some theft, and I brought up the room's camera feed to watch the cleaning crew I'd expected to find. When I saw she was still there, and treating herself so well, I hadn't been able to look away from the screen.

Watching people have sex had lost its appeal a long time ago. And while there was a laundry list of things I could claim as my personal kinks, voyeurism wasn't one of them. It didn't do anything for me personally. Not even porn had been able to trip my proverbial trigger. Not for years now. Cold, clinical, and impersonal would never be anything that interested me.

Nothing about this woman was any of those things. Whoever she was, though, she kept my interest. Most women I knew weren't that dedicated—in any area of their lives. Angry or not. But she persisted, doing what needed to be done to make sure she got the outcome she wanted. Assuming the guy I almost plowed over in the hallway hadn't gotten her to that sleepy, sexy state, she took matters into her own hands. And from my count, it took a bit more than a single orgasm release to get her sated.

Poor guy never had a chance.

Her independence was sexy even while it made a vague anger wash through me. She was complex. Intricate. Which was more than I could say for ninety-nine percent of everyone else who came through the doors of Subterra.

Checking the reservations sheet, I saw that the room had been reserved for the entire evening. My brows winged up. Whoever she was, she wasn't hurting for money. It cost more than a month's rent to reserve a room here for that long. And that knowledge added even more mystery to her.

Most wealthy women I knew couldn't be bothered to do anything for themselves. Up to and including chasing their own orgasms. They took the term pillow princesses to new and terrifying heights.

The door on the other side of my computer screen slid open with barely a sigh. My finger stalled in the air above the button that would close the screen. A single tap would give her privacy, shove her back into the void with the other nameless, faceless patrons in Subterra right now.

I willed myself to hit that button. It should have been easy, routine. Nothing but a flick of my finger, a single motion I've done a million times before.

But I didn't move.

My arm tensed—a fraction of an instant too long. A moment of hesitation I had no business entertaining. My chest tightened, something hot uncoiling in my belly. Not just attraction…no, this was somehow deeper. Something dangerous.

She looked soft. Touchable. A contrast too sharp to ignore

Sebastian 'Det Cord' Baumgartner stood in the open door. His dark blond hair scraped back off his face, his brown eyes a little wild. "Keys, we've got an issue." His big frame took up almost the full doorway for a short moment, then he spun on his heel and fled back out the door.

His words shook me back to myself.

Watching her was a mistake. One I corrected with a sharp stab of my finger on the mouse's button. She was just another woman using one of my businesses. I would enjoy the revenue and move on to the next objective.

Getting up, I followed after him. If Det was spooked, then something must be really wrong. My second-in-command didn't get anxious about anything. Being a demolitions expert in our past lives had cured him of that very quickly.

Pushing out into the office section of our multi-business building, I saw the rest of our old platoon and now business partners—my brothers—scattered around our usual meeting place during the work week. The eight of us probably seemed a bit scary to the casual observer. For those in the know, we were deadly.

"What's the problem?" I looked around at each face, saw similar lines of...anticipation? My heart rate bumped up a few notches.

"SRD is back on scene. And we've got positive contact," Iggy, our tech guy, said. He flicked his hand over the touch screen that served as the main table in our private conference room. That table was his baby. I'm pretty sure he treated it better than the women he fucked.

"Show me," I demanded. The Sisterhood of the Rising Dawn was the one target we'd been unable to take down. It also resulted in all of us getting booted from the only real family we'd ever known.

I didn't have to make the demand a second time. We all knew and understood our objective, our mission. The tension in the room shifted as postures straightened and focus snapped into place.

"Lights," Iggy called out. With a few taps of his fingers, the space over the table lit up and filled with holographic surveillance photos.

The room immediately dimmed—none of us had time for doubt, for uncertainty, for hesitation. Doubt got men killed. Uncertainty made widows. Hesitation filled coffins. We had a score to settle and we wouldn't be losing this time.

Solana Nicollier and her lover appeared to be having all kinds of fun traipsing around Venice. Long black hair in her signature braid hung to her ass. It had been just above her hips the last time I saw a picture of her. Amazing what time could do. And the fact that it had been at least two years since she wiggled through our grasp infuriated me.

"Who's that with her?" Judging from his height compared to the diminutive Solana, I put the male at about six-foot even. Blond hair, blue eyes, tats flowing out from under his rolled up long sleeves to twist and twine around his fingers. Not quite the muscular build of Det—the resident powerlifter—but he wasn't slacking. This guy took care of himself.

"Viktor Valek," Iggy replied. "Czech national with ties to just about every game in the EU and Sand Pit. He's a dealer."

"Specialization?"

Iggy shook his head. "Whatever he can get his hands on. He's not picky."

"What does Uncle Sam say?"

"My contact's got nothing on Valek," Aidan said. Our communications guy had contacts in every part of the government and most corners of the world. If he didn't know it, it wasn't worth knowing. "SRD is still not considered a terrorist organization, though. Just so everyone's on the same page."

Scoffs, snarls, and growls sounded from around the room. "Those fuckers are worse than ISIS and the Church, but they're not terrorists?" Markus asked from across the room where one of our chairs groaned under his immense size.

Aidan shook his head. "Not as of yet. And we still don't have the evidence NorCom requires."

Grinding my teeth, I just nodded. The evidence we'd already gathered should have been enough. More than enough, really.

"I still say someone's dirty," Markus voiced what we were all thinking.

"Add it to the list, Squirrel," Aidan said. "We don't have any info on that either. But one of my Twists *might* have gotten a sniff. The faintest of whiffs." He held up his hand before anyone could say anything else. "I'll let you all know as soon as I do."

Biting back the words that gathered at the back of my throat, I knew better than to pester him. Aidan might have a call sign of Banshee, but he didn't speak until he had something to say. If he said he would share when he had something, I would have to wait until he was ready.

"Where are we with Nicollier?" Turning, I asked our company sniper, Beck Maddox. The gentle Irishman sat off by himself. The smallest bubble of space surrounded him, but he was still an integral part of our group. He'd saved all of us more than once.

"While it's not as extensive as Banshee's, my network doesn't have anything either." Beck shook his head.

Shit. No one had anything on this bitch? Nothing? How could that be, especially in this day and age of information transfer and surveillance?

"I think we might need to go about this a different way," Jay offered. Our medic lifted his head and met each of our gazes with his blue one. "If what we've been doing hasn't been working—and it damn sure hasn't—then we need to think of some other ways to attack. That or we're going to be even farther up the creek and still using our hands for paddles. I, for one, am tired of shoveling shit out of our path."

"And what do you suggest we do?" I asked, crossing my arms over my chest and leaning against the wall. "We've tried just about every approach imaginable."

Jay shook his blonde head. "No idea, Keys, but we're running out of time. And the stack of bodies is getting higher."

Like we all didn't know that. We'd lost more than a double handful of our own to this bitch. Not to mention the hundreds and thousands we could attribute to her group.

"Any movement on the cocktail?" I asked. We had to stay focused on the steps. The minutiae. If we got caught up in the hopelessness of the bigger picture, we would fail, just like we had before.

Iggy nodded and flicked his hands over the screen again. "Yeah, we actually did. And I verified it through five different independent labs. All of them came back with the same result."

Finally, something new to use. I jerked my chin at him. "Then read it off."

"I've got that part, Keys." Jay stood up and moved to the desk. "Essentially, we've got a two-step system. First up is what looks like a massive bacterial infection involving the central nervous system, kidneys, lungs, and liver. They run all kinds of tests, including ricin panels. But it's not ricin. No, this is done by none other than the Flame Lily."

Iggy brought up a picture of a pretty pink flower that looked like one of those upside down claw hands in the grocery store machines. Spindly pink leaves curling up over a spaced crown of delicate red spikes with flower parts at the tips. It looked like something my mother would have in her front garden.

"Then, when you're whining and crying about not being dead, the real fun starts," Jay added with a slight laugh.

We all rolled our eyes. Our medic had a sick and twisted sense of humor, which had helped earn him the call sign Giggles.

"The second step: you spike a fever. This isn't just any kind of fever, though. Your skin starts to blister. Then your skin starts bubbling up, kinda like a volcano. But instead of shoving pus and blood out the top, a black ooze rises." The characteristic smile that decorated his face vanished. "These fuckers have somehow managed to weaponize a flesh-eating bacteria and hooked it to a poison that disrupts and enlarges vital organs."

I blinked as I tried to organize the information in my head. "So you're saying that you get sick with what looks like some kind of food poisoning on steroids. It does substantial damage to your body including enlarging vital organs. Then, when you wish you were dying, your body literally eats itself from the inside out, feasting on said bigger organs?"

Jay nodded. "And you get to live with that pain for another four days while your body dies around you. Here's the kicker, since no one knows you have a bastardized version of necrotizing fasciitis on the inside until your body erupts in black volcanos, all they can do is sit around and watch you die. In the cases they've managed to autopsy, the secondary bacterial infection is so pervasive there is no way they could remove all of it."

"So intense pain followed by gruesome, horrific death," Markus said.

Jay dipped his chin. "And no amount of morphine is gonna help."

"Just a bullet to the brain," Beck said.

Jay turned, looked at our sniper, jabbed a finger in his direction. "Exactly."

"Are the bodies contagious after death?" I asked.

Jay shifted to look back at me. "Yeah, Keys. The people who did the autopsies lost four of their own before they realized what was happening. Full HazMat gear is now standard to cut up the dead. We still don't know how long the pathogens are active after death. From the last successful autopsy, we're at six weeks post-mortem and still fully contagious."

My mouth dropped open. "Six weeks and still going?"

Jay just looked at me.

"Shit." I shoved my hands through my hair, distantly realizing I should probably get another haircut at some point. "Can we burn them? Freeze them? How the hell are we supposed to contain the viruses? We can't just let them stay out in the open."

A red light strobed through the room before anyone could offer an answer.

Iggy's fingers danced over the table's keyboard. "Metal detectors went off in Subterra. We've got at least five guns trying to shove out into the open areas."

"Everyone, suit up," I barked as we turned for the lockers lining the far wall. Without having to look over my shoulder, I knew every single one of my men was spinning the dial on his locker and opening it.

Ninety seconds. That's all it took.

Kevlar bit into muscles, settling into place like a second skin. The weight settled—familiar, grounding. A shield and a promise.

Knives whispered into their sheaths. Mags slammed home. The scent of sweat sharpened the air. The line between lovers and predators was separated by the thinnest margin. But this time we weren't dressing for battle. We were dressing to kill.

The air changed—just like it always did right before we stepped into those boxes where our killers lived. The quiet, the calm, the awareness. It sparked through the room like a lit fuse.

Just before we pulled our thin masks down over our faces, I looked at my men. My brothers. I knew beyond any doubt I would die for each of them and they for me.

"Play the game," I called out.

"Beat the odds," they replied.

"All in," we said in unison.

We were predators, and someone threatened what was ours. There would be blood in the water before this night finished.

Shoving out into the hallway in a tight, silent line of death, we crept down the hall toward the entrance to our private club. Someone thought of disrupting not only our patrons but also our business?

I snorted mentally. The people coming in better have some damn good answers. I've gutted men for less and the fish near the docks don't ask questions. Hell, at this point, we probably had an entire lake of pets.

The long line of hallway from the business office to sex club never ceased to amaze me. It was like walking between worlds, just like her owners. We lived, breathed, sweated, and bled in this building. And we would continue to do so, no matter who stormed our gates.

"Section two, Keys," Iggy called out through the bone conduction ear piece.

"Copy that, Azalea," I said over our closed communication line. The microphones were threaded through the material of the masks we wore. A fine invention of the collaboration between Iggy and Aidan.

"On your six, Keys," Markus said.

I stepped out of the way for Squirrel, our breacher. The man could get through any barrier—even ones we didn't have dedicated access to. He certainly didn't know the meaning of the word locked, that was for damn sure. And a better man to have on my team, I didn't know.

Squirrel lifted his hand in a fist and we all lined up behind him. Left hands on the guy's shoulder in front of us, we waited for him to get us through the door. He had the door and the immediate area just beyond it cleared in less than ten seconds.

He swirled his index finger in a tight circle, our signal to fan out beyond the door. I squeezed his shoulder and felt Det squeeze mine. I knew that every man had signaled his acceptance of the command. Just like we'd done a thousand times before. We'd probably die giving that signal to the man next to us.

Squirrel pushed open the door and the thumping bass smashed through my chest. It was go time.

Moving through the door first, I took the lower spot and swept the area with my sidearm out and ready. "Clear," I said softly, knowing the microphone would do its job.

Moments later, the rest of my team came in from behind me. They filtered out into the jagged edge of an arrow, all but two of us pointing down the north hallway. The last two covered our trail.

Crossing the first hallway junction, I tested each door on the left side of the hallway while Squirrel did the same on the right side. When all the doors remained locked, we continued on our way to the common area.

A single thought went to the sated and sleeping woman I'd watched on the camera in one of the rooms we just passed. I prayed she stayed asleep through whatever was playing out right now. It was bad enough we would have civilians in the line of fire. If we could save even one, I would be thankful.

Up ahead, the massive mingling area loomed. Low lighting, comfortable couches, and heavy tables all curl around the centerpiece of the massive bar that served protein drinks, water, snacks, and soda of all flavors. We didn't sell alcohol in our club. Ever. And if someone got caught being drunk, they were kicked out and given probation. We didn't play around with the safety of the people who put their faith in us.

"Spread out into eagle position," I said as I waited at the entrance for the group to come up behind me. Once I felt that squeeze on my left shoulder, I moved into the room and sank into a steady crouch position.

Det and Giggles rushed by me as I dipped the barrel of my gun out of their way. I saw the exact moment when the patrons realized something wasn't quite right. But we would deal with that later. Right now, we needed to neutralize the threat.

My side of the room was cleared by Det and Giggles, leaving Squirrel as doorman, Banshee and Azalea served as clearing team for the right side. Which left Schnauzer and Critter as tail team. Before Det and Giggles could call the room clear on the left side, Schnauzer came up, his back to mine. I knew without looking that Critter had done the same to Squirrel.

"I've got two," Det called out. "Giggles, secure them."

"We've got the other two," Banshee said through our comms.

"That leaves us with one," I announced.

"Got him," Squirrel said.

Out of the corner of my eye, I saw him lift his hand and bring it down in a hard strike that I knew would either kill the guy or make him wish he were dead.

"Pull them out, guys. I'll talk to the club," I said as I stuffed my firearm back in its holster. Pulling my thin mask up and off my face as I got to my feet, I walked out of the murky shadows and into the low lighting. "Members and guests of Subterra, if I could have your attention, please."

Walking around the bar away from the guys who were being escorted from the common area, I made sure to keep the attention of everyone not involved focused on me. "Thank you for keeping your cool. This has been a test and you all passed with flying colors. For those of you in the common area right now, see Samson at the bar and he'll get you your comp pass for your free private room voucher."

Turning, I nodded at our head monitor and bartender. The man looked much like his biblical namesake: huge, bronze, and long-haired. His black vest and triple black ribbons around his bicep seemed to suck in all available light around him. Samson nodded back and got his clipboard out from under the bar.

Walking backwards, I kept my gaze on the room, gauging the vibe. Nodding as business returned to usual, I felt Squirrel tap me on the right hip. "All clear, Keys."

Finally turning around, I waited for him to head back down the hall in front of me.

First in, last out.

Always.

"Let's go see what trash we collected."

Chapter 3
Neva

I woke up too fast. My mind already swept for threats before my breath even hitched. I flung myself off the far side of the raised bed, muscles locking down, braced for an attack.

Unsecured area. Unfamiliar surroundings.

"Stupid, Lark. Stupid."

As I basked in my relief and idiocy, I winced as the aches and pains in my body blared their annoyance at me. They weren't as quiet as they had been ten years ago.

But, then again, I'd put my body through a lot in the last decade.

Standing next to the table, I got cleaned up with some of the available wipes before sliding into my clothes. Gathering up my toys, I tossed them all into my gym bag and headed for the door.

Casting one last glance around the room to make sure no traces of me remained, I pushed open the door. Angling to the right so I could use the side exit, I started booking it out of there. And smashed into someone's hard body.

"Oof!" I rubbed my nose and glared up at the mountain.

Hard hands settled on my shoulders. "Easy there, pixie." He helped steady me before I could get tossed into the wall from the rebound.

"Pixie?"

"You're short."

A man standing next to him groaned. "Squirrel, you dipshit, we *talked* about this. You can't just blurt shit out like that." The other guy slid around the mistakenly named Squirrel. "Sorry about that, ma'am. He's a neanderthal."

My lips pursed. "I prefer Pixie to ma'am, I think." I hoisted my bag's strap higher on my shoulder. "And no worries. I shouldn't have just burst out of the room like that."

"Keys, we've got something you're gonna wanna see," another man called out from down the hallway behind me.

Turning, I saw a group of heavily armed men standing guard around a smaller group of men all dressed in black. But it was one face in that full crowd that made me feel like I needed to throw up. And made me forget every second of my training.

"Jax?"

Hard hands clamped down on my shoulders, and I knew without a doubt that I'd just said the wrong thing. "You know one of these guys, pix?" Mountain Man asked, his tone left no room for disobedience.

The slightly shorter man came around on my left side and peered into my face. Moments before I could change my expression. "Bring her with us, Squirrel."

Shit. I had to salvage this. Had to get out of here. Right now. I had more important things on my plate than dealing with a stupid ex. Especially one who left me for some stupid, skinny bimbo who couldn't be bothered to learn how to read.

Rubbing my eyes, I gave a chuckle. "Wow. The lights are playing tricks on me. I thought that was one of my exes." Shrugging, or trying to, I moved to turn.

Squirrel Mountain wasn't having any of it. "Nice try. But we'll get a little better acquainted and then see where things go."

Sighing, I nodded. Fine. If the fastest way out of here was through whatever this shitshow was, then consider me a piece of corn. "He really is an ex."

The guy named Keys chuckled. "Anything you have left to say to him? Need to slap, kick, or punch him?"

Walking down the hallway closed in on every side by hard slabs of male muscles, I looked up at this guy. "What happened to male solidarity?"

Both Keys and Squirrel laughed. "He's not one of us. And if he let you go, then I can only assume that he's a fucking ret–" Squirrel said.

Keys winced, rolled his eyes. "Squirrel, for fuck's sake. You can't say that either."

Squirrel laughed. "I'll say what I want."

My lips twitched. "Honesty will also go farther with me than being polite."

Keys groaned. "Don't encourage him, pixie. Just don't. He's already insufferable."

"Hey, I'm right here," the big guy said.

"I'll say what I want," Keys snapped back.

Squirrel's head tossed back as he laughed. "That's the spirit, boss."

We reached the other group and made our way from the darkened hallway into the eye-searing light of the business side of the building. Blinking away the stars that tried to blind me, I kept up with the group.

A grand total of eight men moved in familiar silent patterns. Gritting my teeth mentally, I tried to keep from ripping myself a new one. Fucking Navy SEALs. You had to join the club run by Navy SEALs? Just fucking great, Neva. Awesome. Really racking up the good points on this mission.

The five unsubs with them moved like they had some kind of training, but nothing like the eight horsemen of my personal apocalypse. And certainly not if Jax was with them. He'd barely survived basic training and then moved into Military Intelligence. If he was here, then he was the so-called brains of the operation.

"Isa," the asshole said as soon as I joined them.

Rolling my eyes at him, I had to thank my lucky stars that I'd never given him my real name. Call me untrusting, but there were a grand total of four people in this world who knew my real name. And this fucker wasn't on the shortlist. He's just proven why he wasn't there, too.

"Isa?" Keys asked from beside me.

I shrugged, neither confirming nor denying.

"Let's all go have a chat, shall we?" one of the SEALs said, palming open another door. He had blond hair, brown eyes, and tats that crawled over every inch of visible skin from his neckline to his fingertips.

The group of guys with Jax all looked like they wanted to fall through the floor and die of embarrassment. If they were with Jax, I could only pity them. Stealthy and capable of undercover work, he definitely was not. If they were hiding something, I hoped Jax didn't have the knowledge.

Wait. Maybe the SEALs would let me stay and watch the interrogation. I snorted mentally. That could prove fun and entertaining.

Mentally tracing my way through the floor plan, we walked down another hallway, and finally ended in a huge room holding a table that seemed to run at least thirty feet. Sleek polished wood reflected the lights from the ceiling and gave another layer of light to the big room. In addition to the chairs that looked like you could sleep in them and not get a kink in your neck, there was a long console table running along the north wall. An empty glass pitcher and stacked glass cups decorated one end.

"Have a seat, pix," Mountain Man said. He pulled a chair out for me and waited for me to sit down before he slid me up to the table. The damn thing made me feel like even more of a tiny human. Did they all have to be giants?

Grumbling, I curled my legs up under me and straightened my spine as much as possible. I had nothing to be guilty of, and certainly nothing to be ashamed of.

"You do know what kind of club this is, right, Isa?" Jax asked, a sneer in his voice.

All the men around the table laughed.

I smiled at the idiot who'd shared my bed for almost a year and never once made my mind quiet. "Yeah, and I'm getting better service here in two days than I ever did with you. So you might want to keep your mouth shut." I crossed my arms under my tits.

The moment I'd kicked him out was the last time I'd allowed myself to feel bad for needing something more in my bed. Too bad I still hadn't found it, but this jerkwad certainly didn't need to know that.

Keys watched me for a long second, but said nothing.

"Welcome to Locke Securities and Subterra," one of the other guys said, a laugh lurking in his tone. He was the one covered in tats who invited us to join him for the talk. "I'm Jay Waterman, one of the owners of said establishments. These are my colleagues and partners." He had a beautiful smile. And on someone else, it might have worked. I saw something flash in his eyes that didn't quite match the humor on his face.

He waved a hand around the table. "That's us. Now it's time for you to introduce yourselves." He drilled a finger in Jax's direction. "We'll start with the biased idiot. You are, sir?"

Jax's mouth contorted in a sneer as he tried to look tough and in charge. "That's classified."

Internally rolling my eyes at his blunder, I smiled widely. Maybe I did still have something to say. And it might get me out of here faster. Win, win. "That's Captain Jax Mathis. Army Intelligence. Or at least he was a couple years ago. I have no idea what he's doing at this point in his life. Nor what he's doing with this group." I made sure to study every face, check it against my internal roster of bad guys.

"And that's Isa Guari, primary school teacher." Jax crossed his arms as if he'd just dropped a truth bomb on the group.

Jay, the guy officiating the meeting, burst into huge gales of laughter. "You couldn't get your kindergarten teacher girlfriend off?" He slapped his hand to the top of the desk over and over, much like an animal seal when he clapped.

The rest of the SEALs all snickered and laughed to varying degrees as Jax's face flushed crimson. My ex wiggled in his seat as if he had ants in his pants.

"Or she's just a cold, frigid bitch who ca—" Jax started.

Jay's laughter cut off like a sword sliced his vocal cords. He reached out and slapped a casual, brutal hand across Jax's cheek. "Don't ever disrespect a woman in my presence. You couldn't handle her needs, you own that shit and work to be better. But you will never talk about her like that again, not where I can hear it." Jay leaned down, that demonic smile stretching his mouth as he got in Jax's face.

Jax nodded immediately, his hand up holding his cheek, his cornflower blue eyes wide as he stared at the bigger man. "Yes, sir."

About damn time someone put this idiot in his place.

Jay straightened. "Apologize to the lady." He crossed his arms over his chest. The soft *tap, tap, tap* of what had to be his foot against the cement floor seemed to bode poorly for Jax if he didn't start talking.

Jax looked down the length of table at me, glared. "I'm sorry, Isa."

I nodded and waved it away.

Jay shifted to look at me, his eyebrows raised.

I smiled and shrugged.

Jay rolled his eyes and turned back to Jax. "Well, Crappy Tan Jax Mathis of Army Intelligence. What are you doing invading Subterra with weapons? Any and all weapons are forbidden on our property. And since those rules are posted at every entrance you have to cross to get into the member's only area, don't say you didn't know that."

My lips twitched as I watched Jay start questioning. He had an interesting style, that was for sure. I wasn't sure it would be effective, but who knew? I'd witnessed stranger things.

None of the infiltrators said a word.

Bummer. It seemed Bad Guys and Good Guys were Even Steven at ones.

And I really needed to get out of here. Make it back home so I could get some good sleep before I went to that stupid teacher in-service day. Why the heck they scheduled them in the middle of the week, I didn't know. But no one had asked me.

"Since my part here is done, I'd really like to leave. I have no idea who the rest of them are." I waved my hand down that way.

Everyone turned to look at me.

I allowed my cheeks to heat. "I've got a teacher's training day tomorrow, starting at seven in the morning. Before that, I need to get my workout in, which means my day starts around five. If you had to deal with the beautiful screaming demons known as spoiled, pampered kindergartners for eight hours a day, you would understand my need for sleep."

"Nap wasn't enough?" Keys asked softly from beside me.

I barely managed to keep from jolting. Turning to look up into his face, I felt a new kind of awareness slide over my flesh. I hadn't been wrong. Someone had been watching me behind that little red light. "I need more than that," I answered, my voice just as quiet.

He narrowed his eyes at me for a second before a half smile pulled at his mouth. "I'll keep that in mind."

Holy hot flash, and I wasn't even close to being menopausal. Too bad this guy could never know me as anything more than Isa Guari—a legend I'd slipped out of soon after ditching Jax. And running two legends at the same time could be dangerous. Like get me killed dangerous. There was a list of reasons I hadn't been back to New York for three years.

"Whaddaya say, Keys?" Jay asked.

Keys dipped his chin at his man without looking down at me. "You're free to leave."

Not wanting to outstay my invitation to go, I put my hands down on the table and pushed my chair back. The huge guy who seated me hopped to his feet and held my chair while I stood up. Reaching down, I grabbed my gym bag back up and hooked the strap over my shoulder. "Gentlemen," I smiled at the room in general and headed for the door.

Keys got up and trailed after me, cutting off the other guy from following after me. "You'll need someone to show you the way out."

I really didn't, but they couldn't know that. So I just dipped my chin and waited for him to take the lead.

Scooting around me, he paused to pull the door open before letting me cross through first. These guys were a breed all their own, that was for damn sure. I hadn't seen manners like these since before middle school.

My heart tugged, but I pushed the old pain away. It didn't belong here, and I had other things to focus on. Like getting out of here with as little fuss as possible. I would also have to make sure I didn't come back too often. Some space was necessary between me and these owners. No reason to keep me forefront in their minds when I was supposed to be nothing more than a memory to those around me.

We walked down the hall in silence. Not even our footsteps made noise on the cement floors. Just two silent shadows drifting down the corridor. When we finally made it through to an open space filled with desks in a communal area, I blew out a stream of pressure in my chest I hadn't known I was holding. This guy took up more space than he probably should.

Without thinking, I pushed open a door marked MAINTENANCE. We walked through and continued into a gigantic staging area.

"You're a bit of a mystery, Isa Guari."

I bit back a laugh. "That so?"

He stopped.

I stopped.

He moved. Fast. *Too* fast.

A blink—he was there. Close. *Too* close.

Instinct took over. I matched him, countering every shift of his bigger body. That razor-thin breath of air between us?

Shrinking.

Vanishing.

His heat brushed my skin. My chest tightened.

I ripped my gym bag off my shoulder, looped the strap around his wrist, and dropped. A quick pivot—fast, fluid.

A blink and I was behind him.

His hand caught at his waistline.

Too late.

Fuck. I should've seen that.

"That's how."

Chapter 4
Rome

My lips twitched as I imagined her cupid's bow mouth twisting in chagrin…right before she wiped her expression clear. She was good, I'd give her that. But I'd trained hard to notice the little things.

With my hand still caught behind my back, I tipped my weight back toward my heels. Let's see what she did with that.

Just before I would have smashed into her small body, I was yanked to the side, my arm out straight. I allowed my body to follow through with the movement. With a quick jerk of my fingers, I caught the strap of her bag and hooked it around her, catching her against me as I rolled into a controlled fall.

We crashed to the floor, her on top. With my arms full of this woman, I had to keep my focus on ferreting out her secrets instead of how she felt in my arms. My breath caught in my lungs at the feel of her draped over me. My fingers twitched as I stared up at her while she studied me.

She was an unwelcome weight on mine…and fuck, she felt like heaven. But it wasn't the press of her body that rattled me. It was her eyes—sharp, knowing. Like she saw through the layers of control I needed and fucking smiled.

Her green eyes went wide. A sharp inhale, a flicker of something real. Then—gone. She wiped her expression clean, her armor fully back in place. She revealed herself in the nanoseconds before her brain reengaged. She wore lies like a second skin that was starting to slip.

Her legs splayed wide over my hips as she caught herself against my chest. "Well, hello there, sailor." Her gaze dipped down to my mouth as she rubbed her crotch over mine.

But her flirtation felt cold. Like spikes of ice trying to masquerade as heat. I wasn't buying her bullshit. She'd looked more passionate with her toys on camera than she did right now.

One of my brows quirked up. "Sailor?"

She struggled to keep her façade as she nodded. Leaning down, she slid her lips over my neck as she whispered again. "Sailor." Only this time, it wasn't a cold invitation. It was a dare.

Her hips rolled in another wave over my dick, her breath hot against my skin. I should have pushed her off, but my body betrayed me, caught between the desire to dominate and the pull of her reckless confidence.

Fuck. Distraction is definitely, exactly what I didn't want or need right now. Locking control over my body at the feel of hers, I pushed all physical sensation from my mind. She had secrets. Ones I needed to know. Ones that stupid ex of hers didn't have a single inkling about.

My fingers threaded into her hair. Rough. Tight. A quick twist—just enough to pull her up, away from my throat. She would give me the answers I wanted, I'd make damn sure of it. "Not soldier?"

Her pupils blew out, the emerald of her eyes nothing but a thin ring. Then she blinked, and she was back. This feisty woman who lied with her mouth and spoke truth with her body.

She snorted softly. "Please. I know a SEAL when I see one." She put her hands up in mock surrender, gave me a little pouty face even as her eyes danced with mirth.

Gripping her hair tighter, I tugged her face closer to mine. The plump flesh of her lips taunted me, but I wasn't interested in whatever game she was playing anymore. I wanted the truth. And I would make her give it to me.

She held my gaze steadily from inches away, a curious blend of heat and ice that flickered through her green eyes.

No sudden movements, not shifting or twitching. She sat there, almost peacefully.

I slowly loosened my grip on her hair, finally allowing her to sit back. She understood who was in charge here, no matter who sat on whom.

Then she dropped her bag on my belly, and the damn thing started vibrating. A laugh burst through her mouth before she caught her bottom lip in her teeth. Her eyes danced with mischief. She gave a little shrug, but didn't make any motion to turn off the toy that shimmied its way over my abdomen.

She didn't do a single damn thing except settle deeper against my cock. She crossed her arms, tits framed high and plump. She wasn't selling sex. She was testing me.

Sweet fuck, she looked and felt delicious.

Images of her in the private room tried to dance through my head again, but I hadn't become the commander of my unit by getting distracted. So, even though I wanted to indulge in every fantasy flirting with the edges of my mind right now, I stayed focused. "Quite a collection you've got in there."

I could have bitten my tongue off. Hadn't I just said I needed to stay focused? What the fuck was wrong with me?

She shrugged. "They get the job done." She didn't say anything else, seemingly content to sit there straddling me.

"Well, Isa Guari, even though that's not the name on your membership, what about that early morning you're running late to prep for?"

Her weight settled a little harder on my pelvis, her eyes narrowing the slightest bit. "Oh, are we done already?" She heaved a sigh. "Story of my life," she muttered under her breath.

My brows dropped. "Don't lump me in with that idiot ex of yours. You haven't rid—" I stopped the words before I could finish the thought.

Fuck.

She raised a single brow. "I haven't...what? Ridden you yet?" She bounced on my pelvis, the muscles of her legs flexing and relaxing at the bottom of my vision. "But I have. And so you will get lumped." Reaching out, she patted her bag. "The ones, the only." She bumped a single shoulder up into the air, a forlorn look on her face. Right before she seemed to shake herself and a fake, bright smile pulled at her sexy mouth.

35

"Can we get up now?" I asked, unwilling to discuss anything along that particular train of thought anymore.

"You first." She nodded, but didn't move.

I didn't move. Hell, the only thing moving right now was the furious tick of my watch. Thirty minutes of this? An hour? I snorted mentally. That was a game she would never win against me. No one had the patience to outlast me—not even her. In some cases, I'd waited years to get my targets. Some small, sexy woman sitting on my dick was not a hardship.

I crossed my arms, loose. Ready. My fingers stayed clear—just in case. I was this close to crossing my ankles, but the same precaution prevented me from doing that as well. Pushing the annoying vibration against my chest out of my mind, I gathered myself for a long game of Who Could Outlast Whom.

After fifteen minutes, she huffed a sigh.

I smiled at her. They weren't my knees getting smashed into polished cement. I could lay on this floor for a month and not feel any negative effects. Hell, it was better than some beds I'd claimed in my fifteen years in the Navy, which said nothing of the beds I'd taken as a SEAL.

She started shifting slightly from side to side at thirty minutes. As my mind ticked over to the forty-five-minute mark, she finally rolled her eyes and rocked back to her heels. Using slow motions, she put her hands down to my belly and used my hip bones as leverage to get up to her feet.

Eyeing her closely, I caught the wince she tried to hide as she straightened to her full height of still short. With her out of the way, I shifted until I could grab her bag, stand up, and still maintain my distance from her in one fluid move.

The vibration had long since stopped in the bag. I handed it to her. "Might need to do some recharging."

Her nose wrinkled as she bit at her lips, but she didn't say anything. She nodded and hooked the strap over her shoulder. "Do me a favor and just operate as if I am Isa Guari." She dipped her chin and moved around me like she knew exactly where she was going.

Turning, I didn't acknowledge her comment. I was too busy watching to see if she actually knew how to get out of the maze of the building we'd created. Stalking her quietly in the dark, I made sure she left.

She walked out as if she sketched out the floor plan herself. Her movements were smooth, easy, and confident.

Not once did she falter in her forward direction. It hit me then—she wasn't just some woman with too much training and a fake name.

She was fucking amazing. I needed to know more about her. Fuck, everything about her.

The heavy door slid shut behind her. Shadows swallowed the room whole. I stood there, pulse slow, steady. "Who the fuck are you, pixie?" The words barely made a sound.

She was a puzzle, a mystery, a fucking enigma. The temptation she presented…it might be the single thing in this world to test every ounce of my patience. And that thought shook something deep inside me where I didn't want to look.

My control was absolute. Always. It had to be.

"Yo, Keys?" Markus's voice cut through the quiet.

I didn't turn, my gaze stayed on the door almost as if I could still see her. She was gone, but not gone.

Finally, I exhaled, rolled my shoulders, and answered. "Yeah."

"We've got some intel."

Focus, damn it. On SRD, not the woman who made your fingers itch. She was a problem for later.

She was definitely a mystery. A smile pulled at my mouth. Just call me Sherlock.

Right now, though, I had work to do.

Squirrel met me in the hallway where our two businesses merged. He hulked in the doorway, his frame cutting off all ambient light from the hall behind him. He lifted his chin as if he couldn't see over my head. "Where'd she go?" His brows furrowed. "And why did you take her out this way?"

I shook my head. "I didn't. She walked out of here like she personally drew up the plans." Motioning for him to move ahead, I pulled the door shut behind me. Pixie was going to be getting a thorough run through Iggy's systems, that was for damn sure.

"Bring me up to speed," I said to Squirrel as we walked down the hall to the corporate conference room.

Squirrel laughed, the sound more reminiscent of the animal he was named for. "Gigs's got 'em on the ropes. They falling all over theyselves trying to plug up the holes they keep poking in their own stories. Idiots."

The big guy didn't have a lot of good to say about military intelligence in the first place. This was probably hitting home for him like vintage SNL. The guy loved stupid humor. The dumber, the better.

We pushed back into the conference room, and I took in the scene with a single glance. Fighting back the urge to roll my eyes at the stupidity playing out from a group of grown ass men who should know better made me glad that Pixie had left already. That woman didn't need any help in identifying or understanding the shortcomings of my gender.

"Sit the fuck down and shut the hell up." I didn't raise my voice, but you would have thought I shouted it through a megaphone.

Four of the five infiltrators fell back into their seats, wide-eyed and twitchy. They didn't just look guilty. They looked like they knew they wouldn't be leaving alive.

My team, thank the gods, held their mettle a little better. But I could tell Beck was about to put everyone into his version of time-out. Since we didn't have the time to find a cleaning service this late, it was good I arrived when I did.

"Azalea, go." I pointed to Iggy.

Two of the idiots snorted.

"Your call sign is a flower? What a little bitch," one of them snickered.

Jay moved before the guy finished exhaling his laugh. A flash of steel, then the sickening crunch of blade meeting bone.

The idiot screamed, body jerking like a fish on a hook.

Jay leaned down, voice casual. "He's no one's bitch. But he could make you his, if you're so inclined."

The guy curled in on himself, crying like a little girl.

I sneered around the smile. Giggles might do a lot of questionable things, but one thing he didn't do…politely tolerate disrespect.

Giggles ripped the blade from the guy's hand and then slapped him on the cheek with the flat of the bloody metal. "And stop screaming. Talk about a little bitch." He rolled his eyes as he wiped his blade on the guy's shoulder.

"Now that we're all here and ready to share like big boys, how about we try this again?" Iggy said. "Keys, we've got an advance welcome team. Say hi to some idiot's version of a black bag test to join their little soiree of bag guys."

I raised my brows as I took my seat.

Iggy nodded. "Yeah. Seems Crappy Tan Jax Mathis has severed his ties with Uncle Sam. He's now on the side of money and selfishness, with a fondness for murder and mayhem. To his right, Bloody Hand McGee here is Christian Gray. No, not that one—he could only be so unlucky. Former Force Recon, also on the wide and curvy road. Next to him, we have Corbin Foote, grunt of some kind with a nose for tech. He's not as good as me, but no one really is."

I crossed my arms over my chest. There were truly few as talented as Iggy when it came to anything with a motherboard and circuitry.

"Across the table there, we have Gantry MacDonald. He doesn't have a farm, but he came from one. A former CIA officer, specialized in Eastern Bloc, got punted for drugs and too many dead hookers. And his happy sister beside him is Bertrand Manswith. BM there is a bit of a mystery. Nothing on file, other than his name, which is a sleeve of some kind. Give me time and I'll give you the particulars."

The black man introduced last said nothing, did nothing. He was breathing, but that was about it. The guy didn't wiggle in his seat, didn't heave sighs or roll his eyes like his compadres. Nothing. Still and silent as a statue. He was the one in charge.

"Well, then take out the trash and let's deal with the dispatcher." I jerked my chin at Critter and Schnauzer. They each grabbed the man closest to them, and with vicious twists, snapped necks like bubble wrap.

The remaining three all backed up in their seats. Even Manswith seemed slightly alarmed by our actions. Gone were the days we played by anyone else's rules. It had gotten us nothing but damaged reputations, being dropped like burning shit, and clawing our way back to some semblance of life. These idiots should have thought of that before they came in here and tried to hurt our business.

"Who's next for a neck massage?" Critter asked, his mouth caressing the words like a lover.

Palmer DeMio was our linguist and could talk to just about anyone on the planet. His bronze skin, dark hair, and cold blue eyes painted a striking picture. The shortest of us, but one of the most brutal, he enjoyed long walks on the beach and killing motherfuckers.

Manswith still didn't respond. Not verbally or physically. It was as if he inhabited a different room than we did. He was doing nothing but watching something on a screen somewhere. No honor or loyalty to the men he'd brought with him. He just sat there and waited for us to make our next moves.

"Crappy Tan, your neck is calling my name." Critter cracked his knuckles as he moved around the end of the table to Pixie's ex. A long string of Farsi flowed from between his lips. I winced at the single word I understood. Crappy Tan would be pleading for death in moments.

Jay stepped up and stabbed a syringe full of something into Jax's neck. The guy went limp instantaneously, slumping against the table before he crumpled to the floor with a rough clatter of bones on cement.

"Damn it, Gigs. He was mine," Critter whined.

Jay shook his head. "Not this time. Not after what he said to the lady." He kicked out, the sound of flesh meeting flesh familiar in the quiet.

Critter huffed, but nodded. We were all well familiar with Giggles's reactions to the men disrespecting ladies. "Fine, but the other one is for me." He stepped over Jax's limp body as if it had no more importance than a felled tree.

The remaining bad guy shoved his chair back hard from the table, the wheels gliding easily over the bare floors. "Fuck that." He sank down into a fighting stance.

We all burst into laughter at his bluster. There was no way this ended with him as anything but dead. He was just giving Critter a little fun before he expired.

"Sit the fuck down, Gray," Manswith said.

I smiled. Patience was so often the name of the game. That and finding the right trigger. Either these two had a personal connection or Manswith didn't want to go back home as the sole survivor of his team. I didn't care which way he leaned, I just wanted some damn answers.

Manswith turned to me, his dark eyes shuttered and observant. "We need a job done." His tone didn't change, didn't waver.

He glanced at the bodies cooling on the floor, then at Gray, the only one still breathing. Then he rolled his eyes, like this was an inconvenience. "Pay's ten million."

I didn't react.

"Each."

I continued to give him blank face.

"The fuck you say, Bert? We were only going to get five hundred K each," Gray bellowed. He launched himself over the table, but he was a little squirt of a guy. He really only made it about halfway before Critter got his hands on him.

Without watching the scuffle, I knew Critter stabbed a spear hand into Gray's windpipe right before he clamped down on the guy's carotid and jugular veins with his fingers. Within a minute or two, Gray was dancing with the Ferryman.

Manswith sighed. Not defeat. Not fear. Just…patience. Like a man waiting for the inevitable to happen.

"We're still listening," I said.

The guy in charge of the Idiot Brigade scrubbed a hand down his face. "You couldn't have left me one of them?"

My guys erupted in snorts and smirks. It was all the answer the question deserved. We didn't play for ego. We played for keeps. Always.

"You have five minutes before you join them. I'd make the most of your time left on this earth," I said.

Iggy gave me a signal from the other side of Bert.

I smiled. "Looks like you're too late."

Schnauzer, still within lunging distance to the guy, eased to his feet. He reached out and caught Bert's collar.

"I have something you want."

I snorted. "No. You really don't." I jerked my chin at Beck. Our sniper knew more ways to kill than just shooting someone.

"I know who's dirty in the CIA," Bert said, not quite shaking in Schnauzer's hold. He held himself still, but I saw the slight trembling of his arms. "Deputy Director Lucas Theodore."

I caught myself before I gave away my surprise. "Clean your own house. We don't play with the government anymore."

"Do you know that one of his mistresses is a Sister?"

"Where'd you get the intel?" Aidan asked, shoving forward between Iggy and Beck to get in the man's face.

Manswith shook his head. "Not if you're going to kill me. Why would I?"

Well, fuck. Glancing again at Iggy, I gave him a long stare, silently asking his opinion. I might be in charge, but we only worked as well as our weakest link. And we had no weak links because I made damn sure we were all strong.

Iggy whispered to Aidan. A moment later, the crack of knuckles on bone shattered the silence.

Manswith hit the floor like dead weight.

41

Aidan flexed his knuckles, his voice dry. "Yeah, he's staying."

Chapter 5
Neva

Back at home, I slumped against the door. Exhaled slow. Steady. Well, shit. That could've been a disaster.

I tipped my head back, smirked at the ceiling. Definitely could have been worse. Something finally tipped in my favor.

Shaking off the club, I pushed from the door. No new scents, no unfamiliar sounds. The shadows and air remained unbroken around me. Darkness pressing in, I could've scrambled my senses, forced myself to take the long route. But tonight? I just wanted bed.

After a long, hot shower.

Wipes at a sex club weren't nearly enough to feel clean. And since I didn't have to worry about being shot, raped, or killed by unsubs or targets in my family home, I was going to take the time to indulge myself.

Walking straight through the foyer, I rounded the landing of the short stack of stairs that led to the bedrooms on the upper floors. Climbing the steps, I blocked any memories from rising along with my ascent.

Tonight was for cleaning and sleeping.

No whispers, no screams, no nightmares. Just fresh, clean restoration. However short it might be.

Turning left at the top of the stairs, I angled off for my bedroom. The scent of lavender and Chanel No. 5 still permeated the space. Every time I stepped in here made me feel like I could turn suddenly and see her one more time. That the tinkling sound of her laugh had faded seconds ago instead of decades.

Shaking off the familiar encroaching misery, I slid the pocket door shut behind me. My eyes hard and dry as bone left out in the sun too long as I flipped the extra locks I'd installed. Moving into the dressing room, I stripped off everything until I stood naked in front of the mirrors that covered each of the five sections of beautifully restored original closets.

I saw my mother's reflection in the mirror: short, curvy, long dark hair in a mess. Heavier than socially acceptable, but curvier than a pinup from the 50s, I no longer hated what I saw in my reflection. Honestly, it saved my ass more than once.

I smoothed a hand over my soft belly, nodded. Moving into the bathroom, I smiled as I always did when entering this particular area. Whoever the trust had hired to renovate had done a superb job.

A huge clawfoot soaking tub stood sentry along the far wall, while the other wall held a room-length shower with multiple heads and jets. The double vanity bisecting the room into halves made the room cozy instead of stark. Dark wood, white granite, gold rimmed mirrors all complimented the gray penny tile floor.

In the shower stall, I flipped the handle and exhaled a long sigh as hot water gushed from six showerheads all at once. Tankless water heaters were a gift from the gods. I stood there for a good ten minutes as I felt the day wash away. By the time my skin turned a hazy red from the heat, I finally got around to washing my hair and scrubbing my body.

As my eyes tried to close the last time, I slammed the handle. Ice sliced through my skin as my breath hitched, nerves screamed. My brain blazed. My body locked, breath strangling in my throat.

Thirty seconds later, I wrenched the handle, cutting off the frigid water. Snarling like a wet black cat, the shower mocked me, steam curling like a smirk.

Holy bleeding hearts, I hated cold plunges. If they weren't so good for me, I'd have ditched them long ago.

Stepping out of the shower enclosure, I ripped the heated towel off the wall rack and bundled myself up like I was going to go visit the Tundra. As my body worked to get back to a normal temperature, I grabbed a second towel and rough dried my hair.

Now that I wasn't in danger of becoming an icicle, I moved to the vanity and took out my hair dryer. No reason to go fancy since I was going to get up and go for my morning run, so I just hit it with some heat until it lay in lazy curls around my face.

Slathered up with lotion, I slid into bed. Snuggling down, I thanked the universe for letting my mind go quiet tonight. It would have to last a couple of weeks. A handsome face flashed in my mind's eye before I shoved it out again.

Shaking my head, I went back to my thankful list. As I worked my way through it, I felt my mind settle and go silent as sleep took me into her capricious arms. Here was hoping the night would be quiet.

**

Light stabbed through my eyelids. The fuck?

Unwilling to alert any possible intruder I was awake, I kept my breathing slow and normal. Shifting as if I were simply moving to my other side, I rolled off the edge of the bed, smooth, quiet. Gun in hand before my breath caught, finger brushing the trigger. "Pu—"

The room—empty. But sunlight speared through my window, slicing through my pillow, right where my head should've been. Shit.

Dropping my gun back down to my side, I flicked my gaze to the bedside table. "Shit!" I'd slept through my alarm. I had eight minutes to get to the school.

Tossing the gun on the bed, I raced around the big piece of furniture and into my dressing room. Ripping down the first available dress, I shimmied into it. Grabbing my hair up, I started braiding it as I went into the bathroom. Wincing at the sight in the mirror, I finished off the braid and grabbed my toothpaste. Squeezing a small bit of the paste onto my finger, I shoved it in my mouth and started swishing.

Stuffing my feet into shoes, I ran for the door. On the way out, I hooked my arm through my purse strap and dug out my phone. Thanking the universe for the forethought to

45

keep several extra chargers at school, I ordered an Uber and started running down the block.

Just as I rounded the block, my left foot snagged on something, tipping my entire body toward the street and into oncoming traffic, I felt a hand slide around my waist.

"Easy there," a laughing male voice answered.

I wiped the glare from my face before I turned to give the asshole a reaming he wouldn't soon forget.

Turning, I looked up, and my stomach dropped.

My mouth dropped open, but I shut it fast. "What the hell are you doing here?"

The guy named Keys from last night smiled down at me. "Saving a pretty kiddie teacher from being flattened like a pancake under cars." When he leaned forward slightly, the sound of him inhaling quickly rose to my ears.

"Did you just—" I blinked. "Sniff me?"

He pulled back, hand sliding away. "Yeah. You smell good. Like sunshine and…" his gaze dragged over me, slow, searching. "Something. I'm not sure what."

"Glad we got that figured out. What are you doing here?" I asked again, getting myself back together. Pulling on my professional mask, I made sure none of my dread or readiness to attack leaked out of my nonverbal reactions.

He raised a single dark brow. "What are you doing here, Ms. Guari?" His tone mocked me with the fake name.

Damn this man. "I live around here." A thought occurred. "Which you knew if you pulled my file." I narrowed my eyes. "Are you following me? Who sent you? Are you on assignment?" The questions fell from my lips before I could catch them. Shit.

Both brows winged high on his forehead as he stared at me in silence for a long moment.

I felt my core twist in a low curl as I tried to read his blue eyes. My fingers tingled as my breath backed up in my lungs.

"No, no one, and no, again. Are you typically followed by people in your line of work?"

Fuck. Forcing out a laugh, I got myself back under control. "Of course not." Tipping my head to the side, I smiled. "Unless you mean divorced billionaire fathers or the random sexy uncle." A laugh built in my chest. "Or the odd au pair who wishes I played for the girl team."

Settling into the familiar skin, I felt all the pressure and stress melt away. I could do this. I've done it a million times; this would be no different.

He looked a little nonplussed at the idea for a moment before he shook it off. Saying nothing else, he simply stood there and watched me from a couple feet away. When he allowed more time to slip by without a single sound, I smiled as my phone buzzed.

The car slid up to the curb just as I turned. The driver opened his mouth, my name probably resting on his lips. So I opened the door and got in before he could say it. "Hi. Thanks for getting here so quickly." I rolled up the window as I urged him to drive to our destination.

Not allowing myself to look back at the poorly named Keys, I pushed everything from my mind. Aneira de Witte didn't do late. Ever. She was punctual, prepared, and pleasant at all times.

We rolled up to the school with fourteen seconds to spare. Rushing from the car, I told the driver thank you and assured him of the five-star rating. I made it through the doors of the school right as the morning bell rang.

"Ah, Ms. de Witte," Ms. Bellington said as she stepped from the door of her office. Her arms were laden with stacks of paper and a laptop on top.

Stepping forward as if it had been my plan to help the headmistress all along, I smiled. "Good morning, Ms. B. I've got that for you." I shifted the bulk of her items into my arms and walked along beside her. "Great morning we're having."

The woman smiled at me, the apples of her cheeks flushing red with delight. "Indeed, my dear. My irises are looking so beautiful. I've got pictures to show at our first break."

I smiled, genuinely this time. I loved plants, even the non-poisonous ones. Plants were pretty simple in their needs, and they gave their lives to their beauty. Nothing was purer than that. "I can't wait to see them."

We walked the rest of the way in silence as the sounds of the other teachers could be heard in the library where our in-service trainings took place. If people thought elementary school students were bad, they clearly hadn't played at the teachers' table.

Worse than the students they taught, these people were only interested in money and used children to get it. I'd already sent a few of their names and information to one of my contacts in the NYPD. If they weren't being exploitative yet, they were primed to do so in the very near future.

After helping Ms. Bellington get her stuff situated at the front of the room, I took my customary spot near the middle left. Since I wasn't here for anything more than target acquisition, I didn't spend the energy to make lasting connections. I was reliable, but aloof. The recent widow I currently played allowed me a certain lenience in my solitude.

A quick skim of the clock told me I had just enough time to run to my room and snag a charger. Rising from my chair, I lifted my phone and shook it in Ms. Bellington's direction when she gave me a questioning glance. At her smile, I hurried off, then managed to slide back into my seat just as she dimmed the lights.

"Today's topic: Trauma-informed teaching," Ms. Bellington began.

My phone vibrated in my hand as I plugged it into the charger. When it continued to dance, I looked down at the device. UNAVAILABLE scrolled across the screen. Probably another spam call, so I hit the down volume button to silence the buzzing.

Just as I was about to put the phone on silent mode, a message dinged through.

> I know who you really are. You should be more careful; you never know who's watching.

The words seared into my brain. My pulse lurched, once, twice. Too fast. I sat there in stunned disbelief, blinking at the screen in the dark. There's no way anyone could know who I truly was. I barely remembered my real identity these days.

Who the fuck could it be? Mr. Keys? A scammer? Brantley? Someone watching—waiting?

No good answers. No time to dwell. I shoved down the panic, deep, where it belonged. Silenced the phone. Looked up. Focused. No one was going to throw me off my game. Not today.

Control reestablished, I smiled at the familiar topic. I knew all about trauma: causing it, enduring it, capitalizing on it, manipulating it. But sure, let's add some more tricks to my playbook for learning how to effectively teach children who've experienced it.

Chapter 6

Rome

Smiling, I walked through Locke Security's main door. When I'd run the woman's information last night, I hadn't thought I would run into her again. It hadn't dawned on me that we lived on the same block, just different ends and corners of it. But watching her almost launch herself into traffic this morning had been a fairly welcome surprise. Not the whole pavement spatter part of it, but the getting to get my hands on her body part.

"When the hell did you have time to get pussy last night?" Squirrel squinted over his sludge-green drink.

I arched a brow.

He snorted. "You're smiling. Only two reasons you do that: mission success or pussy. And I don't see no blood." He took a huge swig from his cup and grimaced as he lowered it again, wiping his mouth on the back of his wrist.

I glared at him. "I smile."

He shook his head, polished off his beverage. "Fuck, these never get better." He set the glass down on the lobby countertop. "Who was she?"

I shook my head. "I didn't get pussy; I'm just having a good morning." For fuck's sake, it wasn't like I was a Gloomy Gus or anything.

Squirrel snorted. "Yeah, because it involved pussy." He sat down behind the high-top desk and started turning on lights and electronics.

"Where's Brooks?" I scanned the empty reception desk.

Squirrel shrugged. "Critter got a message saying Brooks was out sick with his baby girl. Something about the sweetheart chucking up her tiny little guts all night. We're on our own today."

"I'll work up a sch—"

"Here's the schedule," Aidan said as he strode into the room. "Squirrel, you're up first for two hours." He slapped the sheet of paper down onto the desk. "I'm up next."

I grabbed the sheet and skimmed it, nodded. "Good job, Banshee. What else do we have on the line for today? Any other breakthroughs from last night?"

Aidan shook his head, his brown skin gleaming as if he'd just used some steel wool to wipe off his face. His high and tight fade of coiled hair seemed to consume the surrounding light. "Nope, but with the new info from BM, I've been able to nudge some of my Twists."

I nodded. "Excellent. Let me know as soon as you have something." Giving them both a nod, I turned and headed for the back of the huge warehouse where we'd entertained our guests last night. Which reminded me. "Iggy in yet?" I turned, asked at the same time.

"Yeah, he's with his bitch," Squirrel answered.

I rolled my eyes. There was zero hope of trying to correct the large guy. He did and said whatever he damn well wanted and to hell with the rest of the world.

I traced my way through the maze of rooms. But my mind wasn't on the mission. No, it was on her. She wasn't Isa Guari, not a fucking chance. And if that dickhead ex of hers thought he had her real name, he was even dumber than I pegged him. I wouldn't have told that man shit, either.

Making the final turn, I saw Iggy at his desktop console. The lights were dimmed, and he had his hands in the air like a conductor as information and data streamed over the pale blue waves of light in front of him. The man consumed information the way the rest of us breathed.

Waiting for him to finish his current task, I leaned against the doorframe and studied the guy. He and Aidan could have been brothers with their brown skin, piercing eyes, and high and tight cuts. But having met both of their mommas, I knew they couldn't have been raised farther apart in terms of privilege.

Iggy seemed to come to himself as he dictated a note into one of his ubiquitous files. "Save, encrypt level three." He sat back, rubbed his fingers into his lavender eyes. "Come on in, Keys. Thanks for waiting. Lights up."

"All good. Get what you wanted?" I sat down in my customary chair at the far end. It had the perfect vantage point.

"Not all of it, but we're getting closer. I've started the deep crawl around DD Theodore. Once I get the non-standard runs, I'll bring everyone together." He rubbed his eyes again.

My brows furrowed. "You good?"

He sighed, nodded. "Just dry eyes. This time of year in the city kills me." He leaned up to one hip, dug his fingers in his pocket. When he lifted a small white bottle and uncapped it, I watched as he dropped two beads of clear liquid into each eye. He blinked a little, smiled. "Oh, fuck yes. That's so much better."

Thank fuck. We would be down and out without him. "I need a run on the lady from last night. She's not what or who she says she is." Giving him a brief rundown of our interaction, I watched him simply consume the knowledge before he reacted or responded.

When I finally finished, his dark brows winged up. "She, a short, kindergarten teacher, took you down with her gym bag?"

Gritting my teeth at the joy in his statement, I simply nodded.

He bleated a laugh, tried to turn it into a cough. His pale purple eyes wide as he struggled to hold in his hilarity.

I rolled my eyes. "Get it out of your system." I waved him on.

He burst into huge gales of laughter. The man didn't understand the idea of quiet laughter, so it boomed from him and seemed to bounce around the glassed-in situation area.

I just shook my head and waited him out. Pulling my phone from my pocket, I double-checked the time, wanting to make sure my mental clock and my schedule for the day were still in sync. I had three appointments today, and one of them was off site. Thankfully, Aidan had taken that into account when he created the schedule and my time behind the desk in reception wouldn't bump into that appointment.

"What the fuck's all the racket?" Jay said, a smile already pulling at his face. "Why's he laughing like that?" He jerked a thumb in Iggy's direction.

Which made Iggy's dwindling laughter spring back to life. "She took him down. With her bag." The words stopped and started between his guffaws.

Jay turned to me, his dark blond brows furrowed. "What?"

I gave him the whole story, too. It would make the rounds before the day was out, might as well hurry it along so I could get back to work.

By the time Jay dissolved into laughter, his signature giggles filling the room, the rest of the guys had joined us. Minus Squirrel. It would take an act of God or an active shooter to move him from his post before his shift ended.

It took a good twenty minutes for everyone to laugh it out of their systems. Why it was so funny, I wasn't really sure, but here we were.

I'd been very careful not to let last night's encounter trip through my head. At least nothing outside of the sitrep that I just gave the guys. I employed the same dedication to avoiding remembering the feel of her across my lap now.

The final laugh wrung itself dry and everyone slumped in their chairs like survivors of some kind of war. It hit me then that we'd taken on too much too soon. We'd all been in the same recruitment year around the nation and found ourselves in the same class at BUD/s. After some shifting of teams and deployments, we were settled on to one team for the last eight years of our careers.

Now, two years after our dishonorable discharges, we were still working just as hard as we had back in the Teams. Harder, really. Running two businesses while working on finding the evidence necessary to take down SRD, we'd slammed ourselves into walls and demanded we push through them.

We all needed some time away. And more than just a vacation.

"Oh fuck, that was good," Giggles said as he wiped his eyes again. "I knew that little lady was more than what she claimed, but good enough to take down Keys?" He shook his head, his blond hair flapping from side to side against his face. "Damn, I would have paid good money to see that."

"Ask and you shall receive," Iggy said. He hit a series of buttons on his holo keyboard, and the camera footage of that hallway last night glared to bright life. "Lights, fifty percent."

My guts twisted watching her on screen. She was tiny—five-three, maybe five-four—but fuck, did she move like she owned the place.

She was short, but damn was she packed in the perfect package. She looked like a kindergarten teacher. If kindergarten teachers belonged in high-end porn instead of classrooms. Curves for days, tits that swayed naturally as she moved, and thighs that rubbed together in her leggings. Her belly had my dick going hard under the desk as I got to watch her in action.

Shoving my physical reaction to her body aside, I studied her movements. Her actions were a hint from being second nature. She thought them through instead of relying on her body to do what was required. That hesitancy to trust her instincts and training would be the way to get through her defenses.

She lied with her mouth, but her expressions and body gave her away.

"Tell me she felt good straddling your dick." Sebastian groaned as he continued to watch us lay there on the ground while we played the waiting game. "She looks like she'd feel so damn good."

Giggles made a warning sound in the back of his throat.

"I mean that in the most respectful of ways, Gigs. She's fucking perfect," Sebastian said, his eyes wide as he stared at our medic.

Giggles nodded, but I could tell he was on edge. Which was strange for the guy. Nothing really set him off except rudeness and disrespect.

While Det's statement could be considered disrespectful, we all knew the man essentially worshiped women of every size and shape. Why this small woman taking me down would set him off was a puzzle.

Jay turned to me. "So? You claiming her?"

Not "is she fair game" or "I call dibs." I should be beyond marveling at his words when it came to women, but then he went and did something like this that always set me on my heels for a moment.

"And if I did?"

The muscles around his eyes flinched for a brief moment, but he nodded. "You need to make it clear." He jerked his chin at the rest of the guys. "I don't want to beat the shit out of any of them."

My head tipped to the side the slightest degree. "You good?"

He shook his head faintly. "She's breakable."

I huffed a laugh. "She dropped me, sat on me, and didn't flinch. You think she's breakable?"

He shook his head again, his mouth twitched up. "Yeah, she did. But that's not how I mean." He stared at me for a long, silent moment.

Shifting back to the video, I studied her again. Saw the same mesmerizing woman who'd knocked me flat yesterday. Turning back to Jay, I shook my head. "I don't see it."

Jay knocked his fist against the table. "Fake name. Ditched her ex. Alone in a sex club when she's got a morning gig. And she put you down, but didn't finish the job. That doesn't ping your radar?" He stared at me again, expectancy weighting the air around the table.

Whatever he was trying to put down, I wasn't picking up. "You're going to have to spell it out, Jay. None of that adds up to breakable."

"She's one of three things: rebuilt, undercover, or after you," Schnauzer said for our medic.

Giggles nodded. "Exactly."

My brain tried to twist itself into knots trying to logic my way through that one. "That makes her breakable?"

Both Giggles and Schnauzer nodded. "Yes."

"In what universe does that make her breakable?" All I saw was a woman imminently capable of taking care of herself, no matter the danger.

"Assuming she was a victim, she's damn sure not cowering away now. She took me down and then sat on me for close to an hour, calm as apple pie on a Sunday in the summer. Assuming she's working undercover, she can do whatever the fuck she wants in her off time. Why not go to a sex club with rigid rules of anonymity and nondisclosure contracts? And if she's trying to get close to me, then bring it the fuck on. I'd love to get closer to that." I stabbed my finger at the video footage.

Giggles's broad smile had my belly twisting in dread. "You fucker."

He hooted a laugh. "Oh please, you're so pent up you're over there with a stiffy and heavy breathing over a video of a woman taking you down. You needed to answer

it for yourself, everyone else here already figured it out."
He jerked his head in the direction of the guys all facing
me.

They nodded in unison, knowing looks on their faces.

"You all can shut the fuck up and keep your noses out
of my bed."

"Not that it matters because no one, including you, is in
your bed. You're uptight, moody as fuck, and starting to get
soft," Beck said, his red hair and blue eyes sparkling under
the lights. "That woman is what? Five-three, five-four, and
maybe a buck seventy? Ninety on the outside?"

He shook his head in dismay. "She shouldn't have been
able to get you on your back, let alone straddled you for an
hour. We've been going up against a group of women who
would rather slice your dick off and feed it to feral rabbits
than look at you. But you're going to play Street Fighter
with some unknown from Subterra?"

"And watch her walk away as if she owns the joint?"
Iggy said as he drew everyone's attention back to the
screen. "How the fuck did she even know where to go?"

With all of their eyes on me, I had to admit that they
were right. Something about that woman screwed me up. "I
don't know. It's one of the reasons I told you about her in
the first place. We need a run on her. I pulled her file last
night when I realized she was staying in one of the private
rooms…for the entire night."

Beck shook his head, pinched the bridge of his nose.
"How did you find out about her initially?"

I fought the heat that tried to crawl up my neck and
into my cheeks. Fuck. "She rented out the room. The one
we've been getting reports of theft in. I slammed into her
partner by accident in the hallway as he exited; he said that
it was occupied, and I would have to wait. I went back to
the office and turned on the camera to watch her leave and
the cleaning team come in and watch them."

"And…what did you find out about the cleaning
team?" Sebastian asked.

Shit, I had to confess something else. Again. I shook
my head. "They didn't go in. That's when I found out she
booked the room for the entire night."

"Well hell, that's what you shut off as soon as I walked
into your office last night," Sebastian said. "You were
looking guilty as shit."

"You watched her?" Giggles asked, a threat in his tone.

Damn it. How had we gotten here from watching the footage of her taking me down last night? "Yes. She finished, fell asleep."

My entire team, minus the too blunt Squirrel, gaped at me in horror.

"What? Why are you all staring at me like that?"

"You've never used the cameras to spy on patrons. You're the one who set up the rules to make sure it never happens. But now, not only are you watching, but you're also escorting the same woman from the building. She put you fucking down and all you're concerned about is her name," Aidan said. "That's fucked up, Keys. Even for Squirrel, that would be fucked up."

Nods all the way around the table.

Well, shit. Looking at it from their perspectives, I could understand where they were coming from now. I looked like a weak pansyass and was taking my team down with me step by step. All because some woman had caught my eye.

I forced out a breath. "Fine, someone else can take point on her." The words tasted like fucking poison.

"I'll take head," Critter said, a menacing smile on his face.

Gritting my teeth at the mental image his words brought, I just nodded. The fucker had probably done it on purpose, too.

But no way in fucking hell was I going to dig my grave any deeper. Not over some unknown woman. Losing the respect of my team wasn't worth that. Worth anything. They were all I had left in this world.

Giggles turned, eyes dark. "Critter, you so much as breathe disrespect, I'll break you and leave you in pieces."

Critter dipped his chin. "Scout's honor." He raised three fingers and gave a mock salute.

Fuck. I was screwed.

Chapter 7

Neva

Rubbing my eyes as the lights came back up, I brought my mind back to the room around me. None of the information Ms. Bellington had shared was new. Honestly, I wasn't even sure it was recent. Trauma was a given these days, but she made it sound like winning the world's shittiest lottery.

"Since none of you had questions, it seems we'll get to give you back some time in your days. Thank you all for your attendance and your dedication to our students. We appreciate each and every one of you," Ms. Bellington said as she got all of her supplies stacked back together. A considerably smaller pile now that all of the handouts had been dispensed to us.

As if she'd blown a horn at the Kentucky Derby, teachers flew out of the room. There didn't seem to be a noticeable difference between my students or their teachers when it came to leaving campus. Stupid animals.

Picking up my handouts and notepad, I made a mental note to grab the scribbled equations from my notepad and take them home with me. While Ms. B droned on about psychotropics, my brain brewed up something better.

I was sure I could improve on the dosing and strength options without a lot of the side effects. Mother Nature was a crafty bitch and no lab-made chemical could outdo her.

"Ms. de Witte," a grizzly masculine voice asked from behind me.

Turning, I smiled at our librarian.

"I have that book you asked me about." His fuzzy eyebrows were high on his weathered face. "You'll have to do better if you expect to stump me." He offered me a small book, no bigger than the size of his hand. "Although I do admit that this one was a bit more obscure than the others. Happy reading, my dear."

Taking the book from him, I added it to my pile. Hitching my bag's strap up on my shoulder, I walked from the library to my classroom. Setting my stuff down, I stuffed the book and notepad into my bag. Filing the handouts into the folder with other in-service information, I kept myself busy for an hour or two trying to catch up on the actual business of teaching children.

After my neck protested the constant looking down, I got up and stretched. Shifting my focus out, I tried to tell if anyone was left in the building. When it sounded like the coasts were clear, I gathered my stuff to leave. Locking my door behind me, I made my way to the administration office.

Smiling at the empty, dark room, I went inside. Barely any light filtered through the high windows that lined each wall, but I made my way to the secretary's computer without having to turn on any lamps.

Ms. Ernestine Holowitz was a dragon when it came to protecting the privacy of the students' information. At any other time or setting, I would applaud her dedication to her duties.

The last few weeks were definitely not the right time or setting though.

Luckily, she was also getting soft when it came to password retention. Someone had suggested the grand idea of password management. Ms. Holowitz had taken up the habit of writing those pesky little details down on a sheet of paper in her nearly indecipherable cursive handwriting and locking them in her desk.

Who said I couldn't be helpful?

Taking a seat at her desk, I had her desk locks open and her computer humming through its opening sequences in a matter of moments. When the newest string of cursive characters on the sheet allowed me access to her secured device, I could have shouted for joy.

Bypassing all of the educational software, I went straight for the database I'd been trying to get into since I found out about it.

It seems, in the higher tax bracket settings, certain institutions could pay for services that would allow them to track children. All done with the permission of their parents, of course. These trackers helped with kidnapping insurance premiums, and provided parents a—false—sense of security.

I'm sure that whoever designed the software originally had planned it for only altruistic uses. But in the hands of someone in need of actual information about sensitive subjects…well, a lot of damage could happen.

The best way to keep your loved ones safe? Don't have any.

And look at me out here, killing it all friendless and alone.

Snickering at myself, I found the information I needed. Sending a tracking link to my phone, I removed any traces of being in the program. As my phone buzzed in my purse, I nodded and turned off the computer.

Putting Ms. Holowitz's password cheat card back in her desk, I locked it up, cleaned everything off with a Clorox wipe, and left the building. The solid thud of the lock latching behind me brought a slight twitch to my lips.

Sketching a glance at my watch, I smiled at the idea of my upcoming run. It would be hotter than the blazes in the late afternoon instead of the early morning, but at least I would still be able to get it into my day. After the day of sitting in chairs listening to bad information, I was more than ready to move my body.

Walking back home, I enjoyed the sun beating down on me. Even the humidity, noise, and overpopulation couldn't drag me down. Not today. I finally had a way forward. And nothing and no one was going to get in my way of finishing this last mission.

I could almost taste my freedom. The knowledge that I wouldn't have to look over my shoulder every day. Try to remember which lie I lived and all the details that could get me killed if I forgot them.

Hell, I might even be able to get a cat.

Well, maybe a pet rock would be better. No sense getting attached to something living.

61

As I approached my home, I noticed something on the top step. Since I rarely ordered anything that could get shipped and tracked, I paused and pulled out my phone as if I'd just gotten a call. "Hello?"

Waiting a few seconds, I pulled the phone from my ear, put a quizzical look on my face. With the camera facing the entrance, I snapped a couple shots as I faked tapping the screen in frustration.

When I put the phone back to my ear, I gave a fake smile. "Oh, hey, there you are. Sorry, I think my phone's about to die. Where are you?" Moving toward the street, I looked both directions. Shoving delight onto my face, I waved at no one. "Absolutely. I'll come down right now." Dropping my phone back into my bag, I hurried down the street, joy and openness on my face.

Inside, I fumed. Someone had come to my home. Disturbed the sanctuary of my space. And not only that, but they added insult to injury by leaving their traces all over it.

Crossing the street, I made my way into Prospect Park. Heading down the trail, I found a bench that was hidden around a slight bend of the walking path. It also happened to afford me a somewhat broken sightline of my front door.

Pulling my phone out of my bag again, I pulled up the pictures I'd snapped. Zooming in told me I had a couple of packages in plain cardboard boxes. None of the familiar dark blue tape with royal blue smiles. No labels that I could see at all, actually. Just plain brown sides with what I was assuming was glossy packing tape at the seams.

Closing the photos, I pulled up the program for my security system. Having to give precise instructions for the installers had been a bitch, but I'd managed to piggyback a secondary system that only I had access to onto the original.

Backing up to watch myself leave that morning on the camera, I ground my teeth together when the primary feed went to a black screen for forty-seven point six seconds a couple hours after I left. Catching the time marker, I pulled up the secondary system footage feed.

My stomach overflowed with angry bubbles when I saw someone who looked slightly familiar smirk into the doorbell camera. He even gave a little finger wave. Leaning down, he put the package on the porch. Just as soon as he hit the bottom step, he turned back and waved again.

That fucker. Closing both programs, I breathed through the rage.

What kind of business were they running that they thought this would be a good use of their company resources? And what the fuck was in those packages?

Getting to my feet, I had the information pulled up on my phone and the number dialed before I could take a beat to settle down.

"Locke Security. What can I do for you?" a now familiar voice said into my ear.

Bracing against the shivers that wanted to race down my spine, I stiffened it instead. "Why the hell did you have one of your grunts leave shit on my doorstep?"

A hard second of silence came through the line. "To what do I owe this pleasure, Ms. Guari?" A taunt lived and breathed in his tone.

I ground my teeth together. "I'll show you pleasure, bastard. What kind of racket are you running over there?" These fuckers were going to get me killed or I would kill them. In the end, there would be death, and it would be all their faults.

"Ms. Guari, is that you? Or should I call you Aneira de Witte?"

Fuck. Tactical error. I'd rung their bell one too many times, and now they weren't just answering—they were inviting themselves in.

"Or maybe you're feeling frisky and want to give me your real name?" He let the question dangle in the air and for the first time in almost twenty years of clandestine work I wanted to actually share it. To have someone know me, not the lies I lived or the legends I wore. But the real me.

Then I brushed it off. I had a job to do. One more. The last one and then I was free. I could go live somewhere and just be around plants and nature and leave people to their own downfall. "Yes, this is Aneira de Witte. To whom do I have the pleasure of speaking?"

He chuckled, a single note of humor before he cut it off. "I think you already know that."

I bit my lip to keep from telling him the truth. I didn't know him or anyone else in his little band of merry men.

Other than studying the building that held Subterra for exits, I hadn't bothered to learn anything else about them. It seemed I needed to rethink some of my education in this area.

I cleared my throat. "Why do you have one of your guys leaving stuff on my doorstep?" I'd called for a reason, damn it. And I wasn't going to be deterred.

He heaved a huge sigh. "I don't know what you're talking about, but I can certainly ask around. What was left?"

Glaring at someone stupid enough to try to cut me off as I exited the park, I made my way back to my home. "A couple boxes. Care to tell me what's inside?"

"You haven't opened it?"

"Why would I open any boxes from an unknown male?"

"How do you know it was a man?"

"Doorbell camera." I didn't tell him that the footage came from a secondary system. He didn't need to know that.

His chuckle was drier than dead leaves at the end of fall. "Ms. de Witte, if we had left something for you at your front door, do you really think we would allow ourselves to be seen by something so mundane as a doorbell camera?"

"I don't know what you or yours do at all. Why would you feel the need to take out a doorbell camera on a private citizen's residence?" Stomping up the steps to my front door, I grabbed the packages and cradled them in my arm while I unlocked the door with my free hand. They were pretty heavy, which raised my internal alarm a little louder. "What's in the boxes?"

So badly did I want to yell at him, but I refused to call him Keys and let him know I didn't know his first name.

"Like I said before, why do you think the package is from us?"

"Because the guy on the footage looked like one of the ones I saw last night." Getting through the front door, I set the package down on the entryway table. Tossing my bag onto the hook, I stepped out of my shoes.

"Well, then it definitely had to be one of us, I just don't know which one. I can check with my guys. See if they've...contacted you." The hesitation in his tone had something prickling over my skin.

"Am I now a target for your group?" My entire body tensed as I waited for his answer. There was no possible way things could have degraded this quickly. Not after one single weekend in Subterra.

"You use very distinct terms not commonly found in the field of kindergarten teaching, Ms. Guari."

I caught the dig at my other assumed name. I just had to hope and pray that he hadn't gotten a hold of my real identity. "A life long lived. Please answer the question. I need to know if I should get the authorities involved."

He heaved a long sigh. "No, Ms. de Witte, you are not now, nor have you been, a target for my group. I don't foresee you being a target in the future either. Have you at least opened the package yet?"

Why did he keep saying package? As in the singular, when I'd distinctly said the plural form? Glaring down at the three boxes on my entryway table, I pulled my phone down again and looked at the doorbell camera footage.

"Ms. de Witte?"

"Hold on. I'm checking something." Hells bells, the man was bossy. Watching through the remainder of the footage at double speed, I saw two other black screens on my primary feed. "Shit." Two other deliveries had been made.

"If you have nothing else to offer, maybe I should hang up. You seem a bit preoccupied."

I let out a low snarl. "Jeez, are you always this antsy? Hold on, I said." I rolled my eyes.

"I'm incredibly patient, if you'll care to recall," he said, his voice low through the speaker phone.

Shutting my mind to the remembered feel of him between my legs last night, I just hummed an answer. Finally, I watched myself approach the front landing of my home not even ten minutes ago. "I have three packages. Are you all so clumsy that you can't send your packages all at once? I can't say that bodes well for your logistics team lead."

Something was off. Three boxes, three different deliveries. Too precise to be a mistake. My gut churned. I knew better than this.

"Ms. de Witte, again, I didn't send a package, and I'm reasonably sure no one in my company did either. Maybe you saw this man in the club or out in public somewhere. I'm assuming you do more than just come to Subterra and go to work. You run. Perhaps your mystery man is a sec—" he cut the words off before he finished his sentence. "It wasn't us. I can assure you of that."

Gritting my teeth, I pulled open the drawers on the entryway table, grabbing a letter opener that could double as a knife if necessary. Setting that to the side, I lowered my head to the side of each box. None of them ticked, but in today's world, that didn't mean a whole lot. Chemical terrorism was at an all time high—I should know, since some of the agents were my own design.

Reaching into my purse, I pulled out a little device of…well, not quite my own making, but close enough. The actual manufacturer had done it all according to my specifics. When the readout on the front came back with a zero read on most known components of poisons and toxins, I set it aside.

"If you didn't send me the packages, who did?" Shit, I needed to learn this guy's name.

He sighed heavily. "Why would I know that? How would I know that? Other than the fact that you live on the same block, have a body built for sin, forged names, and work with children, I don't know anything about you."

I snorted softly. Picking up the letter opener again, I cut through the tape. Easing the edges of the box up, I bent down so I could see if any trip wires were attached to the tops.

"Because you're angry that I—"

A faint metallic click—wrong, sharp. My pulse stalled. Then mist exploded in my face.

"Oh fuck." The coughing started immediately.

"Aneira? Talk to me. What just happened?" Keys asked, his tone hard and bright.

I tried to answer, but all I could do was cough again. Lifting my elbow to cover my nose and mouth, I waved at the dissipating cloud. My cheeks felt like they were on fire, just like my lungs. I could feel the muscles in my chest tightening down.

Shit. This wasn't good. I coughed again, felt something goopy slide up through my throat and splat against my elbow crease. "Shit."

"Aneira. Say something. What's in the box?" Keys's voice felt like nails against a chalkboard through the speaker of my phone.

"Well, I should have been a little more careful," I said to myself as I felt my vision start to waver around the edges. "Who knew it would have been poison that took me out?" My laugh rattled my chest as my brain slid sideways. "Oh, momma, if you could only see your little girl now. You'd be so disappointed."

"Ms. de Witte!"

I tumbled to the floor, the phone clattering to the hardwood beside me. Blinking, I saw her spectral form near the stairs. "You left me too soon. Took all the best parts of me and left me alone." Her dark brown hair like thick molasses, her creamy white skin that held the smattering of freckles I'd counted when I was a child. The sparkles in her eyes when she danced around her beakers and crafted new and interesting poisons in the depths of her laboratory.

"Hold on, Aneira. I'm almost there."

Chapter 8

Rome

Transferring the call from the office line to my cell phone, I waited for my mobile to pick it up. Hissing at the guys around me to shut up, I shoved my phone closer to my ear. I raced from the reception desk down the hall into the loading area.

"Gigs, on me. Bring your gear." I listened to her talk to her mother, but whatever the other woman said in response, I couldn't hear.

"What the fuck, Keys?" Squirrel said as he rushed up in my wake. "Where's the damn fire?"

I couldn't explain the urgency, but I trusted it. "Get in or get out of the way. I don't have time to explain it right now."

Jumping behind the wheel, I pulled the door closed as I hit the button for the garage doors to open. All of the doors opened around the vehicle and my entire team flooded in. Just as the massive door reached the top, the backdoor of the vehicle slid shut.

"Start talking, Keys," Det said. I recognized the tone in my second in command's voice. He wasn't going to take silence for an answer.

I gave them a rough rundown as I streamed into traffic. "Iggy, see if you can pull up her information. She mentioned a doorbell camera. See if you can hack it, give us some kind of idea of what we're walking into. Gigs, she was muttering about poison and her mother being disappointed in her. I couldn't tell if her mom was there or if she was going crazy."

The phone call finally linked into the van's speaker system. "Aneira, can you hear me?" I bit out through the live call.

"You're so pretty, momma. Why? Why did you leave? You could have stayed. Should have stayed." She sounded either drunk, higher than a kite on a windy day, or like she was taking a bad acid trip.

I looked at Gigs.

His usually smiling face was drawn down into a tight line of concentration. "When did she start talking to her mother?"

"A couple seconds before I bolted for the van," I answered. "Aneira! Can you hear me? It's Rome."

"Rome."

I felt my belly tighten at the ache in her voice.

"Rome is so pretty in the summer. The buildings, the architecture. Splashing in the fountain at midnight."

I shoved my bruised ego aside and refocused on her. "Aneira!"

She snickered, wet and wrong, then broke into coughing so raw it made my lungs ache. "Such a pretty red. The best flowers are red. Some are purple though. You loved purple most. So do I. Did you know that?"

Her chuckle sounded sad and slightly deranged. "Of course you don't know that. You're dead. You've been dead for a long time now." She coughed again, but this time it sounded dry and normal. "Oh shit. This is bad. This is really, really bad. Fuck. How did I end up on the floor?"

"Aneira de Witte! Can you hear me?" I bit the words off, felt them cut like glass in my throat.

"Who is this?" She sounded closer to the phone.

"Rome Whitlock," I said. I wanted to shout at her, but I kept my cool. "From Locke Security. We're on our way to you now. I think you've been poisoned." The tires screeched as I took a turn too fast.

"Yeah, pretty sure I have." Sounds came through the phone that I couldn't identify. "Come on, baby, almost there. Come to momma."

Flashes of watching her on the camera footage from Subterra flicked through my mind. I clicked my teeth together to keep from saying anything inappropriate.

"Oh yeah, so close. So fucking close. Come on, you can do it."

Hisses and snorts went through the van. Gigs turned around and glared at everyone in the back. The van went quiet.

"What are you doing, Aneira?" We're trying to get coherent conversation and she's sexy pleading with something or someone.

"Trying to get my bag." She coughed again, the sound back to wet and syrupy. She snickered. "My purse has more poison in it. I need to dose myself." Her laugh was bright and crazy. "Give myself more so I can live. Poisons are silly that way."

Gigs turned to look at me, his blue eyes wide. He shook his head. "I wouldn't be doing that, darling. Not if we don't know what you got dosed with in the first place."

She snorted as if she were offended by the very idea. "Oh please. Poisons like me. I like them. We're a match made in hell." Her words fell off into an off-key rendition of the marriage march.

"What kind of kindergarten teacher knows about poisons?" Gigs asked, his tone overly happy and bright.

"The kind who doesn't only teach babies." She sighed, aching and longing in the low rush of air. "I never got to have babies of my own. Never wanted them, really. They can be used to hurt you, or they can be hurt and that hurts you, too. I don't have any, but I love the ones I have. Too bad their daddies are mean and bad people. She shouldn't have to live with a daddy for a monster. But don't you worry, I'll save her. Save her from the bad man. And then I'll get to be done."

I bit back another rush of words, but for an altogether different reason this time. This woman had a lot more going on than anything I'd imagined so far. And I'd imagined quite a bit.

"I've still got point, Keys," Critter said from the back. "Don't go forgetting that."

With a quick glance, I speared him a death stare in the rearview mirror.

Before I could open my mouth, Gigs shouted. "Keys, road!" He slammed his fist down on the dash as I flicked my gaze back to the street.

71

I narrowly missed smashing into a group of kids crossing the street. Gritting my teeth, I weaved around them. Something in my jaw popped, but I shook it off. I needed to concentrate on getting to her house. Everything else could be sorted once we got to her and got her stabilized.

"Keys," Aneira said softly. "I've got a lock for you." She snickered before a heavy thump came through the line. "There you go, baby. Just like that. I knew you could do it. Such a good boy for me."

My body warred with itself as I tried to stay focused on the situation and not just the words coming out of her mouth. She was going to kill me.

Critter's warning sounded in my head again.

Fuck. I either had to step up or step away. And I needed to make that choice hard and fast. There could be no faltering, no wishy-washy bullshit that could endanger my team any more than I already had.

We finally turned the last corner. "Last on the right." The van screeched to a halt as I stomped on the brakes. We all jolted forward and were out the doors before the vehicle stopped rocking. Just as we always did in an active situation, we lined up and made our way smoothly and quickly to our target.

Double stepping the stairs, I made it to her front door and knocked. With the phone left in the car, I didn't know if she was still coherent or not. But I couldn't go barging in with it still being daylight outside. Having a group of big men smash through her front door could lead to bigger issues none of us, including her, wanted to deal with.

"Honey, I'm home," I called out. Praying the door had been left unlocked, I tried the handle. It turned easily in my hand. The band around my belly loosened. Shifting slightly, I pulled my weapon from my in-pants holster.

The guys were joking and messing with each other as if nothing was wrong in the world.

Gigs came up along my right side, Det on my left. "Clear, Keys," they both said together.

Nodding, I lowered my hand and let Gigs push the door open for me. Clearing the front room, I rushed to her. "Clear."

The rest of my team filed in behind me. The outward signs of joking and joviality were easy to see. But as soon as the door closed, they dropped the act and filtered out through the house. Guns out and ready. The call of 'clear' came from every one of my guys.

Gigs met me at her side. "Honey, can you hear me?"

She nodded, her green eyes sleepy. Splotches of red dotted her lower face. "You're Mr. Giggles."

He smiled at her. "That's right, peaches. Where does it hurt?"

She shook her head, almost pitched herself sideways to the floor.

Reaching out, I caught her against me. She felt like she was on fire, the finest sheen of sweat coated her skin where I held her.

"My chest. My heart rate's too fast, but it's starting to slow down. My lungs hurt and my lips, mouth, nose, and eyes burn." She lifted red-stained fingers to her lips, but didn't touch the rubied skin. "Get my bag for me."

Gigs turned and hit the table. Three boxes fell to the floor beside him. A small plume of mist erupted into the air.

"No!" Aneira launched herself from my arms and smashed into the man, throwing both of them back, away from the aerosol.

Before I knew how she did it, she covered his entire face with cloth of some kind. The mist settled over her like a sigh and she shuddered. Turning her eyes to me, red started overtaking the white. "Get us outside. Now." She fell against Gigs's body and went limp.

"Squirrel," I shouted as I got her rolled off my medic. Launching her up into my arms, I ran for the front door.

"Keys, this way," Beck said from behind me.

Turning a quick one-eighty almost blew out my knee, but I kept moving. He pointed down a set of stairs that led to an all-glass door covered in decorative metal.

Critter yanked the door open, his gun pointed toward the floor. "Private garden area with headcover. Squirrel's getting Gigs."

I nodded and rushed past him. "I need info from Gigs on how to treat them both." Looking around the space, I saw a small seating area with a loveseat kind of thing. Sitting down on it with her, I peered down into her face. "Aneira? Can you hear me?"

Aneira shifted in my arms, blinked at me slowly. "Sec flur, rmm 'ight. Ox'gen. Purp 'ag." Her slurred speech descended into hacking coughs that shook her entire frame. She grabbed a handful of her dress, raised it to cover her mouth. Her bloody-looking eyes apologetic over the fabric.

"Second floor, a room on the right, oxygen tanks, and a purple bag. Get it down here," I barked out. Heard one of my guys race through the home.

Squirrel brought our medic out to the garden as well. Gigs was coughing and he looked a little pale, but he didn't seem any worse for wear. It looked as if Aneira had taken the bigger hit of the second puff of whatever this was.

Once all my guys gathered, we almost filled the small outdoor space completely. Banshee rushed forward, the small tank and giant bag in his hands. "I've got the stuff, Keys."

Gigs reached out, grabbed the tank. Lurching forward out of Squirrel's grip, he pulled the clear tubing off Banshee's wrist. "Open the tank, we need to get her some clean oxygen to breathe."

They worked together and settled the cannula into Aneira's nose, the slight hissing of the oxygen tank opening the only sound other than nature and Brooklyn surrounding us. We all waited with baited breath as we watched Gigs give her a superficial examination. He was careful to keep his skin away from hers.

He coughed once or twice but managed to push through whatever had gotten into his system. "She's gotta be something other than just a kid teacher, man." His words were soft as he finished checking her pupillary response.

I nodded. "Yeah. Once she's better, we'll get it figured out."

"I think you mean I'll get it figured out." Critter's gaze flicked between me and her, his usual smirk nowhere in sight. "She's my mission, Keys. Unless you're saying otherwise."

"You better be talking about something other than me when you use words like that," she said, her words still sleepy and slurred.

"I've got her." The words came out too fast, too final. The words settled like steel, locking into place before I could take them back.

She shifted her bruised green eyes to me, blinking sluggishly, as if fighting off the drag of exhaustion. "You've got ten seconds to tell me why I'm in your lap and you're all in my house." She shifted her gaze. "Or my garden. No one comes here."

Gigs blew out a breath and sank into one of the chairs surrounding a tiny, useless table. "Thank fuck, peaches. You scared the shit out of me." He coughed again, winced a little.

Aneira pushed up too fast, her fingers gripping my thigh harder than necessary—steadying, but also reluctant. A sharp inhale, a half-second hestitation—then she forced herself upright. She ripped the cannula off her face and almost shoved it straight up into Gigs's brain via his nose. "Here. You need this. What the fuck are you doing, treating me before yourself? That's a good way to get killed." She wilted all over him, like a wet sheet in the breeze.

He chuckled as he caught her. "You need to be taking your own advice, sweets." He pulled the oxygen tube from his face and put it back on hers. "Now don't make me paddle your ass. Keep it there and we'll be square." He glared at her as he shifted her around to sit on his lap instead of covering it like a fungus.

I glared at him as my fingers started itching. Seeing him touch her set something off in my chest. Not rational, not reasonable. Just raw. Which was utterly ridiculous. I'd seen him more involved in helping other women and not a single time in the past had it bothered me like it did now.

I glared at her, every inch of me blaming her. She made me reckless. Unfocused. Weak. And I'd be damned if I let her see it.

Shifting to look at Critter, I shook my head. I'd kill them all if I had to watch each of them handle her. And she wasn't that important, so I would take care of it myself. No harm would come to these men. Not by her, not because of her.

Critter nodded and gave me a small salute.

The band around my chest loosened. One down, six to go. "Gigs." The steel in my voice had every man turning to watch me. "I've got point."

He cradled her a little closer, dipped his chin. "Same rules apply."

I nodded.

"Since you're all dying soon, I guess I won't have to worry about lambasting you for thinking of me like property," she sniped. Pushing her way off Gigs's lap, she stumbled to her feet.

Each of my men lurched forward as if to catch her.

I let out a low snarl, felt it vibrate in my chest. Mine. The thought came out of nowhere, uninvited. "You called me, Ms. de Witte. Not the other way around. And you damn near passed out doing it." I crossed my arms over my chest, waited for her to look at me.

I didn't have to wait long. Seemed the tiny teacher didn't enjoy being told what to do. Deep inside, everything inside me eased out into smooth lines and clear patterns. Bringing sassy women to heel made places inside me giddy like a little boy.

"I didn't ask you to come. And by coming, you've put me in danger. So thanks for that. All of you need to leave." She turned to look at each man. "Now." She stabbed a finger at the door when she turned back to me.

I sank my weight deeper into the cushions holding me. "I think not, Ms. Guari."

Critter hesitated—just for a second—before leaning in, his smirk tight. "What was the other name you called her?"

Looking over Aneira's head, I caught his gaze. "Aneira de Witte and Isa Guari."

"And she plays with poison." He laughed again, not even trying to hide it..

Aneira flung herself at him. "You! You're the one who left the boxes on my front step."

Squirrel caught her midair and wrapped his long arms around her much smaller frame, the fabric of her dress bunched up under her tits, lifting the hem a good handful of inches.

Damn, she had sexy legs.

"Easy, pixie. That man is an asshole, no lie. But he didn't go leaving no poison on your porch. Now tell Big Daddy Squirrel what's got you all riled up, because one thing you won't be doing is hurting me or mine."

She glared at Critter as she tried to wrestle her way out of Squirrel's arms. All she did was exhaust herself. It took a couple seconds for her to realize she wasn't going anywhere.

"Why did you leave boxes on my step?" Her breath panted between the words, her entire rib cage shuddering.

I shifted to look at my medic, my eyebrows raised.

He shook his head. "The air is the best thing for her. We'll need to keep an eye on her for the next few hours though, make sure whatever it was is out of her system." His words were barely a whisper.

"Well, spit it out. I don't have all day," Aneira said, drawing my attention back to her with the amount of venom in her voice.

Critter lost his laugh as his dark brows fell low. "Just like Squirrel said, I didn't leave anything on your step. Box or anything else. Why the hell do I think I did anyway?"

"Because she has a secondary surveillance system hooked to her doorbell cam," Iggy said from his spot near the door. He had a tablet in his hands, his brows low as he watched something on his screen. "If I didn't know for sure it wasn't you, I'd blame you, too, Critter."

He turned the screen and hit a button. A wide angle picture of her front porch came into view. A man who looked like Critter's twin came to the door. With a little wave and a smirk, he settled the box in his hands on the stoop.

We all looked at Critter.

He shook his head, confusion and irritation plain to see. "The fuck that's me." He stabbed a finger in Iggy's direction.

"Camera's don't typically lie, you little shit. Why did you bring me poison? I won't ask again," Aneira said.

Something in her tone had all of us going still and quiet. There's no way she could have anything on her.

Right?

Gigs had given her an exam and he knew well enough to frisk her while he was doing it.

An unholy amount of anticipation saturated my system at her threat. She had something up her proverbial sleeve. Something sneaky and wickedly dangerous.

"Ms. de Witte, whatever you're thinking or planning, I would suggest you stall it. We're not your enemy. I can promise you that none of my men would have sent you the package, and I sure as hell didn't either. Come up with different options before you get one of us hurt." The threat threaded my tone so clearly a deaf man could have heard it.

She stilled in Squirrel's arms and turned to me. "What makes you think I have an outside option?"

I smirked. "Just a feeling I have. Belay its deployment and we'll all get to the bottom of this. If you're cleared by Gigs, we'll leave, and you'll never have to see us again. But if someone is out there running around with a face similar enough to one of my guys that even his brothers were fooled for a second, I need to know it. You obviously need to know who is leaving you dangerous packages. Let's team up for a minute and figure out what's really going on."

I watched her work through the problem in her head. Saw her run scenarios and outcomes, watched as she

77

considered and discarded each one. Eventually, I saw the truth of my words hit her. The acceptance took the steel from her spine.

"You can let me go, Mountain Man." She tapped a finger to his arm, her hand looking more like a doll's than a small woman's against his huge paddle-sized paws.

Squirrel chuckled as he let her go. "You're fun to hold, so if you need cuddles any time in the future, you give me a call. I'll cuddle you right up."

Her lips quirked before she got her expression fully under control. She turned up to him with a glare on her face. "Thank you, but no. I don't cuddle." She backed herself up until she hit the slim space of blank wall. "Well, let's get brainstorming. You really can't be here." She looked down at her watch, winced.

"Man coming home?" Gigs asked her, one brow raised high.

She rolled her eyes. "I'm not telling you that. I just need you all to leave. As quickly as possible."

The fact that the first time I saw her was after what could only be termed a failed encounter at Subterra and her subsequent satisfaction at her own hands, I had to assume that she really didn't have a man in her life. At least not a good one. The male who could leave this woman high and dry hadn't earned the title of man.

"Are you safe?" The words slipped out before I knew I was going to speak them.

The muscles around her pretty eyes flinched for the briefest second as she shook her head. "Yes, I'm safe. Why wouldn't I be safe?" The exasperation in her voice told me to leave it alone.

The mixed messages from her body language and her actual words told a different story.

"Buttercup, you need some muscle?" Squirrel asked. He flexed his huge arms. "You don't even have to give me cuddles in payment. No woman should be made to feel unsafe in her own home. I could teach him some lessons for you." He slid his index finger over his neck in a short motion. "Just give me a nod and he'll be flower food."

She spluttered a laugh. "Flower food?"

He nodded, jerked his chin at the arboretum's worth of flowers in the garden area. "Unless you know of some feral cats."

She shook her head. "I'm safe. But the longer you lot stand around, I won't be. You have to leave, as soon as possible, so let's get brainstorming." She lifted her chin as if that closed that particular subject.

Shifting, she looked at Critter. "You say it wasn't you. If not you, then who would be wearing your face? Or at least a really good fake of your face?"

Chapter 9
Neva

The man looked just as confused as I felt. "I have no idea. I don't have any uncles or brothers. What's left of my family is female and they aren't as sexy as I am." He bumped a shoulder up, a smug smirk on his face.

Chuckling at his ego, I shook my head. "Good to know you have a working relationship with humility." Pressure clenched down on my chest, ruining my smile with another cough. Thankfully, I didn't feel like anything was going to come rushing up from my lungs this time.

Which reminded me.

Shit.

I turned my elbow out, the bloody sputum stark against my skin. A fresh prickle of heat ran up my arms, my muscles tensing like they knew something I didn't. Whatever had been in that gas…it was still inside me. Still working.

And I was losing time.

Fast.

Spinning, I bolted back into the house. I needed to get a sample of whatever I'd been dosed with, see if I could run it through my system and identify its parts. Instead of going up the short stack of stairs, I went straight and headed down into my home lab.

"Aneira, wait!" The guy in charge called out.

Hurrying faster, I slid into the room and locked the door before anyone could follow me into my secondary sanctuary. Heavy fists pounded on the other side. "Get your tiny little ass out here, Aneira. Right now." His words were muffled, but I smiled at his compliment.

Just for that, I wasn't going to turn on my sprinklers laced with an aerosolized plant sap that would make them want to cut their flesh off their own bodies for days.

Shutting them out of my consciousness, I sat down at the table and pulled on a pair of blue nitrile gloves. Once I had that precaution out of the way, I took a scalpel and scraped at the bloody stain in my elbow.

Sliding the sample onto a glass slide, I got a cotton swab and rubbed it over the specimen. Setting up the solution and getting the gas chromatography-mass spectrometry machine started, I also did some sample collection from my face and a particularly bloody section of my dress.

Keys continued thumping on my door. "Last chance, Ms. de Witte."

I snorted. There was no way he was getting through that door. I didn't care if he was coming with a battering ram, or even a wrecking ball.

The lock clicked over, the sound loud in the quiet. My stomach dropped as my shoulders tensed. A shadow shifted in the crack beneath the door.

Too late.

A second later, the door swung open. Mountain Man stood there, a small set of tools in his hands and a wide smile on his face. "Hiya, pixie. Want to cuddle yet?"

My mouth dropped open. "H-h-hho…" I looked behind him to see the smiling faces of the rest of the group. "How the hell did you pop my lock? That's impossible."

He snickered as he put his tools in his pocket. "No lock can keep me out, sweet cheeks." He opened his arms. "Let's cuddle in acknowledgement of my accomplishment."

The audacity and inanity of his remark had a laugh bursting out of my mouth before I could stop it. Too loud. Too genuine. Too real. That wasn't right. Something in my brain was…loose. Off-balance. I clamped my lips together, shaking off the ripple of wrongness slithering down my spine.

I bit the laugh off, acutely conscious of the dichotomy of my thoughts and actions. My brow furrowed as I ran through my plant knowledge. Whatever I'd been dosed with had some very peculiar properties. And ones that weren't typically found in your garden variety poisons or toxins.

Which meant it was a designer compound.

"Where is Mr. Giggles?" I asked, trying to see around the big guy. He really was more of a mountain.

"I'm here, peaches," he slid to the side, shook his hand. "Whatcha need?"

"List your symptoms, please." I picked up a pen without having to look and grabbed my handy pad of paper. My eyebrows raised in expectation as I waited for him to respond.

If I could get some supporting information from a second victim, then I might be able to get a better picture of the compound before the computer gave me the answer.

Besting my computer was one of my favorite pastimes. It just didn't happen very often. The jerk.

"Coughing, burning fingertips and nasal passages. I think you smashing into me kept me from getting too much of it." He shifted and moved farther into my lab. His blue eyes wide as he studied my setup. "What the fuck kind of kindergarten teacher are you?" He swung his gaze back to me.

"The special kind. Any other symptoms? How long did you cough? How severe was it? Are you running a fever? Has the burning in your fingers or nose gone away?" I jotted notes as I did a visual inspection of him. He looked fairly normal, or as normal as I could claim for a relative stranger.

He shook his head. "No fever, no more burning. Like I said, I think you took the brunt of it. I coughed my head off for a couple seconds, felt a tight band go around my chest, but that went away almost as soon as Squirrel got me to the garden."

I spluttered a laugh as something finally dawned on me. "You call Mountain Man Squirrel?"

Everyone nodded.

So did Squirrel. "Yes, ma'am. On account of deez nutz." He twirled his hips in a tight circle, bit his lower lip in a paroxysm of bad porn face.

His team groaned as I laughed out loud. "I'll take your word on that, Squirrel. Do you want a cookie?" Steve Carrel's voice from the animated movie about wildlife animals getting the boot so a new housing development could take over kept flashing through my mind.

His whole face lifted in joy. "You got one?"

I shook my head, laughing slightly at the sorrow that fell over him. "No. Sorry. Just reminded me of a movie."

He nodded, but kept pouting. "Can I get a cuddle now?"

"Ask me again later." I couldn't bring myself to shoot him down again. Not with that face being all sad and sappy.

I made another note on my pad. Distinctly altered characteristics. My brain whizzed into high gear again as I tried to come up with the compound that would give me such widely varying side effects.

There was no other explanation for my drastic change in behaviors. Especially with a group of men I knew could kill me in less than a second. I narrowed my gaze as I studied all of them I could see. Squirrel was still making a better door than a window at the moment and half the team was obscured from view.

"How long did it take you to build this room?" Mr. Giggles asked.

I shook myself back to the here and now. No need to get lost in my brain while I was amongst unknowns. "Not answering. Do you have any other symptoms to report?"

He shook his head. Wandering farther into the room, he stopped at each piece of equipment, gave it a thorough study. "How long have you been a pathologist?"

"Not answering." The GC-Mass Spec gave a little ding that it was ready for the first specimen. Loading it into the chamber, I hit the button to begin the sequencing. I prepared the next sample.

Running through all the common possibilities left me with some gaping holes in my theory, but I couldn't get over the suddenness of the onset of symptoms. That was the biggest stumbling block for me. It had been almost instantaneous. It usually took at least a few minutes for even the most fast-acting poisons to start working.

Edging my ass onto the stool, I turned to the table and got down to the real business of phytotoxicolgy. There weren't too many of us pure plant poison people out there in the world. Which kinda made it even better for me, honestly. I enjoyed the rare, the hard to find, the exotic. Mundanity and normalcy had never really tripped my trigger. Not to mention that some of the deadliest things in this world were masked as delicate petals and beautiful blooms with heady scents.

"Ms. de Witte!" Key said, his voice loud in the quiet room.

I jolted. "What? And damn, no need to yell." I glared up at him. "I'm sitting right here."

The group burst into collective laughter.

"I called your name no fewer than eight times, you failed to answer." He smirked at me. "But now that I have your attention, what are you doing?" He gestured to the whole lab.

"Running experiments. What does it look like I'm doing?" Ask a stupid question, get a stupid answer. I went back to my notepad, chemical scribbles decorated the front page.

I blinked. Oh damn.

Popping up from my seat, I bolted for the door.

And smashed into Keys's chest. "Oof."

He caught my shoulders and steadied me. "You've really got to look before you leap, Aneira."

"Neva." The name blasted through my lips before I could catch it.

"What?"

"Neva," the man who I'd accused of leaving the packages on my door replied for me. "A derivative of neve, which means snow. Guess what de Witte means?" He pumped his dark brows at his leader.

One of the quieter men of the group, the only one with red hair, started chuckling. "Now I get the poison part."

"White. Her name literally means Snow White," the other guy answered before anyone could make a guess. "So does Isa Guari."

Eight gazes zeroed in on me. I felt the expectation, the judgment, the weight of every single one. But my momma hadn't raised a little bitch, so I stiffened my shoulders. "And? What of it?"

"You work for the CIA. With those kinds of names, your apparent skill with poisons, you get to pick your legends, don't you?" Keys asked.

Pokering up, I gave him a blank face. I didn't owe these men anything. Certainly not answers to my true identity.

"One Neva Bylur, nee Kendrick. Your name officially changed at the age of twelve," one of the Black men said from the corner of the room. He had the tablet in his hands, but he didn't bother looking up from the screen.

"Your mother, Lilla Kendrick, died around that time. You went to live with your grandparents." He kept reading off data as if he wasn't talking about the worst time in my life.

"Iggy," Keys said, his tone cool.

The man stopped talking finally.

I shook back my hair. "And now you all need to forget you ever heard any of that." I pushed my way through them. It was like trying to make my way down a forgotten forest path; they were all so damn tall.

Pushing everything about my past away, I focused on my bag. On getting my chemical notes from earlier today from it. With everything swirling around in my mind right now, I couldn't think in straight enough patterns to make heads or tails out of anything.

Stupid assholes thinking they could just come in and tear my life apart. I'd have survived the poisoning, and even if I hadn't, then I'd be dead, and it wouldn't matter. They were doing nothing but making everything worse.

I couldn't call Brantley, certainly couldn't call the police. I was alone with eight highly trained men who wanted answers. And I needed the same answers, so I couldn't just wait until they left either. I'd been dosed twice, right in my face. If there were potential long-term side effects, I needed to know it.

I heaved a sigh. My only option was to get them what they wanted as soon as humanly possible and pray that Brantley didn't do another of his ridiculous spot checks. Rushing to the foyer faster, I found the bag and grabbed it up.

Unwilling to hit the first box and potentially dose myself again, I kicked the other two boxes out of the way so I could grab them. Those would be opened in a secure clean area in my lab so no one else got hit in the face with anything.

My bag knocking against my rib cage, I hurried back to my lab. No telling what those animals were getting into. And with Squirrel's skills with locks, and the ever-not-helpful Iggy with his tablet, I couldn't leave them alone for too long.

Just as I cleared the last step, I heard one of them say, "For fuck's sake, Keys, she's working for them. We've got to take her out. She could identify us, get us all killed."

I stilled just outside the door, held my breath. They were plotting to kill me? In my own home? What assholes! And to think I was going to try to help them. Well, they could take a long jump off a short bridge for all I cared.

"Critter, pushing me won't change my answer. We're not going to kill her, you idiot. Over and above the fact that she's fucking living as a kindergarten teacher right now, we don't know what her job is. Because we all know she shouldn't be working on US soil for the Company, that's for damn sure."

"Fine," the first man said.

Assuming he was this Critter, I was sure I could come up with some non-fatal chemical bath for him. Help him change his attitude.

"And I was just fucking with you. If you'd gotten any closer to her, you would have hit her with your dick."

The rest of the team seemed to agree because they started ragging on their leader as well. Before I could decide what to do, the door whipped open and revealed me standing there. Wiping my face clear of any expression, I walked into the room like I owned the joint. Because I did. These jerks needed to remember that.

"Unless your dick runs on batteries, I'm not interested. None of you know how to use them anyway. And damn straight you're not gonna kill me, you assholes." I glared at all of them. "Which of you is Critter again?"

The man who looked like the guy from the footage raised his hand, gave me a smile. "Palmer DeMio, at your service, Snow White." He sketched a quick bow.

The audacity on this guy. I smiled at him, visions of him patchy and red entertaining my brain. "Easy there, Dopey. Don't need you getting your idiot all over the room."

The men boomed into laughter so loud I felt it in my chest. Putting my bag down, I moved to the containment isolator with the two other boxes I'd found on my porch. Opening the hatch, I put both of them in, closed the door, and hit the button to sterilize the field.

"What the hell are you doing?" someone asked from behind me.

In short order, I had a wall of heat at my back. Over my head and shoulders, weak reflections of their faces stared back at me in the thick, shiny plexiglass of the isolator. "I'm doing my job and since I don't want another cloud of poison in my face, I'm doing what I should have done earlier."

Picking up one of the scalpels I'd placed in there after my last experiment, I slit open the boxes. One of them produced another chemical cloud and the other didn't.

"Thank fuck you did that in the machine," Keys said from directly behind me.

I couldn't actually feel his body against mine, but if I took a big enough breath, I had no doubt that I would. The man had no concept of personal space, apparently. Or he just really liked a front row seat to the isolator show.

"Yeah, amazing what I can accomplish when I'm not irritated and distracted by you lot." Pulling open the box containing the second poison, I noticed something smudged on the inside of the cardboard. Which looked suspiciously shiny. Too shiny for cardboard.

They all chuckled behind me. I didn't know if they thought I was kidding or not, but right now, I had other things to worry about.

"Someone hand me that pair of scissors." I jerked my chin at the far end of the isolator.

A hard scuffle jostled me into the machine. "Hey."

"Sorry, Snow. Dopey was trying to beat me; I had to put him down," Mr. Giggles said as he slid his hands and arms into the second set of inward facing gloves.

"Don't call me Snow but keep calling him Dopey." I took the scissors he held out to me. "Thanks."

"Why do I get called Dopey?" Critter asked as he shuffled to the far end of the isolator. "You don't know me well enough to give me a nickname."

"If I have to explain it, you can't handle the truth. Now everyone shut up so I can focus. If you can't, you're all more than welcome to leave." Shutting out the whole group from my consciousness, I focused on the shiny lining of the box.

"Holy shit, is that gold?" Mr. Giggles said, his words more breath than sound.

I nodded without looking away, my brain tripping into overtime with all kinds of reasons and possibilities. "Yes, Happy, it is. A barrier to keep the poison intact until it could be released into the air when the box opened. Negates the need for a capsule or vacuum tube, too. Wouldn't do shit for scanners or imaging, but they did leave it on my doorstep personally."

The room was quiet behind me.

So quiet, I turned, my hand still stuck in the gloves. "What?" I looked at each man, their expressions stuck somewhere between quizzical and outraged.

"He's Happy?" Dopey jabbed his finger in Mr. Giggles's direction. "The psychopath gets to be Happy?"

I shrugged. "He has a nice laugh, when he's not threatening idiots." Turning back to the isolator, I tried to peel the gold from the cardboard. My brows rose high when I realized how thick the lining really was. "Damn."

"What's wrong now, Neva?" Keys asked from his spot at my back.

Jolting at the sound of my real name, it took me a second to focus again. Shaking it off, I shifted to the side, tapping the edge of the lining with the scalpel in my hand. "Do you see how thick that is? That's got to be at least two hundred sheets deep. Why would someone use that much gold leaf to line a package?"

Behind me, the room went still—the kind of stillness that precedes gunfire. A breath held. A muscle tensed. A chair leg scraped against the floor, abrupt and wrong.

Then Keys spoke, low and sharp. "Because whoever sent it wasn't just protecting the poison. They were protecting the message."

My breath caught in my throat for a long moment as my fingers and toes went to ice. No one moved. The air in the lab felt too still, thick. It was a message. Not just a toxin, not just a hit.

Someone wanted me to see and understand whatever this was as a whole.

Shit.

I still needed answers. We all did. Shaking off the heaviness in the room, I moved back into my position, scraping at the layers I could see. "From my best guess, that's twenty-four karat."

"Look again, Snow. Those aren't layers. At least not leaf," Happy said.

Glaring at him out of the corner of my eye, I saw his smirk.

"Hey, you're going to give us Seven Dwarfs monikers, you get to be Snow." He jutted his chin back at the isolator. "Those aren't separate layers; those are hammered melt lines."

"Can you take a sample?" one of the guys asked from the group at my back.

"After I get a couple swabs and I neutralize any residue," I bit the words off. They were in my space, trying to give me orders, disrupting my groove. I was used to working on my own with no one else telling me what to do or interrupting my thoughts.

"Are we in your space, Snow?" Keys whispered, his voice a low hum against my skin. The kind of whisper meant to unravel, not reassure. "Distracting you?"

Chills ran up my spine, and for a second, I didn't shake them off. The heat of him. The scent. The weight of his presence behind me, pressing in. Too damn close. Too damn easy to lean into.

I caught myself mid-breath, already leaning before my brain caught up. Too fucking close. Too fucking easy.

I forced myself to move. Shook him off. Again.

I had a job to do and none of them, especially their leader, were going to throw me off my game. "And you're all done. Time to leave." I shook my hands free of the isolator gloves and turned around.

Keys hadn't moved, so my face slid across his chest like a kid with her face to the candy shop window. The scent of him invaded my nose; clean laundry and man. No discernable cologne or anything else.

Just him. The heat he pumped off would have activated any chemicals he had put onto his skin or his clothes, so I had to assume that he didn't wear any.

My mouth went dry. But I shook it off, shook him off. Again.

No. Not happening.

I had goals that didn't include any of these men. In fact, they were going to get hurt if they stayed around me. So I needed to shut this down and shut it down hard and fast.

"You don't have what it takes to really distract me, so you all might as well leave. And that wasn't a suggestion. Get out of my house. Thank you for the assist" —even though I hadn't really needed one— "and, please, lose my number."

Turning back around, I pushed them from my mind and tried to focus on the work in front of me. Once I was done with this last job, I would be finished, and my life would finally be my own.

Chapter 10
Rome

Gritting my teeth at the cold shoulder and brusque dismissal, I curled my fingers into fists. It would take nothing to close the space. Nothing to grab her, press her back, make her look at me—make her see. Turnabout's fair play in my book.

Giggles shot me a look that promised bodily harm if I did anything. He jerked his head toward the door where the rest of the team had filed out. Bunch of pussies, letting one small curvy woman tell them what to do.

Giggles pushed up into my space, physically using his body to shove me out of the room. "Don't make me hurt you, boss." There wasn't a trace of humor on his face.

My lips twitched as I remembered Snow's moniker for him. "Sure thing, Happy."

I spun on my heel and went down the short hallway to see my men ranged out in her living room. Stretched out on couches, languishing on chairs. Schnauzer sat on the short stack of stairs that led up to the second floor.

"I'm not leaving until that little b—" Critter started.

Giggles lunged for him.

Critter jumped back, hands up in surrender. "Babe, Gigs. I was gonna say babe. Jeez, I'm not wanting to die today. Fuck. I'm not leaving until that *babe* can tell me why my face is on her security system for dropping off packages we all know damn good and well I didn't leave." Critter stepped forward, lowering his hands.

"I've run her entire system," Iggy said. His tablet had been in his hands the whole time, his nose almost brushing the screen. "Both of them, actually. There are no signs of hacking, no signs of intrusion at all. For all intents and digital purposes, Critter, you did drop those packages."

Critter spun, his color high. "The fuck I did, Ig."

"Can you grab some stills and run them back at the office?" Banshee asked. "If we can analyze the face on the footage, we might be able to do something with that information."

Iggy nodded. "I've already sent a couple shots to my unit back at HQ. I'm waiting for my system to run some preliminaries." He looked back at Critter. "And I'm not saying you did it. Not your style and definitely not in your schedule today. I'm saying that if it were someone else running her footage and they ID'd you, most people would testify that it was you. The skills of the guy leaving that shit on her doorstep are top-notch."

Critter eased back, then fell into a chair that creaked under his weight.

We all tensed up to see if it would hold up under the guy. When it held, we all blew out a collective breath.

"Thank fuck. I don't want that angry pixie poisoning me." He rubbed a hand down his face.

I nodded. Killing her for poisoning one of my men would make me a little sad, I'll admit. She was intriguing, challenging, and mysterious. Something so unique shouldn't be snuffed out for stupid reasons.

"What else did you find on her, Iggy?" I asked, needing to get the image of her cold, dead body out of my head.

"For her public face, she's going under Aneira de Witte, kindergarten teacher at some fancy-ass private school for kids. Lives alone, no family of record. Pays her taxes on time, has a single late fee at the library. Honestly, if this was all that was in her legend, it's no surprise she made it through Subterra's vetting process."

He smiled slightly. "Thank fuck you guys made the connection on her names, otherwise I wouldn't have found her at all. Even her Company history is super spotty. Literally all I've got are the highlights. She's been in since eighteen after she graduated college early. Company footed the bill for her doctorates."

"Doctorates? As in more than one?" Giggles asked.

Iggy nodded. "Yeah, pathology and toxicology with a specialization in plants."

"Why did we never work with her, then?" Schnauzer asked. "We were a specialized team for exactly that kind of shit. She never once got hooked in with us while we were in Teams."

Iggy shook his head. "Haven't drilled down that far yet. I have to be careful, there's something odd about her file. It has some kind of marker on it I've never seen before. I don't want to trip any triggers and get her flagged."

"We certainly don't want to let anyone know we've met her now," I said. "If she's still in, we might be able to use her to get some information."

Everyone turned to me, calculation on each face.

"You're really going to turn her into a double agent?" Critter asked. "Not even this morning you were getting pissy because I used suggestive language when talking about her and you almost got her pregnant in her lab with your stiff dick. But you're going to set all of that off and try to run her on the side?"

I rolled my eyes at him. "I'm not trying to turn her into a double agent. Besides, if she's a legit agent, then taking down dirty actors is part of her job description."

"She could also help with the SRD poison. With the lab she's got downstairs, she might be able to synthesize something to help us out," Gigs suggested.

I waved a hand in his direction "See? We need to help her keep her legend intact and see if we can get into her good graces."

"Like finding out who sent poison to her," Critter offered.

I nodded. "Exactly. Information for information."

"And you're hoping that's enough for her to change her mind on your dick," Squirrel said. "Admit it, Rome. There's something selfish in wanting to keep her close. At least admit it to yourself."

I glared at the big man. "Fine. She's off limits."

Satisfaction sat on every single one of my men's faces.

I rolled my eyes. "When did you guys get so concerned with where I put my dick?"

"When you started thinking with it. And the fact you're a moody bitch when you're not getting any. And believe you me, you've been a super moody bitch lately," Squirrel answered for the group.

When the guys all nodded along with him, I had to bite back my snappish reply. Maybe they were onto something with the moody bitch part.

"We've got incoming, Keys," Iggy said, his voice hard. "I'm still in her system. Someone is approaching from the front."

As a single unit, we got to our feet and fell into our customary positioning. Moving to the front, I took the lead. Without having to look behind me, I knew everyone other than Det had taken some sort of cover while out in their staggered spots.

"Five," Iggy counted down.

I pulled my weapon from my inner-pants holster and checked the slide and chamber.

"Four."

I heard the softest whispers of metal on metal as my team did the same checks for their own firearms.

"Three."

Taking up position to the right of the door, I waited for Det to take up the left position.

"Two."

Iggy set down the tablet on the entryway table and pulled his gun. The doorbell rang as he fingered off the safety.

A rushing hustle came from the back of the house where Snow's lab was. She hurried through, her head down as she pulled blue gloves off her dainty hands. "Coming."

"It's cuddle time, pix," Squirrel whispered as he caught her up in his arms, slapped his hand over her mouth.

I'm pretty sure it was the only thing that saved him.

Fire lit her gaze an instant before she seemed to relax into his grip. Watching him whispering into her ear, I had to bite back the snippy response to get his hands off of her.

Definitely a moody bitch, damn it.

He set her down so her feet were back on the floor. She smiled up at him, patted his hand like he was her faithful puppy, and walked forward more sedately. Once she made it to the door, she glared at me like I'd set said puppy on fire and danced around the pyre. "We'll talk about this later."

Reaching for the doorknob, I tapped her hand out of the way. Pulling her up against me, I tucked her under my shoulder, settled my hand at her hip, and opened the door as a couple. "Yes, can I help you?"

The man on the porch stepped back a couple feet before he rocked to a halt. About six foot even, he was a very pale skinned mixed race guy with the ugliest dreads I've ever seen on a human head. He glanced between us for long moments, then glared at Snow. "Baby, who the fuck is this?" His saccharine tone ruined by the twist of his face and hate in his eyes.

Snow bit her fingers into my waist. "Who are you talking about, lover?"

The pleasant befuddlement in her tone caught me off guard. Had I not been standing right here, I would have assumed the man was simply mistaken about someone else being in the vicinity.

The guy shifted his gaze up to me, back to Snow. "The giant man holding you entirely too close to his body."

Snow tipped her head to the side, a faint frown marring her brows. "I have no idea what you're talking about, Brantley. Do you have someone with you?" She even pushed up to her tiptoes to see down the porch.

Brantley blew out a big breath through his nose and shoved forward. "Get the fuck out of the way, Larkspur, or I'll take you off this case so fast your head will spin."

She stepped into his direct path, icy fury on her face. Though she was a foot shorter than me, I would have backed up too with the gleeful promise of violence on her pretty features. "You remember my rules, don't you, Brantley? Step one foot inside my home without express permission and you'll be drinking your meals through a straw for the foreseeable future." She pulled her hand free from my hip and intertwined her fingers at her waist as if she were a 1950s mother on a commercial.

Brantley stopped dead in his tracks, his gaze sliding over her smaller frame with intent focus. "You won't get me to play that game again, you bitch." He acted as if he were going to mow her down.

She lifted her chin, leaned forward slightly. "Try me." Her voice was soft, almost lilting in the late afternoon sun.

He hesitated for another long moment, rocking back on his heels. Then he changed his tactics from bulldozing to more questions. "Who the fuck is in your house?"

She narrowed her gaze. "How do you know I have anyone in my house, Brantley? You're my handler, not my keeper."

His smile was greasy and made my fingers itch to cut it off his face. He shifted his gaze to me again. "Do I need more proof?"

She didn't bother looking in my direction at all. "Yes, actually you do. Photographic proof of wrongdoing. You know the drill. And if it can't be verified by an unbiased third party, remember the outcome." She stepped back, shoving me out of the way of the door swing with her luscious ass, and closed the door softly in his face. "Fuck. Fuck. Fuck. Fuck." She wrenched on her fingers until her knuckles went white.

After a long moment of watching her spin out of control, she glared up at me. "Get the fuck out of my house. Right now."

I snorted, shook my head. "Not happening. You know he's not going to have his proof. We could both smell the power games he was playing. And if he's your handler, then you need to come stay with us, or we'll move in here. He'll sell you for free down any river he can find. He just needs a reason at this point." I crossed my arms over my chest, smiling down at her.

"I know that. I knew that when he was assigned to my case," she bit the words off and spit them out at me.

My brows furrowed. "Then why the fuck are you playing his game?"

She raised a single dark brow. "Vinegar and honey, sweets. Vinegar and honey."

My laugh spluttered out. "And which was that?" I jerked a thumb in the direction of the door.

"Honey." She gave me a steady look.

I felt my dick twitch at the savage brutality in her eyes. "Then color me very curious about your vinegar."

Her lips twitched the slightest degree before she turned back to the main room of her house. "Why the hell are you guys still here? Are you all deaf? Stupid? Lacking women? Hobbies? Pets?" She jammed her fists on her hips and glared at each of my men as they came out of their spots.

"What the fuck are you?" Critter demanded.

Giggles growled low in his throat.

Critter waved him off as he stepped up into Snow's space. "Can it, Gigs. She's rude, I can be rude back. Those are *your* rules." He looked down the length of his nose at her. "So...what's your deal? Are you really this bitchy? Are you on your period?"

My eyes widened as the man signed his own death certificate. I wouldn't even be mad at her at this point. My guy was aching for a beat down.

"And you ask why you're Dopey." She sounded so sad as she shook her head and weaved around him.

Critter caught her arm and spun her around to face him.

We all got up close and personal, snarls and growls sounding from the tight circle we'd formed around them. "Take your hand off her, Critter." I had to force the words through the rage in my throat.

Critter shook his head without looking away from her. "No." He had ego riding front and center as he leaned down to get in her face.

"Shoulda listened, Dopey." Snow spun in a tight circle, her hand going up to grab her necklace for a short second. As she faced him again, she feigned her knee to his junk. When he raised his leg to counter, she shoved her hand into his face. As he struggled to right himself, then she jacked him in the dick with her knee.

He bleated out a high-pitched whine, his hands cupping his crotch. "Bitch."

She wiped her hand down his face, slowly, deliberately, a bright smile on her own. Sweet, cruel, the tiniest touch of humor that made my stomach twist in fear. "Thank you, sweetie. I'm so glad you noticed."

A hush fell as we watched the marks bloom—five perfect streaks, his skin rising in angry lines across his cheeks, forehead, chin. His nose went cherry-bright, sweat beading on his brow.

Then, he coughed.

Hard.

We all took a giant step back.

"The next one who touches me gets the same treatment," she said, her voice hard. "I tried telling you all to leave. I'm done being nice."

"Snow, I'm not sure how to tell you this, but this isn't nice," Giggles said. "Fix him. Now."

She rolled her eyes. "He's fine." She jerked her chin in my fallen brother's direction. "See?"

As we all watched from our safe distances, the redness turned more of a pink color as he continued to cough. But even that reaction slowed and decreased. His nose no longer resembled Rudolph's.

We all turned back to look at her.

Holy fuck, this woman was terrifying.

She had her arms crossed over her chest, her chin held high. An air of royal displeasure settled in the room like we were in the presence of greatness and we just annoyed her.

"Told you so. Stop being such babies." From queen to mean girl in the space of a breath.

"What the fuck was that?" Critter demanded from his spot on the floor, still holding his junk in his hands.

"A personal formula I made for just such occasions. I didn't give you permission to touch me. Make damn sure you don't ever touch me again." She glared at Critter before lifting her gaze to all of us. "He needed to learn some manners. I taught him a lesson. That's all."

Since we'd been on the verge of giving him a smackdown of our own for touching her in anger, I couldn't really fault her logic. "Maybe just the junk jacking next time."

She lifted her chin. "There won't be a next time, will there, Dopey?"

He shook his head, cringed away from the tiny terror. "No, Snow. I won't touch you again."

Her smile made my chest ache. Then she showed her teeth, and my balls drew up in fear.

"Sweet fuck, you're terrifying." Critter shuddered.

She giggled like a little girl. "I know. It's great, right?" With that, she spun on her heel and left the room. "Shut the door on your way out."

I snorted. "We're not leaving without some actual answers, Snow. Might as well come back—without your poisons—and have a chat." I jerked my chin for the men to all take up their original positions.

Everyone but Critter found their spots on the couches, chairs, and stairs once more.

She trailed back into the room, head lowered, her cheeks pink with outrage. "What did you just say to me?"

I cleared my throat, felt a zing of adrenaline and lust wash through me at her anger. Fuck, tangling with her got me jacked in all the good kinds of ways. "We're not leaving without some actual answers, Snow. Might as well come back—without your poisons—and have a chat." I leaned against the wall, arms crossed, a brilliant smile on my face.

She studied me for long moments, then dipped her chin. Not submission. Not surrender. Pure calculation.

Just before she moved, her lips curved—but it wasn't a smile. It was a fucking challenge that lit her eyes.

"Fine, Keys. Let's play your game."

Then, with an exhale, she folded her legs and settled onto the floor. Not wilting.

Waiting.

Chapter 11
Neva

The fading burn in my hand kept my mind focused as I tried to think through the implications of this shittastic day. From the missed run, all the way through to having to use the last of my necklace serum on that jackhole's face. Distilling some more of the mixture was going to take at least a week, assuming I had enough free time in the lab.

"We're waiting," Keys said.

I looked up at him through my lashes. It really was too bad that he oozed such sincerity and sex appeal. Had he been just an outright asshole, things would have gone a lot smoother. But no, he had to step in and help me. Hell, tried to save my life—even if he did make it a lot worse in the doing.

"Waiting on what?" I asked. Leaning back on my hands, I stretched out my legs. It had taken close to an hour, but I finally felt normal again. No more hacking cough or tight pressure around my chest. Everything was status quo.

Except for the forest of too tall dwarfs scattered around my living room. If they would leave, I could carry on my way without any more issues. Too bad I had a feeling I wouldn't be rid of them for a long while.

"For some damn answers," Dopey said from his spot on the floor. He kept running his hands over his face, glaring at me between his spread fingers.

"You literally have the same information I do. And since I'm sure your techno wizard over there knows more about some stuff, you're the ones in the lead. Find your answers on your own." Rolling to the side, I got back to my feet. "If you can't offer anything but blank looks and stupid remarks, you're free to leave. Like I keep telling you." I glared at each of them.

Squirrel just smiled and wiggled his fingers at me in a coquettish wave that was more suited to a teeny bopper in the late '80s. I had to bite my lip to keep from laughing at him and his antics. Smart alecks had a special place in my heart.

"What are you working on?" Keys asked. "For the CIA? And why the fuck are you on US soil doing it?"

"Who said I'm working with the CIA right now?" I asked, raising one eyebrow high.

Keys just smiled and tipped his head to the guy with the tablet. "Iggy verified."

I smiled. "Then you have bad intel as well as bad hearing. I can suggest some good audiologists, if you need one. Let me know, I'll text you the information."

Keys's eyebrows winged up. "You have my phone number?"

Now more than ever I was sure it had been him who texted me earlier today with vague threats. I rolled my eyes at his juvenile attempt to lie. "That's all you've got? Feigned confusion?" Some of my kindergartners lie better than this.

This time, his dark brows fell into a line of blatant confusion. "I'm not lying." He shook his head. "Why would I lie about asking you if you have my phone number?"

I narrowed my gaze at him. "You didn't text me earlier today?"

He shook his head. "Why would you assume I had?"

"Get her phone," Iggy, the apparent Tech Lord Supremo, instructed. The men all got up and started moving around my living room like they owned the joint.

"I'll check the lab," Squirrel said. He rushed by me, a huge goofy smile on his face. It was a little disconcerting that the giant man was almost silent in his passing.

"Got it," Happy called. He crossed paths with Squirrel and they both rejoined the group. Happy gave my phone to Iggy.

I just sighed at them. When would they learn they couldn't just run roughshod over me and expect me to take it with a smile? "You have twenty seconds to give me my phone, without unlocking it, or you're all going to get an itch bath you won't soon forget." I examined my cuticles as I waited for one of them to entertain some common sense and hand me my device.

Critter leapt forward and snatched the phone from Iggy's fingers before he practically threw the thing at me. "Don't douse us."

I caught the heavy rectangle against my chest and marveled at his aim. The guy had some skills with throwing weighted objects. I'd have to keep that in mind.

Stuffing my phone in my bra, I crossed my arms and studied the room. "What will it take for you all to leave?"

"Answers, Snow. We already told you that," Keys answered.

Gritting my teeth, I weighed my options. Give them just enough to make them go away so I could finish this job in peace and never go back to the club, or keep trying to stonewall them and hope they got tired and left on their own.

Looking at each man, I knew the latter would never be an option for them. Ever. Especially as former SEALs. These men didn't know the definition of the word quit. As a gender, as a species, as former operators, they were disinclined to quit anything.

"If I give you information, what will you give me?" I wasn't really in the market for anything at the moment, but you never knew when information would come in handy. And since I wasn't getting out of this situation without at least a little quid pro quo, then they had to offer up something to get mine.

All heads turned to Keys in deferred silence. The man in charge continued to watch me. A little too closely, if I were being honest. I didn't like being so seen. It made me itchy.

"We'll tell you our names," he offered.

I raised a single brow. "Are they state secrets?"

No one answered. Which probably meant they weren't.

I smiled. "You can add it to the pile then, but I'm gonna need more." It was the story of my entire freaking life. But I pushed those thoughts away. No need to devolve into a puddle of pity and tears.

"We have a new poison you probably haven't heard of," Happy offered when Keys didn't say anything else.

I turned to the man with a psychopath's smile. "Oh yeah? What's the base? If I haven't heard of it, I'll tell you something you want to know."

Happy turned to Keys for a long moment, his head cocked to the side.

Keys finally nodded, his arms crossed over his chest again. He kept his eagle eyes on me.

Turning to Happy, I smiled in welcome. "Well?"

"Flame lily."

Well, shitsticks and rose petals. There's no possible way they could know about that. It was still in testing and production.

"You've heard of it," Keys said before I could even blink.

Damn it. He really needed to stop watching me.

I dipped my chin. "Yup. Got anything else?"

"In your version, what's it paired with?" Happy demanded.

I had to tread carefully. "Why do you think it's paired with anything?" They must not have a very good idea of what flame lily could do all on its own.

Happy's smile blossomed into a true grin of happiness. "Ours has necrotizing fasciitis. We win." He gave me gimme-gimme fingers and pumped his blond brows.

I blinked as I tried to organize my thoughts. A flesh-eating bacteria had been added to their flame lily? How the fuck was that even possible? And why the hell would someone want to create it in the first place?

My mind started zipping and zinging with different solutions and reagents, but I couldn't get a cohesive chemical formula to come together in my mind. That combination was utter craziness.

"We're waiting, Snow," Keys said softly, demand a living thing in his voice.

Shaking myself back to the present, I glared at him. "You're so fucking bossy; do you know that?"

The men all burst into laughter as Keys merely smirked.

"Look who's talking, lady," Critter snorted out between laughs.

I nodded, I'd give him that. "Fine. I'm working with the FBI on special assignment to help with bioweapon identification. Seems there's a new dealer in town."

"Did they supply your lab?" Happy asked quickly.

I shook my head, but didn't say anything more. "How long has your poison been in circulation?"

Keys slashed his hand through the air before Happy could answer. "Not nearly enough information for what we gave you. You've got to give us something else."

I blew out my breath and shook out my shoulders. Damn him. Casting my mind around for something else I could share and not ruin everything I'd been planning for the last year, I stalled for time. "What do you mean? I gave you good information."

He rolled his eyes and crossed his arms again. He looked like he was going to stand there until he became a part of the house. A living tree made of flesh and blood. But he didn't say anything else.

Damn it.

"Brantley is my cover boyfriend. He's also my FBI handler for this mission. As you probably noticed, he's more worried about optics and power displays than catching anyone."

Keys shook his head, said nothing again. When the rest of his men followed his example, I gritted my teeth. I could definitely see why Keys was in charge. And I really needed to figure out his real name. Calling him by his call sign without a relationship of some kind could make things even more awkward.

"There have been some anonymous reports of harassment and misuse of power by Brantley. He thinks they came from me, so now he's all bent out of shape and wants to screw me over." I held my breath, prayed that would be enough.

Keys rolled his eyes. "I don't care one flying fuck what that ratfaced bastard does or thinks. Actionable intel, Snow. Or get ready for some long-term guests."

"If I could interject," the tall guy with red hair said. Not quite as big as Squirrel, he had the presence and withdrawn energy of someone who was incredibly comfortable behind a long-range weapon.

Keys waved him forward.

Tall Guy shifted to look at me directly. "I'm Beck Maddox." He dipped his chin with a soft smile. "And we're offering to work together, Ms. Bylur."

107

My eyes widened momentarily at hearing my real last name. Just as I was about to freak the fuck out, I remembered Iggy saying it while we were in the lab earlier. "To what end, Mr. Maddox?"

Keys snarled low in his throat behind his man.

He grinned, shook his head slightly. "Either Beck, Maddox, or Schnauzer. Never Mr. Maddox."

Not wanting to risk a glance away from the man in front of me, I narrowed my focus. Nodding, I said, "Maddox. To what end?"

"We're no longer in Special Operations, Ms. Bylur. We are now providing personal security for individuals and businesses. The poison Giggles—or Happy, as you call him—referenced is one we've been tracking since our time in the Teams. You seem to be an expert. If you could help us, we would do our best to help you."

I smiled at the slightly formal tone, but couldn't fault him for cutting through the posturing bullshit. "Thank you for answering fully, Maddox. I appreciate that."

He dipped his chin. "We can do quite a bit outside of the lines of law and government as private contractors. There are admittedly more of us than there are of you. And we would be loyal to you—assuming you're not doing anything to harm innocents."

I blinked at his words. "All I have to do to get your help is not harm innocents? Not follow the rules, mind the law, do what I'm told by my superiors?"

Beck shook his head, his blue eyes twinkling. "We learned hard lessons about rules, chains of command, and laws that help the guilty. Are you now, or planning to in the future, hurt innocents?"

I shook my head. "I'm planning to save them." Shit. I hadn't meant for that to come out of my mouth. What was it about this group of men who made me do and say shit I hadn't planned on?

They were going to be the death of me. If not literally, then figuratively.

...and probably literally, too, damn it.

I needed to watch myself better than this. I walked a very precarious edge and falling either way would spell my certain untimely death. There were more things I needed to accomplish and fix before I could meet my eternal rest.

Otherwise, I would have taken out a lot of people already.

I smiled a little at the mental picture of all the faces of the people who would find their end with my help. The list of people aching to die kept getting longer and longer. I was only too happy to help do my part.

"That's fucking scary. Stop smiling like that," Dopey demanded.

Oh right. Still had people in my house. I wiped my expression clean. "Don't tell me what to do, Dopey. I'm still pissed at you."

He backed up, his hands lifted in surrender. "Fine. No wonder you called Giggles Happy. You're two peas in a fucking psychotic pod."

"You're planning to save innocents, which means we can be on the same team. We could share information and put our respective problems to bed that much faster." Beck smiled slightly. "Sound like a plan?"

Honestly, it sounded amazing. A group of men who knew how to handle themselves without having to worry they were working for someone else? That was a magic wand wish right there. I'd known going into this last job I'd be on my own. Nine times out of ten, I preferred it that way.

But this time, I just couldn't shake the feeling that something wasn't quite right. I knew, better than most, what could happen when it came to bioagents. And while the FBI wasn't on the top of the ladder when it came to poisons, the slapdash method of working this case left quite a lot to be desired.

We were no closer now than we had been almost six months ago. Granted, my clandestine efforts to get placed here had taken time the country really didn't have to waste in bringing these fuckers down, but to have a full team of agents since that time and still not make any progress? Something was off and it could cost too many lives.

Shifting to the side, I looked at Keys. "You on board with your man's offer?"

Keys nodded. "If you're really as good as what Iggy says and have the ability to help us, I'll help you take down anyone you want, Snow."

"We all will," Happy offered.

It was a very tempting offer. But I couldn't just make a blind leap. That's what landed me in this mess in the first place. "How about this? I'll run you through a program I have."

Keys shook his head.

I blazed on as if I hadn't seen it. "It's not one linked to any databases under US government control. I'll run you through those. If I'm good with what I find, then I'll join Team Tall Trees."

Keys shook his head again. "If you run us through any program that even flirts with the US government, you'll raise flags we can't afford. Especially right now."

My brows winged up. "Are you on the run?"

Once again, Keys shook his head. "Not like that. We're hunting moles."

My lips quirked. "You're mole hunting in the US government?" I laughed. "Hell, who isn't these days? What makes your moles so special?"

"We can't tell you that without you coming on board. And that's for your benefit, too, Ms. Bylur," Beck said, drawing my attention back to him. "In this particular case, you're an innocent on our side of things, too."

I sighed and shook my head. "Aneira, Ms. de Witte, Larkspur, or that stupid Snow. I can't have one of you slipping up and leaking my real name."

"Were you really named Neva at birth?" Iggy asked softly.

I nodded. My mom loved winter and snow. She also had a little thing for Snow White as a bedtime story, but the one I got read to me every night couldn't be found in any Disney show, that was for damned sure.

"What program were you wanting to use to run us?" Iggy said, breaking into my thoughts. "I can send you our records, let you do some snooping that way."

"A program a friend of a friend has access to." It might be better to leave her alone, though. From what I heard on the news these days, she could be in over her head at the moment.

"How about a happy medium?" Iggy suggested.

"I'm listening."

"I can give you an access point to a group of third-party enthusiasts. Give them our names, have them run the data. That way, there's no link between you or us."

"How would I know their data is any less biased than yours?"

Iggy smiled a bit wolfishly. "In your time with the Company, have you ever heard of The Collective?"

Blinking at him, I felt the humor rush up my throat. I swallowed it back before I could start laughing. "I have."

They were the owners of the program I'd suggested in the first place.

"Will they suffice as DJs for you?"

Nodding, I smiled. "Yes. They will be fine as go-betweens."

Almost every single set of shoulders belonging to these guys relaxed at my answer. They were really keen on having someone with my skillset on their side it seemed.

Iggy smiled back at me. "I sent you an email."

My brows furrowed. "How do you know my email address?"

"I hacked your doorbell cam account." He said it so nonchalantly that I almost passed over the infringement on my privacy.

"Stay out of my data."

He smiled even brighter. "Sure, I can do that for you."

Which probably meant he'd already copied everything he could get his grubby little hands on. Assholes. The whole, damn lot of them. Too bad they mostly made me want to laugh instead of kill them.

Firmly pushing down the smile at their take charge and give zero fucks attitudes, I glared at them all. "Then tell me names, call signs, and jobs."

"You already know Rome Whitlock, Keys. He's the bossman extraordinaire," Squirrel started, pointing at the guy.

I finally had his real name. And got it in a way that wasn't suspicious at all. My day was suddenly looking up.

Squirrel put his giant hand on his chest. "I'm Markus Lowman, Squirrel. Breacher. The poorly named Happy is actually Jay Waterman, Giggles, medic."

Happy waved a hand covered in tattoos that I noticed for the first time. The artistry in the designs was awe inspiring.

"Iggy Mathis, Azalea, tech," Squirrel continued.

My lips quirked. "Iggy Azalea. Rap or poison aficionado?"

The tech genius blinked at me for a long, silent moment. "Poison?"

I nodded. "Must have been the artist you enjoyed then. Just a little FYI, your call sign namesake is extremely poisonous. Signs of toxicity include salivation, watering of eyes and nose, abdominal pain, loss of energy, depression, nausea and vomiting, diarrhea, weakness, difficulty

111

breathing, progressive paralysis of arms and legs, coma, and eventual cardiac failure."

The men just stared at me for a while in stunned silence. Looks of horror, bemusement, and a certain pride shown in their various gazes.

"What?"

"You just rattled off the toxicity signs like you read them from a fucking card," Happy said. "You keep all your plant data in your head for ready access?"

I shrugged. "The ones that can cause death, usually, yeah. It's something I've always been able to do. I enjoy my work." So sue me. Geez, it wasn't like that was all I was good at.

"I guess so," Happy said. He waved Squirrel to resume his intros. "Get the rest of them."

"Aidan Bradford, Banshee, communications." The other Black man waved a hand. I was pretty sure he hadn't spoken a single word since entering my home. Or if he had, it hadn't been within my earshot. The quietest guy on the team was named after a mythical shrieking creature that foretold death? These guys were interesting, I'd given them that.

"Palmer DeMio, Critter, AKA Dopey, linguist," Squirrel said.

I narrowed my eyes at the guy. "Linguist." Obviously, he was some kind of savant when it came to name meanings. And he thought I was weird for having plant poison information readily available in my mind. At least my data was pertinent to my job. Why did he need to know name meanings at all?

His smile was huge. "I know fourteen languages, Snow. And I'm working on a couple more. But you keep hiding behind your legends. I'll find the rest of them."

I had more legends than he probably had pairs of underwear. Dipping my chin, I welcomed his challenge.

Shifting to look at the one guy who wasn't Beck Maddox, I smiled. "Did he save the best for last?"

The group snorted as the guy nodded.

Blond hair shoved back off a high forehead. Aside from his face, almost all of the skin I could see was covered in tattoos. Even his fingers. "Sebastian Baumgartner, Det Cord or Det."

"Let me guess: explosives," I completed his intro.

He nodded with a laugh. "Gotta end with a bang."

Turning to the tall red headed Beck, I sized him up. "Sniper."

His teeth flashed in a smile as he dipped his chin. "Yes, ma'am."

Looking back over the room, I studied and memorized faces and names. "Call sign or name preferences."

"Either works for all of us," Squirrel said. "Although I might get on board with the Snow White and Seven Dwarfs bit."

I chuckled. "There are eight of you, big man."

He shrugged. "Just call him Prince Charming." He jerked his thumb at Keys. "You ain't get kisses from any of the rest of us."

Spluttering a laugh at the remark and the inference, I looked at Rome, one eyebrow raised high.

The man just watched me, not rising to the bait. Although he did flash Squirrel a quelling look that would have made lesser men tremble.

Squirrel just laughed and shrugged. "Might as well tell her up front."

"Yeah, predatory anticipation really gets me going," I deadpanned, my tone drier than the desert.

Squirrel just snorted another laugh as the other guys joined in this time.

Every one of them except Rome. The man was patient—something I'd become well acquainted with last night. But the way he watched me now…It did something to me deep inside where he had no business being able to see. And certainly no business affecting.

In the end, I raised my chin and met the unstated challenge in his posture. We were going to work together. My past had taught me that mixing business and pleasure was a surefire way to get someone killed. So, in the end, it didn't matter.

"Like I said before, unless your dick runs on batteries, I'm not interested." That kind of disappointment I really didn't need in my life. Especially right now. I had other things to worry about and accomplish.

Not to mention the fact that if we were working together, I wouldn't be stepping one single freaking toe back into Subterra. Which fucking sucked. I wouldn't miss the money. I would miss the outlet, even if I had to finish everything by myself.

So, it was back to my toys for my only release and mental quiet. I shrugged mentally. Oh well. It wasn't like I hadn't had to live with that knowledge before.

Besides, maybe this would end faster since I had help in the form of eight highly trained killers. That had to matter somehow. Even in just catching Jorgenssen faster.

"Fine. You want breadcrumbs? I'll give you a full fucking feast."

I gave them a beat of silence, really letting them feel the full weight of shit they didn't really understand.

"But you're not the only ones tracking this poison. And if I end up in a ditch, you can bet your last fucking bullet my backup plan will make sure all your names land in the worst hands possible."

I just prayed I was making the right decision because the universe knew I couldn't trust anyone on my temporary FBI team. Or the CIA. The former were clueless outside of their rigid rules and hard lines. The latter were hiding something. Something big and destructive. I couldn't morally walk away from this one.

"Before you jump into that," Happy said. "If we can get you a sample of our poison, would you be able to run analyzes on it here in your home lab?"

My brows furrowed as my brain jumped to a different mental track. I bumped my shoulders up. "Sure, I don't know why I wouldn't be able to do that. Why do you need it run, anyway? You already said you know what it's been hooked to for a carrier."

Happy shook his head. "No, I told you what had been added to it, not what the carrier is. We're still missing a lot of significant information. We have the route of infiltration into the body and damaging effects, but that's about it."

I blinked at him as I tried to wrap my brain around the kind of spotty chemical assay. "How is that even possible?"

"We've had to use segmented information, various labs, and independent pathologists. No one can agree on anything but route and damage," Rome explained, his voice low and almost vibrating.

I heard what he didn't say. His sources weren't exactly trustworthy, in addition to not wanting the information to get out as a whole. Then something else hit me between the eyes. "You said you're mole hunting. So what is it—bait or target?"

Silence.

Heavy, knowing, brutal silence. Rome and his men exchanged looks.

"Neither." Rome shook his head.

The air in the room seemed to contract around that single word.

"It's the weapon."

Chapter 12

Rome

I watched her expression, noting every single twitch and relaxing of her muscles. She either had no idea what we were really working on, or she was an incredible liar and actress. I had to pray for the first and guard against the second.

Something about her responses didn't ring true. They weren't out and out lies, but something else hid just below the surface. Whatever it was, we'd bought ourselves enough time to figure it out.

And time for other things, as well.

She smirked and shrugged. "Yeah, poison is usually considered a weapon. But is someone trying to buy-slash-sell it or using it as a method of manipulation?"

My guys all shared a look. Confusion and irritation were the top two expressions.

"Does the why matter?" I finally asked. We knew what the SRD were using it for, but I guess I hadn't really thought beyond that. We just had to neutralize both the poison itself and the SRD.

"Of course it matters. Poison is a very intimate killing mechanism. If you're wanting pain, anguish, suffering, and abject horror inflicted on your victims, poisoning is the way

117

to go. If you just want someone dead, there are easier and cheaper options available." Neva plopped her fists on her hips, her tits pushing out against her dress. "So, which is it?"

Shifting my focus away from her tits that made my mouth water, I blinked at her question. This woman really didn't beat around the bush. In any situation or circumstance. It was fucking refreshing, honestly.

"From what we've seen of it and how it's been used, manipulation," Beck answered for me.

We all nodded as Neva took in the information. She tipped her head to the side. "Is the who a group or a person?"

"Group," I answered, bringing her attention back to me. Where it belonged. "That's all we're sharing without an agreement of some kind." It seems we needed to be digging a little deeper into SRD and their function outside of just killing hundreds, and possibly thousands, of people.

Neva nodded. "Fine. But once you get that information, tell me. I can help you build a profile for the group and some possible targets or outcomes."

"You got a psych degree in there somewhere, too?" Critter asked, a sneer in his voice.

I sighed. Maybe we should all start calling him Dopey.

"You fucktard," Squirrel sighed. "She's literally in the business of poisons. Why wouldn't she know why people poison shit and how and what they poison?"

At least the slapback had come from Squirrel and not me. As smart as Critter was when it came to languages and killing shit, he really didn't use his brain very often when it came to stuff outside of those two arenas.

Neva just smiled. "What Squirrel said."

"To get us back on track, Snow, what information were you going to share with us?" Giggles asked.

She flicked her head to look at our medic, her hair shifting back over her shoulders. "Right. Current target is Oskar Jorgenssen. Swedish native with a penchant for international travel as an antique broker."

"Why is he the target?" I asked.

Neva turned to look at me. "Because he recently moved to the US after being overseas all his life. He's been on my radar for a long time, but I never had access to him."

"On your radar how? And why do you have to team up with the FBI to get him?" Giggles asked.

"Someone in Jorgenssen's network has been supplying designer poisons to anyone who can pay. I finally identified Jorgenssen about two years ago as the courier. He kept killing his own men for some reason, and now he does the majority of the shipping and handling himself. As to why the FBI, you said it yourself, we're on US soil. I'm one of the few SMEs in phytotoxicology outside of the WHO and the CDC."

I absorbed the information. If she was on the up and up and any deeper runs Iggy could do on her turned out clean, then she could be the missing piece we've been needing to take down SRD.

Holy fuck.

Deep inside, I rejoiced at the realization of keeping the promise of finally bringing down that band of crazy bitches. I also couldn't deny my excitement at having such a sexy woman on my team who could actually help us do that. A fucking win-win.

"You mentioned your poison with the flame lily was hooked to a fast-acting nerve agent. Which one?" Giggles asked. The man was on fire with his on-point questions.

Neva cocked her head to one side, a considering look in her eyes. "I didn't, actually."

Giggles smiled. "It seemed the most logical choice from what I've been able to gather on our end of things."

She studied him for so long I got itchy between my shoulder blades. Then she shrugged everything aside and blew out a breath. "A bastardized version of ricin. Not as deadly, because why would they want to actually kill someone with it when they can use it to demand any price they want?" She bumped a single shoulder into the air. "I personally call it ricin lite, but that's just me. There are a lot of similar characteristics to ricin, except the whole fatal part, like I just mentioned. And none of the symptoms are as elevated or exaggerated as ricin. They've put some kind of inhibitor or internal kill switch on it. And it degrades so quickly there's usually nothing left by the time someone figures out what it is, so we haven't been able to fully study it yet."

I snorted mentally. If someone was out there with a cool new weapon, it had been studied. Especially if they were getting more than one agency involved. Her higher ups just hadn't shared that knowledge with her.

"Do you really think that's true?" Beck asked. "That they haven't run it through every possible machine and study imaginable."

She rolled her eyes. "No. I think they know exactly what it is, how it works, and already have an antidote for it. There's no way this could be anything except lab-created with intention. Of course they know, but I have to pretend I don't because nosey neighbors get nixed." She drew a single finger across her throat. "I'll admit to not knowing a lot of things in this world, but the shadiness of people in power?" She shook her head. "I'll always count on them only looking out for themselves and how to get more power."

Everything inside me relaxed. The knowledge that I didn't have to find her rose-colored glasses and smash them into pieces to make her see reason put another point in her column.

Anticipation and excitement bubbled to life in the pit of my gut. If we could really get her on our side, have her expertise and knowledge base, then we might be able to end this shitshow with SRD sooner rather than later. Who knew the number of lives we could save.

"Oskar Jorgenssen, age fifty-eight, six foot even, blond hair, blue eyes, Swedish native. Pulls in over twenty million a year from his antiques business," Iggy interrupted.

Everyone turned to look at our tech guy.

"His data at the school lists him as fifty-one, six-one," Neva said. "What data did you pull?"

Iggy smiled, shook his head. "We all have our wheelhouse, this is mine."

"You're undercover as a kindergarten teacher to get close to Jorgenssen?" The words tumbled from my lips before I could think about it.

She turned back to me. Her green eyes sharp. "How do you know I'm a kindergarten teacher specifically?" Her gaze went hazy for a split second before it cleared again. "You ran my file at Subterra." She crossed her arms, boosting up her tits with the movement.

I nodded. "You walked through our staging area like you owned the joint. None of those files are readily available information. Of course we ran you."

Her mouth twisted as her brows furrowed low over her nose. Her lips moved, but I was too far away to hear what she said.

Squirrel's chest bumped up and down as he chuckled. "Too good for your own good, Snow. Might need to keep an eye on that."

She rolled her eyes up at the big man. "If he wasn't so freakishly observant, it would have been fine." She turned and glared at me like it was my fault.

I pursed my lips to hide the smile. She was feisty and acerbic. I really fucking loved it. But I did have more important things to worry about right now. "Why a kindergarten teacher to get to Jorgenssen?"

She blew out a breath, the small rush of air disturbing the hair around her face. "Because his daughter has some idiopathic medical conditions. She's my in."

From the way her features tightened, I knew she had a problem using a child as bait. But I also saw the determination to see her project through.

"To him, I'm nothing other than a silly kindergarten teacher with extracurricular knowledge in plant-based and natural medicine." She gave the epitome of an innocent smile, even batted her lashes. "Harmless, sweet, personable, loves children."

Critter snorted derisively.

She whirled on him, stabbing a finger in his direction. "Fuck you, Dopey. I am sweet."

The room shook from the guys' laughter.

"Of course you are, pix. Nothing but honey, sweet tea, and tulips on a spring afternoon," Squirrel cooed, sliding his arm around her back, tugging her against him.

I curled my fingers into fists to keep from lashing out at him. He wasn't allowed to touch her. None of them were. She was mine, damn it. They'd all acknowledged it when I called her off limits.

He must have seen something on my face, because he dropped his hands like he'd touched an open napalm flame. He even took a couple steps away from her side.

She looked up at him, confusion on her face. "What, do I smell or something?" She raised her arm and bent her head like she was about to sniff her armpit.

He caught her arm and pushed it back down to her side. "Not at all, Snow. Just got a little chilly in here."

I could almost see the confusion wrench her brain into knots at his answer. As long as he took his hands off her, I didn't care what he said. As I watched, he put his hand back at his side.

Then, I stared in stunned wonder as he tucked them up into his armpits.

He shook his head, shoved his hands into his pockets. When that didn't seem to make him happy either, he stepped backward until his ass hit the wall and leaned back against it, his hands trapped behind his lower back.

By this time, Neva was staring at him with her mouth hanging open. "What is wrong with you?" She shoved her fisted hands onto her hips.

He shook his head, careful to keep his gaze off me. "Nothing, Snow. Like I said, just a little chilly in here."

She turned, found our medic's gaze, and jerked her chin in Squirrel's direction. "You might want to check him out. He's acting funny, because it's not chilly in here. If anything, it's way too hot with all of you crowding my space."

With that, she turned back to me. "I have to see it through with him, too. If I bail out now, I'll lose the only progress the team has made."

I shrugged. "I'm not looking to derail your case, Neva."

She flinched the slightest bit between her brows, but she didn't correct me about her name. Without saying anything else, she turned to Iggy, opened her mouth, closed it again without uttering a single sound.

"Why is that the only progress the team has made?" Beck asked into the silence. "Did you guys just form into a unit?"

She shook her head, sighed. "No. We've been working on this for almost six months now."

My mouth fell open. "Six months and the best you've got is that you're a kindergarten teacher at his kid's school?"

Her mouth tightened at the corners as she nodded. "Yes."

I looked at Iggy. He wore the same expression I did. There was something wrong going on with her investigation as well. There had to be. I understood the purpose of going slow while being undercover, but six months with nothing to show but being in the same proximity as his daughter? That didn't add up.

"How much does this Brantley get in the way of you doing your job?" I asked.

Her shoulders inched up as she glared at me through her lashes. "Way too much. Whatever else is going on, I have zero trouble believing he's involved in it."

"So you think something is wrong with the team," Beck said.

She nodded. "I feel the same way about it all of you seem to. There's no reason it should be going this slowly or seeing so little payout. But every time I get the green from Jorgenssen to go to his house to help his daughter with some possible naturopathic medicine or private lessons, Brantley puts the brakes on."

I had to shove aside the instinctive urge to tell her she couldn't go to the man's house. Alone or otherwise. She wasn't allowed to go see this man if he was her target. "Does he say why?"

She shook her head. "No. Other than to say it's not the right time. But as soon as I have to turn Jorgenssen down, he always comes back to the school with more suspicions in his eyes. He's colder, and not just because I stood up his daughter. It's like he's being fed information about me and can't decide if it's true or not."

As she finished speaking, I could almost see the weight lift off her shoulders. "You've been working on this alone this whole time, haven't you?" No wonder she had trouble getting off at the club. Why her partner hadn't been able to penetrate that sphere of stress eating through her.

That slightly feral part of me grinned. She needed some education on how to live and work with a team. And since I claimed her, I would be her teacher. She just needed to realize and know that I could handle anything she wanted to dish out and it wouldn't break me. Hell, it would probably give me some fucking relief—I just didn't examine that last part too hard.

She nodded, shoving her shoulders back. "I usually work alone. This is nothing new."

I snorted mentally, bringing myself back to the conversation at hand. Yeah, but there was a huge difference between working alone on your own and working alone on a team.

Oh, dewdrop, the things I'm going to teach you. "Do your runs on us. You have thirty-six hours. If I don't see you at Subterra Friday night, I'll assume we didn't pass your checks."

She spluttered. "I'm not going back to the club." Shaking her head, her dark brown hair went flying around

123

her shoulders. "No. If we start working together, then I can't be in the club." She continued to shake her head, her green eyes wide. She even took a step back.

Before I could stop myself, I moved forward. It was like she was some kind of magnet, and I a flimsy piece of iron. "Yes, you will. It will be less obvious than all of us coming here."

I continued my progress until I entered her personal space. "It will be the best cover. Especially if Brantley is working against you. If he tries to enter the club, or Locke Security, we'll know it. He doesn't have current access, so we could flag his face for our system. Instant alarm. You can't say the same here. Nor do you have the computing power to set up that kind of warning system, I'm guessing." By the time I finished talking, I could feel the heat of her body along the front of mine.

Her head tipped all the way back, she glared at me. "No. We can come up with an alternate venue. I'm not going back to the club. Brantley is already suspicious of me. If I start going to a sex club regularly, he'll find some way to kick me off the team."

Iggy snorted. "If he wanted to do that, then he would have done it already. You're the boots on the ground, he could lay the lack of progress directly at your feet. The fact he hasn't done something to switch things up is all on him. I agree with Keys, you'll come to the club. Sex is good self care. Besides, in today's world of snowflakes, they couldn't say shit about it."

She continued to shake her head. "No. Find somewhere else." She eased back, crossing her arms again, creating a barrier between us.

I ground my back teeth together to keep from reaching for her, moving her arms physically. She didn't get to put up blocks. Not against me. She was fucking mine.

"If I have to come here and hogtie you to get you into that club, it will create more issues, Snow. But don't think I won't do it. It really will be the best place for you. And for us," Squirrel said.

Gasping, she turned to him, defeat and betrayal in her eyes. Right before she narrowed them. "I'd like to see you tr—"

I slid my hand up, over her mouth, my fingers and thumb spanning from ear to ear. Listening to her bait Squirrel into touching her wasn't something I could handle at the moment. "I'll do more and worse than hogtie you, Neva." My voice was whisper soft but threaded with steel.

Her pupils dilated for a moment before she seemed to sink into herself.

I waited her out. I'd watched her enough now that I knew she wasn't giving in this easily. Nothing about this woman was going to be easy. She was a challenge. One I was looking forward to more and more.

Shifting my pelvis to the side just in time, I caught her upthrust knee in my thigh. Thank fuck I'd shifted. My balls would have been up in my abdomen with the force she put into that strike. For a small woman, she packed a fucking punch.

With a quick twist of my free hand, I caught her leg up against my hip and hauled her up. Walking forward, I pushed her up against the wall.

The entire room and the men in it fell away as I held her pinned with only the weight of my body against hers, our gazes level. She hung there, mouth open in shock under my palm, the humid heat of her breath puffing against my skin.

That's right, my little flower, I'm in charge here. Always.

"Say yes, Neva. It's the only answer that gets you out of this without punishment." I kept my voice low.

The fire sparked in her eyes, turning her green irises into heated emeralds. I felt her lips pull back under my palm just as her teeth sank into the fleshy pad under my thumb. I grunted and leaned more of my weight against her.

"Wrong answer." Without looking away from her, I turned my head. "Get out."

"Keys," Giggles started.

I turned to see him just over my shoulder. "I said, get out." There was no mistaking the order in my voice.

He shifted his gaze to look at her.

I snarled low in my throat as he tried to check in with her. He was trying to go around me, shove himself into the picture where he had no place.

I called dibs. We all knew what that meant between us.

"Now, Gigs." I brought his attention back to me. "Stay here, I'll take it out on her."

His expression firmed, but he stepped back. He opened his mouth, saying nothing before he turned away.

"Clear," Squirrel called from what sounded like the second floor.

Shifting my attention back to Neva, I smiled down at her. "We're going to talk, you and me."

She tightened the grip of her teeth in my flesh.

My skin threatened to give way under her attack, but I didn't let her go. "Let me give you some advice: the next time you taunt, tease, or trick one of my men into touching you, I'll take it out on your body, then I'll beat the shit out of my brothers." I felt my lip curl up. "Do not make me hurt one of them. Do you understand me?"

She released her teeth and nodded. Pleading up at me with her eyes, I lowered my hand slightly. She licked her lips.

When I saw her eyes shift from beseeching to hard, I slid my hand down and wrapped it around her throat. "Think very carefully about what you say next, Neva." I curled my fingertips and thumb around to either side of her neck, pressing into the delicate structures below to slow the blood flow to her brain.

For whatever reason, I had a hair trigger around this woman and I couldn't afford the lapse in my control. Not right now. Not when the guys were still within earshot.

"I don't like being touched." She flicked her gaze down to my arm and back up. "So get your fucking hands off me before I rip them from your body and beat you to death with them."

I laughed. Right in her face. "You're more than welcome to try. But we both know you're too small to do that successfully."

One corner of her mouth kicked up in a smile. "Just remember you said that, Rome."

My belly fluttered as her tongue and lips shaped my name. I vowed at that moment that I would make her bloody my ears as she screamed it while I wrecked her entire world from the inside out. "Bring it on, dewdrop."

Leaning in, I pushed my face to hers. With only enough room for air to pass between our lips, I waited. She was small enough that I could break her with one hard squeeze around her slim throat. One squeeze and a twist that would send her to whatever god she believed in. She would learn that she couldn't push me around, couldn't force me in a direction I didn't want to go.

I hadn't planned to taunt her. Not like this, not yet. But all of the barely leashed violence in her tiny frame made me a stupid man in her presence. I might say and do things I hadn't planned on around her, but that didn't mean I wasn't in control of myself. Of her.

The faintest whiff of fear swirled through me. If I wasn't careful, I could lose myself completely in this woman.

I pushed the thought away. The day a woman broke my control was the day I cut off my own dick with a rusty knife.

She rolled her eyes at me. "I'm not afraid of you, Rome."

Smiling at her, I studied every inch of her face. "Maybe that's your mistake." When the only thing I felt on my skin was the breath panting from between her lips, I tightened my fingers the slightest degree more.

"Maybe it's yours." Her tone could have flash frozen the desert. Her jaw clenched as her body flexed for the briefest moment against mine. It almost felt like she was fighting herself internally.

But whatever her body was saying, it didn't matter. No, I was watching her eyes. And once again, her pretty green eyes gave her away. Her pupils constricted for the briefest moment, then they blew out. It felt like I was falling into her soul, and in seeing so deeply inside her, I noticed something else.

It was as if she wavered on some kind of precipice, the tension I saw in her gaze was reflected in her admittedly delicious body. The tension was complex, just like the woman herself. Sexual, definitely. But something else quivered through her small frame. Some…thing that had me waiting patiently like the predator I'd been trained to be.

Time drew out into long moments between the beats of my heart. I felt the answering thud of her heartbeat against my fingertips. Each beat called to me, spoke my name, chanted through my mind. With my ring finger, I traced that thumping line of blood just under the thin skin of her throat.

She was so fucking close. Almost there, dewdrop. Almost there. Give me what I want.

A shudder rolled through her body before her lashes drooped ever so slightly over her stunning verdant eyes. The smallest, prettiest crack in her armor. I felt the way her pulse jumped against my fingertips, the way her mouth parted—just barely.

Just enough.

And then I took it. Took her.

The fiery heat in my belly exploded as I flicked out my tongue and swiped it over her lower lip. I hovered there, feeling the sharp inhale against my mouth, feeling the way her body tensed—ready to run, or ready to fall. Then slowly...so fucking slowly...I sucked her lower lip between mine. Savoring her flavor, feeling it imprint itself in my mind.

And then I bit down.

The softest moan that was more air than sound wafted over my upper lip as I pulled back, her lip still between my teeth. With her flesh stretched tight between us, I nipped the edge of the soft skin.

Shoving everything back into its box, I take a steadying inhale through my nose. I could take her right now. Hell, right now, her body and mind were ripe for the plucking. I could strip her bare, break her apart, make her accept the truth she saw coming for her.

But where was the fun in that?

No. I wanted her to hand it to me. Make her give herself to me, piece by fucking piece, until she couldn't deny it anymore. "That's what I thought."

She gasped, and her leg jerked against mine before hanging like a dead branch from a tree. Her green eyes cleared for the briefest moment before some kind of shutter came down, blocking me out. "Let me go, Rome. I'm not playing this game with you." Her cold tone was like being dropped into a hole for icefishing.

Chapter 13

Neva

Shit, shit, shit.

I had to get out of here. Away from him. No fucking way had I just been closer to coming with a man in my entire life, and all he did was shove me into a wall, wrap his hand around my throat, and bite me.

Nope. Not today, Satan. Not any day, but certainly not on the day I just agreed to work with these assholes.

Absolutely not happening.

The phrase was becoming my anthem.

I tucked it all away. Or tried to. I couldn't remember being this turned on in the whole of my existence. My body felt all jittery, my mind clouded and hazy. It felt like someone alternated pouring ice and then lava in my veins as the shock of it all swamped through me.

Left gasping, I struggled to put my shields back in place. Put some kind of armor on so nothing and no one could reach me.

I wouldn't let what just happened matter. Nothing was going to happen with anyone. It certainly wasn't going to happen with him. This bossy man bitch who couldn't figure out how to ta—

"What did you just say to me?"

My breath backed up in my lungs as the threat in his voice snaked through me like poison invading my body. Devil's cherry. I needed to get away from him.

Now.

"Let me go, Rome." I have no idea how my voice came out so steady or cold, but I could only thank any gods still out there in the universe that it had. "I'm not playing this game with you."

He cocked his head to the side. "What game is that, Neva?"

My mind skittered away from the challenge in that small question. Chills and tingles swept down my spine as my real name swept over his lips again. No one called me that. I barely remembered it was mine on a day-to-day basis.

But he kept shoving it in my face. Kept speaking it. Kept drawing me in.

I shook my head. "Whatever this dominance display is. I didn't consent, and I didn't agree."

He snorted. "If I'd asked you to sub for me, I would actually take your words into consideration. I haven't, and I won't."

My breath caught in my chest as humiliation fired my cheeks, my throat closing around the taste of metal as I flinched back. I blinked and fought not to gape up at him as it felt like he dropped a gallon of icy water on my head. Man, talk about stabbing a girl while she's down. Damn. "Good. I wouldn't agree, anyway."

He just stared at me, laughter lurking in his blue eyes.

The fucker. I was going to cook something up that would make him think of me for the rest of his natural life. And it would never bring him joy, that was for damn sure. Lifelong jock itch, here we come.

While I watched, his eyes frosted over. "None of this is a game to me. The lives of my men and brothers are not pieces on a fucking chessboard to me. Saving potentially thousands or millions of lives is not a game. There is no game. There is life and there is death."

His words sliced through me like the sharpest blade. No notice until the sting sent you to your knees as pain crashed through you once your brain caught up.

"Do not get in my way about helping them. Do not make me choose between millions of lives and theirs. They will win. Always." His fingers tightened on my neck again, the wavy lines around the edge of my vision telling me this

130

man had far more control and knowledge than I had accounted for.

"You don't own me, Rome." My voice came out scratchy as the guilt pressed in on me. But I pushed it away.

I'd promised myself long ago that no man would ever again get to make me feel bad for having boundaries. Maybe I'd gotten the whole thing between us wrong, but no man would ever get to treat me like trash again. And if this man thought he could simply skip over my boundaries because we were working together, then I would be more than happy to give him a real education on how to treat a woman.

His chuckle flicked at my nerve endings. "Oh, dewdrop, I do. I really, really do." He leaned forward, pressed his lips to my ear. "And what's better is that you'll let me own you. You'll fucking beg me to keep owning you before all of this is over."

I blinked as my brain twisted. Who the fuck says something like that?

Now I was more confused than ever.

But I locked it away with everything else this psycho kept spouting off. More for some Future Neva to examine and dissect.

With that final threat, he stepped back. Without his grip or weight to keep me up against the wall, I tumbled like a little kid falling down a slide. Only his hand around my throat kept me from smashing into the floor completely.

As I came to rest on my ass at his feet, I watched him squat down over me. My chin rested on his wrist. "Keep that in mind the next time you try to make me jealous. I don't share. Ever. And anyone—outside of one of my brothers saving your life—who tries touching you, no matter what they pack between their legs, will die."

I spluttered up at him as he straightened to his full height. He dusted his hands together as if ridding them of dirt.

The man was giving me whiplash.

First, it was a game, then he talked about saving millions of lives. And now we were back to him claiming me. I couldn't keep track of whatever conversation he was having.

In the end, it didn't matter. I wouldn't let it matter. They were helping me, I would be helping them. We were nothing to each other but a means to an end. Transactional, professional. Cold.

131

Which reminded me…this man needed a lesson in how he would interact with me. I narrowed my eyes. Acting like I was going to slump over, I stiffened my ankle and swept his feet together.

Or tried to. The fucker just chuckled again and stepped over my attempt to knock him down a few levels, literally and figuratively. The bastard. "Keep that spirit, dewdrop. You're going to need it."

Rage ate through me again at that stupid nickname. He probably had no idea what he was even saying. "Do you even know what a dewdrop can do, you fucking asshole?" I glared up at him.

He shrugged. "Don't really care. But I think the name fits you, Neva." He snapped his teeth at me.

"Try to bite me again, you'll find out really quick how lethal a dewdrop can be, Rome." I'd make damn sure he knew that the unassuming little flower could pack more than just a punch. It could kill him.

He smiled as he walked to the short stack of stairs at the north wall of my family home. "I look forward to the education." He gave a short two-tone whistle without looking away from me. "Oh, and dewdrop?"

I clenched my fists as I fought not to scream in impotent rage and bloody his fucking ears. "What?"

His smirk deepened. "You didn't tell me to let go." The words ghosted over my skin, sank straight into my core. Like a blade coated in poison, I felt the weight of those words echo through my entire being.

Within moments, I heard the tromping footsteps of his men. And considering I hadn't heard any of them leave, I knew they were making all that noise for me. My eyes burned with tears. The assholes.

Dopey came down first, a cocky smile on his face as he saw me heave myself up off the floor. "Have a nice nap?"

Just like that, my eyes were drier than a bleached bone forgotten under the desert sun.

"Critter, can it, or I'll fill it for you," Rome said, his tone as hard as diamonds.

Dopey smirked and moved out of the way for the rest of his brothers to come down the stairs behind him. "Sure, Keys. Whatever you say." He strode off with a pep in his step that I was going to remove at my earliest convenience.

The rest of the men came down in near silence. Which, considering how creaky the stairs were, was almost impossible.

It wasn't until Squirrel came down last, each step sounding like thunder, that I knew exactly who had been giving me a warning that they were coming back.

I curled my fingers into fists and squeezed until I felt my flesh give way under my nails to push back the tears. That giant man could kill me in a multitude of ways, most of them probably without breaking a sweat, and here he was, trying to give me a warning that I was about to have an audience once again.

"Ready for those cuddles yet, pix?" he asked as he finally stepped down the last stair.

My gaze slid to Rome. Even though I told myself he was bluffing, there was the smallest part of me that just wasn't sure.

But come on, there was no way he would ever hurt one of his own for touching me. A literal stranger slash tentative ally. He'd spoken not even two minutes ago about choosing them over millions of innocents. I'd lost my innocence too long ago to remember, so I certainly wouldn't be the choice anyone chose.

"Cuddles are off the table, Squirrel. Stop trying to get her in trouble," Rome bit out.

Squirrel pouted. A full on teenage girl who just got her phone taken away from her pout. "But Keys, she's so cuddleable."

Keys shook his head. "No."

Squirrel looked at me with such sorrow in his eyes I found myself moving toward him without thinking about it. The big giant smartass looked so dejected, something inside me needed to comfort him.

A quick breeze of movement and I was flying through the air. I landed on the couch with a blink and a gasp just as the first sound of fists pounding into flesh floated to my ears.

"I said no." The tone sounded more like he was turning down another roll at the dinner table. Rome landed another blow into Squirrel's belly.

That was it. I didn't know who this guy thought he was, but he was about to find out that I wasn't some kind of damsel in distress, nor was I his. I didn't care what he said. Until I wanted to belong to someone, I belonged only to myself.

I crawled to the back of the couch and launched myself through the air. Landing on Rome's back, I stabbed my fingers into the vulnerable parts of his underarms, aiming for the bundles of nerves there.

He just laughed and kept throwing punches at the mountainous Squirrel.

"Snow, you're going to make it worse for Squirrel if you keep trying to get in between them," Happy said.

I flipped him off over my shoulder. No one would ever stand in the gap for a beating that was mine to take. I didn't care how big and tall the asshole was. It wasn't his fault I'd instinctively offered comfort to the overgrown man-baby. It was my own.

And I needed to take care of this whole shitshow and get back to the business that brought me to this godsforsaken city again in the first place. "You land one more punch on him, I'll poison you to make your dick fall off." I shouted the threat and felt the world stop moving as Keys caught himself in mid motion.

The other men whispered, "Is that a thing?"

"Can she really do that?"

"What the fuck? I told you she was crazy." The last from Dopey, of course. That man was the biggest baby of them all.

Squirrel straightened from his defensive pose, standing tall; a good five six inches taller than Rome. "Yeah. Snow won't let you hurt me." His smile was a little bloody, but he didn't back down.

"The next time your wrap your legs around my waist, dewdrop, you better be ready to be fucked until you can't remember your name," Rome said as he caught one of my legs and my opposite arm. He raised my arm and bit my inner wrist.

Damn him. My pussy clenched.

But I pushed it aside. If men couldn't be trusted to reliably deliver orgasms, they certainly weren't trustworthy enough for anything requiring more intimacy or vulnerability. But again, it didn't matter.

Because absolutely no one was getting near my pussy. Certainly not this man who didn't understand that I really wasn't interested in anything resembling dick not running on batteries.

"Keep wishing on those stars, Rome. One of them will surely grant your wish." With my free hand, I tunneled my fingers through his hair and yanked his head back away from my wrist.

The men around us all busted out calls like they were teenagers again.

"I don't need stars for luck, Neva. I make my own." Once again, the man dropped me like a bad habit.

This time, though, I was ready for it. I caught myself on my tiptoes and shuffled back before he could grab me again. "Stop being an asshole. I'm not fucking you; you're not fucking me. No one is touching me. We'll get our respective jobs done and never have to see each other ever again."

"But, pix…" Squirrel whined.

I glared at him, stabbing a finger in his direction. "No. You shut up, too. You're the one getting your ass beat because he's a psycho. Stop it."

He folded his hands over his heart. "You do care." He heaved a satisfied sigh, and I saw the mischief in his eyes.

My lips twitched before I could shift them into a frown. "No. I don't. But I don't want to be down a capable body, especially one as big as you that I can easily hide behind, when we take these fuckers down. Stop it." I narrowed my gaze even further.

Squirrel just winked at me, blew me a kiss. "Sure, pix. Sure. Anything you say, pretty mama."

"Squirrel, shut the fuck up," one of the other men said. "You're not paying attention to the real threat here."

Squirrel and I both turned to see Rome.

Expression colder than a glacier during the ice age, his hands flexed and relaxed into fists at his sides. Had I not seen his nostrils flare, I would have assumed he wasn't even breathing.

Squirrel immediately stepped back, hands up. "Sorry, boss. I was just giving you shit."

I rolled my eyes. "He's not going to hurt one of you. You're his brother."

The entire group, minus Rome, laughed as if I'd just delivered the punch line in a comedy bar. Beck walked up on my other side.

Rome turned to watch his brother's progress as if he were some kind of heat-seeking missile and Beck his new target.

The tall ginger stopped short of entering my personal space. "A little thing you should know, Lady Larkspur."

My brain shifted. Lady Larkspur? I looked up into his blue eyes, my head tilted back as it tipped to the side. "What?"

The slight smile fell from his features like it had never been there. "No one touches what's Keys's. Ever. Not us, not anyone. If he called dibs, and he did, then you're off limits. Don't make him choose."

I wanted to laugh in his face, to say something biting and cruel, and make him regret opening his mouth. But the words stuck in my head, slithered down my spine like a brand I couldn't quite scrape off.

Because, come on, there was no way he would ever truly hurt one of his own for touching me.

…right?

Instead, I rolled my eyes. Forced myself to shove whatever game they were playing aside. I wasn't stupid and they couldn't convince me otherwise.

And honestly, they were all laying it on way too thick. Apparently, they'd forgotten that I'd worked with Navy SEALs before. "Oh, please. You guys have been through hell and back. Together, I'm assuming from the way you move around each other. Almost as if you can anticipate the movements of the brother next to you. I'm a free agent. An unknown, at best. I know exactly where I rate in the hierarchy of things around here. And while I'm at the bottom of your particular totem, I'm at the tippy fucking top on mine. So don't try to sell me some bullshit about him downing one of his own for me. I'm not that stupid. Never have been, and certainly won't be starting now."

I was done with them. Done with this whole situation. The pressure in my chest felt like it was choking me. The burn at the back of my eyes had my hate fires burning hotter. I would kill them before I let them see me break.

No.

Right now, I just needed to get away from them all. Needed them out of my space, my life, my air.

Their loyalty, camaraderie, and familial connection grated on my already overtaxed nerves. It made me angry enough to lash out.

"Get out. If you're not gone in the next five minutes, I'll deploy my security measures. And then you'll all get dragged out by EMS. This is your last chance to choose if you walk out or get dragged out, but you will be leaving." I stalked off, heading down into my lab. After locking the door, I wedged a couple of tools under the door so Squirrel couldn't open it even if he got past the lock again.

On the far wall, I tapped the screen to bring it to life. Watching my first floor from over a dozen camera angles, I waited for them to make the decision: get lost or get doused. Right now, I didn't fucking care which. I just wanted them gone.

Plopping down onto the stool, I heaved a sigh as they finally nodded and left.

Good. I hadn't really wanted to waste my security on them. I would have, but this way I could use the lethal aerosolized serum on real enemies. Like Brantley and Jorgenssen.

When my alarm beeped, indicating the system had been reset, I clenched my teeth in barely suppressed rage. Those fuckers. Especially their techno god. I wanted to destroy his entire system.

Blowing out a breath, I shook my head.

Not important.

Not important.

They're *not* important.

Right now, I had more important things to think about. To worry over. A group of do-gooder hero types didn't really concern me. They might play at being badasses, but I'd learned how to survive from the worst kind of monsters. These guys didn't even earn participation trophies.

Shifting my mind and energies back to the packages full of poison in my isolator, I got enveloped in the science that never made me feel like an outsider. I just needed to focus. Refocus. That's all.

Science didn't bite, didn't whisper threats in my ear like promises, or make my pussy clench without permission. It didn't confuse me or make my body betray itself. It never made me feel like I was better off alone. It called to me. Spoke to me. Told me her secrets. We had a language all our own.

As I ran test after test on the samples I could extract and distill in the chamber, I finally got down to the business of plants, chemistry, and killing people. Whoever put together this particular combination of chemicals knew their shit.

Had the guys not arrived and gotten me to clean air, I probably would have been on a ventilator for the rest of my life. Assuming someone found me at all. Watching the mass spec spit out its findings told me I probably should have been a little kinder to Rome and his men. They had actually saved my life.

My fingers twitched over the keyboard. For a second too long, I wasn't thinking about formulas, or poisons, or the molecular stability of the airborne agent. Rome was the only thing in my mind. Without conscious thought, I lowered my gaze to my wrist where he'd bitten me. My fingers trembled for a heartbeat as they traced the skin he'd abused.

This time, my brain blared a five-alarm alert, shaking me back to reality.

Oh, *hell* no! I didn't care what kind of magic or hormones or anything else that man tried to call from within me. He wasn't going to be successful. Not on my watch, and sure the fuck not with my body. Fuck that noise.

I forced my thoughts back to the problem of poison— where it belonged. Besides, Rome killed any chance of me treating him with anything but brutally efficient professionalism. We could have at least tried being friendly. But not any longer.

Oh well. I had too many things on my plate to worry about him and whatever game he was planning. Case in point, how the hell had a poison I created in secret back in undergrad come back out to see daylight? I blinked at the screen as the full list of elements came through.

Slumping back, I remembered at the last minute that my stool didn't have a back. I caught myself and must have looked like I was being electrocuted. Good thing I was all alone.

I snorted. All alone. The story of my life.

Brushing that mental sidetrack aside, I refocused and leaned forward onto my desk, my elbows smashing into the stainless-steel tabletop. I shook my head again. There was no way; I'd destroyed everything about that workup. The only thing that still existed of it was the note that I created and killed it. In the end, it was too volatile to be useful in any measurable kind of way. The chemical compound was too unstable.

As the rest of the composition ran over my screen, I spotted it. Lurching forward, I stabbed a finger at the monitor. Stopping the flow of information, I read the components and amounts. My brain translated the information as I watched through my mental eye exactly how they reformulated my original structure.

I sat back in awe. Those fucking brilliant bastards. Not only had they stabilized it, but by putting it into a gold-lined box, they made it longer lasting. They effectively made the box into a sealed airborne bioagent canister. Until the internal components came into contact with oxygen, they'd been harmless and stable.

My blood ran cold as I realized the implications. Whoever sent this, and I had to admit the fact it probably hadn't been Dopey, they'd done it on purpose. Not a missed delivery. Not a botched drop off. They'd meant to target me. And I'd fallen directly into their hands.

But who the hell would have the chemical formula for my own poison from so long ago?

And why were they sending it to me now?

I jumped as my alarm sounded again, the bright blaring noise shattering the calm in my home and my head. Jerking my head up and around, I stared at the monitor.

Grabbing up my phone, I called the last dialed number.

"Locke Security. How can I help you?" Rome answered, his professional voice on full.

"Dopey is back on my front porch," I said as I got up from my stool. Running to the door, I kicked the tools out from under it.

Rome heaved a sigh worthy of a nagged husband. "He's with me, dewdrop. There's no way he's at your door."

I rolled my eyes. "No shit, Sherlock. Turn around and get your sexy ass back here so we can talk to the real delivery guy." I ended the call as I grabbed a sealed beaker from the worktop beside the door.

Running quietly up the stairs to the second floor, I dashed for the front of the house. Opening the false wall, I skimmed through to the overhang of the porch. With the camera footage showing on the small display I'd placed up here, I saw the man was still there, fiddling with the doorknob. I watched as he did something to the metal. He sprayed it down with some kind of liquid from a small brown bottle.

Pulling on the shielded hatch, I opened the access panel to the porch ceiling's soffit I'd installed for just such occasions. "Hey, asshole."

The man looked up.

I poured the liquid from the beaker down onto his face. "Gotcha, you dirty bastard."

He stood there in stunned silence for all of three seconds. Then he started screeching and clawing his face.

Smirking, I replaced the soffit panel and wiggled back through into the main hallway. Sprinting back down the stairs, I raced to the front door. Just as I got it open and was going to pull the guy in, Rome leapt up the stairs.

"Keep your fucking hands to yourself, dewdrop. I'll handle him." He grabbed the guy up by his belt and neckline and tossed him into my home.

"Try to avoid the liquid," I said as the rest of the guys followed with quick, but silent, movements.

They all stepped around or over the puddle. Once they were inside, I raced through to the lab once more. Grabbing up kitty litter, I ran back out to the front porch. Tossing the absorbent crystals onto the cement steps, I neutralized everything.

Lifting the hem of the ruined dress I still hadn't changed out of, I wiped off the doorknob. When nothing happened to the fabric, I assumed the liquid wasn't harmful. It was something else to worry about later.

Shutting the door, I leaned against it for a moment. I'd been so close to being free of these men. But here they were again. And I'd been the one to call them back.

I heaved a sigh. I had a feeling this was only the beginning of a really bad pattern.

Chapter 14

Rome

The fury that ate through my fairly famous control should have surprised me. But when I saw Neva rush by, her dark chocolate hair dancing in her wake, I knew control was going to be a precious commodity. Something about her had awakened my more feral instincts.

If she hadn't called when she did, I probably would have alienated every single brother who now stood with me once again in her living room. They'd been this close to chucking me out the door of the van and running me over. Each taking a turn at the wheel.

Shoving it aside, I knew I'd have to deal with them, and my shittiness, later. Right now, we had an asshole to interrogate.

Finally, something that I could unleash on. Throwing him to the floor, I pulled my arm back, fist ready, and more than willing to put enough oomph into smashing it clear through his head.

"Wait, Keys!" Neva raced back through the big space. "He's still got the chemical on his face. It could transfer to you. I just have to hope it didn't get too far into his mouth and damage his vocal cords."

She slid to a smooth stop beside me. With careful, quick fingers, she pulled on thin blue gloves. In her other hand, she held a familiar orange box of baking soda. "I'll hold his mouth open, you dump that into his mouth in a slow steady stream. Someone get a bottle of water from the kitchen at the back of the house. We'll need to neutralize everything and wash it down. His stomach acid will destroy anything else."

"Get me some gloves, I'll hold his mouth open." What part of her not touching other people, especially men, was not sinking in for her?

She glared up at me. "I'm already good to go." She reached forward, her blue covered fingers about to slide through this fucker's hair.

I caught her hand in mine and pulled her away. "You're not touching him. I don't care if he dies right here, right now. We'll get what we need some other way, but you're not touching him."

I felt her bones rub together under my tight grip, but I couldn't make myself gentle the touch. She was demanding I allow another man to have access to her. I didn't fucking care that she wore gloves.

Not happening, dewdrop. Not now, not fucking ever. As long as I claimed her, she would only ever touch me.

Blue gloves slapped me in the chest as Giggles came up. He pried my fingers off her wrist. "You're going to leave bruises." I heard the threat in his voice. Knew I needed whatever beating he would bring down on me for it, so I let him rip my fingers away from her.

"Pix, it might be better if you come over here," Squirrel said. His tone held caution and urgency. "We'll need you to direct traffic, and it seems we've got a bit of a jam."

Neva heaved a sigh and moved to the far side of the intruder. Squirrel carefully maneuvered her farther to the side without touching her. "There ya go, perfect vantage spot."

She rolled her eyes as the gloves snapped down on my wrists. I yanked the infiltrating bastard's head back with a hard pull, feeling some of his hair come loose from his scalp. He yelped.

"Well, at least he can still use his voice," Neva said. She'd pulled over one of the armchairs and crawled to stand up on the oversized arm in order to peer down over the

142

shoulders of my team. Up and away from them, but still able to see and tell us what to do.

Good. Maybe she was learning.

"Mr. Not Dopey, if you would hold your mouth open, I'm trying to save your life. If you'd like to die, please keep whining and crying like a little bitch. Similar to the real Dopey."

"Hey," Critter said.

"I'm not wrong, and you know it. Happy, start your pour. Slow and steady. Who's on water duty?"

"That would be me, Lady Larkspur," Maddox said as he came up on my other side.

"Excellent. Steady hands are definitely what the doctor called for."

Grumbles from some of the other guys came from around the room at the jab, but they didn't pull her attention.

"Happy to be of service," Maddox added as he flipped off our brothers with his free hand.

"Remember Fake Dopey, open wide. Keep it open. Everything will stop burning soon," she cooed, as if she hadn't been the one to put him in his current state.

Giggles and Maddox finally got a good rhythm down and by the time the box of powder and the bottle of water were emptied down the intruder's throat, he sounded like he could actually breathe without pain again.

I smiled darkly. He would find out soon enough that he would have been much better off keeping his mouth shut against the remedy.

Neva got down off the chair, then slid through the forest of trees that were my men. "There now, isn't that so much better?" She nodded, her tone dripping honey and motherly comfort. She came to a gentle halt right in front of the guy and peered down into his face.

He nodded. Or tried to. I didn't let go of his hair because no way I was going to give him even an inch of leash to launch himself at her.

"Yes. Much better." His voice was rough and cracked, but still able to be understood.

Neva nodded. "Of course it is, baby. Of course it is." She reached out her hand as if to touch him.

I yanked his head out of her reach, his body bowed back in a wide arc. He grunted and coughed, his body heaving up and down under the angle.

She glared up at me. "Keys, he's just a poor man who got a little drenched. No worries. He's not going to hurt me." The syrupy sweet tone of her voice didn't match the death I saw written in her eyes.

She was daring me. Telling me without telling to keep getting in her way.

I bared my teeth at her. "Not happening, Larkspur." I put a bite on the sound of her call sign.

If she pushed me on this, I would kill him right here. With my free hand, I pulled one of my hidden knives from its sheath. Holding it down by my leg, I let her see the glint of the blade. "Not happening."

Her eyes widened for a moment before she rolled them at me. "The big, scary man with no boundaries is being a bit of a baby bitch, Mr. Fake Dopey. I apologize for his behavior. Can you tell me your name, pumpkin?" She folded her hands at her waist again, the perfect picture of a 1950s stay at home mother helping children and old people while a scratch-made cherry pie baked in the oven.

The guy swallowed, his Adam's apple giving a grinding, bumpy ride up and down the column of his throat. Between the angle I held his head, the burn, the powder and water combination, I was almost impressed by his resiliency. "You don't need my name, bitch."

Giggles let out a sigh. Then launched his fist into the fucker's face. "Don't ever let me hear you call her that again."

Blood blossomed on the guy's face as he curled in as best as he could under the blow. I smiled as I held him backward, away from any possible reprieve from the pain.

Neva heaved a sigh. "Let's try that again, shall we?" She gave a sad smile once the guy opened his eyes again. "Because if you thought getting punched in the face was bad, wait until I dip your dick into a vat of acid that will eat it away layer by layer." She never once changed the expression on her face or varied her sugary sweet tone.

Fuck, it was hot. Had I not been more worried about keeping this guy from launching himself at her, I probably would have launched myself at her.

"Does that sound good to you, sweetie? You want to play along with me, right? Be a good boy and tell me what I want to know." She smiled again, light dancing in the depths of her green eyes.

He tried to shrink away, tried to lift his hands to shield his junk. But Maddox and Giggles both caught his arms and held them away from his body.

"Now. Tell Auntie Larkspur your name, baby. Just say it. You can whisper it if you want. No one else has to hear." She bent down, her damaged dress still decorating her delicious body.

When he said nothing, I wrenched him back harder, increasing the grotesque angle I held him in. "Larry! It's Larry."

Neva looked a little nonplussed at the name, but she smiled prettily. "Larry. May I call you Lawrence? I had a bad uncle named Larry and you don't want to get mixed up with him in my mind. Is that okay with you, Lawrence?"

Without easing my grip on the bastard, I looked at Iggy.

He already had his iPad out, tapping away on the screen, nodding. If she really did have a bad Uncle Larry, then the man better hope and pray he was already dead.

Lawrence dipped his chin the scant millimeter of room I'd left him. "Sure. Sure, just don't melt my dick." His arms flexed against the hold of my men as if he tried to cover his crotch again.

She giggled, high and light, like a butterfly dancing in the breeze. "Of course, you silly goose. If you give me what I want, I'll let you keep your dick."

Tears sprang to the guy's eyes and flowed down his cheeks.

Not gonna lie, I probably would have cried tears of gratitude as well were it my dick she just spared with that smile. But since I wasn't the fucker caught on my knees before her, I just smirked.

"Now, Lawrence"—her tone turned disappointed—"you've been very, very bad. Why did you bring me those packages? Were you trying to hurt my feelings?"

I bit the inside of my cheek. This woman was scary good at her job. To say nothing of her skill with plants and poisons, she was a truly effective and unique interrogator. Fucking scary as hell, honestly.

Lawrence shook his head. "No. Not really. She paid me fifty grand to drop those off. I don't even know what was in them."

"She's just a mean old lady, huh?" Neva asked, her tone back to sweet and understanding. "Taking advantage of a big, strong man like you. She put you in this spot, got you caught, got you poisoned. It's all her fault. She's the one who should be on her knees on my floor. Not you. You didn't do anything wrong. You had to take the job, had to earn money, didn't you?" She nodded.

Lawrence started moving his head up and down in the same rhythm as hers. "Yeah. I got mouths to feed, don't I? And a nagging lady of my own always breathing down my neck about being good for nothing."

Neva nodded, a sad smile on her face, sympathy shining in her eyes. "You were just providing for your family. Making sure you could keep a roof over their heads and food in their bellies. It's not your fault at all. They made you do it. Always nagging on you, grinding you down. Telling you you're good for nothing, not worth anything. Well, they're obviously wrong. The mean old lady couldn't pick someone stupid, could she? No, she had to pick someone smart and cagey. Someone who could get through my security system and make it seem like someone else entirely. You're so smart, Lawrence. Even the Tech God Supremo over there thinks you did a great job. Isn't that right, Supremo?"

Iggy was too busy making love to his iPad to play his part.

Det elbowed him, jerked his chin in our direction and whispered in our brother's ear.

Iggy jerked, looked up. "Yeah, yup. Yup. Definitely pulled the wool over my eyes. And I can crack the NSA encryption with a laptop. I'm still not sure how you placed the footage or made the computer see a different face."

Lawrence practically beamed. "I'm smart. Smarter than most people give me credit for, that's for fuck's sure." He puffed his chest out, looked up at Neva as if she were his own personal angel. "Not everyone sees that about me."

She smiled prettily, made gooey eyes at him. "Of course, I did, baby. It's so easy to see. Honestly, a blind man could see how smart and talented you are. How did you do it? We're all so confused, not being nearly as smart as you. Would you be willing to teach us? If that's not too much trouble?" She allowed her cheeks to flush, lifted a hand to one of them. "But you're probably too busy, huh? Smart, talented men like you don't have time to teach a silly little girl new tricks."

146

She heaved a sigh, and I felt like the man had just plunged a knife into her chest by the amount of chagrined disappointment floating in her voice.

"That's okay. I understand. I wouldn't want to make your woman jealous. You being so smart and all, teaching some dummy how to do cool things on the computer is probably something you're not interested in." She bumped her shoulder in the air.

Lawrence rushed in to answer as she started to turn away, tears shimmering in her eyes. "Well, I could probably tell you. It's really not that hard. I'm sure you're not too stupid, you could probably learn real fast. Pretty thing like you, you'd pick it up real quick."

I saw the briefest flash in those pretty green eyes, but she recovered well. "Aw, Lawrence. You're so brave. Thank you. If you could tell me, just whisper it real quiet like, I promise I'll memorize every word you say."

She sank to her knees in front of him, a graceful display of femininity that had my belly clenching. "Please, Lawrence. Please tell me. I need to know. I need to know it from you. Only you can tell me, only you're smart enough to have gotten by all my security so easily. I bet that silly man who installed all of it couldn't even have done what you did." She heaved another sigh, looked up at him through her lashes.

Lawrence ate up every single word from her admittedly sexy lips. He poured out secret after secret. And she kept building him up. Just some mope out for some quick money, he'd been a struggling college student who'd knocked up his girlfriend. Dropped out of computer science classes, but that didn't stop him from learning shit on the dark web. So he'd coded out a program that launched on his signal.

"But how did you choose that face? You're much more handsome than the face you used in the camera footage." Neva traced her gaze over every inch of his face as if she were trying to memorize it for her spank bank. "The ugly face you chose..." She shook her head, her lips twisting in disgust as a light sparked in her eyes for a moment. Then they shuttered back down to the doting woman just trying to get closer to her man. "Nothing compared to the one you have naturally."

Out of the corner of my vision, I saw Squirrel clamp his hand over Critter's mouth and hold him in a bear hug to keep the smaller man from jumping forward and defending his honor.

Another one-two punch from the little lady right into Critter's ego. She was good. Damn good.

"The stupid old lady told me to use that face. It had to be that face. It took a long time to code out because it's so ugly," Lawrence said. "And the only place I had pictures for sourcing were from her. So it took even longer. Honestly, I'm smart enough and fast enough that I could have been done and gone by the time she got me all the pictures I needed. But nooooo, she had to have it just the way she wanted."

Neva smiled sadly, her brow furrowed gently. "Some women just don't know a good thing when it's right in front of them, do they?"

Lawrence shook his head slightly. "Mostly they're dumb bitches. But you're nice. You're a nice, pretty lady. Thanks for not melting my dick off. You seem pretty understanding about the whole mix up. I'm real sorry for dropping those packages off to you. I don't know why the mean lady doesn't like you."

"Did you know what was in the packages? Maybe took a peek because of how heavy they were?" Neva tipped her lips into a conspiratorial angle. "I know I would have been tempted, that's for sure. But then again, big, heavy things just really do it for me." She gave a delicate body shiver, her lashes fluttering.

I'd give her something big and heavy.

Lawrence made a sound low in his throat. "I've got something big and heavy for you."

I tightened my fist in his hair and yanked. Clumps of hair came loose through my fingers as I shifted my hand to get a firmer grip on him while he screamed like a baby.

Neva glared up at me as he fought to get himself back under control. One of her brows raised, as if trying to tell me she knew I'd been thinking the exact same thing he'd stated out loud.

My lip curled up, but I kept my silence.

"Oh, my poor, poor baby. Did the bad man hurt you? Do you need a cuddle?" she asked in a voice that held a touch of sorrow in it.

Lawrence nodded so pitifully, I was surprised he didn't dissolve into himself as he bawled like a toddler denied his pacifier. What kind of snowflake, pansyassed fucker was this?

"Of course, you do, baby. Of course, you do." She made little kissy noises. "I'll get you some cuddles right now, Lawrence. Just you wait." She eased back and got to her knees.

Lawrence leaned forward, obviously expecting the cuddles to come from her. When she stepped back, his brow wrinkled. "Where are you going? Don't I get my cuddles?"

Neva giggled. "You sure do, my big brave boy. But my dress is all yucky. I don't want to get you all yucky, now do I?" She shook her head.

Lawrence parroted the motion.

"Guess who loves cuddles?" she asked, her hands folded up under her chin.

Lawrence beamed at her. "I do. I love cuddles."

"Good. So do I," Squirrel said as he came up behind Lawrence. "But no way in hell are you touching Pix there. Not with your stupid hands, fucktard body, or anything else. You're dumber than a box of wet hair." The big man squeezed the intruder in his arms until I heard a couple ribs pop.

Critter came up in front of the men and shoved a ball of fabric into the guy's gaping mouth before slapping a heavy piece of plastic he'd dug up from somewhere over his face. He finished it off by wrapping Lawrence's entire head in duct tape. Round and round and round. "I'm not stupid or ugly, you fucker." He slammed his fist into Lawrence's belly.

Squirrel dropped the guy and we all waited in heavy silence while Lawrence learned that he shouldn't have taken the job from the stupid, mean lady in the first place.

When he finally stopped dancing in his death throes, Critter and Squirrel picked him up. "Out through the garden entrance, please," Neva said, chill as a fucking cucumber.

Studying her, I saw the cost of death in her eyes. But I also saw her shoulder that burden without qualm or comment. She was strong. Fucking strong.

Then her eyes went shimmery as she stared up at me. She spun on her heel, raced across the room, and up the stairs.

Fuck.

She ran and I wanted to chase. To hunt her down, drag her back to me. Hold her still until she understood.

That should have scared me.

It didn't.

149

"Check her wrist," Gigs said. "If I see a single shade of purple or red, it's coming out of your hide."

I nodded as I turned to follow her.

Chapter 15
Neva

Taking a hard left at the top of the stairs, I walked into my bedroom. After sliding the pocket door shut with a soft snick, I made my way through the closet into the bathroom. The breath backed up in my lungs as I tried to swallow down the bile threatening to rise up my throat.

But I was too late and had too little left in reserve. Rushing forward, I barely lifted the toilet seat before emptying my stomach contents into its depths.

Fuck. Fuck. FUCK! Another tick in the dead column I had to atone for.

Clawed fingers tore all the ruined fabric from my body. I tossed it onto the floor, not caring where it landed. Stomping into the shower, I slapped the handle all the way to the hot side. Maybe I could burn away some of the guilt.

I told myself the sobs that shook my chest were covered under the thunder of the showerhead. The spiking heat of the water peppered my face with bites of fire. Too hot, but I stood there and forced myself to accept the punishment. Just like I played that idiot like a fiddle.

Lawrence was smart enough to build what he did—but too stupid to realize the woman pulling his strings had set him up from the start. He was a puppet for anyone with a steady hand.

He got played by a master.

I hated monsters.

Too many years ago to count, I joined their ranks.

Tears mixed with the water streaming down my face. I had to get it out, unleash some of the storm inside me, or I knew what could happen. Especially being undercover again.

Now that I couldn't go to Subterra for anything other than more briefings, I would have to make do with tears in the shower. And rides with my toy collection. Rome and the Seven Dwarfs had removed my last external option.

Damn them.

Lawrence's face burned behind my closed lids. He had zero chance—twenty-five, maybe. His whole life ahead of him and I'd worked him like he was nothing more than a ball of dough and me a five-star pastry chef.

So I stood there in the endless hot water and let everything inside me writhe and stew. It wasn't until I outlined it to the guys I could see how far off the mark this job really was.

Time was rushing down the drain too quickly. If my information was correct, Jorgenssen was scheduled to make another drop-off on Sunday night. That meant I was three weeks behind my infiltration deadline and I hadn't made it to his house once.

Brantley. Fucking Brantley. He should have been jumping for joy at having a clandestine operator with my particular skill set in his toolbelt, but he kept treating me like I had the plague. I gave fuck all about credit; I needed inside Jorgenssen's organization so I could find the fucking maker.

Once I found the maker, I'd be one step closer to the killer who took my mo—

The heat of the water should have been the only thing scalding my skin.

But something else was there. Watching, devouring.

The prickle at the base of my skull turned electric.

My breath hitched as I turned.

Blue eyes.

My stomach dropped.

Rome stood in the entryway, sapphire eyes hard as he stared through the clear glass. One of his hands gripped the header over the door, the other strangled his dick through his jeans.

My body heated and my nerves went molten. He might not be in the Teams anymore, but he definitely kept himself in shape as if he were. Muscles rippled over his abdomen as his hips jerked before he dropped his dick.

"Perv much?" I asked over the sound of the shower.

One side of his mouth ticked up. "It seems to only be with you, dewdrop."

"Get your fill now, Rome. Looks are all you're getting from me." I shifted my face back into the flow of water and prayed he left.

With little effort, I could imagine what being with him would be like. Probably fucks like Gabe—mind blowing and selfish. Better for him and his ego if he found someone else to screw—over.

With my escape ruined, I put my mind to actually showering. By the time I smoothed conditioner through my long locks, everything from this shit day was organized in my brain where it belonged.

No more outbursts. No more getting distracted.

No more—

I smashed the level to the cold side and doused myself, and made plans for the rest of the night. First things first, I needed to reach out to my friend in the Collective and run these fuckers through their program. It would cost me, but the money was a non-issue. Especially if it meant I would have some backup I could finally trust.

When my mental timer struck zero, I hit the water handle and shut the whole thing off. I shivered, turned for the exit—and froze.

Rome was still there, although now his dick was out of his pants and caught in the rough grip of his fist. With the noise of the shower off, I could hear his soft grunts while he fucked his palm with slow, measured movements as his searing blue gaze memorized every inch of my form.

At a grand total of five-four, I was an extremely curvy one-eighty-four. People called me soft—curves, thighs, too much everywhere. But...he never looked away. Not even once.

Feeling very much like prey, I grabbed my heated towel from the bar—slowly. No sudden movements.

He jacked off—slow, deliberate—in the doorway between bathroom and closet. He truly was a beautiful specimen. But it was the heat in his eyes and the tight grip of his fist that drew me in the most.

He'd gotten it into his head that I was his, that he'd claimed me. Nothing but lies. I simply had tits and a vagina they wanted to sample before he moved on to the next set of matching hardware.

If I needed a sign to swear off men forever, this was it.

With the towel secured up under my armpits, I moved across the bathroom. The closer I got, the white his knuckles.

"Careful. Gonna pop that clean off." I eased by without touching him. Once inside my closet space, I fully dried off. Bending in half, I flipped my head and wrapped my hair up in a second, smaller towel to catch most of the moisture.

He made a low sound that sent chills skating down my spine. Fuck, he just had to be vocal. Men who got vocal when they enjoyed themselves...so fucking hot.

I bit my lip. No, bad body. No reaction. Professional colleague. Hotness quotient and vocals didn't matter. Fuck, please let them not matter.

Since I didn't have anything else on my plate tonight except chatting with my friend and working in the lab, I went for oversized and comfy. I grabbed the first set of comfy clothes I could reach and bent to tug the ratty sweatpants up my legs.

Within moments, I was straightened and flattened against the mirrored front of one of the wardrobe doors. Steam from my breath blurred the mirror.

Rome's gaze speared me over my shoulder in the mirror. "What the fuck do you think you're doing?"

I smirked up at him. "You do know jacking off too much makes you go blind, right?"

He snorted softly. "Not at all. Especially when I get to see something as beautiful as you. Why do you think you get to put clothes on?" He continued to stroke his dick, his knuckles trailing up and down my skin from hips to mid back.

I arched a single brow. "Why do you think your opinion matters?"

He radiated heat like a bonfire. And sweet daffodils, if the length of his stroke was any indication, he'd rip me in half—maybe quarters. And gallons of lube? Nobody's fantasy.

His chuckle sent shivers down my spine. "Because I own you, dewdrop. We've been over this part already."

154

My mind's telling me no. But my body's humming yes.

I laughed, right in his reflected face. "You might think you own me, but since I didn't have any say in the matter, your ownership claim is null and void. No one owns me but me."

And my slutty, traitorous body arched into his heat anyway.

His moan hit my spine like a curse. "Fuck, dewdrop. Every time you say that kind of shit, it just makes me more determined. Please, keep saying it. Keep trying to deny me what's mine." He let go, the weight of him resting boldly against my spine, then reached around my body and cupped my right breast.

The breath stalled in my lungs as I fought to push through the heat, the lust. Hell, through all the sensations rushing through me at his touch. Fucking. Pinyang.

No shame, no hesitation. He acted like he did own me—and something in me liked it.

No. His dick, while impressive, didn't run on batteries. He didn't get to go anywhere near my pussy with it.

I held his gaze, raised a single brow. "Then me kicking you out should make you nut enough to feed every Prospect Park squirrel for the winter. Go give it to them and call it a day, Keys. I'm done." I shifted to the side.

Or tried to. Once again, he saw my move before I made it. He caught me with his other hand around my throat, and his thumb caressed my skin. My skin prickled as the scalding heat of his body rested along mine from ass to shoulders. As he massaged my neck, he tightened his hold on my right breast.

Soft and rough.

Hard and gentle.

The only thing I knew for sure was that this man was dangerous. Physically and sexually.

But I shoved it all aside. Even if he made my body weep for him, it wouldn't be enough.

Honestly? Kicking him out was to protect him. Wasn't mad about the spank bank material. I could ride this wave for a while.

I met his fiery gaze with my own cool one. He wouldn't get a rise out of me—at least not one he could use. Just a vacant doll in a sexy hold, I watched him while he fondled me.

"I bet if I slid my fingers through your pussy, they'd get drenched." His words were like fire to kindling.

155

I nodded, no reason to lie about it. "I'm a damn Slip 'N Slide. But like I keep trying to tell you, none of you know how to use your dicks. I take mine battery operated and guided by my own hands, thanks."

Getting hot and wet wasn't the problem. The follow-through was. "I'm trying to spare your ego here, Keys. It's really not personal. I'm sure you're more than adequate in the sack. Fuck knows you're hot enough to get any woman's pussy wet and achy." I shrugged.

The longer we stood there, the quieter she got—back to her usual nothing. Just another body next to mine. No reason to get all worked up about it.

He must have seen something in my gaze because he stepped back, his head tipped slightly to the side. "You're being serious."

Of course he was shocked. I nodded anyway, too fucking tired to care.

"Look, assuming everything turns out clean on the runs, we'll be working together. It will go much smoother if you consider me some kind of sexless auntie."

If it would save him from constantly trying to get into my pants and piling on more disappointment, I'd wear ice panties.

He burst into laughter. "Sexless auntie?" He shoved his still mostly hard dick back into his jeans and zipped up. "You've got to be kidding me with that shit."

Turning, I pulled my sweatpants up the rest of the way, then elbowed on an equally ratty hoodie I'd stolen from one of my past partners.

He glared, hands fisted on his hips. "Do you really think putting on another guy's sweatshirt is going to help your case?"

I rolled my eyes. "Not. Personal. And what I wear has absolutely zero to do with you. Look, I'm sorry you got all hot and bothered by watching me shower. I wasn't putting on a show. I didn't know you were there, and then, once I did know you were there, I thought you left. You getting all handsy with yourself is on you, not me."

He snickered. "You're funny. I know you probably don't mean to be, but you do make me laugh."

I held my bored expression. "So happy."

He laughed—then his brows furrowed. "How long were you with your partner at Subterra before you took matters into your own hands?"

My mouth fell open at the question. He wasn't even trying to hide the fact that he'd been spying on me with that camera. The audacity of this guy.

"Come on. Not personal, right? One semi-friend to another." He crossed his arms and backed up to lean against the door frame. "From all appearances, you're a sex kitten waiting for a lion to pounce."

I snorted a laugh. "Of course, a man would say that." Heaved a sigh. "Seriously, you couldn't handle being my friend, Keys, so let's not even try. We'll be polite professional killers taking down some truly terrible people. Let's leave it at that. Once the job is done—separate sunsets. Participation trophies all around."

His lips twisted. "I couldn't handle being your friend?"

Men had the most fragile egos about the silliest things. "No. You couldn't."

I shoved at the corners of my towel turban.

"You're a former SEAL. You made a brotherhood, a fucking family, with the guys downstairs. Everything about you runs on community—on having that safety net. You are a pack. Your pride-ful lions."

"Me? I'm a solitary creature; the grumpy, grouchy indoor cat who ate the nice old lady after she died and didn't leave me enough food in my dish. I'm feral, don't like being touched, and am safer, saner, and less dangerous by myself."

I bit back everything else.

"We're not the same."

Something inside me broke off and turned to ash to say the words, but they were true. I'd learned to live with it, even embraced it sometimes. Didn't mean I accepted it all the time.

On good days, I liked that I was so independent. On bad days, I went searching for it. For that fleeting moment of connection with someone else. Hence my membership at Subterra.

And just like that, I was exhausted. Every part of me. A moment was coming—I wouldn't be able to outrun it. Wouldn't release the weight inside me. I'd break. And I'd take too many down with me.

His expression shadowed with sadness as his gaze searched mine. I'm pretty sure he flinched away deep inside where he didn't want me to see. He opened his mouth, corners turned down. "Neva, I'm so—" He closed his mouth, agony wrenching in his eyes.

He was going to pity me?

Me!?

I'd just told him I was better on my own and here he was trying to play Sad Sack Sam like he knew me. His audacity was enough to make me see red. Animosity lit my stomach, set my veins to blazing as he tried to offer some kind of platitude.

As if he'd set off a string of Black Cat fireworks, everything inside me went pop, pop, pop. I launched myself at him.

"Get the fuck out, Keys. Get out!"

Blind with anger, I attacked him. I hit, kicked, punched. Everything I'd learned in my twenty years of clandestine operations, I threw at him.

He caught me against his body, then curled in so I couldn't do as much damage. And that just made me rage harder. How dare he pity me—and still not stand there and take his beating like a man? My vision went crimson as I tried to get through his protective barrier.

For just a moment, there was a break in his guard. A sliver of space for me to land a strike.

The grin. The light in his eyes…my mind went blank. I let go—sank into the adrenaline-soaked animal inside me, survival the only thing that mattered.

Chapter 16

Rome

I had to give it to her, she was skilled. For a moment, I wasn't sure I could hold her at all. She was small, but the hell in her skin and veins, made up for it. If I wasn't at least fifty pounds heavier and stood close to twelve inches taller than her, she probably would have done some real damage. As it was, I would be carrying some bruises, scratches, and pain for a while.

That wounded look in her green eyes as she tried to get rid of me this last time sank through me again. Just like her fist into my right kidney.

Fuck.

This woman would rather bleed than break.

Hell, maybe that was the point.

I grunted as I allowed the pain to wash through me before sliding it off to the side. She better hope I didn't piss blood tomorrow.

As she wedged herself away, I scrambled to grab her arms. Just as I thought I got her under control, she slammed the point of her elbow into the back of my neck. Stars filled my vision—not a single thread of Old Glory though.

Damn, for someone so soft and abso-fucking-lutely sexy, she had some lethal points on her.

The rush of feet up the stairs told me I needed to get her under control before my men tried to step in and get her off me. They wouldn't hold to the no touching rule if they thought I was under attack.

She rewarded my distraction with a well-placed finger lock. With a grip like a seasoned Strongman, I felt my belly begin to revolt when she tried to pull it from its socket.

Gritting my teeth against the pain, I locked back into the fight in my arms. This tiny she-devil wasn't going to bring me to my knees. Not with my men coming up the stairs to save me.

That would be the single injury I never lived down.

I finally got my free arm up and over hers, squeezing her wrists between my biceps and my rib cage. I exhaled hard, blew her dark hair out of my face.

I should've been pissed. Out for fucking blood. Her hair clung to my jaw. Her wrist still jerked in my hold. But all I could think about...I wanted was to know what broke her—and who I had to kill for it.

Her face was white—except for the twin points of furious red blooming on her cheeks. She narrowed her eyes, and I swore I saw the attack before she actually moved.

I snapped my head back—she still clipped my chin. Pain sparked tears, but I shoved them down. Damn, she was relentless.

As she regrouped, the sound of a gun being cocked filled the space. She went still in my arms, her eyes narrowing down into slits as she turned her head slowly toward the door.

"Get off him, Snow. Slowly," Gigs said. There was no mistaking the promise of pain in his voice if she didn't comply. He didn't have the gun pointed at her, which was the only thing saving him from a future beating. He did, however, have it out and ready to draw down on her if she moved too quickly.

Without taking her eyes off him, she sank her nails into my rib cage.

Yeah. Dewdrop was done playing nice. She maintained and increased the pressure until I felt my shirt and skin give way to her sharp talons. I inhaled a sharp breath.

Fuck, where they lined in steel or something?

I bit back a wince, the warm flow of my own blood down my sides should have surprised and angered me. But she reminded me too much of a feral animal left on its own for far too long.

She hissed. Snapped. Fought. Scratched. Pushed people away. To force them to leave her alone. I had a feeling she was highly successful at it, too.

"I won't tell you again, Snow. Get off him," Gigs said softly. "I don't want to hurt you, but I will."

Let her fight me. Let her bleed me. I'd still choose this over watching her go numb again.

I bared my teeth at him over her head, but he didn't take his eyes off her. Considering she was the real threat at the moment, I understood his caution. But we'd be having words later.

The team bottlenecked behind him, faces tight with confusion or restraint. Only Squirrel wore that sad, knowing the look—the giant man who didn't give two fucks about anyone outside of our group—that told me her face still held at least some degree of hate.

Squirrel and I shared the same kind of pain—two ends of the same blade. The Navy had made us equals. Our history made us brothers.

One second, she's fighting like a caged animal, like she had fucking fangs.

The next?

Nothing.

Like she'd flipped a switch. Like I wasn't worth the fight—hell, the energy—anymore. Just like that, the storm passed. And it wasn't peace she left in its place—it was absence.

Neva finally extricated her nails from my flesh. She wiped her hands on my shirt, dappled streaks of red, then held them up in the air. Her lower body went soft and pliant, and I had to remind myself that she'd just done me physical damage and it wasn't hot.

When she glanced down at me with one dark raised brow, I had to figure I failed. I shrugged. "Not my fault we both like the way you look and feel." I held still and waited for her to get completely off me.

As she scooted to the far side of the room on her ass, hands still in the air, she rolled her eyes. "Might need to keep the blood up north, Keys. Down south's only gonna get you in trouble."

I snorted softly. She wasn't kidding, but something about this woman took the large part of the decision out of my hands. If she thought I enjoyed walking around like a slobbering dog after a particularly meaty bone, then she needed to have her head examined. I hadn't experienced

161

this kind of reaction to a woman in almost a decade. Hell, if ever.

The soft click of Gigs's hammer released me from the moment. I got to my feet and winced. I would remember her touch all right. Too bad it came with blood, not sweat. Stretching out the aches and cramps, I walked over and put a hand down to help her up.

She looked gobsmacked as she stared up at me.

What now? This woman was going to kill me with her swift mood changes.

She glanced between my hand and my face, like she didn't trust either. Her pulse jumped once under my fingers.

Not weakness. Just warning. Like her body hadn't told her mind she was safe yet.

I held still.

The moment I gripped her wrist, she twitched—just barely. Gone so fast, I almost missed it. Her wrist bones ground against each other under my grip. She was so fucking tiny. But she fought like she was some six-five linebacker on steroids.

Once on her feet, she studied me. A look of guilt washed over her pretty features as she dipped her gaze to my chest. She heaved a sigh. "I'm sorry." The words were soft, almost a moan of tempered anguish, but I heard them.

I looked down—streaks of drying blood. Shrugging, I shifted to look at her again. "Hey, at least I know you can take care of yourself in a fight that doesn't involve cream, gas, liquid, flakes, or serums, right?" I hoped she's smile. Just once.

Seeing her hurt made it hard to breathe.

A muffled snort sounded as she lifted her gaze to mine again. Merriment danced in her green eyes.

Thank fuck. I smiled back at her.

"You're just lucky you're so damn big." The humor vanished as fast as it came.

She spun on her heel and went back into the bathroom. She reappeared in under a minute, a small, battered tin in her hands. "Here. Sit." She patted the bench by the mirrored closet doors.

"Are you going to attack me again?" I asked as I moved to where she indicated.

She shook her head, deadpan. "No, but keep it up and I'll give you something to make it burn instead of heal faster."

162

"Pix, give him another scar. He's too sexy," Squirrel added as the rest of the guys packed the room to the brim towering over her as she told me to take my shirt off.

"If you're going to go all sexy nurse, I demand to stay," Critter said.

Gigs slapped him upside the head before anyone could answer. "We'll keep him quiet."

Beck rolled his eyes as he moved up behind Critter with a promise in his gaze. His lips moved, but I couldn't tell what he said.

Focusing on Neva again, I tossed my shirt over my knee. I felt my nipples bead as the air conditioner buzzed and blew a cold breeze through the room. Fucking hell.

She directed me to put my hands out, palms up. "Hold this and if you value the rest of your life, don't drop it." She put the open tin across my palms with a glare promising that my death would be as painful as she could make it.

I simply nodded. I would never doubt the damage this woman could visit on anyone, least of all someone she'd just warned.

She pulled a tiny cobalt vial from the tin's shallow depths. Barely longer than an inch, it had a black screw-top lid. She opened the bottle, dropping the top back into the tin. She capped it with a finger, flipped it twice. She did it three more times—each on a different finger.

When she was apparently happy with the amount of the golden liquid she'd collected on her fingertips, she bent down, her hoodie caught on my knees. "This won't sting, and it will help kill anything that might have gotten transferred into your body. I might've skipped under my fingernails."

She dabbed the pale golden liquid that rested on her fingertip onto the points on my rib cage where she'd gouged me. And she was right, it didn't sting. Other than the fact that she smoothed the liquid over my skin, I couldn't really even tell that she'd done anything.

My dick didn't care—he just liked her touching us.

A soft floral scent hit my nose as she rubbed whatever remaining liquid she had on her fingertips into her hands like lotion.

It wasn't the oil that calmed me. It was her hands.

"What was that?" Gigs asked, his face a tanned moon over her shoulder.

"Lavender oil with a few drops of tea tree oil. Good for cuts, wounds, bug bites, bruises—calms irritated skin. The tea tree is antiseptic, antifungal, antiviral. Antibacterial, too. Keeps all the goobies out. Creates a barrier. High-concentration cleanse, right where you need it. Not that those scratches were a real risk—but human fingernails are disgusting, so better safe than sorry."

I blinked. Hard. "Goobies?"

She nodded, smiling. "Goobies. The unidentified disease-carrying microbes transferred from my nails into your body that might cause infection or illness. It's a highly technical term."

Yeah. I was absolutely fucked.

Looking at her now, I would never have assumed that she attacked me just moments ago. The hate was gone. So was the anger—the wrenching loneliness I saw before she snapped. Shadowed intuition crept up my spine.

She was a pressure cooker about to pop. What I saw earlier? Just a little steam.

Made me a sick, twisted bastard, but I really wanted to be the one to crack the seal on her. Open her up, explore her deepest depths, and shatter her from the inside out. More than just fucking, I wanted the raw version of her. The one locked away for far too long.

Was she spicy and spiky? Soft and sultry? Somewhere in between? My belly tightened at the idea of finding out.

She didn't know it yet, but I meant what I said. She was mine. I wasn't willing to let her go until I found the true Neva hidden under the legends, the veneers, and the masks.

But if I'd learned nothing else from this last interaction, I knew I needed to go about it a different way. She might be tangentially interested in me, but I was coming to learn that she didn't lie. About anything. Everything she said was the truth—if varying shades of it, due to her job. If she couldn't do so honestly, she just stayed silent.

If she truly thought she didn't want any dick that didn't run on batteries, then there was a whole mess of stuff in her head that continued to get in her way when it came to getting off with a partner.

Since I fully intended to make her come so hard and so often she got addicted to it, to me, I needed to do more than just assume my dick was magical.

I smiled at her as she recapped the small bottle and put it back in the tin. As she took it from my hands, she turned. And ran face first into Gigs's chest.

He jerked back like she was radioactive. "Easy there, Snow. I don't feel like getting beat any more than what I already have coming to me."

Her head tipped to the side, but I didn't see her facial expression. If I had to guess, she rolled her eyes hard enough to see her brain. The woman really didn't understand the no touching rule we all had.

Watching her walk back to the bathroom in the ratty, baggy clothes made my chest twinge. If she had to wear a man's clothes, they damn well better be mine. She should smell like me— wrapped top to toe in my scent, not some other asshole's cologne.

I swallowed the words she'd take the wrong way. I didn't need more puncture wounds right now.

The guys fanned out into the closet, overfilling the small space. What I could see now felt vintage, classically feminine than I would have assumed she enjoyed.

From her personality, she seemed more fitted to a fallout bunker or barracks setting. Still, this felt like her real space, not just something that came with her legend for her current undercover assignment.

What I needed was intel. Real intel. On the real Neva Bylur. But from what Iggy said earlier, there were flags on her file that he'd never seen before. And since I really didn't want her to get killed or burned by the Agency, I needed to get close enough to learn her secrets from the woman herself.

She came back into the oversized closet, her body engulfed in the huge clothes. Skimming a glance down to her feet, I saw that she'd cut off the bottom of sweatpants. No telling how much she cut, but her little toes just stuck out from the rolled edges of the material.

I'd never been into feet. Ever. Too much time in boots for feet to ever be sexy for me. But her toes...they were adorable. It kinda tripped my brain how much I wanted to see the rest of her foot.

"If you're all done staring at me, you can leave now. And don't make me threaten you again, please. Just go. I need to do the runs on you all and get some more work done in the lab." She sounded tired. And more than just physically.

Whatever was wearing her down...I was going to kill it.

Sliding my shirt back on, I stood up. I blinked. The punctures didn't hurt at all. I've been stabbed before, by

165

just about every object that could break skin. The fact I couldn't feel ten fingernail sized punctures on my body amazed me.

"We'll get out of your hair, dewdrop." I jerked my chin at the door for the guys to start heading out.

"Wait," Iggy said, cutting off the exit. "Something you said earlier has been bothering me and since we're not currently in a high-risk situation, I thought it would be a good time to discuss it."

All gazes swung back to Neva. She heaved a sigh, then waved a hand for him to go on. She crossed her arms over her chest and waited, slight irritation pinched her otherwise gorgeous face.

Iggy licked his lips. "You said earlier that you had Keys's phone number. I'm assuming you meant his personal phone number. That's not listed anywhere, for a number of reasons. What phone number do you have that you think belongs to Keys?"

Her jaw ticked as she stared at him for a moment. After a long moment, she shifted her gaze to me. "You didn't text me earlier today?"

I shook my head. "No, I had no reason to message you. I was still trying to track down your information after you slid through Locke's staging area like you designed it yourself."

She bit her lower lip.

Holy shit. I felt that movement all the way through my dick. I forced the image out of my head. How the fuck did she keep doing this to me?

It was crazy.

She finally nodded and turned back to Iggy. "It came from an unavailable number."

My brain refocused immediately at her words. "But you thought it was from me? What did the message say that made you think that?"

She licked her lips, they twisted with chagrin. She unfolded her arms, raised her fingers them air quotes as she said, "I know who you really are. You should be more careful; you never know who's watching."

Angry fire lit my veins. She thought I would send something like that to her?

"You were one of a few options that came to mind. Considering you saw me on the corner, I figured you'd gone back to your offices and ran me."

I blew out a breath. That was logical. Still a little damaging to my honor, but at least logical on her part. "Who else did you suspect?"

Her slumped, deflated. "Brantley. It's so easy to get a burner phone these days, and knowing him, this is definitely something I could see him doing. More power plays and mindfucks. Something definitive he could use to get me kicked off his team for breaching confidentiality in some stupid way."

Her FBI handler just made my list. What kind of fuckwit tried to screw with the people on his own op? There had to be something else at play that she clearly didn't know about. Luckily for her, she had us now.

Me, now.

"Any other players you can think of?" Iggy asked.

She sighed and tossed the towel from her head. She shook out her damp locks. "I thought of everything from bots to scammers to creepy car extended warranty sales callers using new tactics. Keys and Brantley were the most logical of the two." She turned back to me. "That, plus with what happened on my porch, and I was sure it was you playing games for taking you down in your own building."

Again, the logic was going to get me put in an early, brutally painful grave. I'm damn glad she wasn't an immediate vengeance kind of girl. Thank the universe she wasn't the vengeance-on-sight type.

"Now that it wasn't actually Dopey at my doorstep, I'm back to thinking it was Brantley. If not him, I have zero idea who it could be." Worry flitted over her pretty face for a moment before she shrugged. "If they pop up again, I'll handle it."

The unstated, 'by myself,' hit the room like a bomb.

Squirrel snorted. "Hate to break it to you, pix, but if you run us and we vibing Gangnam style, then we'll handle it for you."

A ghost of a smile pulled at her lips even as she shook her head. "I've undoubtedly made a lot of enemies in my twenty years with the Company. Don't worry. If something comes up, I'll deal with it."

Did she really just say she made enemies working in the CIA, but being doxed was just a another Tuesday? She was taking the whole lone wolf bit a little too far, if she truly thought that. I was going to shake her.

She wasn't bulletproof. But she sure as hell acted like it.

167

And I was getting real tired of watching her walk into war alone.

"From the syntax and verbiage used, did you recognize any specific phrasing?" Critter asked.

She blinked at him, her mouth dropping open slightly.

He flushed slightly. "Hey, I'm a linguist. I know shit about words and speaking patterns." He muttered something that cracked the guys up.

"I'm just surprised is all, Dopey. Sorry," Neva said. "And to answer your question, no. Too generic. Nothing stood out."

"Any ex-lovers, bad blood in your family, some kind of shirttail relative you pissed off?" he asked.

She shook her head. "You all met my last lover. Did you leave him in any condition to send me a message?"

I snorted loudly. Unless he accessed a cell phone with 5G capabilities in hell, he certainly wasn't dancing his fingers over a screen. "No, dewdrop. It wasn't him."

She shrugged, shaking her head. "Then no. I've mainly stuck to short-term partners at various sex clubs I've been a member of." Her lips parted—then shut. Whatever she almost said, she swallowed it.

But even with that phony ass smile on her face, for the tiniest fragments of a second, she seemed to wilt in front of me. Less than a heartbeat, but there none the less.

Then it hit me. I would have to go track every one of those fuckers down. If any of them thought about coming back…I'd make sure they never got the chance.

She's a member of various sex clubs and not a single guy could give her what she needed? Is that why she was so dedicated to her toys? Damn. My little dewdrop needed rewired from the inside out.

"And now that you're all partially aware of my sexual history, you need to leave." She crossed her arms again. Smile gone. Expression flat. Then she shook her head, arms dropping down to her sides as if they weighed too much.

"Now." The word cracked. Her arm lifted like it weight a hundred pounds, finger slicing the air.

She wasn't trying to push us away. She was trying not to shatter in front of witnesses.

Chapter 17

Neva

I felt like such a freak standing in that thick silence. Keys now knew for sure that I was some kind of broken doll.

Not that it mattered, I reminded myself.

Battery boyfriends. Battery boyfriends. He's nothing but a new colleague.

Someone cleared their throat. "If you get another text from an unavailable number like the first one you got, will you send it to me?" Tech God Supremo asked.

I nodded, arm still raised. "Yes. Leave. Now. All of you." I started walking toward them. If they weren't allowed to touch me, maybe that would make them leave sooner in an attempt to avoid physical contact.

I snickered silently. This no touching rule could turn out to be a real boon for me. My gaze slipped to Rome, and I mentally pouted.

Well, mostly a boon for me.

If he thought he could touch me whenever he wanted, there was still something wrong with it. But he'd learn, eventually.

They always did.

Following them down the stairs to the main level, I watched them walk out the front door; Rome followed at the back of the pack. At the door, he turned. "Be at the club on Friday night, dewdrop." He said nothing else, simply spun and headed down the steps back to their huge van.

I slammed the door behind him. What made him think he could give me orders?

I would go to the club if I wanted to, or I would stay home if I wanted to. His thoughts on the matter meant absolutely nothing to me.

Locking the door and resetting my alarm, I wandered through the living room. Setting the armchair upright reminded me of Lawrence, and a pang of guilt slithered through me. Until I remembered he'd delivered a package full of poison.

Which reminded me of something else. Hurrying to the lab, I grabbed up my phone and hit the button for the last dialed number.

I wasn't going to chase him. I just needed the number. That was all.

"Locke Security, this is Rome Whitlock."

Ignoring the flutter in my belly, I said, "I need your actual number, not the business line."

He laughed softly. "Stop flirting with me, dewdrop. It makes me all tingly when you gush on like that."

Next, I messaged the Collective. My contact there could run the full file on the team—quietly and quickly. And I would need every hour she could spare. But first, I had revisit the poison Lawrence had left on my doorstep.

Pulling up the right file, I studied the old formula. Aconite, with a touch of corn cockle and a sprinkle of belladonna. Dosages in the microliters—fast, fleeting, brutal. Whoever created the newer version had adjusted the dosages of each singular part and added some kind of inhibitor.

Flipping between the mass spec readouts and my own notes from almost twenty years ago, I was caught between professional jealousy and personal anger. No way anyone found my notes. Or the recipe. But I was looking at the evidence right in front of me.

Skimming through the rest of my notes, I checked to see if I had anything in the original formula that would make sense for what they added to make it stable. I shook my head after reading through the list a couple times. What they put together obviously worked, but it shouldn't have. Not according to the chemistry staring me in the face.

Shoving my rolling stool to the mass spec computer, I ran the results again. There had to be something I was missing. Some kind of additive. Removing something would have made it more unstable. The gold didn't stabilize it. Just housed the aerosol.

I ran through a ton of options while I waited for the mass spec to do her business and give me the missing ingredient. Standing up from the desk, I moved back to the isolator. Maybe there was something else in the box.

The box.

I smacked my forehead with my palm and raced for the front entryway again. This was the second box, not the first one. I just hoped there would be enough residue left in the first box to get some results. I skidded to a halt in the foyer.

There. Tucked in the corner. Rolling my eyes at my idiocy, I ran back to the lab. Grabbing a ventilator mask and long gloves, I pulled on the PPE equipment. Once again back at the front of my family home, I grabbed the box and held it away from me as I carried it back to the lab.

Setting it inside my second, and last, isolator, I hit the big red button to sterilize the field. A heavy plume of inert gas washed through the small chamber. A big green light blinked on at the top of the machine.

I nodded, smiling. Going through the same process I did for the second box, I gathered my samples. After getting them secured in the mass spec, I went back and started examining the box itself.

Lined in thick layers of gold just like the first one I'd tested, this box held something else inside it. Instead of a low shimmering that uniformly covered the sides, there were jagged breaks in the reflection.

My brow wrinkled. What the hell was that about? Double checking to be sure the field was clean, I grabbed my gloves and pulled the box from the chamber. Setting it on the worktop, I studied it. Roughly four by four by four, the box was relatively small. And some of the internal space was used up by the gold lining itself.

I pulled the cardboard away. Or tried to. Yanking. Cutting. Nothing worked. I finally had to get a brand new scalpel out of its packaging and slice away a small section. I grabbed calipers and measured the thickness of the gold lining.

My eyes widened.

I repeated the process on every side. My mind reeled. Same numbers for each section.

How much did a four by four by four box lined in half an inch of gold cost? And why the hell did someone spend that kind of money to send me my own poison? And even more important, how did they get the aerosol in there without letting it touch oxygen?

Starting at the top of my mental questions, I moved back to the Google machine, completed some scouting for numbers, gold prices, and measurements. I set the box on my scale.

Eight pounds, twelve ounces. Nearly nine. Pulling up the cost of gold based on weight, my mind exploded. Someone spent just under $350,000 sending me a poison of my own that they modified.

Talk about wasting money.

Two fucking boxes.

These people were idiots of the highest order. No one I knew in any corner of the globe was going to spend that kind of money on a poison that was so fast acting and could be mitigated with large volumes of high percentage oxygen. Granted, whoever sent it to me probably hadn't planned on me having a group of guys rush to my aid.

Did the sender expect me to die? Would they be looking for me tomorrow? Would my being alive and working at the school be good or bad?

Shit. There was so much that could go wrong. Too many risks. Not enough intel. Or anyone to fucking talk to about any of the possibilities.

I exhaled. Recentered. Running myself ragged in circles wasn't going to help me accomplish anything. Least of all coming up with coherent answers based on good intel. I didn't have intel, good, bad, or otherwise. Hoping anything was a waste of time. I needed solid facts.

My brain blinked a massive red warning.

I did have some info.

Walking back over to my phone, I texted TGS, asking for the name of the woman Lawrence mentioned.

My phone danced across the counter. Unknown number. I slipped into Aneira's voice like a second skin.

"Hello, this is Aneira."

"Dewdrop, I'm offended you don't have my number in your phone yet," Rome drawled down the line.

I rolled my eyes, felt my shoulders relax. "Yeah, color me surprised that I'm not just sitting here putting all of your information in my phone while I crochet doilies or bake pies. Why are you calling me?"

"Iggy said you had a question."

I waited for him to say anything else.

He let the silence stretch.

"Yes. I did. Why are you calling me?"

He heaved a sigh. "Because I claimed you, you're mine. You want information, you get it from me. None of them are going to talk to you unless it's face to face, encrypted, or a high risk situation." His tone made it sound like I was an idiot who he had to slow down for.

I gritted my teeth. "That's the dumbest thing I've ever heard. They can't talk to me without a chaperone? Let me guess. That's you?"

"Got it in one, dewdrop."

Of course it was him. Gods forbid I operate without a leash.

Glaring, I put the phone on speaker. "What is with the caveman behavior, Rome? We talked about it; we're work colleagues. Nothing more, nothing less."

I rolled my eyes, uninterested in any of his twisted explanations. "Really, I just need the name of the mean old lady Lawrence talked about." Which reminded me, I still needed to check what they did with the body. The lock on the garden gate was impenetrable.

Then Squirrel asking for cuddles as he broke through the lock on my lab rattled through my brain again. I sighed. If they got it open, that's one less thing on my list. That was good.

"NEVA!"

I startled, glared at my phone. "What?! Happy hemlock, Rome. Why the fuck are you screaming at me?"

He blew out a breath—sharp and annoyed. "Because, once again, I've been talking to you, and you couldn't be bothered to answer. Her name is Penni Scoipross." He spelled each name and then started grumbling to himself. Something about contrary women and sexy asses.

"Good. Thank you." I hung up.

Damn, give the man an inch and he took a mile. I tossed the phone back onto the table and sat at my Company computer. Accessing a CIA-owned laptop took less time than hitting the dark web. Not exactly comforting.

Putting Penni Scoipross into the database, I got exactly zero. Well shit. I told the program to check for any spelling variations, derivatives, or aliases. Not hopeful, but I ran it through every program I had.

Waiting for the database to do its thing, I turned back to the box. I still couldn't figure out why the inside of this box looked different from the second. Going over to the first isolator, I performed the same steps to measure, calculate, and cost out the second box. They weighed the same. Give or take a gram.

Looking at the inside of the second box, I noted the glimmer and shimmer were uniform along every side. Even the top flaps were the same. For whatever reason, the first box held something different inside it.

I blinked. A couple grams difference in weight that seemed to be the exact same dimensions? Accounting for the differences in the melting process or cardboard could give that discrepancy. But what if Box One's shimmer was the clue?

Picking up my phone again, I hit the redial button.

"Keep calling me so often, I'm going to think you really want me, dewdrop."

I rolled my eyes. "Do you have a way to cut gold?"

"I'm sure we could rig something up in the shop. Why are you cutting one of the boxes open?"

I smiled. He knew exactly what I planned without me having to walk him through my thought process. I really hoped the Collective run came back clean. It would be nice working with competent people again. Running through my conclusions and reasons why, I waited for him to say something.

"How often were you coming to Subterra?"

I blinked as I tried to follow his mental path now. "The last two weekends."

"Shit. Today and tomorrow are too early for you to come by without raising any flags. Do you think you can wait to bring it with you Friday?"

I shrugged as I finally caught on. "I don't see why not. All my scans say the boxes are inert. Stable. Unless there's some kind of computer virus that lives in gold lining, I should be pretty safe."

"Give me a second." Silence. "Iggy said it's a good idea, but largely science fiction."

I rolled my eyes. "So glad Tech God Supremo can cast his vote to you."

"You wanted an answer."

"And I'll only get them from you," I finished for him. "Yeah, I remember your neuroses quite clearly."

"Good. Less time repeating myself." He paused. The weight in the silence said enough. "Because I remember your...tells quite well, too." He hung up.

Snorting a laugh, I put the phone down. He was clever.

Then I realized I was smiling about an interaction with him.

No. No, no, no, no. Wasn't happening.

"FUCK!"

Chapter 18

Rome

I smiled at the phone then looked up to see the whole group staring at me. I wiped my face clean and put my phone back on the table in the conference room. We were reviewing Iggy's data from the main unit while we were at Neva's.

"What?"

Squirrel snickered. "She gonna show up on Friday, ya think?"

Fuck, I hoped so. Then again, tying her up and kidnapping her to bring her here sounded like more fun.

"We'll see. Assuming this third party gives her good results from their run of us, we should be in the clear." I looked at Iggy, brows raised.

He nodded. "They're good and we're clear anyway, so she shouldn't have any issues coming onboard."

The knot in my gut didn't ease. No, if anything, it shifted into something sharper, darker. It wasn't just about the job.

That was the problem.

I buried it deep.

I knew we were clean—minus the shit that got us all dishonorably discharged. Hopefully, she'd be able to look past what was on paper.

And she would.

She had to.

If she walked away, I wouldn't just lose the op. I'd lose the one person who made this ware feel like it was worth surviving.

She'd be back at Subterra. I'd make sure of it.

I shoved her out of my head and focused on the data dump. I had to admit that I was more than a little excited.

Lawrence's info gave Iggy a new toy. If he could replicate the program that Neva's intruder used, we would be able to slide past almost any surveillance currently on the market.

"Anything on the unknown lady, yet?" I asked

Iggy shook his head. "Not a single byte, domestically or globally. Which tells me it's a deliberate plant. To not have a name show up anywhere on any database I can access?" He pursed his lips. "It was chosen because of that very reason. It was meant to be run. Meant to come up empty."

"Targeting her specifically." I gritted my teeth.

Fuck.

Iggy nodded. "And since I still can't get through the flags on her Company file without knowing what they'll send out, we're at a loss tracking her that way as well."

"Have you found any other legends that match Snow White?" Critter asked.

Iggy nodded. "But there are literally tens of hundreds of options for her to choose from. Without a filter, we're stuck."

"What about her real identity through public records? She has to have some kind of digital record as Neva Bylur, or even as Neva Kendrick."

There had to be something on her. No one avoids the digital footprint—not without serious money, power, or pull.

Even as a Company asset, they wouldn't totally wipe all of her native data. They had to pay her, she had to be listed as an asset. Those things couldn't happen if she didn't officially exist in some digital form.

Unless they're handing over bundles of cash each payday. One thing the government didn't do was hand out cold, hard cash. Well, unless it was to foreign countries for dirty deals.

Iggy shook his head again. "I gave you the basics from her place. I can send it to you, but that's about it. Nothing really new."

Any information I could get on the elusive Dewdrop would be a good thing. I nodded. "Yeah, thanks. Anything on her grandparents? Her mother?"

Iggy shrugged, turned to the screen. "Sure, but unless you're interested in their ancestry or the grandparents' regularly scheduled bridge games every fourth Saturday, you're not going to like what's to be had there, either."

Pictures, articles, police records, everything a person accumulates in the digital age flashed up on screen in cascading windows. There, it was something, even if it meant nothing. She did exist, largely through her relatives, but she was in there.

One picture stopped me cold—Neva, maybe ten, with her grandmother in what looked like a classroom.

"What age did grandma teach?" I asked, my entire focus centered on that little girl.

"Post-grad chemistry," Iggy answered.

I blinked. "Damn. Was she taking classes from her grandma at age…what? Is she even ten in that picture?"

"She's fourteen in the picture, and yes, that's what the article is about. One of the youngest people to audit the class and would've aced the class if she'd paid for the credit," Iggy answered.

"Little Pix gotta big brain," Squirrel said. He turned to me. "Are you sure you're still stuck on the no touching? I just gotta cuddle her once."

I snarled at him. "Hands off."

He pouted and huffed. "Fine. But I'm first if something goes wrong."

"The fuck, Squirrel. Why?" Critter complained. "She's fucking crazy."

Squirrel chuckled. "She reminds me of my Memaw. All spicy and tiny." The huge man gave himself a hug as if he held said tiny, spicy lady in his arms.

"Your Memaw ever try to poison you or jack her knee into your balls like a battering ram?" Critter asked.

Squirrel hooted. "Fuck no, Dopey. You got junk jacked all on your own, you dipshit. Ain't none of us nursing hurt balls or egos, neither. But you keep messing with Pix, you're gonna be a eunuch pretty soon. She'll melt it clean off." He lost the humor in his gaze. "And I'll help her. She's been through enough and you're being the little baby bitch she keeps calling you."

And there it was. The first line drawn in the sand over a potential newcomer. We'd set up the Rules the way we did for this very reason.

Bros before hoes wasn't a joke to us. It was law. It's also why we called dibs and had strict no touching rules.

We didn't all have the same taste in women, our preferences were as varied as our sexual proclivities. Didn't stop some from trying to worm in through our dicks, and we'd been on the verge of falling apart as friends and a family more than once.

After we'd cleared the air and our beds that last time, we'd come up with the Rules. Everyone agreed because we all knew we needed each other more than we each needed any particular woman. The consequences of breaking any of the Rules were pretty harsh. Since we all agreed to the Rules, we also all agreed to the outcomes.

It was blatantly archaic and slightly homicidal, but it worked for us. If anyone outside of our group broke our rules, then…well, let's just say they would never get the chance to learn the error of their ways.

Critter gawked at me like I just handed him a live grenade. "You keep her occupied enough to keep her crazy, psycho brain fixed on your dick. Not mine. You get me?" He stabbed a finger down the long table at me.

I snorted. "Then stop putting yourself front and center in her mind, Crit. You're the one bringing all of her pain down on you, not anyone else."

Squirrel was right, the man just couldn't seem to help himself and it appeared he'd met his match.

Critter let his hand fall, his expression falling into a glower as he mumbled to himself. Since Gigs didn't bash his face into the huge conference table, I had to assume it was at least not disrespectful.

"While waiting for any extra Snow information to come back from my deeper runs, I do have some updates on this Brantley fucker," Iggy said, drawing everyone's attention back to the front of the room.

The screen cleared of the Bylur family info and filled with the life and times of Brantley Higginsworth. Did his parents hate him? I mean, I could totally see why they would, because that name was trash, but it really didn't fit the picture of the man who'd try to bum-rush Neva's house earlier.

"Is he wearing some kind of hairpiece?" Gigs asked, humor lurking in his tone.

Iggy turned to the screen as well, shrugged. "No idea. Maybe the dreads are for his cover?" He shook his head. "If they are for his cover, he chose very poorly."

The guy in the picture looked like some frat boy with appropriately styled brown hair and the standard Finance Bro uniform. The snide smirk on his official photo made my fists itch to rearrange his stupid face. It was just so punchable.

"Starting from the top, Brantley Martin Higginsworth, aged thirty-two, rose through the ranks by kissing ass and fudging reports that smashed his colleagues and made them look incompetent. From the reports of those same colleagues, Brantley here is known to undercut or undermine their tasks, claim they're incompetent, and then hoard whatever accolades remained when he somehow managed to pull a win out of thin air. Recruited out of Harvard, he's the son of a state senator in Connecticut—Lady Rebecca Higginsworth—and one Martin Reginald Hollsthwarpe, a self-made millionaire in the consulting game."

Laughing, I cleared my throat. "Lady Rebecca?" Iggy had to be shitting us.

He shook his head, his lavender eyes mostly blue in the darkened room against the lights of the screen. "Not kidding. She legally changed it at eighteen. Her first name is literally Lady. Of course, she goes by Lady Rebecca."

I shook my head. Talk about ridiculous. I could understand now why they named their kid what they did. "Father took mother's name?"

Iggy nodded. "Yeah, he's all in on the woke, toxic masculinity movement. That's how she rode into office. He's essentially a trophy wife with a dick. She's held it for almost fourteen years now, so she's doing something right. Or buying enough votes to stay in her spot at the top."

"Any cleanups Mommy and Daddy had to do for little Brantley?" I asked. For him to behave as he was in the FBI right now, I had no doubt this fucker had slid through enough civil and criminal charges to make the best frat proud.

"Three charges of battery and assault, nixed. Two rape charges against sorority sisters at Harvard. Got nothing but a slap on the wrist; the girls transferred out with all of their future college bills paid by his parents. Nothing ever officially added to his record, hence his ability to skate into the FBI like he owned the joint." Iggy curled his fingers down into fists, the sound of plastic creaking sadly as the remote in his hand twisted under the pressure.

He tossed it down on the table and paced over and back a couple times. Iggy had some pretty dark stuff in his family's past and whenever something like this came up, we knew it would be a hard day for him.

Luckily, we might be able to stop this guy before he did any more damage to the women around him. Sexually or not, that kind of predatory and manipulative behavior didn't sit with Iggy. Ever.

"Who's the fucker in bed with?" Beck's low, steady voice reeled him back in.

Iggy blew out a breath, punched the air a couple times as he shook out his hands, and retrieved his remote from the tabletop. Victory gleamed in his eyes. "For that answer to have real weight, we need to follow Dickfuck's career trajectory."

I settled back, a wave of relief washing through me. Good. If Iggy could focus on taking Brantley down electronically, we wouldn't need to worry about having another body to hide.

Not that it would stop him, or any of us, from getting rid of it. Cleaner for Neva if we kept this digital—for now.

"Then proceed, Professor," Beck said, waving a hand.

Iggy's smile was all teeth. "Dickfuck's first case upon getting his shiny new, get out of jail free, badge was a drug bust. Stepping on a few heads, he got top points. Next job was a racketeering case. Just so happens that the little drug cartel he busted also owned the racket down in Miami, where he was stationed."

With a silent snarl, his whole trajectory snapped into place. "They bought him off, set him up to keep moving up, and now he's playing for the cartel."

Iggy shot me with a finger gun. "Got it in one, Keys. He's not only playing for the cartel, but the cartel is also using Oskar Jorgenssen for transport. Apparently, they're looking to expand their financial enterprises by venturing out into other revenue paths."

"Weapons," I bit out through clenched teeth.

Iggy nodded. "Any type. Any scope. Any body count. If they can move it along their routes, they're willing to play the game."

"Is the cartel hoping to use Brantley as their front man?" Gigs asked.

Iggy shook his head. "I can't tell yet. From what Snow said about how he's behaving and what we know now, then none of his actions make any sense."

"Do you think Brantley is trying to use Neva as a Trojan horse?" Squirrel asked.

It sickened me to see how easily that could work.

Keep screwing her over when she fumbles trying to get close to the mark so Dickfuck can swoop in, some kind of savior mode, while getting to put his eyes on Jorgenssen. If he got Jorgenssen into custody, he could let him go on some kind of technicality after he made contact on behalf of the cartel.

I lined it out for them. Saw the dawning horror on their faces as they followed along with my mental path. She was a sitting duck, and she didn't even know it. She was nothing but breadcrumbs while the monsters darted through the dark forest around her.

Squirrel turned to me, a hard light in his eyes. "We need to get her and bring her here."

I shook my head. "Not only will Neva kill us for that, but she's still on a mission. Granted, one that's set up to fail, but we can't pull her out of it yet."

If at all. If we did, things could not only blow up in her face, but ours too.

"Then we need eyes on her, at all times. No way Pix gets stung by this fucker," Squirrel bit out.

I nodded, already having come to the same conclusion. "I'll do it." I completely ignored the tiny flame that flared in my gut.

Snickers and sly glances came my way from each and every brother. I rolled my eyes and waved them off. "Fuck off." I jerked my chin at Iggy for him to keep going. "What else?"

"Now that I'm linked into her system, I put myself as an additional user," Iggy started. He gave me a long look. "We can track her that way, no need for in person tracking."

I shook my head. "She's still spending too much time away from her home. No, I'll keep track of her. But send me a link with her credentials, and I'll sleep a little easier."

"We can trick out her place with a full range system. Judging by her lab, it doubles as a panic room. She's got more than enough eyes on the guest spaces of her house." Iggy pulled Dickfuck's info down and up slid a full five-foot by nine-foot picture of Neva's living room. There were at least eleven camera angles lining the edges of the screen.

After the living room flicked off, her entryway flooded into view. Not a full dozen angles, but enough to completely cover the smaller area. The kitchen, lower-level half bath entrance, dining room, and covered garden were all fully covered by every possible camera angle as well.

My brows furrowed. "What's that area?" I pointed to a screen. In the picture, there was a door I couldn't figure out where it went. From everything we'd seen and experienced today in her house, that door didn't look familiar.

"Apparently, there's a full parlor at the front. Other side of the wall from the entryway."

I shook my head. "You're kidding me."

Iggy shook his head. "I searched her address, found the floor plans. Unless she's changed it, there's a full room in there. Pretty big, too. Twenty long by fourteen wide, fireplace, the whole enchilada."

He pulled up a picture of architecture plans. Dated within the last fifteen years. "No permits for renovation or anything else. And she would need them if she was going to do any changes to a load bearing wall."

I'd recognized that the entryway we saw and used wasn't the full span of the width of the house, but I hadn't really given it that much thought. The living room felt big enough.

That will teach me to take things at face value with her. But I shoved it away. "She's got five stories. Do we have video access to any other floors?"

Iggy nodded. "She's got a basic three point setup for each floor's landing and two points in each room. Seven in total, for those counting. Bathrooms, if they're attached to a bedroom, don't have cameras. But that's probably out of modesty's sake. Altogether, she's got almost thirty cameras for just over nine thousand square feet of livable and usable space."

It didn't seem like enough. Not to keep her truly safe. "How many more?"

The words came too fast, too sharp—but I didn't take them back.

No one bothered to snicker this time. Good. I wasn't really feeling like beating the shit out of any of them right now. It was best if they just left me to proceed how I wanted.

Iggy gave me a long considering look, and my skin itched under his gaze. "We can piggyback her current signals. She won't notice the drop in bandwidth since she's getting gig service."

Not enough. Not even close.

I shook my head. "Not enough, Ig. I want more, some that only we control. If someone can override her system, they can lock us out too."

They could lock me out.

I couldn't let that happen.

I didn't know what my problem was. There was no reason I should assume she wouldn't be safe with that much coverage, but even the possibility of it burned in my belly.

Iggy stared at me for a long time. "I'll work up a network. How many do you want?"

I exhaled at his acceptance of my crazy. "I want at least five cameras with full sensors per access point. Two facing interior, two facing exterior, one three-sixty cam inside, per door."

I shifted my gaze to study the floor plan again. Iggy had put little red dots to show where each existing camera sat. I knew he would more than cover whatever else I was missing. The man didn't miss a fucking mouse's whisker twitch when it came to tech. "I want that entire home covered, top to bottom. What about roof access?"

He shook his head, his lips turning down at the corners. "She doesn't have anything up there at all."

Gritting my teeth, I bit back the anger that wanted to spew forward. This woman would learn what real security was, if it was the last thing I taught her. "Add those."

"That's going to be close to wiping out our current stock."

"Order more. I'll cover it. We won't be getting to send out an invoice for this."

"No, we're not. So why the excess?" Det asked. He was almost as quiet as Banshee, but I knew that still waters ran deep in my second-in-command. His tattooed arms were bunched as he stared at me from down the table.

"Because if she can help us take down SRD, I think the personal outlay is going to be helpful. And if something happens to her due to Dickfuck's ineptitude or outright illegal activities, then we need to be there to step in and get her out before anything can truly take her down or out. She could be the fucking key we've been waiting for to bring that group of crazy bitches down."

I made sure to keep it all professional, strictly strategic. And every single point I made was strategic. We did need her and her working knowledge—a fucking library's worth—on poisons to help us out.

"Sure it's not about putting your key in her lock?" Critter bit out.

They all stared at me, expectation heavy in their faces.

I blew out a breath. The question wasn't surprising—or unfair. "Do I want to get her under me? Yes, absolutely. Will I ruin any chance we have to bring down SRD and clear our names to do it?" I shook my head. "Fuck no. Each of us knows exactly what we've lost, what the world has lost, because of SRD. I won't screw up getting to break them apart piece by piece for anyone, except the people around this table. And that's only if the cost becomes too high."

"You're skimming very close to entertaining two masters, Keys," Det said.

My molars ground together. I shook my head. "We need her for SRD."

In my lap, my fingers curled into fists. The fuck? They'd never challenged me like this before. Not once in all of our history.

"If she shows up on Friday at Subterra, I'll install our system. It only gets viewed if an alarm goes off," Iggy said, his tone like granite.

I shot up from my chair, the air in the room going thin as my lungs fought to get enough oxygen.

They weren't fucking with me. They were serious.

"What the fuck is wrong with all of you?" My voice hit harder than I meant it to, but I couldn't stop it now. "You act like I'm some kind of stalker, just waiting for a chance to get her alone—"

I didn't finish the sentence.

Silence vibrated through the room, much like my blood in my veins. Thick. Heavy.

They weren't laughing.

They weren't even moving.

I slammed my fists down on the table. "She's mine, you all fucking know that. She just doesn't yet." The words came out sharper, harder, heavier than I meant.

A chill ran down my spine and landed in my belly.

Fuck.

No one moved.

No one fucking breathed.

The silence was suffocating, drowning me, pulsing in my ears, jabbing into my skull.

Then—

Critter's chair scraped against the floor as he stood, fury written all over his face.

The sound sliced through me like a blade.

My body moved before my brain caught up. Shoulders locked. Fists clenched. Breath short and rapid.

The only sound in the room was my slight panting as adrenaline spiked hard. Sharp. Demanding.

The fuck?

"The *fuck* is wrong with *you*, Keys?" Critter's voice was a gut-shot.

Like a fist to the ribs. A clean, casually brutal hit.

This wasn't some joke, a dose of brotherly bullshit.

They meant it.

Det leaned forward, slow, deliberate.

A blade to the throat. Precise, unshaking.

"You're staking your claim again when we've already acknowledged it. So you tell us, Keys, what the fuck is wrong with you?" His voice was calm and ice cold.

Chapter 19

Neva

The ache in my lower back told me I'd been hunched over my microscope for far too long. Stretching backwards, I sighed as everything inside me moved again. Twisting from side to side, I smiled at the cracking noises shooting up and down my spine. Ah, that was beautiful.

Once my vision returned to normal after all the little fireworks behind my eyes finished firing, I realized my tummy had moved past growling and into howling for food. Locking the notes and samples away for the night, I got everything in the lab tidied up. Turning to leave, I grabbed my phone and keys.

Heading into the kitchen, I made some dinner, made my way into my bedroom to eat, and wind down. House Hunters was my guilty pleasure, the reminder that the world still moved in mundane revolutions around the sun.

By the time the episode was finished, my belly was full, my head was empty from the wine I'd refilled twice, and my body was tired. It was going to be a great night of sleep, I could already tell. I smashed my pillow a bit, got comfy, and closed my eyes as sleep teased the edges of my consciousness.

**

Two hours later, I was still glaring at the ceiling. What the wisteria, man? I was exhausted, but my traitor brain had decided to replay every second of today with doom-level scrutiny.

And of course, starring in tonight's mental theater? Rome. Fucking. Whitlock. That suped-up psycho who couldn't keep his dick, his claim, or his stupid pretty eyes to himself.

I kicked off the covers and shot daggers at the ceiling. That fucker.

But my mind didn't care. It brought back the feel of his hand around my throat—rough, steady, not scratchy. A man who got shit done.

Heat sparked in my belly. I groaned and buried my scream in my pillow. Not now. Not him.

Naturally, my brain doubled down—cue the memory of him stroking himself across the bathroom, the weight of him between my thighs. My breath hitched. Had that really only been last night?

He wasn't covered in tattoos like his brothers, but the ones he had? They made my mouth water. Literally.

My pussy throbbed, and I glared harder at the ceiling. No. I was a grown-ass woman. I didn't bow to slutty cravings.

My subconscious snorted. Liar. It slithered the memory of his dick down my spine, and I shivered.

Nope. Ice bath. Monastery. Nun life. Something.

I forced my thoughts elsewhere. Squirrel. Squirrel was safe. A giant teddy bear who made me want to feed him cookies and rock him like a toddler. Ridiculous, since he could probably lift a car, but the image stuck.

I smiled into the dark. All big and menacing, marshmallow inside.

Finally, my body calmed. I snuggled back into the sheets.

See? Nothing to see here. No dirty thoughts. No sexy psychos. Just sunshine, cuddles, and a very safe teddy bear.

Sleep wrapped around me like a velvet vice. I let her take me. That wicked bitch.

**

190

"Rome," I gasped as I came awake. My hand was between my thighs, the burning tingle in my pussy telling me I'd been playing with myself for a while.

Fuck.

I blew my hair out of my face. Too well did I recognize the throbbing ache in my body. There weren't enough soft and cuddly thoughts to push this one aside. I'd well and truly jumped headfirst into the lake of sexual frustration.

Throwing a quick glance at the clock on the wall, I rolled over and pulled open my nightstand drawer. Grabbing my familiar collection of toys, I glared at the ceiling again.

My cheeks heated with mortification as I got the harness strapped around my thighs and waist. Fastening the clover clamps over my greedy nipples, I let out a sigh as the matching points of pleasurable pain slid through my awareness.

With a disinterested look at the dildo I'd unearthed, I got out of bed and hurried to my secret stash. Ripping open the door behind the mirror, I opened the biometric lock box and stepped through into my toy closet.

Yes, I had a full fucking closet of toys. A deeper burn of humiliation swept through me. Grabbing one of the bigger silicone mechanical rabbits, I smiled as I hefted it up into my hand. Almost as long and thick as my arm, I didn't think about it too hard as I closed the closet and got back into my bed.

My pussy was dripping enough that I didn't need any lube, that was for damn sure. Relaxing onto my back, I worked the huge fake cock up inside me. My eyes went wide at the incredibly satisfying stretch deep in my cunt.

Maybe I needed to switch up my routine. Holy kingcup, that felt amazing. Shudders ran from my clit up to my nipples caught by the clover clamps. Getting the toy hooked to my harness, I laid back with a puff of relief exploding through my lips.

Fuck, that felt good.

Grabbing the loose end of the clover clamps, I slid my fingers down my tummy and over my pussy. Stretched wide over the rabbit, everything felt more intense, fuller.

Of course, it does, you idiot. Snickering at the stupid thought, I caught my clit between my index and middle fingers.

My toes curled as streaks of fire sparked through my core out into the rest of my body. "Oh, shit."

I blinked widely at the ceiling. I'd never experienced that before. Squeezing my fingers together, I refreshed those sparks as I felt my thighs tremble.

With a blind grin at my ceiling fan, I lowered my other hand and slid the final clover clamp over my clit.

My eyes rolled up into my head as a low moan slithered between my lips. Fucking bishop's lace, that was amazing. Fuck, fuck, fuck. For the first time in my adult life, I felt that first orgasm sitting so close I could almost reach out and touch it.

A deeper part of my psyche smirked again. You haven't seen anything yet.

Reaching down, I hit the button on the base of the toy to make the toy heat up and get the internal mechanism rolling up and down its seven-inch length.

I blew out an unsteady breath as my eyes crossed. Snowdrops and spiderflowers, that… Even my mental voice fell off into a moan as a wave of tightening pleasure cramped my muscles into strings of perfect pain.

I might actually get everything I need from just these. Flapping my hand at the wand at my side, I dismissed it. Byrony could wait. I might not actually need him.

Purposely sinking into the hot, slutty part of my brain, I immersed myself in all the thoughts I'd pushed aside before falling asleep. The memories rewrote themselves into my fantasies as I actively courted them.

Instead of just rocking against his dick while astride him at the club, I unzipped his pants. His breath sucked in as my fingers found his hard length pushing against the fly of his boxer briefs. "Fuck, dewdrop."

I wrinkled my nose at the mental nickname. Damn it. Even here, in the safety of my mind, he asserted his will. But I wouldn't let it deter me. Not this time.

"Yes, you need to fuck dewdrop. That's what I'm working on," I said softly into the cool air of my bedroom.

He helped me move to the side as we both shoved his clothing down. When he was free and clear, he grabbed a knife from somewhere and cut away the crotch of my pants.

"I don't have the patience to get you fully naked. Drop that sexy cunt on my dick, baby. Fucking ride me." He curled his fingers into my hips and held me steady as his length invaded my drenched pussy.

We both groaned as I took all of him. It felt like it took forever, but I was finally full. For the first time, well and truly full.

Lifting my gaze to his, his eyes were fierce as he kept his grip on my hips. "Ride me, dewdrop. Take your time, I need to feel you come all over my dick." He set me into a slow grind that had my eyes rolling up into my head.

A heavy hand circled my neck, drawing me down to his chest. "Eyes. I need to see those pretty eyes while you do it. I have to watch you fall apart." His fingertips tightened into my neck until those slight wavy lines appeared at the edges of my vision. "Now fuck me, baby. Fuck me until you baptize my dick with all that cream."

I grimaced into the morning lit room around me.

Laying on my back wasn't going to do enough. Rolling to my side, I stuffed three pillows together and tossed my leg over them. Settling back down on them, they were a poor woman's substitute for his hips. But I needed to work with what I had.

With the thrusting motions of the rabbit, the grinding of my hips mixed with the pinch and pull of the clover clamp on my clit, I rode that pile of pillows like my life depended on it. And fuck, right now, it felt like it did.

Reaching up, I pulled the nipple clamp chain between my teeth before sliding my palm around my neck. Nothing close to what he'd given me, but needs must.

Sucking in a startled breath as I allowed myself to sink back into the fantasy in my head, I rode phantom Rome like a fucking Olympic Equestrian going for gold.

My breath soughed through my teeth as I fought for each gasp. "Rome, fuck." I ground down on the pillows, while in my mind he thrust up from below.

"Yes, dewdrop. Just like that. Fuck. I feel you getting tighter. You make me so fucking hard when your cunt flutters like that. Yeah, just like that, baby. Just like that."

The grip around my throat tightened as he held me inches away from his face. "Say my name, dewdrop. Who owns your body?"

I shook my head.

"Tell me, baby. Tell me who owns your body, and I'll give you exactly what you need."

I shook my head again, the overwhelming pulse in my pussy dimming slightly.

His laugh was dark. "Now, dewdrop. Fucking say my name. I won't tell you again." He squeezed tighter on my throat, my vision dancing at the edges.

"Rome. Rome. Rome." His name burst from between my clenched teeth.

As I allowed myself to break inside the privacy of my head and bedroom, my pussy came back to life like she was hooked up to a power plant. That deep, aching burn of orgasm rushed up from my depths.

"Good fucking girl, dewdrop. Good girl. Take your time, take all the time you need. Give me that cum. Drown my dick in all that pretty cum, baby. Yes, just like that. Fuck, baby. Just like that." His whispered words sank into my mind as my body gave that first delicious ripple of pleasure.

"Oh, you're doing so good for me, dewdrop. Let it come. Give it to me. Give it to me, fuck yeah. Just like that. Damn, you feel so fucking good. Stroking that tight wet cunt all over my dick. Such a good fucking girl."

And just like that, my body locked up as my cunt clenched on the toy thrusting deep inside me. Tidal waves of pleasure racking through me from clit to tit, top to toe. "ROMMMMMMME!"

My voice trailed off into a moan as I allowed the rippling of my pussy to strangle the fuck out of the fake dick inside me.

The soles of my feet started burning as the orgasm continued to wring me dry. Just as I fought for breath, I tightened my jaw, pulling on the clover clamps at every attachment point. My tits buzzed and the nerves in my clit danced under the new assault. With the angle of the rabbit hitting me just right, I felt something build in a rush I wasn't familiar with.

My eyes opened wide in blind stupefaction as my body rode the surge of sensation. The clamp chain fell from between my gaping lips as a rush of wet warmth slid from between my legs.

"Fuck, fuck, fuck." I gulped in air as my body went haywire all around me. Tears slid from the corners of my eyes as all of the stiffness left my body in a single swoop.

I fell to the side, the rabbit still working his way up and down in my pussy. With weighted limbs, I tried to maneuver enough to shut it off. When I couldn't get my arms to pay attention any better, I sucked back a sob and attacked the harness buckle with dead fingers. "Off, off, please get off. Oh fuck." The tears threaded every syllable as I fought with the metal clasp.

Finally free, I pulled my knees to my chest, curled my arms around them, and just tried to figure out where each piece of me was. I felt like I'd shattered into a million shards. Tears continued unchecked over my cheeks, landing into a widening pool on the sheets.

My brow wrinkled. Lifting my head, I looked at my pillows. The top one was soaked, the white pillowcase transparent enough I could read the manufacturer's mark across the fabric underneath.

I let my head fall back against the mattress. "Fucking Rome Whitlock," I screamed at the ceiling.

Once I felt like I could finally move my arms and legs and get them to do what I actually wanted, I uncurled myself. Gingerly removing the clover clamps, I hissed out a breath as all the blood came rushing back into my abused nipples and clit. A hard orgasm rushed up and slapped me in the face, my back arching as more moans fell from my lips, more tears slinking down my cheeks as I glared up at the ceiling.

After the pleasure waned, I eased to the side of my destroyed bed. I narrowed my gaze at the mess. Fuck. "FUCK!" I stomped my foot and spun for the bathroom.

With a quick glance at the clock for the time, I felt all the blood drain away from my overheated face.

That had taken less than fifteen minutes. Fifteen minutes to ruin my entire view of my own sexuality. Fifteen minutes to experience the hardest, most brutal orgasm of my life.

I shook my head, gritting my teeth as I stomped into the shower. Flicking the handle, I demanded water hot enough to scald.

No. Rome Fucking Whitlock would not do this to me. I was in charge of my body. My mind. My fantasies. Not that stupid psychotic fucker with all of his rules and his stupidly hot body and pretty eyes.

"You can fuck right off, Rome!" I shrieked into the universe before I shoved my face into the lava-hot flow of water.

Chapter 20
Rome

"Rome."

I blinked against the darkness of my office, searching for the speaker. When my bleary eyes came back with no suspect, I sat back and scrubbed my hands down my face. Fuck. These sleepless night were hitting harder with age.

Sitting in my admittedly comfortable office chair, I laid my head back and stared at the ceiling. Last night's fight with the guys ran through my head again. I'd barely made it out of there before we all came to blows.

In the harsh light of day, I could see they were right. I'd let her get too far under my skin. Let her pull me out of the path that we'd set ourselves on more than five years ago. There was no way I could ditch everything for her.

"Oh, shit."

Lifting my head, I searched the room again. What the fuck?

Getting up from my chair, I calmly cleared the empty space. There was no one here but me. Why the fuck was I hearing Dewdrop's voice? I knew she'd been on my mind when I'd fallen asleep, and it had been in ways that didn't exactly bring me peace. Especially considering how things stood with my brothers.

Maybe it would be a one and done kind of deal? Maybe?

Even in my head I could hear the hopefulness of that statement. If I was this giddy over the possibility of getting my hands on her again, I knew I was in too deep.

Slumping back down into my seat, I leaned forward, my elbows on my knees. Putting my head in my hands, I tried to shove the now familiar mental image of her naked and wet in the shower out of my mind. "Fuck, dewdrop." My dick hardened as I kept my mind's eye on her curvy little body.

"Yes, you need to fuck dewdrop. That's what I'm working on." Her voice was soft, almost breathy as her words settled over me like a silken fist on my dick.

Jolting upward, I spun to my computer.

My jaw just about hit the tabletop as I saw one of the security camera feeds shift to the main picture, a thin white border around the picture. After a list of promises to my brothers about this very thing, I'd convinced Iggy to give me the codes to her system. I had no idea her security feeds came with sound.

In the high definition picture on my monitor, I watched as Neva grimaced up at the camera as if she could see me.

I held my breath. How the hell had I missed the fact that she had cameras in her private bedroom? And why did she need cameras in her bedroom anyway, especially pointing at her bed?

And holy fuck, she couldn't actually see me could she? I waved my hand in front of the tiny camera of my computer.

Huffing out a laugh at my own stupidity, I realized she was just glaring at her ceiling. The laughter fell away as I really took in the sexy woman on my screen.

She wasn't supposed to do this. Not here. Not where I could see her. Not when I'd just decided to let her go.

She had clamps on her nipples, but from the angle, I couldn't be sure what kind. And a single trailing chain led between her legs. A black leather harness nipped at her waist and gripped her thighs. The flared base of some kind of toy was just barely visible at her pussy.

I licked my lips. Fuuuuuck.

As I watched, she rolled to the side. Grabbing a handful of pillows, she stacked them up and then slid over them like she was mounting a mechanical bull. Her tits pushed out, the glinting of subdued sunlight over the chains of her clamps sent prisms of light over her room.

She settled onto that small mountain of pillows and started riding them. So different from the passive posture she had here at Subterra, she actively engaged as she worked her way up that orgasm hill.

My dick hardened so fast it felt like I got punched in the guts. The head of my cock smashed into the back of my zipper, making my teeth ache.

Fuck, she was perfect.

Sitting back, I had my dick in hand before I took another breath. A faint wash of uneasiness was quickly swatted away when I looked at my office door. Before I could get too worried about it, she shifted on screen.

My mouth went dry as she put the clamp chain in her mouth. Delicate fingers tipped with claws slid to her throat. A startling picture that both drew me in and made my teeth grit in frustration. What the fuck did she think she was doing, touching her body like it didn't belong to me?

I spat and started pumping up and down my length. If I focused hard enough, I could almost feel her tight pussy gripping me. The slick, wet heat of her sliding up and down every fucking inch of me. A low, feral sound slid between my lips.

"Rome, fuck."

The first bead of pre-cum leaked out as my name tumbled off her trembling lips. She was fantasizing about me.

Damn right, it better be.

I clenched my dick like a motherfucker, fought to surge. Fuck. My heart pounding in my chest, I sat glued to that screen watching her fuck herself while she thought of me. Heat scalded my cheeks as I fought through the pleasure.

A distant warning bell went off in my head, but it fell silent as she shook her head, her little nose wrinkled up in irritation.

I gripped my balls. Rolling them around, I panted through the heavy weight sitting in my chest.

Watching every ripple of movement shimmer over her luxurious body, I fought with myself not to drive to her place and finish her off with the real version of me, not some paltry phantom in her head.

She shook her head again, the furrow between her brows making me snarl. I knew that look. She was defying me. Even in her own fantasies, she defied me.

I snapped my teeth at her image on my screen. "Give it to me, dewdrop. Just fucking give in already. I'll make it so damn good for you, I promise."

As if she heard me through the computer, her mouth fell open as her body lost its rhythm for the tiniest fraction of a second. "Rome. Rome. Rome."

My dick jumped as she chanted my name. I moaned, the sound long and low in the quiet office. "Oh fuck, baby, yes. Such a good fucking girl."

As I watched, she seemed to sink into whatever she saw in her mind fully. Her movement smoothed out, the easy grace I knew she carried in her deadly body eased her into the hottest fucking ride I'd ever seen. Her cheeks flushed, her chest ran pink in the bright light of the morning.

"That's my girl, dewdrop."

I sucked in a hard breath as I heard something outside my office. When no one knocked on the door, I shifted my attention back to the screen.

She got that jerky edge against. My grin turned savage. "Fuck, yes, baby. Just like that. Take your time. Take all the time you need." My memory brought back the sight of her in Subterra.

This was not the same woman. That one had been determined, almost passively angry. This one though. "Fuck, dewdrop." I bit my lip. This one simply let her body do what it needed to.

That rush of pink slid over her entire body like a full body blush as she started to tremble. From the top of her head to the tips of her toes, she shattered into a quivering mess. "ROMMMMME!"

My eyes rolled up as I lost control of my own response to this woman. "Fuck, fuck, fuck." I shot rope after rope of cum all over my desk, my breath heaving in my chest as I blinked my vision clear.

Just as my body tried to break apart from the best kind of tension, I watched as her head flung back, her long brown hair tumbling down her back. She shifted her jaw and I watched as the clamps lifted her nipples higher. The slack on the chain running down her curving belly pulled taut in response as well.

I sat there in stunned silence as I continued to watch her. Her eyes flared open, blind, as she stared directly into the camera. My dick jumped in my hand, hard again.

Swiping my hand through the cum on my desk, I grabbed my dick once again. "Wait for me, baby. Wait for me." It was going to be rough and dirty, savage and a little brutal. But I was totally fucking here for it.

As I watched, her pillows became transparent under her sexy thighs. "Fuck, fuck, fuck," she moaned. Tears streamed down from the corners of her eyes.

She was perfect.

Ruin-me perfect.

My hand pistoned around my dick as my lips burned to taste her tears. Fuck, I needed to taste her. Hold her. Feel her cunt twitch and strangle my dick. I needed that woman.

Watching her come back into herself, she shifted to the side as if she had no more bones. Her lush body needed my arms around her. My arms actually ached from the loss.

She fumbled at the apex of her thighs. Her limbs looked heavy and uncoordinated. It was the first time I'd ever seen her so graceless. And the fact I wasn't there to take care of her angered me.

"Off, off, please get off. Oh, fuck." She burst into tears as she got the buckle at her waist undone, tossing aside the toy that had been cradled where I wish I could be.

She curled up, knees tucked to her chest, arms wrapped around herself. A soft, broken sound filled the room—her sobs.

My chest cracked open. My dick jumped again.

Tears after a mind-blowing orgasm?

My hand locked around my cock. The second orgasm tore through me without warning. I gritted my teeth, choking back the sound—white light searing up my spine as I came again, messier this time. Desperate. Possessive.

On screen, she lifted her head. Looked at the pillows. One was soaked. Soaked because of me.

She collapsed back with a cry. "Fucking Rome Whitlock!"

A slow smile pulled at my mouth.

Only battery dicks, huh?

I licked my lips. Not anymore.

Shifting my gaze, I clocked the toy she'd had in her pussy. From the angle and what I knew of her dimensions, I nodded. It was at least close to what I carried. Knowing she could take me—and crave it—lit something black and hot in my chest.

"That's right, dewdrop. All for me. I'll kill anyone else who even tries." I blew a kiss at the screen as she uncurled herself from the little ball she'd taken refuge in. When she was mostly stretched out, her hands lowered to her perfect tits.

My mouth watered in envy.

Then I winced as she took the distinctive design of the clover clamp off each nipple. Oh damn, that was going to burn. Then her hands delved between her slick thighs, the light sheening off their inner surfaces.

Fuck. She'd squirted all over that fucking fake dick.

I glared at her.

Never again, dewdrop. Not unless I put the toys inside you myself.

She pulled the clover clamp from between her thighs, her back arching high as a soundless shriek heralded another orgasm.

My mouth shifted into another dark smile. My girl liked some pain with her sex. "I'll give you all the pain your mind and body can handle, princess. Come for me, dewdrop. Good fucking girl. Give me more of that cum." My whispers were low as I talked her through it.

She flopped back on the bed, the soft pink glow slowly retreating from her skin. Her green eyes glimmered with more tears as she panted up at the ceiling. She lay there for long moments, trying to steady her breathing. By the time she managed to get up and stand at the side of the bed, I had my desk cleaned off and my dick back in my pants.

"FUCK!"

My gaze darted to the screen as she actually stomped her tiny little foot before spinning and storming off.

Hurriedly, I grabbed the mouse and switched the camera feed to keep track of her. While I watched, her ass jiggled as she stomped into the closet area. A light flicked on, brightening the space.

Gritting my teeth at not having any options for camera angles in there, I made a mental note for Iggy to rig something in those two particular rooms. I would need to come up with a good reason as to why, but I was more determined than ever to make sure I could watch her every breath.

"You can fuck right off, Rome!" The shrill words were little more than a whisper through the camera.

I sat back, smirking. "Game on, dewdrop. Game fucking on."

Over the edge of my computer, my door swung open.

"We need to talk," Det said, his expression grim. He eyed me for a moment before disbelief sank into his gaze. Rushing to my desk, he caught my hand, knocking the mouse out of my reach.

"For fucks sake, Keys," he roared. He grabbed my monitor and spun it around. His dark gaze searched the full screen, but when he saw an empty closet, I hid my smile.

Thank fuck he'd come in when he did. I'd have had to kill him for even hearing Dewdrop as she fucked herself to fantasies of me.

He turned the screen back around, confusion on his face. "Why are you watching her closet?"

I shook my head. "I'm not. I was doing a quick run through the footage to see if everything was good. She's probably in the bathroom since her bed's empty." I shrugged like I hadn't just busted a nut on my desk twice in less than ten minutes.

He reached over, grabbed the mouse, handed it back. "My bad, man."

I shook my head again, pushing the guilt of lying to him away. "What's up?"

He looked around my room. "Did you sleep in here last night?"

I nodded, easing back into my chair. "Yeah, working on getting everything ready so I can run surveillance on Snow." I should have been embarrassed how easily the lies fell from my mouth, but I wasn't. There was nothing that would keep her from claiming her as my own.

Not now. Not when she'd given herself to me in her mind. Settled in with the knowledge that I was about to become unbearable for just about every person in my life, I smiled at my brother. "What's up?"

Det sank back into one of the visitor's chairs. "I'm sorry, man. Last night, everything just blew up and I feel like shit." He rubbed a hand over his neck. "I know you'll do the right thing by her." He looked up at me, grief in his dark eyes.

Well, fuck. Confronted with the agony my previous actions caused my brothers, I had to rethink this whole claiming shit. If they were getting this upset about my behavior, I wasn't sure I could put them through anything else.

Damnit.

I waved away Det's words. "We're good, bro. I know I was in a little deep with her yesterday. It must have been the forced proximity of being in her house most of the day, trying to make sure she didn't die." I bumped a shoulder into the air.

It was the answer I'd come up with last night, at least.

He nodded, blew out a breath before shooting me a smile. "Yeah, she's a fierce one." All the tension left his body as he leaned back and propped one ankle over the opposite knee. "I've never seen Critter run scared from a woman before. Usually, he's trying to flick them off with his shitty assholeness."

I choked out a laugh. "You're not wrong."

Over the years, we'd all watched women flock to the linguist among us. The man was pickier than a Karen at the high-end supermarket, so he didn't really get along with most women. The ones he did choose…well, they weren't exactly the laid-back and easygoing types.

"I'm pretty sure he crossed himself and said his prayers last night, hoping that Snow wouldn't somehow manage to sneak in and melt his dick off." Det laughed, his inked shoulders shaking under his tank.

I laughed at the visual. It would probably do Critter good to realize how strong women really were on their own. We men were the ones who usually needed them. Not the other way around.

When I finally clocked his workout wear, I realized I missed our regular morning routine. Fighting to keep from glancing at the screen, I stood up. "Sorry for missing the workout this morning." Nothing had been further from my mind this morning, in all honesty. Luckily, I was the only one to know that.

And it had to end here. From this point forward, I would be the epitome of professional. No spying, no jerking off while she masturbated. Just one guy looking out for his soon to be new colleague.

Keep her safe, protect the mission.

Anger rose up through me that was swiftly quashed. I'd claimed her. She was fucking mine. Mine to do with as I pleased.

No, get yourself under fucking control, Keys, I mentally berated myself. Keep her safe, protect the mission.

Det got to his feet as well. "All good. It gave me time to think." He shrugged. "I'll talk with the others, let them know that you're really working on doing the right thing by her."

Ice twisted in my belly, but not enough to make me confess. It was a onetime thing. Never to be repeated. There's no reason to confess. It wasn't a betrayal. Not really.

Just…surveillance.

Please, fuck, let it be a onetime thing.

I smiled at him. "Thanks, man. I appreciate that. Professional Mr. Whitlock is on the job."

He snorted and rolled his eyes. "Yeah, because who doesn't want to deal with a fucking tightass with control problems, huh?" He turned and walked out of my office.

My shoulders drooped as I blew out a breath. Tapping a fist to the bridge of my nose, I muttered, "Keep her safe, protect the mission."

Maybe if I said it enough times, it would magically happen.

That was a thing, right? Miracles and all that fluffy unicorn shit was a thing.

Right?

Manifestation. That was it. Keep her safe, protect the mission

The pit of my belly twisted.

It could happen. Right?

Chapter 21

Neva

Getting out of the shower, I made my way back into the wardrobe. After pulling on my running gear, I purposely didn't look at the bed as I made my way downstairs.

Didn't happen.

Just a regular woman on a regular run. No noodle limbs or buzzy head, here. Normal.

Everything was. Fucking. Normal.

After stuffing my phone in my bra, I grabbed my spare house key and headed for the old service entrance at the back of my home. Shoving a piece of spicy cinnamon gum in my mouth, I grabbed the handle and ripped the door open.

See? Normal.

Locking the door behind me, I dashed up the steps and out onto the sidewalk. Inhaling a huge breath of Prospect Park and Brooklyn in the early Autumn morning helped steady some of those less than normal parts inside me. But it was still all normal. Nothing I hadn't done a thousand times before.

Heading for the park across the street, I set my gaze fifteen feet in front of me and dug into the workout. Miss one run and I was completely off. That's definitely the problem.

The first lap around the inner loop was slow and easy. As the bright early morning sun sliced through the buildings, I pushed everything else away and focused only on moving my body. The familiar pounding of feet against pavement eased some of the tension in my shoulders.

Good and warm, I kicked my speed up a couple notches. Not quite a full out sprint, but close enough that my body didn't really notice the difference. Other than the fact I wasn't literally running for my life, it felt pretty comparable.

With the same measured focus, I made my way around the three-and-a-half-mile trail again. With today being a Thursday, I had to make sure I got to the school on time so I could get everything set up.

Thursdays were for story time, creativity hour, music, and recess. Little faces flashed through my memory as I rounded the last bend of the loop. They drove me crazy quite often. But they were smart, funny, wise beyond their years.

Jamie Winston's boyish smirk filled my mind. Okay, maybe they weren't all wise beyond their years. That one was going to be a lady killer by the time he grew up. Witty, flitty, and such a sweetheart. Whoever he captivated in the future was going to be one lucky lady or gentleman.

When I passed the familiar bench that signaled the start and end of my little journey through the park, I dialed my speed back so it was more of a meandering trot. Breath not quite billowing through my mouth, I managed to finish the morning ritual in a decent amount of time.

Shaking my legs out as I did some light stretching off the paved path, I checked my surroundings once again. There weren't typically a ton of people out here this early. Not wanting to delve into the reasons why it was so empty right now, I just smiled at the knowledge that I had the park mostly to myself.

Making my way back home, I pulled my phone from its resting place between my boob and bra. Wiping sweat off the screen onto my pants, I nodded at the fact there were no notifications. Maybe I should get up this early all the time.

Checking traffic, I crossed the street. Making sure my front porch was still empty, I smiled slightly and moved down the block to reach the service entrance. Just as I put my key into the door, hard hands grabbed me from behind.

Instinct kicked in, and I slammed my head back as hard as I could. I grinned through the stars that broke through my brain, and went limp to fall to the stoop as dead weight.

The assailant grunted, which was a little unnecessary, the asshole.

Turning into a quick spin, I knocked the ankles of the other person together. Jumping up, I landed on their falling body and rode it to the ground. As I finally got my first good look at them, my smile was dark.

"Brantley, you fucking idiot." I smashed my fist into his solar plexus, then shot a spear hand into his throat.

While he gasped and bucked for air, I got back to my feet, dusted off, and went into my home. Locking the door behind me, I walked through my house and up to my bedroom. That fucker. What did he think was going to happen? He better be glad I used the rest of my necklace serum on Dopey's face yesterday.

Heavy pounding sounded more like a distant bass beat as I dragged off my wet sports bra, yoga pants, and panties. I spit the now flavorless gum into the trash.

Smiling like a loon, I stepped into the shower. Tapping the handle to the tepid middle of the dial, I took my time washing the sweat and morning idiocy of my body. But as I went through my hair care routine, my smile melted.

What the fuck was he doing here? And trying to scare me? He'd never done that before. Maybe because of having the guys here yesterday?

I shook my head. With Brantley, it could be anything and nothing, the man wasn't exactly stable when it came to being blown off.

I'd known working to get on his team would carry some risks. His record at the FBI—while nice and professional on paper—was not all it was cracked up to be. Before seeking out his team to work on, I reached out to some friendlies between our agencies and got the scoop from people he worked with in the past. He was exactly the kind of guy I hated in any position of power.

Hopefully, all of my reports and evidence during my time on his team would help knock him down a couple notches on the corporate ladder. He shouldn't be anything more than a janitor, honestly. I doubted anything I submitted would derail his life that much, but I couldn't do nothing.

After my hated cold plunge, I wrapped up in my towel and went back into the closet. Getting down another day dress for work, I got dressed before heading back into the bathroom to deal with my hair. After it laid in nice, loose waves, I used minimal makeup, brushed my teeth, and grabbed my shoes on the way out of the closet.

I still avoided looking at the bed. Later would be soon enough to deal with all of that. Since my alarm didn't go off, I knew Brantley hadn't made it inside my house. But since I also didn't hear any more pounding, I held my breath as I made my way downstairs.

He could be even worse when he was in a bitchy mood, and me knocking him on his ass was a surefire way to make sure Bitchy was Brantley's first name. He didn't do too well when anyone bested him, but certainly not a woman on his op.

As soon as my foot landed on the main floor's hardwood, the pounding picked up again. This time from the front door. Looking over, I saw Brantley with his face smashed up against the glass, his ugly dreads creating crazy shadows on the floor of the entryway.

Walking to the door, I waved at him through the glass. "What do you want, Brantley?"

I didn't open the door. I didn't have time in my schedule for another shower and dress. He might get to do whatever he wanted as team lead, but I still had to maintain my cover at the school.

"Open the fucking door, Larkspur." He jiggled the handle.

"No, I don't have time to argue with you. What do you want that couldn't wait for our regular chat later?" I put my stuff in my bag, making sure all of my school paraphernalia was inside. With a nod, I waited for Bitchy to answer.

When I looked up again, he was gone. My brows furrowed. What the fuck was this guy's problem?

I flirted with the idea of telling my superiors at the Company, but I really didn't have time to get into the whole thing right now. With my bag hiked up onto my shoulder, I made my way back through the house. Grabbing a protein bar, and an iced coffee from the fridge, I decided the service entrance might be a better option for leaving the house.

Taking a couple seconds to confirm Brantley wasn't lurking somewhere on the street within view, I smiled slightly and went through the door.

"You better be glad you're teaching babies wearing sexy shit like that, dewdrop. I'd have to kill all the horny teenage boys," a familiar voice said behind me.

My body, traitorous bitch that she was, went hot. But I slapped her back.

No, down girl.

Turning the key in the lock, I mentally braced myself to see him again. And the fact I had to brace anything to see this cocky asshole was enough to set my teeth on edge.

Lifting my chin, I grazed my gaze over him. "Mr. Whitlock. Out for a stroll this morning?" I hitched my bag higher after sliding the protein bar and coffee into the gaping opening. Determined to ignore him, I eased by and walked down the street the wrong way.

"Not really, Ms. de Witte. Just getting home from a long evening. Are you off to work this morning?"

I rolled my eyes at the obviously stupid question. "No, just off to join the war effort." What else did he think I was doing wearing a dress with a gigantic bag hooked on my shoulder?

"I'm sure the USO could use some ladies like you. You'll definitely raise the morale of the troops. You're so kind and generous to share your time with those serving our country." He caught up and walked beside me.

Just leave me alone, you fucker.

Fucker. Fuck. Fuck Rome. My brain tripped over my fantasy, causing me to stumble as my legs went a little wobbly. Shit.

"Whoa, easy there, Snow," he said softly, catching me against his big hard body. "What's wrong?"

I shook my head, shrugged him off then shifted as far away as the sidewalk would allow. "Uneven sidewalk. Thank you. If you've been up all night, you must be tired. Don't let me keep you from finding your bed. Have a good day, Mr. Whitlock." I dipped my chin in his general direction and put a little pep in my step.

He kept pace with me. "You're heading in the right direction, Ms. de Witte, I think I'll walk with you and take the long way home. I don't really get to see this side of the block. The park sure is pretty this time of day. Good morning for a run, don't you think?"

Looking at him out of the corner of my eye, I saw him watching me, his lips quirked at the corner.

"Seems a little late to be running right now." I cast my glance up at the bright sky. "But if you're a runner, the park is a good spot."

Refocusing my attention, I pulled my phone from my bag. Opening the Uber app, I called for a ride. Since I never called for an Uber from the same spot two times in a row, I had to walk a little further today to reach a new corner.

"I bet you know a lot of good spots," Rome continued, something dark and sinful in his voice.

Brushing him from my awareness, I didn't bother to acknowledge him. He could play dark and mysterious with someone else. I had a job to do.

Two of them, technically.

Crossing the next street, I stopped on the corner and waited for the Uber. "You can go now, Mr. Whitlock. Enjoy your day." I entertained myself on my phone.

All of this junk email wasn't going to sort itself, now was it? And was that an ad for dentures? Yes, I definitely needed to learn more about those. It was never too soon to think about good dental care.

"I think I'll wait with you. A woman can never be too careful in a city like Brooklyn." He slid his hands in his pockets and seemed to just sink into a stance he could probably hold until the zombie apocalypse.

Not paying him any more attention than what I absolutely had to, I wasn't quite prepared for a black SUV to rock to a jarring stop right in front of me.

"Get the fuck in this car, Larkspur," Brantley hissed at me. His eyes held murderous rage. And from the bruising on his throat, I was going to go with the idea that he was a little peeved with me.

"I don't take rides from strangers, but thank you." I waved him off, then glanced back down at my phone.

"This is your last chance, de Witte. Don't make me pull rank." From the anger in his voice, I was a little surprised it came out so calmly.

"Hey, lady, do you know this guy?" Rome said, overly loudly. He pushed in front of me, jabbing a finger in Brantley's direction. "Man, she doesn't know you. Move along before I call the cops." He pulled his phone out, made a big show out of it. "No wonder women are scared to be walking alone these days." He raised his voice again. "Get lost, pal. She doesn't know you."

He'd drawn a small crowd of onlookers, some of them pulling their phones out and pointing them at us. Since the

SUV had tinted windows, they had no idea who was actually inside. But I also couldn't let this completely kill our op.

I backed away from both men, letting fear and weariness blanket my features. "I don't know either of you. I'm just going to leave. I'm sorry."

Keeping my head down, I hid my smile as I dropped Rome into the social gaffe he lumped on Brantley. Two birds, one stone. Without a backwards glance, I joined a small group of other women with looks of solidarity on their faces. "Why are men such assholes?"

A round of affirmatives went around as they accepted me into their little tribe until my ride showed up. "Give 'em all hell, honey. Don't let any man try to lock you in or down," one particularly rabid woman said as she continued to glare down the street at Rome who was standing alone after Brantley zipped off quickly while I walked away.

Rome gave a small salute as I dipped down to get into the waiting car. As I pulled the door shut, I caught him spin on his heel, hotfooting it back down the street the way we'd come.

Blowing out a breath, I leaned back against the seat and tried to get everything back under control. Doing some deep breathing exercises, I centered myself and tried to think through all my current problems in a logical fashion. My biggest issue right now: Brantly. His visits—as in fucking multiple—spelled nothing but trouble.

Pulling a second phone from my bag, I sent an email to my department lead. There was no way Brantley would get out of this one. My upper management could pull the data from the cell phones without an issue and see I'd done everything by the book, especially in the face of such blatant disregard for procedure that Brantley had shown.

We made it to the school just as I put the phone back in my bag. "Thank you." I slid out of the backseat, having already given the driver a five star rating. With my huge bag on my shoulder, I crossed the street and made my way through the doors of the school.

It was nothing like any of the schools I attended growing up. Even for my doctoral programs, none of my educational institutions had been this fancy. I had to hand it to the administration, though. For what they took in for tuition—even with the disbursement of financial aid—they were raking in millions a year.

213

Not that they handed any of those funds down to the teachers, though.

That would be heresy.

I had nothing but respect for real teachers. Even just playing one was draining, I couldn't imagine being this invested on a day-to-day level for years on end.

Mimi told me that teaching was a calling. There weren't a ton of benefits if someone was just wanting an 'easy career.' So the people who put their time, effort, dedication, and money into being good teachers…they had my undying appreciation.

Making my way to my borrowed classroom, I put my stuff away and started pulling the chairs down from the desks. Getting the room ready, I took a few minutes to mentally prepare myself for the onslaught of constant energy that was about to bombard my immediate space. By the time I had the chairs set, the windows open, and the music on at a low volume, I was ready.

And just in time.

The room started to fill with the little humans who had somehow managed to infiltrate my heart, the cold, hard shell that it was. They had such innocence and curiosity and joi de verve that it made my own blossom for a short while.

Once the morning bell rang, all of my kiddos were in their seats. Jamie Winston sat at his station, already bedeviling Margaret Maidenwood beside him. He tugged on her hair and poked at the bows on her shoulders. "Don't worry, Maggie, I'll kiss you one day."

Of course, he blurted it out at one of the few rare moments of quiet in the room. He let out a sigh more reminiscent of a love sick puppy and put his head in his hands, not at all ashamed of his crush. "Hi, Ms. de Witte."

I buried my smile. "Hi Jamie; let's keep our hands to ourselves, please. Did you have a good Wednesday?"

He nodded. "Yeah, Maggie and her momma came over for tea."

Maggie rolled her brown eyes. "I don't want your kisses, Jamie Winston. You keep those yucky boy lips to yourself." She crossed her arms, shooting daggers at the little guy next to her. "Boys are so gross."

I snorted mentally. I had a feeling she wouldn't always think so. "Keep thinking that way, Maggie." I cleared my throat and moved around to the front of my desk. "I think today we're going to do all of our work and then have a creativity day. What do you all think?"

Loud cheers went up around the room.

"Excellent. So let's jump in. We're going to work on letter F today. Who knows words that start with the letter F?"

One particular word starting with that particular letter sprang to mind. But I successfully pushed it aside before I could get myself into too much trouble thinking about the act that accompanied those four letters.

"Fart!" Jamie yelled from the back, drawing another glare from Maggie.

I laughed at both of them. "Yes, that definitely starts with an F. Anyone else have a word?"

Chapter 22

Rome

Walking around the full block one more time, I found myself back at the rear entrance to Neva's home. What I was doing here, I had no fucking idea, but here I was.

She smelled like sunshine and…whatever that hint of spice was again. It curled through me like black threads, locking me into every single thing that was Neva Bylur. Almost like hyperfocus, but a little more feral than that.

As I stood outside her house, the same black SUV rocked up to a halt at the curb. Brantley fucking Higginsworth got out and rounded the big vehicle. "Who the fuck are you, man? Why are you all up in my girl's business?" He shoved forward, obviously leading with his ego more than any intelligence.

Burying my smile at getting a chance to deal with him alone, I merely raised a single brow. "From where I'm standing, you're interfering with my girl. Who the fuck are you?" I crossed my arms, drawing my left hand up to my hidden knife along the inner surface of my arm under the overshirt I wore.

His mouth dropped open. "Y-y-your girl?" He burst into laughter. "Oh, bruh, you couldn't handle her. Believe me. Just drop any interest you have in her now. She'd just as soon kill you as look at you."

Both of my brows raised at this little remark. "If that's true, why are you keeping her?"

He stopped laughing with a hard cough. "I like the danger." He tried to look like he was some kind of bad boy.

"Oh, yeah?" I gave him a once over, still finding him severely lacking. "So do I. So why don't you just bow out and let the real man handle the woman. Besides, she didn't seem too happy with you just a bit ago. If she's as crazy as you claim, I wouldn't want to eat anything that woman put down in front of me at the dinner table."

He snorted. "It ain't the food on the table I'm interested in eating, if you know what I mean." A sick, almost psychopathic look slid through his eyes. The look didn't match the innuendo, either.

My vision tunneled.

My body went tight, my teeth locking, every muscle primed for the kind of violence that came from deep primal instinct. He said that. He actually fucking said that about her. About Neva.

To me.

A deep, sick heat bloomed in my chest, thick, suffocating. I should walk away, brush it off.

Should play it co—

Before I knew it, my blade was in my hand and I was moving. Fake trip. Blade forward, straight into his soft, weak, stupid fucking body.

"Oh fuck, man. I'm so sorry." I stabbed him again as I used his belly for leverage to get back to my feet.

Stepping back, I helped him up. "Oh *bruh*, you're bleeding. Do you feel okay? Do you need me to call someone for you?"

With my blade hidden out of sight once again, I raised my voice. "Help, help. We need some help over here," I shouted. With my free hand, I pulled my phone from my back pocket, I hit the buttons to call 911.

He looked down at his body as his face went a little gray. He swept his gaze back up to me, confusion in his eyes. "What the fuck?"

I shook my head, fake horror alive in my gaze. "I have no idea. Are you okay? I'm calling the police. Hang on." I caught his shoulder in my grip, squeezing harder than necessary.

218

The sound of rushing footsteps came from a few feet away. Looking over, I saw two beat cops coming down. "Someone called for help?"

"Yeah, yeah, man. He's bleeding." I made a face like I was about to puke. "Oh fuck, he's bleeding."

I staggered on my feet, fell against the wrought iron fencing that framed the green space of Snow's property. "I don't do well with blood, man. He's bleeding. He's bleeding." My pitch got progressively higher. As I stumbled along the fencing, I dropped my blade down into Dewdrop's garden area.

"Hey, man, you okay?" the other cop asked. "You gotta stay here. You can't leave yet."

I dry heaved in the plants growing up from Neva's green space, my hand out, nodding to indicate I'd heard the cop. "Just...I can't handle the blood, man." I dry heaved again.

"He's gonna be fine. Just sit over there, sir. Just sit over there. I'll get your statement after we get him settled," the cop said.

I plopped down onto the raised curb where the fencing was embedded in the cement. "Sure, sure." I waved him off again, my hand over my mouth.

Behind my fingers, I smiled as they got Brantley down to the ground, his shirt up and away from the wounds. The crimson streams flowing from his body filled me with a particular feeling of joy.

Then his words rambled back through my brain, and I had to tell myself that stabbing an FBI agent to death for hinting that he ate Dewdrop's pussy wasn't really keeping under the radar. I'd have to live with the damage I did and hope none of it came back on me.

Or that Neva found out.

All of sudden, I was filled with joy again. Dancing a couple rounds with that woman made more than just a few feelings lift. Her bland answers as we walked to the random corner she chose today drifted through my mind.

She tried so hard to play it off, to act like nothing was wrong. Tripping over uneven pavement, my ass. I've made enough knees weak in my time to recognize when the woman I wanted to devour had the same affliction.

The feeling of her warm flesh as I caught her to keep her from falling. Fuck. I flexed my fingers as I studied them. There was nothing different about them, really.

219

Nothing that would indicate they'd touched the softest skin they would ever know.

I blew out a breath.

This was bad. This was really, really bad. I knew my reaction to her was way out of left field, but right now, I didn't care and didn't want to fix it.

Watching the EMS roll up and work on Brantley, I hid a wince. Or at least a grimace. I would never feel truly bad about stabbing that fucker. But it just went to show, once again, that I was way too far gone over Neva. I needed to wrap it up.

"Sir," the cop said as he came toward me. "I'm Officer Kevin Barrone. I need to take your statement."

I nodded, working to put a harrowed look on my face. From his reaction to me, I'm guessing it was mildly successful. "Sure, I was just walking down the street. I tripped." I allowed my cheeks to heat, not meet the cop's gaze. "When I finally righted myself, I saw that man just standing there. He was bleeding." I covered my mouth with my fist and bit back another dry heave. "Is he gonna be okay?"

Office Barrone nodded. "Sure, the EMTs think he should be fine. Why are you in this neighborhood?"

I nodded a couple times, making a real show of swallowing hard. "I live on this block." I jerked my thumb in the opposite direction. "Had a long night at the office, needed to walk off some stress before finally heading home."

"Do you have any ID on you, sir?"

I dipped my chin as I pulled up to one ass cheek to grab my wallet from my back pocket. Handing him my driver's license, I waited for him to copy down my information onto his little pad.

He would find nothing of interest or importance when he ran me. Although, if he looked too hard, my reaction to the scene wouldn't make a lot of sense if he understood my former career choice. I made damn sure not to draw this kind of attention. I would really have to be careful moving forward.

"Did you notice anyone looking out of place? Like they didn't belong? Anyone you don't normally see in this area?" He handed my ID back to me.

I shook my head, put the wallet back in my pocket. "No, officer, I'm sorry. I'm just glad I was here when I was, who knows what could have happened to that guy."

Cop nodded, put his notepad back in a pocket on his vest. "He's probably going to be thankful as well. I'll let you go, Mr. Whitlock. Have a good rest of your day." He dipped his chin and wandered back to his friend, sweeping his gaze from side to side as if searching for some kind of implement.

Which reminded me.

I got up, dusted off my ass, and walked around to the front side of Neva's home. With a few quick taps on my phone, using the access Iggy had given me, I blanked out her system and entered the house using the set of tools Squirrel gifted me.

Locking the door behind me, I felt adrenaline rush into my entire body like a flood. The only times I could remember getting this excited were right before HALO jumps back in the Teams.

Creeping around Neva's house without her knowing...shivers raced up and down my spine. I had to remember to clear out my presence from her camera feed storage, but since I had full access, it shouldn't be too hard.

First thing first, though. Walking through the living room, I made my way through it to the small stack of stairs near the back.

Pulling the door open slightly, I waited and listened for the cops. It seemed like they were back at the street, so I made my way forward in a silent rush. Grabbing up my knife, I had it stored back on my body within seconds. With another quick moment to listen, I cleared the open area and moved back into the house and had the door locked.

There. All clean. Not a trace or a weapon for them to find. And Brantley was safely out of commission for at least a few hours while they treated him at the ER. And ERs in Brooklyn were crowded on most days. He might be there the entire day.

Smiling widely, I made my way back into the living room. Without a second's hesitation, I moved up the stairs and took a hard left into Neva's room. The pillows and sex toy paraphernalia were still scattered on the bed.

It took all of my self control not to go over and scoop up that fake dick and throw it down her garbage disposal. But I couldn't touch anything in here. Not without her knowing someone had been in her space.

Another thought dug through my brain. Pulling my phone from my pocket again, I accessed her security system and wiped the entire section of me approaching the

221

building. She would show a short five minute glitch. And that's if she even bothered to look and review the footage.

Which meant I had to leave.

But I came in here for a reason. A sick, perverted reason, but a reason nonetheless.

Stalking into the bathroom, I scanned the room until I found what I was looking for. The white lace panties she wore yesterday. I stuffed them in my pocket and headed back out of her personal space.

It wasn't about the panties themselves. This was about understanding her. The way her scent clung to the fabric, the chemical markers her body left behind—all of it was just data. Biological data that would help me understand what she needed.

Not allowing myself to think about it anymore, I gritted my teeth to keep from stealing that stupid toy from her bed. I rushed down the stairs and straight out of her home, making sure the door locked behind me.

What crazy woman didn't have a deadbolt on her door?

Once I was out of view of her front porch, I reset the alarm and made a note to put a damned deadbolt on her front and back doors. Iggy could add it when he came over and installed the new system tomorrow.

Sending myself a voice note, I made my way back to my own home—which was safely secured, by the way. Two deadbolts, fingerprint scanner, and physical key all to get in the front door. The back door didn't really do anything except open into a high-walled garden and covered patio holding my grill and two chairs. There was no external or outside access from the alleyway. Just individual plots of a massive green shared space.

Once inside, I blew out a breath. Even knowing what I was about to do was beyond stupid, I didn't even try to stop myself from doing it. Walking through the short entryway, I took a sharp left and hauled ass upstairs to the third floor. After another sharp left, I walked into my secondary office. Skirting around the edge of the large desk, I sat in the chair and booted up my computer.

My desktop popped up almost immediately. It definitely paid to have a tech genius set up your home computer network and systems. Pulling up the webpage for her security alarm provider, I input her credentials and watched as the interior of her entire home came into view once more.

It wasn't just about watching her—it was about keeping her safe. If I don't do it, who would? No one else could understand what she needed. Not the way I could.

Completely ignoring my better self calling me a psycho, I made sure to add myself as a user to her account. If she ever went into more than just her dashboard, she would definitely see me, but I was figuring she wouldn't. At least, not until after we had our own, better, system installed tomorrow night.

This would work for now. Tomorrow though…I blew out a long breath. Tomorrow, I would have full access to her. And then I could relax.

But that meant a couple more tasks for today before I got a shower, a meal, and went back into the office. Doing some digging with the programs we used for Locke Securities, I found the security company for the school where she worked. A little longer search brought me to their IT page.

With a little help from a digital friend, I fired off an email that would allow me to access their system as well. I'd only be able to watch their feeds, but if it allowed me to keep an eye on my little dewdrop, I was fine with that.

My conscience well and truly silenced at this point, I scanned the different views until I found the three placed in Neva's classroom. My belly tightened as she bent down to help some snot nosed kid with his piece of paper. The top of her dress gaped open enough that I could see her tits.

That fucker better be glad he's under the age of ten. I curled my fingers into fists and looked up at the ceiling as I worked through the admittedly insane rage I felt toward a child for being in the same room with her.

The kid probably didn't even know what tits were good for.

Right now, I couldn't even make that fucking matter. I was furious he got to see her in person, while I had to settle for a picture from over twenty-five feet away with no way to zoom in. He got to smell her. Bask in the glow of her smile. Listen to her sexy voice.

For the briefest, blackest moment, I considered it. But no—too messy, too much attention. And even I wasn't that far gone.

Right?

"Get your fucking head on straight, man." I glared up at the ceiling as scenario after scenario blazed through my head.

Then it dawned on me that I was fantasizing about removing children from this earth because they were near the woman I claimed. I *really* had to get my shit together. A lot better than this. "I'm trying." Blowing out a low breath, I counted to ten.

Then twenty.

By ninety-two, I was feeling much better.

I looked up and saw that the room was empty except for Ms. de Witte. As she bustled around each of the tables, a little smile covered her pretty face, though there was a touch of sorrow in her green eyes as she moved. Gentle fingers traced over jagged and broken lines on each page of paper.

As I watched, she stiffened and turned. When I couldn't see what she was looking at, I hit the button to switch the camera angle. A rumbling snarl slid between my lips. A man stood there, looking like a stupid limp noodle in his khakis and polo, his light brown hair shoved back off his forehead.

They talked for a moment, but I couldn't see her face and watch him at the same time, so I had to settle for watching this ugly motherfucker talk to her. The look of outright lust in his eyes made my fists curl so tightly something in my hand popped.

Pulling up the screen clipping tool on my computer, I took a screenshot of his face. Shifting, I uploaded the picture into a program we owned. I would have his entire life in my email inbox within twenty minutes. He better hope nothing even tinged in gray showed up.

With a smarmy smile, he nodded and moved away. "About fucking time, asshole," I snarled as I clicked back to the camera feed with her in it.

She sat at her desk, a strange look on her face. She didn't seem upset, which was the only thing saving that dipshit from meeting me in a dark alley one night very soon. But she just sat there, looking off into space.

I had my phone up and her dialed before I could think about it. On screen, she startled and grabbed up the phone. A sly grin stretched her mouth as she answered. "This is Aneira de Witte. To whom am I speaking?"

I bit back the laughter. "Oh, I'm so sorry. I was calling for Isa Guari. Would you happen to know if she's available?"

On screen, I watched her roll her eyes. "No, I'm sorry, you've got the wrong number." She hung up on me, tossing her phone down with a triumphant smile.

At least she didn't look disturbed anymore. And maybe it would keep me in her mind for a while longer. She was constantly in mine; it was only fair that I was in hers.

But she was smiling right now. That was good enough. And would allow me at least a couple minutes to go grab a quick meal, shower, a change of clothes, and get back to the office.

Just as I was getting ready to turn off the whole system, a ding sounded from the speakers. Shifting to glance through my notifications, I saw an email landed in my inbox. Since it was way too soon for any of the programs to be spitting out results, I frowned as I pulled open my email.

Mr. Whitlock,
You don't know me. Let me be clear: it's in your best interests to stay out of my way and my business. Leave Ms. Aniera de Witte alone. This is your only warning.

Without clicking on anything else, I grabbed my phone and punched in the button for Iggy's speed dial. He picked up before the first ring finished. "Go."

"Email from unknown. Threatening me to leave Aniera de Witte alone."

"Which account?"

Shifting my gaze, I gave him the information. "Personal for junk." My brows furrowed. "Why would they send it there?"

He made a low humming noise over the line. "Almost in."

I waited in silence as I let him do his thing. Shifting my phone, I pulled up the footage to the camera at the school again. Then breathed a silent sigh of relief when I saw the kids were back in the room and Neva was doing her kindergarten teacher routine.

"Got it," Iggy said, interrupting me from memorizing her figure in a pretty sundress.

I fought not to bark at him for it.

"Burner address that's already shut down. Don't do anything else to your system. Do you have it set up on the alternate server from Locke's?"

Gritting my teeth, I answered truthfully. "No. I got the alert and opened it after doing some work here at home. It's on the same server system."

I withstood the tongue lashing he gave me. I knew better than to be checking anything personal on the system

225

we used for Locke Securities. Blowing out a breath, I listened to the familiar refrain about cybersecurity and operational procedures that I helped create.

He finally wound down. "Let me partition your system. Then you wipe everything on that rig. Full, hard wipe. Don't make me come over and do it for you, either." He hung up without saying anything else.

I winced. Damn it. He was right, there were no two ways around it. But wiping the full thing? I heaved out a sigh. For fuck's sake.

Oh well, it wasn't like I wasn't going to be spending hours upon hours getting it set up again with everything I needed. There were worse things to do with my time. And I still had my personal computer, so I could watch Neva.

Keep her safe, at least.

Scooting back in my chair, I pulled out a laminated sheet of cardstock Iggy demanded we each keep in our homes. It held detailed instructions for just such an event. Thankfully, this didn't happen often enough that I had it memorized. And from this point forward, I would make damn sure I didn't have to use it again.

Damn it. I didn't like being watched.

That was my job.

Chapter 23

Neva

Smiling goodbye to each child as they once again fled for freedom found through the heavy doors of the school, I ground my teeth together and tried to make it look like I wasn't attempting to hold in terrible gas.

During the day, Brantley sent me no fewer than twenty-three text messages, fourteen calls, and had three of his lackeys come down to the school and demand to see me in the principal's office.

What the fuck got stuck up his butt?

The final student safely in the arms of his father, I allowed the doors to close behind me as I made my way back to my classroom. I didn't care what Brantley had to offer in terms of excuses, this was beyond unprofessional. And he was threatening his own op.

Mentally preparing my speech to our respective bosses, my heart skipped a beat as I crossed into my room and saw the man himself slouched onto an entire section of chairs in the middle of the room.

Rolling my lips in so I didn't do more damage to our lovers' cover story, I shot him a glare as I shut the door, barely catching it before it could slam shut, bringing more attention to us.

Spinning back, unable to bear the idea of my back to his man, I made sure to catalog the furniture around me. A handful of possible weapons were within reach, and I waited for him to speak. Knowing Brantley, it wouldn't be too long before he needed to hear the sound of his own voice again.

"Who the fuck was in your house yesterday, Larkspur? And why was he escorting you to school this morning? This isn't a fucking sorority or some Hallmark Christmas movie, this is international weapons and millions of lives on the line." He bit the words out, his tone weak and a little breathy.

My brows furrowed as I studied him.

He didn't look any worse for wear, other than a shade or two paler than usual. Then again, it could be the dreads he wore giving him the sickly grayish pallor against the dark blue of his hipster clothes.

"Again, I don't know what you're talking about, lover. I had no guests at my house, and I certainly don't need escorting to the corner like some damsel in distress." They hadn't been guests. Not really. In the end, the Seven Dwarfs were more like white knights.

So badly did I want to cross my arms, but knowing I needed to keep them free in case Brantley made a move, I began easing my way toward the desk where some very pretty flowers sat in vases of what looked like regular water.

The flowers were the best silk simulations I'd ever seen, and the water was actually a gel serum that could do a lot of damage on contact. The vases were discretely glued to the surface of the desk so little hands couldn't accidentally topple said containers. But, if necessary, I could fling those drenched faux flowers at Brantley if he got too amped up.

And call me crazy, but something told me he was very amped up. And about Rome, of all people. The two run-ins he had with the admittedly infuriating man shouldn't have cranked him this high. This reaction was wildly out of proportion to what actually happened.

"Last chance to tell me the truth, pumpkin." He bit the pet name out through clenched teeth. "Tell me who he is, or I'll have you off this case so fast and up before your professional conduct board that you'll wonder what happened. Do. Not. Fuck. With me." Each word sounded more and more breathless, as if he were a slowly leaking balloon. A ragey balloon, but hot air filled latex, nonetheless.

Rage coiled low and tight, heat licking up my spine. Another fucking man telling me what I can and can't do.

Like I owed him an answer.

Like he had a fucking ounce of control over my life.

My foot edged closer to the desk's hidden mechanism. One touch and this conversation would end permanently.

I exhaled, slow and even, forcing my words to stay level. "You can't get me off this case, you little pissy bitch. Your boss put me on and I'm not the one behaving inappropriately." That was skimming close to a lie, because my boss was the one to demand my involvement after I made the case for it.

Squaring up behind the desk, I slid my foot to the edge where it hit the foot of the heavy piece of furniture. As Ms. de Witte, I had an anxious sentimental attachment to the desk, so Ms. Bellington had allowed me to bring it in since it reminded me of my recently lost fake husband.

The filigree lining the front face of it had beautiful silver accents dotting and swirling through the elegant arches and sweeps of master craftsmanship. Not only was the wood molded and shaped by a master's hands, the intricate system of poison distribution also spoke of masterful design.

If I did say so myself.

"You have no idea who you're playing with, bitch." Brantley heaved himself to his feet, his cheeks losing all color before they flushed with crimson as he righted himself from a slight sway.

"Say goodbye to your career. I'll end you and whatever that fuck's name is that you hooked yourself to." He bent forward, a light in his eyes that I'd seen a time or two in my time in clandestine operations. Pure narcissistic psychosis. This man had surely lost the fucking plot.

Lifting my toes, I readied the system in the desk's interior. He wouldn't make it to me alive if he made a try for it. A soft thunk of pressure landed over the bridge of my foot as the system in the desk lowered the firing mechanism now that it was ready to fire.

A heavy knock sounded at the door. I didn't bother looking in that direction, nothing would make me take my gaze off Brantley. Not when he looked like this, acted like this. He was definitely the greater threat, no matter who or what stood outside the door.

"Ms. de Witte?" Oskar Jorgenssen called out through the heavy wood barrier.

Brantley's eyes went huge as he stumbled back, fear and something else running through his gaze. His mouth gaped, but no words escaped.

"Ms. de Witte?" Oskar called again. "Ms. Bellington told me you were in your classroom. Are you there? Do you need assistance?"

I raised a single dark brow, waiting for Brantley to make a decision.

His mouth firmed down into a hard line, fury eating through the fear in his gaze. "I'll kill you for this." He shuffled forward to the door, unlocked it, then backed up again.

"Sorry, I was keeping her…occupied." His tone left nothing to the imagination as he passed the other man on his way into the hall. "She's free now."

I didn't move from my spot, making my body language easy to read that there had been nothing sexual or even desirous happening between us. Jorgenssen shifted his gaze between us as he stood there in silence for a long moment. His lips moved, but I was too far away to make out any words.

My gaze sharpened.

Was he muttering about assholes like Brantley? Talking to him? Commiserating about the female species? What the hell did he just say?

Brantley's chin dipped an infinitesimal degree, a look of victory raising his shoulders slightly. I was very familiar with what success looked like on that man's body. He was forever shoving his successes in everyone else's faces. But why would he be feeling victorious at whatever Jorgenssen said?

"Yes, Mr. Jorgenssen. I'm sorry to have kept you waiting. That's Brantley Higginsworth, my partner. He was just leaving." I kept my spot by the desk, watching each man for signs of familiarity. And when I saw Brantley's entire body pucker and a sly smile stretch Jorgenssen's face, I knew I was in deep shit.

Very, very deep shit.

Jorgenssen's mouth moved again. Only this time, he didn't try to hide the fact he was speaking to the other man. Jorgenssen lifted his hand and drew it out back toward the classroom as if waving Brantley inside with him.

It seemed like we were going to have a different kind of parent-teacher conference.

Fuck.

I shook my head at Brantley, feeling everything inside me go ice-cold as I saw the moment he decided to handle the Larkspur situation on his own. Slowly, he moved back into the classroom. A smirk stretching his mouth out of sight of Jorgenssen. "Shoulda listened, de Witte."

The door closed behind Jorgenssen with a soft snick of the lock. "Higginsworth, the name sounds oddly familiar."

Brantley moved farther into the room. When he didn't pull his gun or even grab for his phone, I knew then that he'd come here without his usual coterie of hangers-on. He came to teach me a lesson privately, it seemed. The smirk from moments before straightened out into a hard, thin line. Fury rose through his features once again.

Hey, if I was going down, I was taking as many people as possible with me. Even if that was only this asshole who made my life so difficult for the last six months. He was evil, he could die with me. And, hey, on the bright side, Jorgenssen would die, too. All three of us chucked off to hell where we belonged.

"She misspoke, that's not actually my name," Brantley said. He wiped his expression clean as he turned to the arms dealer. "That's the name I gave her, but you already know my real name."

I snorted loudly. "Yeah, did he also tell you he works for the FBI?"

Jorgenssen laughed, a genuine laugh if the lines darting out from his eyes and bracketing his mouth were any indication. "So neither of you understand true loyalty." He nodded. "This is good."

Angling to keep Jorgenssen in my sights, I allowed my foot to lower back to the ground at the foot of the desk. No need to get fatigued and then not have the ability to activate the switch when the time finally came to disperse the poison.

"There's nothing about me you haven't already verified, Mr. Jorgenssen. I have doctorates in both plants and diseases—a wealth of knowledge about how those plants can be used. Ones that can help your beloved Ada. I've studied extensively in various parts of Europe, China, and more remote sections of India."

"And she works for the CIA!" Brantley blurted out.

I rolled my eyes at him. "I've explained that as well." I smiled at Jorgenssen. "If you care to recall, I did mention I have done some consultation work for the American Central Intelligence Agency. I've also worked closely with the World Health Organization, the Centers for Disease Control, and many other organizations both foreign and domestic."

Going into this job, I needed to work under the idea that at some point my affiliation with the CIA would come to light. It was almost a guarantee with someone like Brantley on the team. The man wouldn't know loyalty if it ran up and bit off his dick.

Brantley's face went white before it flashed back to crimson. "You bitch." He launched himself at me.

Jorgenssen sighed, almost disappointed, and kicked Brantley's knees out from under him. "You really should be nicer to those working for you, Mr. Carsten, or rather, Mr. Higginsworth."

The gun was in his hand before I could blink.

A whisper-soft click, a low metallic cough.

Brantley's head snapped back. A fine crimson mist painted the desk, the air stilling as if even the room itself held its breath.

The silence that followed was almost reverent.

Jorgenssen barely even glanced at the body. He only looked at me. His gun still raised, this time in my direction. "You're correct, Ms. de Witte. I did run you. Extensively. Which is why I struggled so hard with your association with this man. He is not a good man. Why would a lovely lady like you willingly be involved with such scum?"

I swallowed back the burst of inappropriate humor as I allowed a tremor to ripple through my hands. Fear…or at least that's what Jorgennsen would see.

"Y-y-y-you shot him." I let my gaze dart to Brantley's lifeless body, back to Jorgenssen, lips parting like I couldn't quite form words.

"You shot him."

Jorgenssen nodded, a single dip of his chin as he shook out his arm and releveled the gun in my direction. "Answer the question, Ms. de Witte." He smiled. "Please."

I licked my lips, allowed my mouth to work open and closed, open and closed. Swallowed a good half dozen times, coughed. Red rushed to my cheeks as I furiously thought through the available answers. "He seemed the best choice at the time."

Jorgenssen snorted, loud and derisively. "You're a beautiful woman, Aniera. Can I call you that? Such a lovely name. Surely you could have done better than this man. A liar, a cheat, a fraud. A man loyal only to himself and to hell with everyone around him."

I shook my head again, at a loss. My gaze glued to the man bleeding out on the floor, the man who shot him close enough to remain in my periphery. He hadn't said anything that wasn't true; Brantley was all of those things. And more. So much more.

Jorgenssen heaved a sigh and lowered his gun. "Do you know that your partner was trying to sell you to me?"

That cleared my brain. I jerked my gaze to the Swede, narrowed my eyes.

Jorgenssen nodded. "Yes. He introduced himself as Brantley Carsten the day after I invited you to my home the first time. He showed up the next day and told me he was the reason you were unable to attend." His jaw rippled as he clenched his teeth.

"He walked right up to my front door and blithely told me he was the reason my Ada was still in such pain, such distress. That he demanded you stay home under threat of violence so that he could vet me." Without taking his gaze from mine, he pumped five more rounds into Brantley's dead body.

I gulped at the ice in Jorgenssen's gaze, feeling the first curls of true fear slide through me at the idea of being alone with this man. He might be a monster, but he cared greatly for his daughter. I needed to remember that.

"When he saw the resources I have at my disposal, he slyly insinuated you were untouched by men. That he had been grooming you for a seller he had in mind. But if I were of such a mind, he would be willing to sell you to me and pocket the shipping fees, as it were." Jorgenssen studied me from less than ten feet away.

My upper lip curled as I snapped a glare down at Brantley. Good thing he was already dead, the fucker. He got off easy with Jorgenssen taking him out with a single shot. He'd have gotten no such mercy from me.

Drawing my gaze back up to Jorgenssen, I waited for him to get to his main point. There had to be something more than him just killing Brantley for giving him a fake name and delaying his daughter's potential cure.

"Then I'm glad he's dead." I raised my chin and shook back my shoulders.

"He left that day, gave me a number to call and a price for you." His gaze slid over my body as if I were nothing more than a piece of the antique furniture he supposedly dealt in.

When he finally raised his gaze back to me, I saw the disgust in his eyes. "I don't pay for sex. Ever. I've never needed to. And I'm certainly not going to start with a woman well past her prime and keep her in slavery. Especially when it's one I need to keep alive for any length of time."

Well, thank all the gods for that, I breathed mentally. "I'm not a virgin, by the way." Why I felt compelled to defend myself on something so stupid was anyone's guess. But here we were.

He shook his head. "I couldn't care less, Aniera. What I do care about? You helping my daughter." He raised the gun again. "Can you do that or are you working with your partner for the FBI trying to trap me for something?"

"I can certainly do my best to help you, Mr. Jorgenssen. You and Ada. I have some ideas from being able to watch the progression of her symptoms while here in class day in, day out."

He motioned with the gun.

Licking my lips, I gave him a weak smile. Pulling up the relevant plant information in my head, I gave him a brief rundown. "Honestly, I think she has a bleeding disorder that's emphasized by adrenaline, dopamine, and cortisol. There are some plants, in specific combinations, which could help with all three biological neurotransmitters without creating any long-term negative side effects. It could be that she'll grow out of the condition once she hits puberty. If not, we'll need to look at some longer lasting combinations you'll be able to titrate as she ages."

He studied me for a very long time. "Why have other medical professionals not given me such a prognosis?"

I shrugged. "I can't tell you that; I'm not them. Nor have I been in their offices during the times you listed her symptoms or signs. I'm simply giving you my best educated guess from what I've seen here in the classroom."

"You will come to my house tonight. You will talk with Ada in a more comfortable setting, and you will bring these plants to treat her. If something happens to her that harms her, you will die. Do you understand me?"

Licking my lips, I cleared my throat. "If you want me to guarantee her health, we will be looking at incremental progress with whatever I can create in my home lab. I have no idea of her allergies, her tolerances, her sensitivities. You are looking at possibly months or years if you hold my life as ransom for causing her harm."

Rage, and the tiniest smidgen of respect, floated through his blue eyes. "Are there tests you can do to mitigate these limitations you mentioned?"

I nodded. "I can do scratch tests for allergies. We would need to run a full genetic assay and blood profile on her for the other two. Has she undergone GeneSight testing?"

He dipped his chin. "Yes to the GeneSight testing. We had that completed last year for possible pharmacological interventions. No to the other two panels."

A curl of triumph eased through me. "If you can arrange for the full genetic assay and the blood profile panels to be completed as soon as possible, that will allow me to make the best possible matches for Ada specifically. I will be able to tailor any herbal or botanical remedies for her with the least amount of discomfort. My showing up at your home tonight will not hurry that process. And could, in all honesty, induce more stress on Ada. This could increase her cortisol levels and create another bleed."

He seemed to chew on that for long moments, the gun still aimed in my direction. "Are you truly a kindergarten teacher?"

I nodded. "Yes, I teach kindergartners." I waved my hand at the empty classroom. "Whatever Brantley told you about me is categorically untrue. Ms. Bellington has my personal and professional history. The school demanded it, along with full federal and local law enforcement background checks. Did you see anything untoward in my file?"

He shook his head. "No. But in this day and age, that doesn't mean a lot. You could be a hired killer with excellent electronic skills. You could work for the FBI, CIA, MI6, Mossad, any number of intelligence agencies. What can be found on paper is not always trustworthy. My life is the perfect example of this."

I nodded. "You're right. But if I have all of these skills, these connections, why would I be at a school when I could be out doing real work that makes the difference in millions of lives instead of only twenty?"

Heaving a sigh, I continued with the truth. "Sometimes, Mr. Jorgenssen, life has a way of beating us down, cutting

235

us into pieces, setting all those pieces on fire, and then dumping us into hell. I work at this school because it calls to me. I serve a purpose higher than death and destruction these days. I work to ensure the best possible future of the lives of the children I see every day."

I let the truth of my words shine from my eyes. He didn't need to know I meant it in a broader sense. That these children were but a small fraction of the lives for which I wanted to ensure best outcomes. I was called to this school because his daughter was here. I'd spoken no lies, merely fragments of truth.

He stood there in silence for what must have been ten full minutes. Not speaking, not twitching, barely breathing.

When he finally roused himself, he dipped his chin. "You are not wrong, Ms. de Witte. But if you are seeking to harm my daughter, I will hunt you down to the ends of the earth and kill you. Then I will make every person who even tangentially knows you feel the same terror and pain."

I laid my hand over my heart. "I have no desire to harm your lovely Ada, Mr. Jorgenssen. She's far too important for that."

And once I got rid of him, she would be even safer.

He studied me for a long time again, the wheels of his mind covering every possible outcome shining through his bright blue eyes. There was no way he could account for this particular situation, but I had to give him props for trying.

Finally lowering his gun, he unscrewed the suppressor, and pocketed both. "Unless you wish to be part of the cleanup for this little tableau, I suggest you leave." He pulled his phone from his pocket. After stabbing his thumb at the screen, he shot a line of bored Swedish to whoever answered.

When he finished, he slid the device back into his pocket and turned to me fully once again. "I'll get the required tests for Ada completed as soon as possible." He eased back and rested his ass on the edge of one of the desks behind him. "Go. Now."

Jerking his chin at the door, he watched me with careful eyes as I gathered my things as quickly as possible.

Just as I was pulling the door shut behind myself, he called out, "Do not disappoint me, Ms. de Witte."

"I'll do my best to fix everything, Mr. Jorgenssen." I shut the door before he could see the triumphant smile stretch my mouth.

I turned too fast, barely processing the movement before I crashed into something unyielding. A heartbeat, steady and slow. A scent, dark spice and heat that curled through me like smoke.

Rome.

Fucking.

Whitlock.

Chapter 24

Rome

My arms locked around her like I could fuse her to me, but I was still shaking. Lungs burning, vision tunneling— fuck. Fuck. FUCK!

Too many ways I could have lost her. Too many ways I still could. My body was short-circuiting, every survival instinct snarling for control.

When I felt like I could finally breathe normally, I grasped her arms and set her away from me, my heart still pumping a mile a minute. Skimming my gaze up and down her body, I blew out a mental breath and felt everything inside me relax.

She was safe. Thank fuck. Thank fucking fuck.

The drive over here was nothing but a blur. On my last check of the camera feeds at the end of the school day, when I saw Brantley shove his way into her room, I'd sprinted from the office out into the van.

Then, on my phone's too small screen, I saw the tall Swede interrupt them, only to shoot Brantley in the fucking dome. I almost wanted to kiss the man himself for saving her by killing that federal asshole, but I had other things to worry about right now.

Walking forward, I double checked the door to make sure it closed all the way. Pulling my phone from my pocket, I noted Jorgenssen was still in the room on his phone. He was pacing back and forth in front of Brantley's body.

While I couldn't be sorry that douche was dead, I was annoyed that Jorgenssen got to do the deed. That asshole's death had been written in my particular stars. Pushing aside the disappointment at not getting to kill him, I turned back to Neva. "What the hell, dewdrop?"

She stood glaring up at me, my death now in her pretty green eyes. "You've been watching me?" Fury ate through the whispered accusation.

Internally, I winced. I knew I was going crazy, I just didn't know how to stop it.

Without a single twitch to give her away, she jolted forward and ripped my phone from my hands. She stared down at the screen, the muscles in her jaw working overtime. "You stupid piece of arrogant trash."

She flung the phone down so hard it bounced, skidding across the tile. Then her heel came down like an executioner's axe. The screen spiderwebbed—almost like my nerves on the way here—but the image of the feed still flickered through the broken glass, taunting her. She stomped again, harder, the shattered screen as black as my death in her eyes.

When she raised her face to mine again, I stopped breathing. Her rage was a tangible thing, coiling tight around my ribs. Every cell screamed danger. Holy fuck, she was going to kill me. Then my dick twitched like it had been branded with electricity.

Holy hell.

I was dead.

And I was hard.

"Ms. de Witte?" a woman called from behind me.

Neva's face cleared as if it had never darkened in her life. "Ms. Bellington. Are you okay? Do you need any help?" She slid around me like a tight end through the D-line. Her hands held out in supplication, she seemed to shrink in on herself, as if she pulled every bit of her large personality into a tiny box that could fit in her palm.

Turning slightly, I catalogued the woman in charge of the school. White hair seemed to drift around her head in a cloud of loose curls. She looked at me, and the rest of the men behind me, as if we'd streaked fully naked through the gymnasium at a pep rally. "Not at all, dear. I was just checking on you. Did Mr. Jorgenssen find you?"

Neva stalled the older woman's progress by angling her toward the other side of the hallway. "Yes, he did. Thank you for directing him to me. He had some questions about Ada."

Ms. Bellington came to rest about five feet from Neva's classroom door. A vague smile graced her pretty face. "Then who are your visitors? They didn't check in at the office." She eyed me and the boys again before turning back to Neva. "All visitors are required to check in, Aniera. You know that."

Neva gave the older woman a chagrined look. "Yes, sorry about that. They were coming to help me move some furniture. In and out. I didn't think it would hurt anything, especially since the kids have all gone for the day." She shook her head, sorrow and guilt marring her features.

Ms. Bellington gave a little tut-tut, but patted Neva's hand. "Just this time. Are you allowing me to replace that desk of yours?"

Neva squeezed the older woman's hand, a bright smile on her face. "No. They were going to help me rearrange the desks. But Rome here hurt his back today. Doing something extraordinarily manly, I'm sure. He isn't able to help. And you're right, Ms. B. They shouldn't be here without checking in through the office. When Rome is feeling better, I'll make sure the lot of them come through the office first."

Hurt my back? Was she insane? And I'd personally show her something extraordinarily manly, but it sure as hell wouldn't put my back out. I might blow hers out, come to think of it.

Ms. Bellington gave me a once over. Her gaze searching out any weakness. I'm pretty sure she had some kind of x-ray vision because her upper lip curled ever so slightly. "He doesn't look hurt to me."

Neva turned to me, another promise in her eyes. She raised a single brow.

Controlling the urge to roll my eyes, I put my hand to my lower back and leaned forward the smallest degree. "Ouch. My back. My back is so hurt. I might need medical intervention." The Sahara had more moisture than my words.

Ms. Bellington snorted, then turned back to Neva. "You're not sneaking in a man and this collection of large sexy human trees for anything scandalous, are you, my dear?" This time, her eyes twinkled with an entirely different light in them.

Neva's face flamed as her mouth dropped open. "Ms. B! No! I wouldn't do that on school grounds. And certainly not with any of them." She stabbed her finger in our direction.

Squirrel heaved a huge sigh. "Way to break a man's heart, Ms. de Witte."

Neva glowered at him. "Shut it. Not another word out of you." She turned back to her boss. "I promise. They were going to help me move some furniture. But we've changed plans. I've already locked up and planned to head out." She lifted her bag and gave it a little shake.

Ms. Bellington examined all of us guys for a little too long, that devilish gleam in her eyes. "Uh, huh. Well, make sure you secure the exterior door behind you." She patted Neva's hand without looking away from any of us. "Gentlemen. Please make sure to use the front door from now on."

A chorus of "yes, ma'am" filled the hallway.

The principal smiled prettily and turned away. "Good night, Aniera. Enjoy your…evening." She spun on her sensible heels and walked away.

After Ms. Bellington cleared the corner, Neva moved over, pushed up into my face. "Get out. Now. We'll be discussing this later, you son of a bitch." She stabbed her little hand over my shoulder as if I'd forgotten where the door was.

From the sounds behind me, the rest of the guys filed out the door in single file. Probably didn't want to stick around for the fireworks when I told her what she could do with her demands.

"Aww, pix, don't be like that. We're just here to help you move some furniture," Squirrel cajoled as he came up beside me. "That's no way to treat your man." He leaned down, sniffed her shoulder. "Why do you always smell so good?"

I was this close to shoving my elbow into his eye socket when the door to Neva's classroom swung open.

Jorgenssen stood there, a look of surprise on his face. "Ms. de Witte?"

Taking a step back to give myself more room if he attacked, I wasn't quite prepared when the Swede smiled widely at Squirrel.

242

"Ah. You must be Aniera's real partner." Jorgenssen's smile was slow, assessing—like he'd just confirmed something. His gaze flicked to Neva, back to Squirrel. "Please tell me you take better care of her than that unfortunate man on the floor there."

Squirrel had his hand out and shaking Jorgenssen's before I could utter a single sound. "She's definitely mine."

What the hell?

He moved as close to Neva's body as he could get without actually touching her, his huge presence almost covering her entirely from Jorgenssen's sight.

"And you are?" I asked, bringing the Swede's attention to me. I was this close to telling him that Neva was mine. The words perched on the tip of my tongue when Neva beat me to speaking.

"Baby, this is Oskar Jorgenssen. He's the father of one of my students." She eased up beside Squirrel, her tiny hand landing on his belly. She leaned against him, staring up at Jorgenssen. "How did you know?"

Jorgenssen snorted. "No way a woman like you is actually hooked up with a weasel like Brantley…Charles." He shook his head. "Whatever his name truly was. You were baiting him, weren't you? Have a real man on the side, while dragging that asshole along until you found something to really punish him with?" The joy in his eyes was a little weird as he described the completely wrong scenario, but at least it gave Neva a way out.

She nodded, a slight blush pinking her cheeks. "You're right, as usual. I've known something was wrong for a while now. I met this mountain at a club and couldn't believe a man like him actually existed." She petted Squirrel's belly again.

Something sharp and feral tore through my ribs, white-hot and all-consuming. Mine. Every inch of her body against his was a personal fucking insult.

A declaration of war.

Jorgenssen laughed. "Good for you." His gaze turned sly. "Is he the real reason you postponed coming to my place tonight?"

Squirrel nodded immediately at the exact time that Neva shook her head. "Of course not!"

Damn right she wasn't trying to get with Squirrel. Even the idea of it had my fingers curling down into fists. I was going to kill him. Actually kill him.

Jorgenssen laughed. "Of course not, indeed."

Neva glared up at Squirrel, then turned back to the Swede. "No, I really do need those tests done. Ada needs me to have the results. I don't want anything I do to hurt her."

Squirrel's face fell into somber lines. "I'm sorry your daughter is sick. We're working on making our own brood. I can't imagine the pain and fear you're going through right now."

Jorgenssen looked pissed for all of two seconds before his expression smoothed out. He nodded. "I'll do anything to make her better. I hope you never have this feeling of absolute uselessness."

Everyone stood there in silence for a long time.

Again, I opened my mouth to set Jorgenssen straight. I didn't care what other lies we had to tell, but no way in hell was I going to let this man, or any other for that matter, think Neva belonged to anyone but me. Ever.

"You said you met at a club. Which one?" Jorgenssen asked abruptly.

I could have bitten off my tongue, I snapped my teeth together so quickly. Why the fuck did that even matter? Honestly, was he going to join up? I snorted mentally, there was no way in hell we'd let him through the vetting process.

"Subterra," Squirrel answered.

Dead. Murdered. Extinguished. By my own hand, one of my brothers was going to meet his maker. Or the devil. Either or. Right now, I didn't care which.

"Ah." Jorgenssen's eyes gleamed with a new kind of awareness. "I wouldn't have assumed you to be a party to such goings on, Ms. de Witte." He trailed his gaze up and down her small body.

Squirrel made a noise in the back of his throat and stepped between them again. "Don't ever look at her like that again. I don't care who you are. She's to be treated with your utmost respect." Gone was the jovial giant who looked on the verge of perpetual laughter. Now, he was an elite killer bred from the fires of hell itself.

Damn it. Now I couldn't torture him. It had to be a clean, fast death. The fucker. Stealing all my fun.

Jorgenssen raised his hands, stepped back. "I apologize to you." He eased to the side, searched out Neva's face. "I apologize to you, as well."

She waved it away with a glare on her face.

"I myself am a member at Subterra. Under a different name, of course. No reason to sully my reputation in the day-to-day. Perhaps we could meet there tomorrow and discuss any other needs for Ada?" There was a tone in his voice that didn't allow for much opposition. "A place like that could guarantee our secrecy and involvement together, yes?"

Squirrel's eyes flashed wide for a moment, but he kept his cool. Turning, he allowed Neva back into the conversation. "What do you say, pix?"

He was looking to her to figure a way out of using one of the most secure places in the city to *not* discuss business with a shady arms dealer? Really?

I smiled. And he was back to being tortured before I killed him. The night was beginning to look a little brighter again.

Neva stared up at Squirrel, heat in her eyes. "I don't think that's quite appropriate." She turned back to the other man. "I'll be in your home on my own, Mr. Jorgenssen. For the purpose of helping your daughter medically. I'm not sure meeting at a sex club is going to be conducive to our arrangement. No need to muddy any lines. We're professionals working to keep your daughter safe and healthy, after all."

Jorgenssen's brows dropped. "Yes, we are professionals. And since you so clearly have been doing things underhandedly"—he tipped his head toward the classroom where Brantley's body still lay—"I think this would give us a perfect time to complete the final vetting, yes? Because clearly no one working for the US Government would be a member of such a club. At least not out in the open. Nor would any teacher associated with the highest morals and values as found in this establishment. There would be too many opportunities for blackmail and leverage."

The moment stretched, the silence too controlled. Too knowing. Then it hit—this wasn't a test. It was a noose.

And he just cinched it tight around our throats.

Neva's mouth worked, but no sound came out. Horror flashed through her pretty green eyes before it was carefully banked. She gave a strained smile. "Sure, Mr. Jorgenssen. You're right. It would be a good final test. As I have nothing to hide, it would seem a logical place to conduct any visits that aren't in your home with Ada."

She leaned into Squirrel's body. Behind his back, her fingers clenched into a fist. Anger dancing in the white knuckles. "Let's say tomorrow at ten?"

Jorgenssen nodded, a brilliant smile on his face. "That will work perfectly." He dipped his chin. "Now, if you could leave, I have a crew coming in. The less interaction you have with them, the better." Meaning he didn't want Neva to know what any of his team looked like.

Shooting a quick glance over my shoulder, I realized the rest of the guys had successfully cleared out earlier. Thank every known and unknown supernatural presence for that. At least not all of us had been ID'd by the guy.

"And bring your third." Jorgenssen jerked his chin in my direction. "He will be vetted as well." His tone offered no way out without sending up more alerts.

"He's nothing but my driver," Squirrel said. "And my head of security."

I glared at him before I cleared my expression as Jorgenssen looked over at me.

"Good. I'll make sure my security personnel are with me as well. No reason for things to be unbalanced, right?" Jorgenssen waved us away as he looked down at his phone. "Leave. Now." He stabbed his finger at the door behind us, just like Neva did long minutes ago.

Neva shot him a tight smile. "I'll see you tomorrow night, Mr. Jorgenssen." With her hand in Squirrel's back pocket, she shoved him before her.

I brought up the rear, walking backwards. No way was I going to give this fucker a chance to take us by surprise. And it kept me from having to watch Neva's hands on that dead man's body. It might have been neck and neck for which option won on the priority list right now.

The cool evening air wrapped around me as I watched the door shut, the final thud of the lock sounding softly in the darkening light. Blowing out a breath, I turned.

Neva let go of Squirrel and whisper-shouted into his face. "You stupid fucking idiot. Do you know what you've just done?" She stalked him as he continued to back up out of her space. "You've put yourself front and center in his mind. Let alone the idea that he has to come to Subterra. You've become a target. If something goes wrong with my finding a cure for Ada, you're now going to be his ransom." Her breath sobbed in her chest as she continued to glare up at him. "You stupid, stupid man."

Her fingers curled into fists as if she could physically force herself to slow down. Her breath stuttered, shallow, too fast. Her body fighting itself, shaking and spiraling apart.

She was coming undone right in front of me.

And I couldn't do anything to stop it.

"Easy, Snow. Easy," Giggles said as he came up on her other side. "You're hyperventilating."

She turned her fury on him so fast it was like whiplash, her eyes sharp enough to carve through flesh. "You think I don't know that?" Her voice broke over the words. Too raw, too jagged. "You're stupid, too. All of you, get the fuck away from me. You're ruining everything."

Then she bent in half, her head almost to her knees, her hands digging into her own thighs like she could anchor herself back to reality.

No. No, no, no, fuck no

I waved them all away. "I'll get her home."

She turned toward me…or tried to. Her knees buckled beneath her, fingers clawing at her throat, as if something inside her was collapsing.

Her mouth opened, but no sound came out.

A flashfire of fear ripped through me. Something primal, something that tore through the obsession and possessiveness and burned me straight down to bone-deep agony.

She couldn't breathe.

She was drowning.

And all I could do was stand here and watch her fall.

I never felt this helpless in my entire fucking life. Her. Neva. My Neva. She was breaking apart, hurting, and I couldn't fucking fix it.

I should have been able to fix it.

The rage twisted and arrowed straight inside me, gutting me from the inside out. I was a monster. A self, obsessive, unhinged piece of shit. I'd been so tangled up in my madness, my need to claim her, to control her, that I hadn't even seen how close to breaking she really was.

I wanted to hold her.

I wanted to fall to my knees in front of her and beg her to let me fix this.

I wanted to burn the world down for making her feel like this.

But before I could move—before I could so much as reach for her—she moved first.

247

Fast.

She snapped upright, her spine locked in steel, her rage a hurricane rolling through her body. The dying light stole the color from them, but I knew those emerald eyes were a wildfire.

"You, too. Get out of here. I'm sick and tired of turning around to find you in my life all the time. I need to read the dossiers that came back. No one is getting anything from me until you're all fully vetted by the Collective." The words were ice cold, frozen knives against my skin.

The words ripped through me like a fucking bullet.

She wanted me gone.

No.

No.

She didn't mean that. She couldn't mean that.

Her breath still hitched. She wasn't thinking straight. Time. She just needed some time. That was it.

She stuffed a hand down into the black hole that was her bag. When she lifted her arm, she held an aerosol can in her fist, the cap off, and her finger flirting with the nozzle.

Neva.

My Neva.

Holding a weapon on me.

Her hand clenched around the can, her chest heaving as she leveled me with a look that could have incinerated flesh. "You think I won't? You arrogant, manipulative sons of bitches." Her voice was sharper than a scalpel.

Lethal.

Then…then her voice softened the barest degree. "Fucking try me."

Something inside me snapped. I backed away, hands up, lungs strangling for breath. She looked at me like I was her enemy.

For the first time since meeting her…

I was fucking terrified.

"Ms. de Witte?" Jorgenssen called from the door. "Are you in danger from your own men?" A thread of victory weaved through his tone. "Are they not your allies?"

"How I treat my ow—"

Squirrel moved in fast, knocking the canister from her grip before she could do something irreversible. His arms locked around her, his mouth crashing against hers—not for passion, but for silence.

Control.

When he pulled back, he flipped Jorgenssen off behind her back, his expression dark. He caught the back of her head and shoved her face into his chest. "Last freebie, Swede. Keep it up and I'll make sure your daughter finds her way into the US foster care system."

The familiar sound of a gun cocking filled the air. "Don't ever threaten her again."

"Don't threaten me or mine and I won't have a need," Squirrel bit back. "Turnabouts and all that shit." He caught Neva's ass in one hand, hoisted her up higher, and used his free hand to make a sign.

A single heartbeat of silence.

Then—click-click-click…a chorus of hammers cocking, six weapons trained and ready. the night went still, the whole fucking world holdings its breath.

"I don't travel alone. Ever," Squirrel added. "And if you get even a hint of an idea that my girl is defenseless, then you better pray I kill you before she does." From a couple feet away, I saw him wince, but he didn't change his hold on her, or the sign he kept on his hand.

Jorgenssen finally nodded, putting his gun away. "Then it seems we've reached another agreement. I won't tell you again. Leave. My team is waiting to clean up the mess in Ms. de Witte's room. If you want her to retain her employment here, then the situation needs to be cleansed. You are endangering your woman by fighting me."

"I'll never ignore a threat against her," Squirrel said. The honesty in his tone was a living thing. Neva might not know it, but she'd earned herself a lifelong ally. A brother.

My belly tightened. Which meant I couldn't kill him.

Damn it. Would nothing about today go the way it should?

"And I feel the same about my daughter." The Swede shoved his gun back in his pocket; the single light over his head turning his blond hair to silver.

"So we agree. We're heading out. Tell your team to give us five minutes," Squirrel bit off. Turning with Neva still in his arms, he shoved me forward. "Get going. I don't trust him not to do something else."

"I'm going to kill you for this, Squirrel," Neva muttered against his chest.

"Sure, pix. Whatever you say. As long as you're alive to threaten me, you can do and say whatever you want. But save it until we're away from that asshole."

We slid into the van at the curb. The rest of the guys shifted back, their guns still out as they protected our flanks. They finally relaxed when the door slid shut behind Squirrel's huge body.

Neva launched herself out of his arms and straight toward me.

Chapter 25
Neva

Leading with my double spear hands, I was millimeters away from taking out Rome when hard arms curled around my belly from behind. Squirrel's chuckle filled the small area of the van as we turned a hard corner. "Easy, pix."

"Don't you *easy* me, you overgrown dickwad."

Even knowing it was futile, I fought like a demon to get out of his grip. Some internal switch flipped and I needed to do bodily, lasting harm to Rome Fucking Whitlock. Since running into him at the club, he'd done nothing but fuck up all of my carefully laid plans.

And here he was doing it again.

Grunting against the restraints of Squirrel's big arms, I fought and wiggled, kicked and scratched. Nothing I did made a single iota of difference. The man might as well have been made of marble for all the reaction he had.

The breath backed up in my lungs as the pressure in my chest grew until I couldn't see, hear, or breathe anything but rage. Animalistic snarls and high-pitched screams erupted from my throat as I fought against another barrier I knew I would never get around.

My life was full of them. Too many of them. But I had to try, had to give it my best.

Something buzzed in my ear, annoying me. But I shoved it aside. Rome needed to learn he couldn't fuck with me and get away with it. None of them could. I wasn't to be trifled with, and had more than enough training, experience, and knowledge to get the outcomes I wanted. Without any of them.

I didn't need anyone. No one could be trusted, anyway. There was no one else to help me with this. Not for my final mission. No one could know what I really needed to do, what I needed to achieve.

Something buzzed in my ear again. And again, I ignored it. Just added it to the list of things I needed to put aside so I could focus on the long-term goal. Getting into Jorgenssen's good graces was just the first part of my plan.

"For the love of gods, woman, stop wiggling so damn much," a low whispered voice said into my ear. The deep sound buzzing through my head.

Squirrel. Squirrel was the thing buzzing in my ear. The giant, stupid, idiot fuckwit was trying to get me to calm down.

He lowered one of his arms and locked it over my hips, catching me against his torso with a single unbreakable band. In my rage, I must have missed the point when he captured my arms. Because both of mine were somehow caught under his other one and all three clamped against my chest.

I could feel the thundering of my heart in my chest and hear it pounding in my ears. My breath splintered in my throat. The world shrank—too dark, too tight, too much.

My lungs locked up, fingers twitching against the restraints.

No. Not again. Not like this. Not with them watching, dissecting my weakness.

The surge of pure freak out provided an instant of calm in my head. I had to get out of Squirrel's hold as soon as humanly possible. I forced my body to go still. Willed it into submission. Fought every single instinct and emotion until everything inside me went cold and distant.

The place where my killer lived. The place where nothing could hurt me, nothing could touch me, nothing could reach me. Pure ice and cold logic.

"Let me go, Markus," I said softly. Using his real name, I put some extra emphasis on my request. He needed to let me go.

Right now.

The van slid around another corner, then rocked to a halt. Everyone went quiet as I felt eight sets of hard gazes find me in the dark of the van's interior.

I waited with endless patience for the big man to release me. I could wait here forever. The Zen of cold, brutal will flowed through my body as I planned each and every one of their deaths. What I would do with the bodies, how I would break them down into parts. Mulch for my beloved plants. They would help me get to the next level with their decomposing flesh. It was truly the best way they could be of use.

When I lifted my lashes to plot my route through them, I saw Rome was inches away. His blue eyes burned with an odd light. But deep inside where it didn't matter, I merely logged the difference and moved on.

"Last chance, Markus. Don't make me hurt you," I said.

I even managed to smile for Rome. See? I could play nice and happy. Be the perfect little woman who just had a tiny freak out. Nothing to worry over. She was better. All better.

As if they were snakes slowly sliding away from me, I felt every inch of his sleeved arms drag along my front. I gulped back the bile that wanted to spew up my throat. Held back the screams by the thinnest margins.

But I was safe. Safe in the box where no one could hurt me. Hell, most people didn't even notice the box. I learned to make myself as small as possible for a reason.

When I was finally free of Squirrel's skin against my body, I jerked my elbow back in a straight, hard line. Catching his sternum under the point of my elbow, I heard a couple of his ribs shift in their joint attachments with soft pops.

He buckled forward as the breath whooshed out of his mouth, the wind kicking my hair into dancing waves of dark brown. The chuckle he made through the pained exhale shifted the box I lived in by the slightest degree.

A miniscule part of me was glad I hadn't hurt him too badly.

A larger, more psychopathic, part reexamined the angle I delivered the hit for weaknesses. Unless the man had cement for rib heads, it should have disabled him, not just knocked the breath from his chest. I'd have to work on my rear attacks.

Hard hands caught my wrists and yanked me forward. Crashing into Rome's chest, the light in his blue eyes shifted from something I didn't have a name for into pure, unadulterated fury. "Hit any of my men like that again, and I'll kill you myself."

I smiled at him placidly. "You're welcome to try."

Leaning forward, I pressed my lips to his in the softest graze of flesh on flesh. Pulling back, I licked my tongue over his lower lip. "But make sure you get me the first time. Because I'll kill all of you slowly and you won't understand the agony that melts through you while you beg for death."

"Why are you talking in that creepy ass voice, Snow?" Dopey asked from my left. "You're fucking weird and scary as hell when you don't sound like that. We're all fully aware of your skills. No need to paint an even creepier picture for us all."

Turning my head slowly, I smiled at him. He really wasn't as stupid as I called him. Maybe not quite as bright as the others, but every group had to have a weak link somewhere. Too bad he had to be theirs.

"And stop smiling at me like that." He jerked back, rubbed his hands up and down his arms. As he fell back against the seat, muttering to himself, he might have crossed himself then kissed his thumb.

Rome caught my chin, grip just shy of bruising. "Why the fuck did you say Squirrel was your man?" His voice was too even, too controlled—like he was holding something back with bloody fingers.

The moment in the school hallway ran through my mind again. Between the angles of where we were all positioned, it made the most logical sense for a believable story.

"When Jorgenssen came out of my room, I had a direct line of sight to the fourth and fifth windows. That means you weren't in his eyeline. With Squirrel already close—not to mention bending down to randomly sniff me—it was more expedient to agree when Jorgenssen voiced the remark. Why would any man let some other man that close to his woman?" I shook my head.

"It wouldn't make sense, and in clandestine work, keeping lies to a minimum is the way to go. One lie to solve the proximity, unknown male, and unexpected appearance issues all at the same time."

Rome shook his head. "I don't fucking care what kind of issues it creates, you're setting Jorgenssen straight when he comes to Subterra tomorrow."

Blinking up at him as another wave of cold slid through my veins, I smiled. Maybe I needed to examine the possibilities of living in my killer box for the duration of my time with these men.

"No. I'm really not. You created the situation by showing up when you shouldn't have been anywhere near my school. Then you made it worse when you bypassed the locks on the back door and let yourselves in. And then further compounded the issues when you got belligerent with him. Had you kept your fucking mouth shut, you could have been another guy on the outside to help us. Now you'll have a front-row seat to your own sins playing out."

Something shifted once again in his blue eyes; but this time, the coldly logical side of my brain caught it. Possession. This man thought he owned me. That his stupid rule of no one else getting to touch me or talk to me or anything else without his permission was anything but a fantasy in his own head.

The frigid bitch inside me grinned widely. Game on, motherfucker.

Leaning back against Squirrel's big body, I smiled at Rome, raising a single brow. Leaning my head forward the slightest degree, I whispered, "Welcome to the show, Prince Charming."

Instead of getting angry, he smiled back. More teeth than humor, it raised shivers down my spine. "Bring it on, dewdrop. Nothing you do will come close to breaking my control."

The men around us all groaned, long and loud. Then the sliding door smashed open, and a rush of cool air slid over my naked arms. I shivered from something other than Rome Whitlock. Shaking myself clear, I climbed out of my internal killer's box and stretched my metaphorical limbs.

Shifting against the big guy I still leaned against, I tipped my head back and said, "Don't ever lock me down again. Do you understand me?"

He studied me with brown eyes from inches away. Whatever went through his mind had his brows furrowing, but they eventually cleared. "Got it, pix."

I nodded. Shifting up and away from his body, I got to my feet and shuffled by him. Blinking when I saw the service entrance to my home, I ground my teeth to keep from laying into all of them again.

It wouldn't help.

I was beginning to realize this group of men did exactly what they wanted, when they wanted, how they wanted. My threats were nothing but dust motes in a shaft of light of an abandoned room.

Stepping down onto the sidewalk, I turned back to them as I grabbed my purse from the floor of the van. Unwilling to look at Rome, I locked my gaze on Squirrel. "Thanks for the assist today, lover. I'll be seeing you tomorrow night."

"The hell he's your lover," Rome bit out.

Squirrel, fully facing me, bounced his brows up and down. "Oh, baby, I can't wait to feel you in my arms again." He rocked his hips back and forth as Rome punched him in the shoulder.

"Not happening, you dipshit. She's mine. You're not touching her."

Squirrel laughed. "You heard the lady, bossman. This is your own doing. I can't deny a lady in need. And certainly not Pix here. She's my woman, now." He blew me a kiss, grabbed the door, and slammed it shut on Rome's bellow.

Snorting softly, I hefted my purse higher on my shoulder and let myself into my home. My sanctuary. My oasis.

Trekking to the front door, I double checked the lock after I set my stuff down on the entryway table. When everything was where and how it should be, I made my way to the kitchen. After all the shenanigans of the day, I just wanted some wine, cheese, grapes, and to fall asleep early.

Putting together my personal charcuterie board, I shuffled up the back stairs with it. As I passed into my bedroom, my gaze immediately landed on the toy and pillows I abandoned earlier today. My mood plummeted another notch.

That fucker. I was seriously going to maim him. Not quite enough to kill him, but close enough he would finally understand that I wasn't some idiot female who couldn't take care of herself. I'd been doing just that since my mom had died. I certainly didn't need him to come in and try to fix things for me. Especially because he only seemed to screw it up.

Getting my bed put back to rights, I created my little nest for the evening. *House Hunters* popped up on my now descended television and I settled in for my nightly ritual. Just as I finished off the last of the wine, my phone buzzed in my bra where apparently I'd forgotten it after getting my dinner ready.

Pulling it from the depths, I winced as I caught the number scrolling across the screen.

Crap.

I should have known this was coming. The fact I felt unprepared was no one's fault but my own. My op lead was dead, and I sat here blithely unencumbered by that knowledge.

Clicking off the TV and sending it back up into the ceiling, I cleared my throat and opened the call. "This is Aniera de Witte."

"Can the shit, Lark. What the hell happened to Higginsworth? I'm getting reports that he's dead." The man on the other end of the line went quiet. "You didn't take him out, did you?"

I snorted. "No. And I'm insulted that you even had to ask."

The man laughed softly. "Yeah, you would have done a better job of keeping it covered up than this." He blew out a breath, momentarily filling the line with a gust of noise. "Then tell me what did happen."

I gave him the brief, high-level overview, minus the parts about Jorgenssen demanding to meet me at Subterra. I would have to find a way to slide that detail in, though, just so their trackers wouldn't keep flagging me when I started showing up too often.

My handler heaved a huge sigh. "That stupid fucker."

I could almost see the guy rubbing a hand up and down his face before he pinched the bridge of his nose. Salt and pepper hair matched his salty brows, furrowed low over his brown eyes. "But you're in with Jorgenssen. And without the interference of the Feds."

I smiled. One thing my boss didn't like…sharing me with another agency. The fact I would essentially be going this alone moving forward would be a boon. For both of us.

"Yeah. I'll be passing all updates to you. You can choose to disseminate it however you'd like."

"From the last report you sent me this morning, I knew it was only a matter of time before he fucked up. I didn't think it would be quite this bad, but the man did make his bed."

257

"And he's definitely lying in it," I finished. It was a common adage from my superior. Let him sleep a little easier at night. Not quite absolution, but certainly a distancing measure from the day-to-day horrors that we saw regularly.

"You're still good to stay under at the school?"

I nodded, answered, "Yeah. I mentioned that my working there was my calling. So it would be extremely suspicious to Jorgenssen if I just dropped it all of a sudden."

"Good. You'll still be under surveillance with the Feeb team, but I'm not worried about you blowing anything. Especially now that you don't have to worry about Mr. Worthless himself."

I snickered at the nickname we'd been using for Brantley since getting onto this op. He really didn't have too many fans outside of his direct influence circles. Mostly, the intelligence communities hated him.

Smiling at the idea that I would have a lot more freedom moving forward, I asked, "Do you want our normal update schedule? Or keep to the op norm?"

He was silent for a long minute. "Let's go back to our normal. I have no doubts you could do this job in your sleep, and I have zero issues giving you the reins to get what you need to get this done. Do you need anything else from me?"

Everything inside me relaxed at the vote of confidence. I'd worked damn hard to have an excellent relationship with this man, and it was confirmation to know that even Brantley hadn't been able to damage it.

"Not right now. Once I get the information back from Jorgenssen on Ada's genetic assays, you should be able to track down the lab and get samples for our own verification and sampling."

DNA-targeting biowarfare. The world we lived in was a truly terrible place. But if it meant getting men like Oskar Jorgenssen off the face of the earth, I would gladly stuff my morals to make this world a better place for the other ninety-nine percent of humanity.

"Knew I could count on you, Lark." He got quiet for another long moment. "You're still sure this is your last job?"

I smiled faintly into the phone. "Definitely. Every substance has a shelf life. We're reaching the end of mine."

He said nothing else, just grunted, and then hung up. His typical goodbye. The man was nothing if not grizzled and grumpy.

The fact I would essentially be putting his career on the shelf with my retirement didn't bother me as much as it used to. In the grand scheme of things, he would find someone else better, faster, younger, and smarter than me to take my place. I just hoped whoever it was knew what they would be getting with him.

Putting the phone down on my nightstand, I took the time to plug it in and double check my alarms set for tomorrow. With a quick glance at the time, I nodded and got out of my nest for the evening. I needed to go retrieve those dossiers about the guys.

Even knowing they would probably come back as squeaky clean, I was more than a little interested to learn more about them. Individually and as a group. When you had that many Type As in a group, it made for some fascinating dynamics.

Down in the lab, I went through the routine to log into the dark web. There, sitting neatly in my inbox, was a file and an invoice. Once I got the invoice paid, a code was emailed to me to open the other file.

Emailing the file from my dark web inbox to my personal one for junk, I got all the guys' information loaded onto my tablet. Backing out of the dark web, I closed down the computer and walked for the huge steel door.

Stopping just inside the threshold, I turned. Something was making my brain itchy, and its awareness just dawned on me. With careful eyes, I examined every inch of my familiar workspace. Since I was more of a neat freak than a slob, I knew immediately what had changed.

Instead of the two boxes holding the poisons standing open, parts of the sides ripped off each one, the flanges pointing to the sky like I'd left them, they now sat in tidy, closed squares. The hairs on my neck and arms stood up as chills raced down my spine. Someone had been in my lab. My locked secret lab.

Running over various possible scenarios, I immediately discarded the idea that one of the guys came back. Even if they had, my alarms would have gone off. And to add to that, they wouldn't have touched the boxes. Ever. Especially since I was supposed to be taking them with me to the club tomorrow night, anyway. It wouldn't make any sense.

Which meant…someone else had been in my home.

A cold rippled spread through my chest, something ancient and primal. Wrong. My heartbeat stuttered, then slammed back into a rhythm too fast and too loud.

No.

I forced my fingers to still, exhaled a slow steady stream of air.

Fury burned through the creeping panic, scorching it into something I could use. Backing out of the lab, I didn't pull the door shut. Cursing myself for leaving my phone up on my nightstand's charger, I hurried to unlock the tablet in my hands. With a quick swipe through screens, and a final stab with my finger, I had a Wi-Fi call flinging itself through the cyber ether to that group of monsters.

The call connected. "Ms. de Witte."

My throat closed down around the sharp comment I had poised on the tip of my tongue. I had no idea who answered. It certainly wasn't one of the guys. "Who is this?" I couldn't even tell if the speaker was male or female.

A low, husky chuckle came down the line. "If you would like to live through the next ten minutes, I suggest you keep silly questions like that to a minimum. Follow the directions on your screen. If you deviate, call for help, or in any way draw extra attention to yourself, the bombs we have rigged around your home will go off."

The line clicked closed.

Then the tablet buzzed in my hands with a notification.

Chapter 26

Rome

Squirrel heaved a sigh as he posted up in front of me once more. Back in the garage at Locke, everyone poured from the van, trying to escape my explosive temper. Everyone except Squirrel. He pushed into my space, the smirk on his face drawing even more of my ire.

"I'm going, Keys. You heard her. Are you really going to endanger her life, and ours, just for a claim?" He yanked himself back, out of the reach of my swing.

My breath heaved through my chest. "Touch her and I will kill you." I scanned his body for weaknesses. But we'd all trained together for too long, and too hard for either of us to get a real advantage. We were too evenly matched.

He shook his head, danced back. Not once did he let loose an offensive move, only defensive to keep me from breaking something vital on him. That pissed me off even more.

"You might as well wear yourself out here, bossman. I have a feeling that fucking Swede is going to demand a show. And if you can't keep your shit together, then you might as well kill all of us right now." He lowered his hands, stared at me, truth blazing in his eyes.

I pulled my swing at the last moment, knowing he was right.

It didn't make it any easier, but I knew he was right. The van's side panel buckled under my fist, metal groaning, my knuckles splitting wide. I barely registered the pain…just the raw, empty silence that followed. The kind of silence that comes when you've broken something, but it still isn't fucking enough.

It never would be.

My own body was a fucking cage. Too much rage, nowhere to put it.

But I had to lock it down. For now.

A long time later, I slumped against the side of the van. Sweat ran down my temples, slicked my shirt to my back, my blood smeared in streaks, spatters, and spots over the shiny black metal in front of me.

When I took a deep breath, I finally felt like I could see straight. See more than just all the shit that had invaded our lives that fateful night five years ago.

My throat ached, my knuckles throbbed, but I could take a full breath. Seems it wasn't just my guys who had been running themselves ragged lately.

We finally had a situation and an enemy we could touch, fight. And in doing so, we would earn the trust and cooperation of Neva so we could finally take down the Sisterhood.

Hot breath creating soft plumes of humidity on the metal of the van, I rested my forehead on the cool surface. "I swear to all that's holy, if you fuck her, I'll cut your dick off and force feed it to you."

Choked chuckles sounded from behind me.

"You couldn't get me near her vag in a hazmat suit. No telling what she stores up there. Probably some kind of dick eating poison," Critter muttered.

Before I could turn to rip into the other man, the sound of flesh meeting flesh filled the room.

"Talk about her cunt like that again, and I'll rip *your* dick off and feed it to you," Squirrel answered. "Pix is a lady."

Turning, my body still slumped against the van, I saw Squirrel turn back to me as Critter smashed into a workbench a couple feet away. "I'll touch her as little as possible. It will be your job to keep that fucking Swede occupied." His face wrenched into tortured lines edged in disgust. "Besides, she really does remind me of my

Memaw. There's no way I want to fuck my Memaw, so Pix is safe from me."

In all our years together, I'd never heard Squirrel talk about his Memaw outside of saying he had one who he loved. The fact he not only revered her, but that Neva reminded him of her probably shouldn't have been a surprise. Squirrel had a lot of fucking layers to him.

I just wasn't sure I could trust this layer. Not with Neva.

"If it comes to playing the game and keeping everyone safe, you'll do it," Det ordered. "If Jorgenssen runs us, he'll know very quickly who we are and what we were. That spells trouble for Snow and us. Depending on how connected he his, he could take us all out with a single fucking phone call. So if he wants to watch you fuck her, then, buddy, you'll need to pop a blue demon. We aren't dying over this." He stabbed a sharp finger down toward the ground as he gave Squirrel a steady look.

The words landed like a fucking gut punch. My stomach curdled, bile biting the back of my throat. Letting anyone else touch her was already a nightmare—letting Jorgenssen dictate it?

That was a whole different level of hell.

Det held my gaze, unflinching. A silent challenge.

My jaw clenched so tight my teeth ached. But I swallowed the fury. Swallowed everything. Because he was right.

My fuck-up had put us here.

Pushing away from the van, I stood upright, pushed out a slow exhale. "You're right, Det."

All eyes swung to me, various expressions on each of my brothers' faces. But it was the surprise that gutted me. My obsession with her had gone too far, too fast and thrown me off course. That ended now.

"Iggy, we need a deep dive on Jorgenssen. Banshee, get your Twists talking. Schnauzer, you too. Anything and everything we can find on him, we need to know before going into the meeting tomorrow. If we're lucky, it will be just fucking." My belly burned saying the words, but they were nothing but truth.

We'd each done enough sketchy shit to meet mission objectives that watching Squirrel fuck Neva would be on the lesser end of the spectrum. By a very large margin.

I just had to get, and keep, my shit together.

And I promised myself right then and there I would wipe every other man from her mind once I finally got my hands on her. Even my brothers.

Especially my brothers.

When everyone's shoulders relaxed as they nodded, I finally understood just how crazy I'd gone. Since we were in the middle of the shit now, I might as well fess up. Opening my mouth to tattle on myself, I wasn't prepared for Iggy to go stiff.

"What?" My brows furrowed.

Iggy lifted his gaze and stared at me over the edge of it, his pale purple eyes glinting in the bright lights of the shop. "Someone was in her house earlier."

Gritting my teeth, I nodded. "Yeah. It was me." Licking my lips to spill my guts about everything, I braced myself for the backlash. "I went over there earlier today. Stabbed Dickfuck while we were standing in the street when he made references to eating her pus—"

"I'm not talking about you, Keys," Iggy cut me off. He turned his tablet and showed us the screen. "Five unsubs."

My stomach dropped. A slow, sinking cold spreading outward from my ribs. Five unsubs. Five.

And then—nothing.

The static filled the screen, an endless fucking void where her house should have been. My throat went tight.

I locked up when I left, I secured everything.

So why the fuck were there five men at her door?

And why was her security dead?

Reaching out, I stabbed at the small monitor. "Bring it up. What the fuck happened?"

Iggy turned the screen back around. "That's the end of footage. I was going back to make sure we weren't tracked and that no one followed us from the school. Her security went down about an hour before we rolled up with her."

"Get it back online," I demanded.

He shook his head. "We're locked out." Curling the tablet in his hand, he turned and ran. "We're locked out of her secondary system as well. Someone else took control of it."

Racing after him, I heard the rest of the guys follow in our footsteps. I crashed around a corner and aimed for the tech suite where our private conference room was.

"Someone get me a fucking phone." I made a mental note to replace the one Neva broke under her shoe at the school.

"Already on it, Keys. She's not answering," Squirrel said as he moved into the room behind me. "Ringing through to voicemail."

"Why do you have her number?" I glared at him as I took my regular seat.

"I gave it to all of them in case she had an emergency. It's not important right now," Iggy spit out. "Lights, fifty percent." The room darkened around us as he spit out more commands, his fingers dancing like wildfire over the keys. The picture in the middle of the table continued to show nothing but static.

"Anything?" I slammed my fist on the table. What the fuck was going on?

"Nothing." Iggy swiped through screens and brought up new ones faster than I could track. "Her entire system is down, but it's logging as still connected and active."

"Where's her phone? Ping it," Squirrel shot out. The casing of his phone made groaning noises as he held his device to his ear. "I'm still calling. Do you get a ping from it?"

He lowered the cell, slapped it on the table. Stabbing the button to put it on speaker, he sat back. His fingers wrenching together as he glared down at it.

When the call went to voicemail, he reached out and called her again. "Come on, pix. Pick up."

The line rang. And rang. Then clicked to voicemail.

Squirrel's face twisted a muscle jumping in his jaw. He stabbed redial. "Pick up for me. Come on, baby girl. Pick up for Squirrel."

Seeing the ghosts in his eyes and hearing the emotion in his voice, I knew he saw her as some kind of family. Maybe his Memaw, maybe a sister. Either way, I had to be glad it was him and not anyone else who got caught by Jorgenssen today.

"Phone is showing it's in her house," Iggy answered. He looked up at me. "Did you do anything else today when you logged in? Change permissions, settings? Anything?"

I shook my head. Other than watching her masturbate, I'd touched nothing on the system itself. "No, nothing."

Then another thought triggered in my head. "That's when I got the email."

All of the breath rushed out of my chest as I thought back to this morning. Trying to remember the order of events from earlier, I pushed through the fear into that still, focused part of my mind. "Could they have gotten into the system through mine?"

Iggy snarled low in his throat as he switched to a different computer system. "Not likely, but I'll double check."

Waiting in tense silence for him to absolve me of my stupidity, I tried to think of any other factors that could be at play. There was no way for us to have a full picture of whatever she was doing simply because we'd been introduced less than two days ago. It felt like years, but I had to remind myself that it was so little time.

"Any other leads from the crazy woman and Lawrence's breach?" Schnauzer asked. "You said they came back clean, but that was at first glance. Did you have them running anything in the background?"

Iggy shook his head. "No. And, Keys, your system was untouched from the email they sent."

I blew out a breath of relief, but it didn't last long. We were still in the dark about what was going on. "We've got to go back over there."

Squirrel got to his feet, grabbed up his phone. "I'll go on my bike. Draw less attention. Especially since every time we've been there, we've gone in the van." Without waiting for anyone to say anything, the big guy ran from the room.

"Squirrel, wait!" I ran after him. "We'll take the Rover."

"You know I can't fit in that shit. I'm taking the bike. I'll meet you there."

The sound of his voice disappeared from the shop, and moments later, the rumbling bark of his Harley filled the air. One of the side doors for personal vehicles opened. The Harley's engine revved and then faded into the night.

Rushing behind him, I sprinted for the Rover. Gigs clipped into the passenger seat, one of his med bags on his lap. "Let's go get your girl, Keys."

I smashed my finger into the ignition button and gunned the engine. Without another word, we were rocketing back through the streets of Brooklyn on our way to Neva's house. It felt like the route was etched in my brain by this point. Even taking secondary and tertiary streets, I had us to her door in record time.

Gigs pulled his phone from his pocket. "Yeah, Squirrel. We're just about to pull up. Where are you?"

Too late, I realized we rushed off without grabbing any of our regular comm units. We were stuck using civilian methods. Damn it. This woman did my head in. I really needed to get a handle on that.

"Give us two minutes. We're right behind you." Gigs stored his phone, hooked the bag's strap over his head, and pulled one of his pistols from his inside-the-pants holster. "He's taking the service entrance. He'll go if we're not there in sixty. He won't wait the extra minute."

Trying to look like we weren't in a hurry, but still moving quickly, we wasted precious seconds, but we made it to the door right as Squirrel breached the entrance. Lining up behind him, I caught his shoulder just as he was about to charge through the opening.

He stilled and waited for me to move in front of him, then took up second position. He had his gun out and ready to go. "If she's in here, and not hurt, we're all going to die," he breathed.

I bit back a snort. I'd fucking love for this to be a fool's errand, at this point. That spot in my gut told me it was anything but. "I'll be her sacrifice."

His hand on my left shoulder gave a squeeze and we entered the small landing that shot off in three directions. To the right held the kitchen, the left was the way to the living room, and straight forward to her lab.

Ice filled my veins when I spotted light leaking around the seams of the lab's door. That fucker was at least six inches thick of solid steel. No way was any light filtering through the cracks if it had been closed and sealed correctly.

Lifting my free hand, I told the guys using sign language that we were going front first. Another squeeze on my left shoulder and I started forward. Dread filled every inch of space inside me the closer we got.

Lifting my weapon, I saw a shadow move just as I was about to push the door open wider. I stilled all of our movements. Waiting to see what horrors waited for us on the other side of the huge barrier, I strained my ears to hear any whisper of sound.

"I'm gonna kill him. Kill all of them. Each and every one, dead. Slowly. Horribly. Painfully." The door eased open, and Neva stood there, glaring down at something in her hands.

The door eased open, spilling soft light into the hallway. Neva stood there, utterly still. Not tense. Not ready to fight.

Still.

Like something coiled too tight. A thing holding its breath before it strikes.

Her fingers curled around the tablet, so tight the plastic casing groaned. Slowly—so fucking slowly—she turned it toward me. I barely registered the image before her voice sliced through the quiet.

"If I find out who put bombs around my house, I'll kill them, too." She gave me serious eyes as she tapped her ear and then pointed to the tablet.

Fuck. My body jolted at the idea of the intruders leaving bombs in her house.

"I'm going to kill everyone." She kept her voice the same tone, the same inflection, the same volume. It sounded more like she was talking to herself, but I had to guess she was trying to tell me something but not addressing me specifically.

She stopped directly in front of me, pressed her body against mine, lifted her chin.

When I lowered my head, the feel of her lips grazing my ear sent shivers down my spine.

"I have to follow the directions on the tablet. If I don't, they'll blow the house." She stepped back, eyebrows raised as if to ask if I understood.

I nodded. Snaking out an arm, I curled it around her to bring her back to me. When she lifted her head again, it was my turn to whisper in her ear. "Can they hear us?"

She shrugged, her dark hair dancing over my gaze. "Stupid fuckers think they can get to me. Who the hell do they think they are?" Her voice was lower than a whisper. Shaking off my hold, she moved by me down the hall. When she moved to take the turn into the kitchen, I motioned for the guys to follow her.

In a single, silent line, we walked through the large kitchen and through a small entrance that was disguised as a pantry wall. Neva had a secret stairwell. And it certainly hadn't been on the updated plans Iggy pulled.

When we all stood in that narrow passage, Neva shoved the tablet at Gigs. "Do you have a phone?" She made gimme hands and demanded it from him. "We can talk freely in here. It's lined in lead, has an RF cage, no cameras, or anything else."

"What the hell is going on, Snow?" Squirrel demanded. His shoulders brushed each side of the stairwell, but he managed to pull her into his arms. He shoved his face into the space between her neck and shoulder. I could hear him muttering, but couldn't make out the words.

She let out a little bleat of sound as she fought to keep a grip on Gigs's phone. Shock widened her features before she closed it down again. "I'm fine. Just pissed off. How did you know to come here?" Her gaze found me in the bright, industrial lights. Then she narrowed her eyes. "You're watching me here, too?"

For all of twenty seconds I was glad Squirrel was holding her. She'd maim all of us if she attacked in the small space.

But she waved it away. "Shut up, and don't make a single fucking peep." She eased back, still in Squirrel's arms, Gigs's phone up in front of her face. Then blew out a frustrated breath. "Shit. No signal at all." Thrusting herself from Squirrel's arms, she landed on her toes before rushing for the far wall, slapped her hand against a panel.

After a second, a red light engulfed the plate and slid up and down her hand twice. "Print accepted."

A low pop sounded just as another section of the wall snicked open. She stuck her hand in, and pulled out an old handset for what looked like a rotary phone. Her arm moved back and forth, back and forth. The faintest ring filled the space. After two rings, she hung up. Then she picked up the handset and did it all again. Three times. On the last ring, she allowed the call to go all the way through.

"Jimmy's Pizzeria, where we rub your dough real good. What can I get ya?"

My stomach clenched. She wasn't ordering pizza. She was sending up a flare.

"This is Larkspur Kendrick. I'd like to place an order. Four large pizzas. Extra boom sauce."

The guy heaved a huge sigh. "What's the address?"

She rattled it off. "I'll pay extra for quick delivery."

"Sure, honey. We'll see what we can do for you." The line disconnected.

Turning, Neva gave the phone back to Gigs as she slid by him. "Get to the roof. We're getting a ride."

Chapter 27

Neva

Tapping not so gentle hands to Squirrel's arms for him to let me pass, I waited a couple seconds for him to register something other than the terror running through his large body.

I hadn't quite caught all the words he muttered into my shoulder, but a few of them led me to believe this man saw me as something more than just a random woman to protect.

Never had anyone called me baby and made it feel more platonically loving than even my grandparents. Squirrel somehow managed it.

Squirrel's face twisted, the ghost of something deep and painful flashing behind his eyes. Not something small, not a fresh wound—but old. Worn raw by time, scarred over wrong.

His hands twitched, like he wanted to reach for me, maybe to hold onto something solid. Instead, he forced a smile…empty of all the warmth I'd come to expect from him.

I hated it. I hated that I recognized it. I hated that I knew exactly what it meant to shove something that big and dark into a corner of yourself and try to pretend it wasn't eating you alive.

I almost said something.

But then his mask snapped into place, and he beat me to it. "Take me to your roof, pix. Let me watch the stars with you." He jutted his chin for me to direct us.

Nodding, I gave him a smile. I knew too well the scars of soul-deep hurting to try to pick at the scabs of this giant's.

I turned and almost ran face first into Rome's stupid manly chest. This man felt like a freaking magnet and my nose a shard of iron. I was getting fucking sick of it. Glaring up at him, I said, "Get out of the way." I shoved by him and climbed the rest of the stairs to the second floor and my bedroom.

"You guys stay here. I'm going to take the tablet into my bedroom and let the next message come through. While I'm in there, I'll grab my phone, too." I finished speaking right as we stopped at the hidden door.

Rome grabbed my arm before I could move. "You're not going in there. What if they're tracking the tablet?"

I smiled, shook off his hold. "I'm planning on it. It will confuse them when the signal dropped and then picks back up in a different spot since I only have Wi-Fi on this device. Let them know I have resources they don't know about. Keeps them guessing." Pushing open the door to my bedroom, I held my hand out for the tablet from Happy.

"Careful, Snow. If your remark about bombs was true, you have neighbors attached to this house. It wouldn't be just us and you getting hurt." He held the tablet out of reach until I met his gaze.

I nodded. "Believe it or not, this isn't the first time someone has tried to pull shit like this with me. I know what I'm doing. In case you've managed to forget, I've been in this field for two decades."

I saved the eye roll for when they couldn't see my expression. Did they all think I was completely incompetent? Stupid?

For fuck's sake.

The tablet buzzed in my hands as three new messages popped up. Each angrier than the last.

When the fourth one slid onto my screen, I opened it and smiled. "Oh, please. Pull your heads out of your asses. I'm going to do what you want, but I'll be doing it my way.

And since you didn't kill me outright, I'm guessing you need me alive. So stuff the 'me boss, you servant' bullshit."

I had no idea if they could hear me, but I figured it was better to assume they could. Especially since they knew I made a call through Wi-Fi. Which reminded me. Glancing up to my ceiling, I glared at the camera I installed over the window. I flipped them off for good measure.

Lowering my gaze back to the tablet, I opened the security system app and shut the whole thing down. I also disabled my Wi-Fi and internet router on this floor. Let them stew in their own ignorance.

Rushing around the bed, I grabbed my phone. Going through the process to put it in airplane mode, I stuffed it back into my bra. I went into my closet and dug out a pair of running shoes. Once I had those shoved onto my feet, I dashed back into the service entrance. "Come on out, I've shut down the internet. No way for them to reach me anymore."

Rome stood just inside the door, his shoulder leaning against the closet door that kept all my sex toys out of sight. "What about the cameras? Especially the one above your bed?"

My brows furrowed. "I don't have one above my bed. Only over the window." Then the full realization of what he was saying dawned on me. "You watched me in bed?" My cheeks blazed red as I fought through the rage and embarrassment.

He nodded. "I didn't plan on it. And of course there's one over your bed. You installed it."

Swallowing against the guttural screams that burned my throat, I shook my head. Kept shaking it when I couldn't promise myself the ability to speak in normal tones.

That's why he was here this morning. Why he ended up on my doorstep so early. He'd been watching me. Creepily stalking me in my own home. At fucking school.

This morning ran through my head again. The fantasy, the toys, the way I'd touched myself. The words I'd said.

"I'm going to kill you."

Rome's face twisted, his jaw working like he was chewing on barbed wire. "I—" He stopped, blew out a breath, then squared his shoulders like he could logic his way out of this.

"I was trying to keep you safe." His voice was low, steady, measured—a careful construction of justification.

273

"You know you need someone watching your back. Someone who could be there before shit hit the fan?"

My nails dug into my palms. "You mean someone who could watch me get myself off in my own fucking bed without my knowledge?"

His throat bobbed. The flicker of something—not quite guilt, not quite shame—shadowed his face.

"That wasn't—"

"Wasn't what, Rome?" My voice turned sharper, lethal as one of my poison tipped blades. "Wasn't your intent? Wasn't something you enjoyed? Or wasn't something I was ever supposed to find out about?"

His silence damned him.

His face...Even more so.

"As soon as I get a free moment, I'm going to melt your dick off." Shoving by him, I stuck my head into the secret passage a little farther. "Come on. You two can follow me. Prince Charming here gets to die with the bombs."

I didn't look at him again as I backed up. He was already dead to me, no reason to entertain ghosts.

"You can't let him die with the bombs, pix. We need him." Squirrel eased forward slowly, careful not to rush into my space as he stepped out into my bedroom. "You need him."

I snorted. "An unwanted perverted voyeur? No. No woman needs that."

Squirrel turned and glared at his team leader. "You were watching her?"

Rome nodded, his burnished cheeks darkening. "I was trying to tell you guys that earlier when Iggy told us someone got into her house."

As if apologizing to his men made any difference whatsoever to what he'd done to me. More rage filled my body.

Happy stepped through. Without a single pause, he decked Rome so hard the crack of bone-on-bone rang through the space.

Rome hit the bed, head snapping to the side, hand cradling his jaw.

"You sick fucking bastard." Happy's voice was low and more psychotic than usual. "You watched her? And you think a fucking joke is gonna smooth it over?"

Rome sat up, but before he could get a word out, Squirrel stepped in.

His voice was cold. Deadly. "You didn't just fuck up, boss. You broke something. You don't come back from that."

I would have winced in sympathy, but I was still too fucking mad. At this point, I would have helped Happy and Squirrel beat the shit out of him. Served him right, getting smashed in the face by someone big enough to hurt him.

"I promise. I won't watch anything else unless she specifically asks me to." He gave me a hot look from his uncovered eye.

I shook my head, a slow deliberate motion. "This is your last warning, Rome."

He didn't move, didn't breathe. He just sat there, watching me.

I bared my teeth. "You think you've been obsessed with me? If you fuck with me again, I'll show you what real obsession looks like. I'll make your life so small, so painful, that you'll beg me to end it."

I let the words hang between us, let him see the truth of them in my face.

Then I turned my back.

If he was smart, he'd stay the fuck down.

He'd learn. Or he wouldn't. But I'd already warned him of the consequences, so whatever happened from here on out was on him.

"We still need to get to the roof for the exfil team," I said.

Once Happy was out of the way of the secret door, I stepped back through and opened the sealed closet. Reaching in, I grabbed my two thumb drives and slammed it shut once more.

"Whatcha got in there, pix?" Squirrel asked.

"Sex toys," I answered. Shoving the thumb drives into the other side of my bra, I held the tablet in my hand. As long as I had the extra device, I could access any of my accounts, both legal and gray.

"Let's go." Walking out of the main door of my bedroom, I moved to the stairwell that zigzagged up the northern wall of my family home. I really hoped it didn't get blown up, but even if it did, it was just a house. And if someone did destroy it, I'd have more to make them pay for later.

I smiled at the idea. By the time I got to the top floor and opened the door for roof access, I had the perfect formula already created in my mind. It would serve the monsters well to have their bodies be treated like they did my home.

Just as the door closed behind the last man, I heard the thump, thump, thump of an incoming helicopter's blades beating the air. My phone buzzed in my bra, drawing my attention.

How the hell had they gotten through airplane mode? Shoving the tablet at Squirrel, I pulled the device from its hiding spot.

No numbers scrolled over the screen, but I could tell someone was calling me by the button showing on the front. Swiping up over that little green circle, I didn't say anything as the line went live.

"We told you not to deviate from the plan."

I rolled my eyes. "Yeah, and I'm very scared of what you could do to me. Seriously, you should see me shaking right now." I pumped boredom into my tone as I examined my cuticles for the tiniest hangnails. Nope, not a single one in sight.

"Silly girl, you should have listened." The line went dead.

The helicopter moved into position directly over my roof. Just as a spotlight shone down on us, I felt the building tremble under my feet.

Holy monkshood, they really set bombs around my home.

Squirrel lifted me up in his arms, launching me toward the guy zipping down. "Take her!"

Another set of hard arms caught me, and I was held aloft in the sky as a wide, rough band immediately went over my head, my arms pulled up and through, phone and tablet still in my hands.

"Go! Go! Go!" the man holding me barked into his microphone.

"Wait for them!" I shouted, looking down to see the three men jump for the rope holding my savior.

"They're on, let's go." He held me tighter as the helicopter made a quick leap up and dragged us off into the night sky.

The phone buzzed in my hand as the guy holding me caught my legs to keep from creating more movement in the rope we all needed to stay alive. I brought it up to my ear. "What now?"

"You should have simply followed the directions, Ms. de Witte. It would have gone much smoother for you had you done as you were told."

I could barely hear the voice on the other end, but I heard enough to know whoever it was thought pretty highly of themselves. "Yeah, you'll learn this about me if you want to work together: I do what I want, when I want, how I want. Unless you make it worth my while to do otherwise, you won't get a whole lot from me."

"Had we known you were so well connected, we would have approached you differently. Consider us educated and ready for our next encounter. We don't make the same mistakes twice."

I snorted loudly. "Sure. That's what they all say. No one ever follows through."

"You can rest assured, Ms. de Witte, we always mean what we say." The line went dead.

Which was good, because I really needed both hands to get up from the harness and into the helicopter without scraping all the skin off my back. Once I was close enough, I tossed the phone up into the black hole of the helicopter's body.

The guy helping me grabbed the tablet from my free hand and told me how to spin and plant my feet so he could help me up with as little issue as possible. Once I got myself set up correctly, he pulled me in with a hard grip around the harness point. Setting me not quite gently out of the way, he helped the guys up into the belly of the whirly bird as well.

Those assholes didn't need to be told how to get up into the helicopter, though. Fuckers.

Scrambling for the tablet and phone, I made sure they were safe before I did anything else. And since those assholes who bombed my place could get through airplane mode, I switched it off. I would need to make some calls whenever we finally landed.

We each grabbed an open seat and buckled in. Well, minus, Squirrel. He pulled his firearm and sat bitch out the door, his gaze never still as he watched the city disappear below us.

Twenty minutes later, we touched down in an empty field and the guy running the government-funded escort service shooed us out. Moments later, he and the pilots took off again.

Waiting until the blade wash died down, I turned to take in our surroundings.

It wasn't awful. Not quite optimal, but not terrible either. Some kind of hobby airport, if the smaller hangers and single and double prop planes dotting the tarmac were any clue.

I powered on my phone. Before it could get all the way through its startup sequences, it rang again. I smiled as the numbers scrolled across the screen. "Yeah, boss. How's your night going?"

"What the fuck do you think you're doing?"

My smile widened at the grumpiness in his voice. "I'm out for a lovely stroll in the evening. What are you doing?"

"Don't give me that lone wolf shit, Larkspur. Why did an alert for your home just go up over the line?"

I rolled my eyes. "Someone decided they wanted a playdate without asking me first. But while we're on the subject, can you check satellites and tell me if the house is still standing where I left it?"

The loud silence through the line told me my glibness might not be appreciated at this point in time.

My smile died a slow death. All these men so uptight about keeping me safe. While I appreciated the gesture, they were going to smother me at some point. There was a reason I did better on my own.

"Spell it out, de Witte. Now."

I blinked a couple times when hearing my legend's name. This man lived and breathed covert ops. He never broke code. Which raised a couple of questions. "What's going on, sir?"

"One of my best agents almost gets toasted in a fucking bombing and she wants to know what's going on? I'll tell you what's going on, Lark. You've pissed on too many people to be able to stay under as deep as you wanted. Someone obviously knows who you are. Your cover is blown."

I reared back at the insult. The fuck it was. Brantley was the one who screwed everything up. I was out here trying to clean up the mess. "I'm still good. I can finish this."

He let loose a snarl of anger. "No. You can't. Someone just turned your personal house into rubble. I told you using it as part of your legend would lead someone to the real you. You have your fucking evidence. I'm bringing you in. Don't make me send someone to find you."

I laughed, right in his ear. "Sir, I hate to break it to you, but I'm not burned. I'm not caught, and I'm not screwed. What the hell is going on that you would use my name? Have *you* been compromised?"

The silence on the other end of the phone stretched out until it felt like it was about to snap me in two.

"Don't make me send a goon squad after you, Lark. Just come in and we can find some way to make all of this better." He hung up without saying anything else.

I pulled the phone from my ear, staring at the device in amazement. Something was very, very wrong. The quick bracing breeze of the autumn night sent shivers down my spine. Right up until it was blanketed in a wall of heat.

Without turning around, I knew immediately who it was. And I was done fucking with him.

Spinning in a low kick, I took out his ankles. Riding his body to the ground just like I had in the shop, I made a couple of important changes. Instead of landing on his pelvis like a princess, I straddled his knees.

My nails dug into hot flesh, sharp enough to break skin. Rome jerked under me, a hissed breath escaping between gritted teeth.

This close, I felt it—his muscles coiling, his hands twitching like he was about to grab me.

But he didn't. He couldn't.

His throat worked, his pupils blown wide. Not with arousal. Not even with anger.

With something dangerously close to fear.

"Neva—" His voice broke.

I leaned in, baring my teeth in a smile. "What's wrong, Prince Charming?" My fingers flexed, claws raking over the skin of his dick just enough to draw another hiss. "Not so fun when I'm the one in control, huh?"

I squeezed harder until I felt the give of his skin and the warm salve of his blood coat over my fingertips.

He winced, but didn't try to move me. "You're just gonna have to fix those up when you start feeling guilty."

I snorted. "I'm done feeling guilty about anything concerning you, Mr. Whitlock. You've abused my trust too many times, and my mother certainly didn't raise a fool. From now on, I don't care about any fucking claim you think you might have in that twisted psychopathic brain of yours. Touch me again, watch me again, or even think in my direction again without my express permission and I'll take your joystick as a prize."

"Uh, pix?" Squirrel asked from behind me.

"Yeah, honey. What's wrong?" I didn't look away from the man between my thighs.

Rome's eyelids fell low as he glared at me.

"I'm not one to shit on anyone's personal decorating tastes, but I'm not sure a dick and balls are going to really be something you want hanging on your wall or sitting on a shelf somewhere. Don't get me wrong, mine would look great. But Keys's there?" He huffed a sad laugh. "Just not majestic enough."

"Well, his will have to work. I'm not taking your majestic dick. I'm sure some woman or man would be happy to have it put to better use."

Squirrel chuckled, sounding more like his normal self. "Oh, definitely only women getting on to see Valhalla. Men might want, but they can't have."

"Good for you, sweetie." I squeezed Rome's dick tighter, felt the muscles of his legs bunch and relax between my legs. "You should listen to your friend on how to conduct yourself, Mr. Whitlock. Hell, at this point, you could probably stand to take some pointers from Dopey."

With his blood staining my fingertips, I pulled my hand from his underwear. Swiping my fingers clean on his shirt, I got back to my feet.

"Oh damn, boss. She got you on that one," Squirrel said in a low, taunting tone.

Rome stayed where he was, laying before me on the ground like some kind of too sexy sacrifice. The smears of blood over his shirt definitely lent an air of ritual to his offering.

Too bad he was too full of himself to ever be the offering for anything important.

Looking around the darkening airfield, I wished I'd brought a go bag. Blowing out a breath, I heaved a mental sigh. Oh, well. Guess this was going to be good practice for whatever other shit the universe wanted to sling my way. I knew it wasn't nearly done fucking with me yet.

I was still waiting on the dinner it owed me, too, damn it.

Sliding my hand to my pocket, a pretty big realization dawned on me. I might, or might not, have a home to go back to. I hadn't gotten a firm answer from my boss on that one. And with how he was acting, I wasn't going to be the one to open up communications with him again.

"Fuck."

"What's wrong, pix?" Squirrel asked.

Shaking my head, I just gave him a wry smile. "Just thinking about stupid mistakes."

"You already bloodied Keys's dick. What other mistakes are you thinking about?"

I laughed softly. "Yeah, that wasn't a mistake. At least not on my part. You're not mad at me?"

Squirrel moved around to stand in front of me, his handsome face peering down into mine. He waited for my gaze to reach his before he shook his head. "No. That was definitely his stupid mistake. If he really watched you on a camera in your own home, in your own bed, then he deserves whatever you want to dish out to him. Unless you asked him to be your watcher." He raised his eyebrows.

I shook my head, snorted. "Definitely not. I didn't even know I had a camera over my bed." Which reminded me. Taking a few steps back towards the bastard, I asked, "How did you realize I have one there?"

I bit back a laugh at the scene before me: the traitor with his pants down around his knees, his buddy trying to wipe the blood away from the wounds I'd inflicted. They looked like they were acting out some kind of gay medical fantasy in public. Although, I wasn't sure an empty hobby airfield qualified as public.

Then again, I wasn't really up on my public fantasy requirements list.

"Are your fingernails actually claws, Snow?" Happy asked. I couldn't tell from his tone if he was unhappy. Maybe impressed?

I shrugged. "Just regular fingernails. I simply happen to take good care of them." Splaying out my fingers, I saw they were a little crusty around the edges at the moment. But they were pretty good weapons. Especially when I laced them with serums. Rome just better be thankful I hadn't dressed to impress tonight.

"Answer the question, Mr. Whitlock. How did you know I had a camera over my bed?"

He hissed out a curse as his medic did something to his happy handle. "How the fuck do you think I did?" A barking howl of pain sprang from the wounded man on the ground. "Fuck's sake, Gigs. Easy."

"You're going to want to be extremely nice to her while I'm working on making sure you don't get an infection in your dick, Keys." There was no disguising the living anger in Happy's tone this time. "She asked you a polite question after you abused her trust. You answer like the fucking gentleman you should have been, or I'll help her cut this off and put it on her shelf."

Chapter 28

Rome

Gritting my teeth at the stinging pain in my dick, I bit back the rest of the words crowding my mouth. It *was* my fault. She hadn't asked and I shouldn't have done it.

I clawed my fingers into the hard ground when Gigs drenched me with another round of alcohol.

I didn't work too hard to understand what he complained about under his breath, sure I wouldn't come out of any estimation with my character still intact. Hissing out around another stab of pain, I squinted at the sky above us as the final lights of the evening sky melted into the stars. Being this far out from the light pollution of the city meant we could actually see the twinkling orbs.

It was almost pretty.

Fire streaked through my pelvis as Gigs dug into my skin like he was cleaning the damn crime scene of my dignity. If I hadn't already committed to the fetal position, I would have curled tighter, locked my legs together like a fucking chastity belt.

Fucking hell, my little dewdrop was savage. My dick would be writing a victim impact statement after this.

When Gigs dug into my skin a little more brutally than usual, I yanked my gaze to find him staring at me with expectation sitting on his face. "Answer the lady, Keys."

Oh right. I'd gotten sidetracked by pain.

Licking my lips, I answered her. Essentially giving her a play-by-play of what we accomplished and planned to set in place, I waited for whatever other wicked punishments she could conjure up and deliver.

When nothing but silence and birds chirping met my ears, I lifted up to my elbows to see her cuddled in Squirrel's arms.

The sight of her in Squirrel's arms punched through me like a fucking bullet. It started small—a tick at the back of my skull, a coil in my gut, the ghost of a snarl curling my lips. Then it spread, twisting through my ribs like barbed wire, flooding my veins like venom.

I couldn't breathe around it.

She was there. With him.

Not me.

I bit down on the words crawling up my throat. Didn't matter. She was mine. Whether she wanted to be or not. Even if I had to carve my name into her fucking soul to make her remember it.

When the extra sensation washed up my dick and into the pit of my belly, I wished for a single instant to be a eunuch.

That thought quickly passed though.

"Get your hands off her, Squirrel."

Squirrel's muscles bounced in the faint light of dusk as he laughed. "She keeps saying it, and I think I finally believe her."

Like a bull released from the gate, she launched herself from Squirrel's restraining grip, knocked Gigs out of the way, and landed on top of me.

With a knee to my balls, she relocated them up in my abdominal cavity. Before I could do more than blink, she stabbed me in the solar plexus with her dagger fingernails and I felt another section of my skin give way beneath the blades.

"FUCK!" I grabbed her wrists in one of my hands. "Don't make me hurt you, dewdrop."

She chuckled softly, and had my balls not already been up inside my body, they would have run for cover at the sound. She bent down, easing my grip on her by getting closer, and licked her tongue up the side of my neck. "You're welcome to try, Mr. Whitlock."

Exploding her hands up through my hold, she clocked me in the chin. My supporting arm gave out and I crashed back into the cold, hard ground head first. Blinking away the bright sparkles in my vision, I brought my hands up to guard my face.

She was fucking untouchable. A hurricane, a fucking force of nature. I got in *one* breath before she was on me again, fingers in my hair, driving me head into the dirt like she was planting a crop.

I tried to roll, to move, to evade, but she was faster—always faster, her knee pinning my throat, nails into my ribs like she was about to crack me open and inspect the damage.

I'd been so fucking wrong about her. About everything.

She wasn't mine. Never had been. The only the that belonged to me in this moment was my own fucking grave.

I curled up into the fetal position as I tried to hold up under her attack.

Honestly, I deserved it. And at this point in time, I couldn't tell if I allowed her to beat me to shit because I was being nice or because I couldn't get a hit in without taking ten times more damage.

Just as I was about to find out, the blows stopped. Just a slight panting danced in the breeze; or it could have been my heart thumping in my ears. Either way, the shock of no more blows to my body had me lifting my head from the relative safety of my arms.

The toe of a shoe drilling right for my face was my reward.

"Not again, pix. We don't want to carry him," Squirrel said quickly.

She heaved a sigh and pulled her second blow, clipping me in the shoulder. "Thank your man, Mr. Whitlock." She spun on her heel and stalked away.

Had the moon not been full, I wouldn't have been able to see her walk off, but the soft lighting made her ass look delicious in those sleep pants. Thankfully, my lips were too swollen and my mouth too bloody to make me an idiot again by saying anything.

A bright light killed my night vision and blinded me at the same time. "You might want to learn your lesson, Keys. She's not playing whatever game you think she is," Gigs said, bending down, the angle of the light changed. "Squirrel, hold this."

The light shifted to a higher position, and I felt the not gentle hands of our medic lay me out on the ground once again. The number of times he whistled under his breath, he could have written a fucking symphony. I should probably be glad I couldn't see the damage. Feeling it was bad enough.

With his head in the swath of light, I watched Gigs's eyes dance in humor and respect as he patched me up. And he patched fucking every inch, it felt like. I knew for a fact I would be pissing blood at least a couple times with the number of hits she sank into my kidneys. The woman knew her poisons and her anatomy.

"She damaged but didn't debilitate. She's fucking good," Gigs said as he slapped a butterfly bandage over a cleaned gouge on my shoulder. The puncture wound in my belly from her nails felt like she attacked me with a pneumatic nailer.

"Damn, she would have made a good SEAL." Coming from Gigs, that was the highest praise. And I really should take it to heart.

Literally every single person in my life was telling me to get my shit straight, including the woman herself, and I kept stumbling down the path of the dumb, blind, and stupid. Hell, at this point, I was racing for the finish line headfirst.

Whatever it was about her that had me acting like a fucking stupid idiot really needed to resolve itself. My body couldn't handle the upkeep of stupidity.

"You're going to be feeling most of that for the next week or two." He slapped a hard hand to the side of my head as if he suffered from bad aim and planned to hit my shoulder. "But lucky for you, you get to go play known voyeur at the club tomorrow night." He snorted and got to his feet. "I can't fucking wait to watch that show."

"He's not watching anything," Dewdrop cut in as she stomped back over. Stepping into the ring of light, she crouched down, got in my face. "You're not going to be there. You're not going to watch. You're not going to be in the club. You lost your chance to be helpful when you had no one watching, you certainly don't get to help when your sins have come to light. You stay home or I won't show up. I'll go after Jorgenssen on my own before I let you help me."

She stared down at me for a long time. Something more than disappointment in her gaze made the pits of my belly twist and shrivel.

"Pix, Jorgenssen is expecting to see him. If you blackball him now, you could undo your entire job," Squirrel said softly.

Her sexy mouth firmed into a hard line, and I saw the resolution to move forward without any of us. My stupidity had lost us more than me claiming this woman. I'd lost us our single biggest advantage in taking down the Sisterhood.

I couldn't let that happen. Not because of me. And certainly not over this.

Leaning back, I put space between us even though some part of me needed to push further into hers. I crossed my arms when they burned to reach out and pull her to me. Lifting my gaze to meet hers, I put everything else out of my mind and body as I spoke. "Neva."

She jolted before she narrowed her eyes as she glared down at me.

Wincing, I wanted to punch myself in the dick. "Aneira, I'm sorry. I'm sorry for pushing you, for watching you, for being in your space and in your bubble. You've told me multiple times to get out of it and I never listened, thinking I knew better what you needed. That was wrong of me and I can promise you here and now that it will never happen again." I licked my lips. There was definitely more I could apologize for, but maybe she would let me off easy.

When she simply raised a single brow, I felt my respect for her grow.

I huffed a soft laugh, dipped my chin in acknowledgement. "I'm sorry for being a dickhead and shoving my way into your life. I'm sorry for stabbing Brantley and potentially fucking up your op."

She held up a finger, her brows furrowed in confusion. "You stabbed that fuckbait?"

I nodded. "Yeah, after you left in the Uber this morning."

Realization dawned, clearing her expression. "You're why he looked like ass when he came to confront me."

I shrugged. "Probably. I just knew I couldn't handle what came out of his mouth, so I plugged it for him." And a couple more holes into his weak, power-hungry body.

"You don't have to apologize for that one." She smiled. "Thank you. Although I would have liked to stab him myself, I'm glad someone I know got to do it."

Laughing again, I smiled. "My pleasure, Aneira."

To say it burned like acid to not be able to call her by her real name would be an understatement. But she'd put down lines and my continuing to cross them put me in this position in the first place.

Her smile sharpened, bright as a blade. "Oh, don't stop now. This is genuinely the best thing I've heard all week."

Squirrel wheezed out a laugh. "I dunno, pix. His girly screaming earlier was pretty fun."

"Hmm." She tipped her head to the side, smiled. "That was good." Her emerald eyes crackled with fire. "But this? This is better. Watching him swallow his pride whole?"

She sighed happily. "Best. Show. Ever."

I bit back a twisted smile. When I finally got her under me, I was going to make her pay for that.

Squirrel and Gigs burst into laughter as well.

And that. My own men laughing at me while I ate crow. Those fuckers.

I blew out a breath. "Honestly, I'm most sorry for treating you like some kind of helpless victim. You clearly are more than capable of holding your own. You are an acknowledged expert in your field, you don't need anyone to help you with shit, and I apologize for my part in trying to take those from you. I can promise you, right here and now, I'll never underestimate you again."

She blinked at me for a long heartbeat, the fake smile melting away. Her head tipped to the side as if considering my words and the totality with which I'd undermined her. Pretty green eyes glimmered for the barest second with extra moisture before she blinked and shuttered everything away.

Tipping her head back to the sky, she blew out a long breath. When she lowered her head, her eyes were no longer soft and shocked. They gleamed hard and bright in the artificial sun of the flashlight. "Thank you. For all of that. I'll take your marker, but it's the last one.Next time you disrespect me like you've done up to this point, I will kill you."

When she didn't embellish the statement, didn't add any flair or tactics, just a simple declaration of intent, it told me she meant every single word. I would die by her hand if I kept treating her like shit.

I nodded. "Acknowledged, Larkspur. Five by five."

So slowly that I might have missed it, she softened. Not enough to be anything close to approachable, but enough that I wasn't terrified of her slitting my throat in my sleep.

"Then it seems we need to do some disaster management and see what's left to salvage from my op." She pushed back up to her feet and stepped back.

Gigs lowered his hand to help me up and I groaned. Every single fucking place she struck felt like lemon juice in an open wound. Even though I already knew it, this just drove it home some more: this woman was fierce.

I really, really needed to remember it. My body couldn't afford to pay any more checks my mouth kept writing.

Everyone waited in silence while I paced off the worst of the aches and pains. When I got back to the small group, the flashlight was off and we stood under a killing moon. Easy enough to see a target, but still blend in with the shadows.

My favorite kind of night.

"First, I think we need to see if your home still stands. We only felt the one shake and nothing blew as we were leaving in the chopper," Gigs reasoned as he slid the med bag's strap over his shoulder. "I've already called Iggy. Someone's on their way now. If we can get out to a street, we can give precise headings without having to be tagged, just in case they're still tracking Snow's phone."

Dewdrop shook her head. "I turned mine completely off after my boss called. I think I've been burned, so it's best practice to operate as if I have been."

My body jolted in shock. "What makes you think that?"

She spelled out the conversation, shrugging as if it was something she'd eventually expected.

It irritated and annoyed me that she was so comfortable with the idea of being ditched or abused by everyone in her life. Not that I'd given her anything else to think differently of me, but still. She was a highly trained and valuable asset. There's no way she should have been left out to dry.

"Do you shelter in place? Have some safe houses? What's your plan?" Squirrel asked, his big arms crossed over his chest. "You point me in the direction you need something killed and I'll get it done, pix. You just say the word."

She smiled up at him and I bit back the jealousy and grief that it wasn't directed at me. I had a long fucking way to go to warrant a smile, let alone anything more than that.

"Thanks, Squirrel. I've got a few bolt holes, but if I don't have to use them, I'd like to keep them intact. I guess the first step is finding out what's still standing back home."

"Either way, I think you should stay at Locke, one of our safehouses, or with one of us," Gigs offered.

Her slight frame stiffened, and she spent a lot of energy not looking in my direction. "We'll see what's left at home, first."

"His place isn't an option. Not unless you want it to be, Snow," Gigs said.

Her shoulders relaxed the smallest degree. "Like I said, let's figure out what's still available and go from there. We can speculate and make plans all day long, but we need actionable intel, not guesses."

"How far out do you estimate for the guys?" I asked, taking the attention off her and what she might or might not need.

Right now, we needed to get out of the open and away from the last position her phone pinged at, regardless of what else we did.

"Probably another hour. Traffic and everything else, we're about twenty miles out of the city as the crow flies. It's going to take them a bit," Gigs answered. "I linked into our satellite feeds and pulled up our location on my phone. There's a road about fifty meters that way." He pointed off to the right. "We get through there, move over a few streets, confuse any watchers with evasive techniques, and we should be ready for pick up by the time the team gets here."

I nodded. "Then lead the way, Gigs." I jutted my chin in his direction.

"Pix, you're up after Happy. Keys you're next. I'll take flank," Squirrel directed. "I've got your gun, too, by the way. You want it back or your hands free?"

I debated with myself. If Gigs was carrying our med supplies, he would need to protect that. Which left me guarding Dewdrop. A situation I could almost guarantee she wouldn't like. But wounded, I couldn't be counted on to carry out backup without some major handicap points and she was too valuable to waste on my pride like that.

"I'll take the gun and third position. No reason for Prince Charming here to be unguarded," Dewdrop drawled.

The blow snuck straight to my chest and made me wheeze. Damn, she had good aim.

Fuck.

"Not to tell you what you can handle, but you shouldn't be third. Or have the gun. We're all significantly taller and heavier than you. If necessary, you can hide, and we can duke it out with whoever comes calling. Then be around to patch us up. Our ace in the hole," Squirrel said.

"And I should be third, with the gun, because I'm the smallest and lightest. If one of you giants gets taken down, there's no way I can carry one of you. Even wounded you could probably carry me. And, like you said, I can run and ride. But with a gun, I would be in an offensive position, not a defensive one," she challenged back.

We all stopped and stared at each other in turn. Both were good points, and I'd already shoved my foot so far down my throat that I was going to shit rubber, so I was staying out of it.

Coward's way out, yes.

Smart, also yes.

"Besides, Prince Charming here is probably not going to be at his best. So he is the weakest link and needs the extra protection."

She just had to get that last kick in, huh? Just slammed her shoe into my ass and fucked me raw with it while demanding I thank her for the gift.

Squirrel studied me in the soft lighting, his brows low. He winced, nodded. "Yeah, you're probably right."

Tag teamed by my own guy. Oh the pain.

"Honestly, with how much shit you dealt him, I'm a little surprised he's walking on his own," Gigs piled on. The faintest laugh marred the edges of his tone. "See? He looks like he's about to keel over right now."

He came up to my side and shoved me with his entire weight, almost knocking me to my feet.

Squirrel sighed, rubbing a hand down his face. "Fuck it. Snow takes the gun. Keys, try not to die from shame while we're walking."

I bit my tongue. I was bleeding everywhere else—what was a little more?

Squirrel didn't even look at me anymore. He has his arm draped over Neva's shoulder, his voice low and serious when he spoke. "You earned this, Keys. You know that, right?"

Gigs adjusted the med bag's strap and muttered, "Would've let her take another shot if I wasn't afraid she'd actually kill you."

Squirrel nodded, his gaze sharp. "You're lucky she still gives a shit."

But I kept my mouth shut and fell into line.

Dewdrop would have zero issues with me from here on out. I would be a fucking boy scout, an altar boy, and a teacher's pet, if that's what it took. But she wouldn't be killing me or leaving me.

And I could play the long game.

Chapter 29
Neva

Walking across the empty airfield, I kept my gaze moving. I wasn't as highly trained as these guys when it came to night maneuvers—but I knew how to make my weaknesses irrelevant. Darkness played with the rods and cones in the human eye, creating blind spots, shifting shapes, making people doubt their instincts.

I used it to my advantage, tracking movement with my periphery, keeping my breath even.

They wouldn't doubt me. Not here. Not ever.

Finally making it out to the street, I waited for Happy to point us in the right direction. I wasn't really sure what specific area we were in, and it was a little far out from the city to be near any of my bolt holes' locations, so I left it up to the guy who knew what he was doing.

Double-stepping to get even with Rome, I slid my arm around his waist, my finger deliberately skimming the gun into the front pocket of his jeans.

His entire body tensed, and for a second, I swore I felt his pulse hammer through his shirt.

"Don't get any ideas, Charming," I murmured as, curling my fingers around the grip, pressing it against him enough to remind him who held the real power. "Or I'll shoot your dick off."

He jolted slightly, but didn't do anything more than slide his free arm over my shoulder. "Sure, Snow. Just for evasive techniques and blending in."

I nodded, reaching up to thread my fingers through his. Damn right it was for tactics. I would sooner let him bleed out than keep him around, but since he was sticking around, I needed to make sure I could protect him like I said I would.

"Hey, man, let's try that bar up on Oakridge," Happy called, adding the slightest sway to his steps.

"Fine by me," Squirrel slurred back. "Beer tas'es li'e beer no mattah weer Iyam." He gave a hiccup that sounded like something came up with it.

I shuddered at the idea of that giant man drunk enough to hiccup bile.

If Squirrel fell in a darkened room and no one else was around, did he still make noise? And heavens help the bed that had to catch him. Hell, even the floor would take a beating under the size of that man.

We stumbled along to the next street. As soon as we turned the corner, we assumed new personas. We carried on switching and flipping characters as we zigzagged our way through the suburban neighborhood.

At one point, I somehow ended up on Squirrel's back as he bucked around like a pony. Happy and Rome walked a little faster during that little show.

Just as we were getting ready to turn the last corner, Happy's phone rang. He dragged us into an alley and put the phone on speaker. "Go."

"Coming up from the south. Stay where you are, I'll come to you." The call dropped before I could fully identify the voice.

It dawned on me that even though it felt like I'd known these men for more years than I wanted to admit, it had actually been less than a freaking week.

My, how time flies when having fun.

I snorted mentally. I could count on no hands how many times I'd had fun with this group.

I tipped my head to the side. Well, that wasn't right. I could count on no hand how many times I'd had fun with Rome. The leader definitely soured my feelings on the rest of them. I even preferred Dopey to Rome right now.

Moments later, a car rolled into the far end of the alley. The lights flashed bright before they turned off, leaving the orange run lights still visible.

"That's us. Let's go," Happy said. He readjusted the med bag on his shoulder and nudged me forward. "Ladies first."

Had I heard the slightest flicker of amusement in his tone, I would have put a round in his ass. But since he sounded nothing but serious, I just nodded and moved toward the vehicle. I didn't mind being treated as a lady in a chivalrous way. Although, I'd probably kill anyone who tried it outside of this group of men.

The vehicle waiting for us was a full-size sedan. I blinked at it as I registered the make and model. Stopping just shy of actually getting even with the doors, I bent down and checked to see if I recognized the driver.

Beck dipped his chin at me, gave a smile.

Sliding into the middle of the backseat, I waited for the guys to come and join. "I wouldn't have expected this kind of car for any of you."

Beck chuckled. "Not all of us like to bring attention to ourselves."

I smiled, nodded. It made a lot of sense that their sniper was the guy actively working to blend in, even on city streets. And this car would have fit in any city in America.

"But don't let her fool you, she's got more under the hood than your typical Ford Taurus." He petted his hand down the steering wheel as the guys finally pulled the doors shut after shuffling in.

Rome took the front seat, his face showing signs of stress. We walked for quite a while. I almost felt bad about his condition.

Almost.

"Let's get out of here, Schnauzer." Rome winced as he buckled his seatbelt.

Beck's eyes were wide as he studied his leader. "What the hell happened to you?"

Squirrel barked a laugh. "Oh, trust me, you're gonna wanna hear this one, Schnaze." He let loose a cackle. An honest to God cackle. "Snow happened to him. Ask him why. Do it. Do it. Ask him."

Rome flicked a black look in Squirrel's direction.

"Why do you look like shit, Keys?"

Rome's shoulders sank as he mumbled under his breath.

Beck's brows furrowed as he caught my gaze in the rearview mirror.

I smiled at him, said nothing.

He looked back at Rome. "I didn't quite catch that."

Even in the backseat, I heard Rome grind his teeth. "I perved on her while she was home in her own bed."

Beck didn't even hesitate. No warning, no twitch of muscle Just pure, unfiltered retribution. his fist cracked into Rome's face so hard, his head ricocheted off the window, leaving a streak of red where his skull hit.

"From the cameras you promised us all you wouldn't use for that shit?" Beck's voice was quieter than I expected.

Deadlier.

Oh, damn.

He blinked rapidly for a few seconds as he nodded. "For fuck's sake, Beck." He ran his hand over the back of his head, looked at his fingers. "I don't need a concussion on top of everything else she did to me. She already beat me bloody, as you can very well see."

"Good, she should have. I punched you for lying to us. Don't ever do it again." The echoes of something deeper sat in Beck's voice as he put the car into gear. "Ever, Keys. Get me?"

Rome nodded. "I'm sorry. It won't ever happen again."

Beck studied his brother for a long minute, finally nodded. "I won't follow someone I can't trust."

Rome winced, taking the proverbial blow on his chin.

I blinked as I realized this was aberrant behavior for Rome. The truth of it should have rung a little sooner when both Squirrel and Happy laid into him about his treatment of me, but I hadn't really put it all together. Apparently, Rome had gone off the deep end with his chosen family, as well. It wasn't with just me.

"It will never happen again, Schnauzer." Rome's words were soft, but honed steel with promise.

Beck nodded again. "Good." He put the car into motion. The tension in the car's interior was heavy.

Until Squirrel laughed. "You gotta check out his dick. She put new holes in it with her Wolverine claws. At one point, she wanted to put it on her mantle, like a vase or something. I told her it wouldn't look very good, certainly not as good as mine. But then again, whose would? I think that's why she didn't rip it off with her bare hands."

Everyone laughed.

Except Rome. He turned and glared at the huge man beside me. "That's not why she didn't cut it off with her bare hands."

I raised a single brow. He knew why I didn't castrate him? "Oh, please, Prince Charming, do tell."

His lips twisted before he shut his mouth and faced forward, his shoulders up around his ears. He just shook his head, drawing even more laughter from his brothers.

Had I been any other person, I might have felt bad for him. As it was, I felt the tiniest of bubbles most closely resembling pity drift through my chest.

Then it popped and I sighed.

Oh, thank goodness. No way was I going to let him off that easily. He had a lot more to pay for than just being arrogant.

"I'm not going to check out his dick, Squirrel, I'll just have to take your word for it," Beck answered. He shuddered a little as he caught my gaze in the rearview mirror again.

I smiled, shrugged.

"Did Iggy check out her house?" Happy asked, drawing us all back to something other than Rome's shame.

Beck nodded, shifted his gaze back out the windshield as he pulled onto the street, heading us back toward the city. "It's still there. He and Banshee got in, found a sonic device. Probably what made it feel like the house was being blown."

My brows furrowed. "A sonic device? Where?"

"Two actually. One was in an empty corner of the attic. The other in the basement, near your lab door."

My heart stalled in my chest. "Was the lab okay?"

"Yeah, all clear. Iggy got the devices down. He's going to run them for prints and whatnot back at his lab. Everything else checked out clear."

Something niggled my brain. "How did they get in?" Not that I would have gotten the alert on my phone telling me the alarms had been tripped, but I couldn't imagine they would be flirting with the police either.

Not a single man said a word.

I bit my tongue to keep from lashing out at the group of them. They copied my security system data. Somehow, someway, they bypassed my entire alarm system and just made themselves at home in my fucking house.

How dare they think they could do whatever they wanted. Especially with my life! "All of you knew and not a single one of you thought it would be a good idea to tell me?" I looked at each one.

When I looked up at Squirrel, I saw the agony on his face. "Pix—"

I held up a hand, cutting him off. Blowing out a low breath, I counted to fifty. "This is the last time. Do you all understand me? I will disappear and you can forget about me helping you with anything. In fact, keep this shit up, and I'll start plotting against you, see how you assholes like it."

All four men winced and hunched their shoulders.

"Promise me," I spit out.

They tripped over themselves, blurting out the words. I couldn't make out a single coherent statement, but at least they'd given me something to show they were listening. The jerks.

"In the interest of full disclosure…" Rome began.

I made a noise in the back of my throat.

He turned to look at me, chagrin on his handsome face. "I'm already beaten, so unless you plan to actually kill me, I'd prefer you add whatever punishment to me now rather than later."

Narrowing my eyes at him, I contemplated if I could stand to hear about any other betrayals he wanted to confess. When I realized it was better to learn them all now, I simply nodded at him.

He blew out a breath. "Are you going to hurt me some more?"

"Depends on what you say." I raised a single brow.

He licked his lips. "We—"

The three other guys made rude, disgusted noises.

Rome winced again. "Fine, *I* was going to have Iggy install more cameras and sensors in your home. Five for each access point. We weren't going to tell you or give you access to the tertiary system. You wouldn't have even known about it."

Rage unlike anything I'd ever experienced before in my life smashed into me like a tidal wave. "Tell me, Prince Charming"—I put a sneer around the words—"were you going to put them in my bathroom? My closet? My shower? Were you going to destroy any privacy I had in my own fucking home for your own neuroses, for this ridiculous claim you think you have?" The last sentence was snarled as I fought back the urge to leap over the seat and thrust his head through the windshield, face first.

"I wouldn't have allowed him to put them in your bathroom, pix. You gotta believe me on that one. And absolutely no number of promises or logic would have moved me on letting him do it," Squirrel said softly.

"Agreed," Happy added.

Beck dipped his chin. "I didn't know you had a camera over your bed. It wasn't listed on Iggy's schematic of your system. But there is no fucking way I would have allowed one in your, or any other, bathroom."

I blew out a breath, fighting through the red haze in my vision. "Tell me any-fucking-thing else, Rome. This is your last chance to come clean. If I find you've held bac—"

"That's it. I swear, Neva. I swear on my mother's grave." He looked back at me, his eyes wide.

Squirrel, Happy, and Beck all sucked in noisy breaths.

I studied Rome Fucking Whitlock for a long time.

"I swear those are the only plans I had. Nothing more. I promise."

In the intermittent passing of the streetlights outside the car, I saw the earnestness in his gaze.

So many thoughts ricocheted around in my head, but I caught one of them. "One day soon, I'm going to give you a drink, Rome."

I tilted my head, studying his face, watching the hesitation bloom behind his bloodied features.

"And you're going to drink it without hesitation Without question. Without second-guessing whether or not I laced it with something that will make you wish you were already dead. You'll get to see, feel, and experience what it's like to not only be plotted against, but to have your trust trampled on, your privacy removed. And all by someone who said they wanted to help you, someone who said you could trust them."

Leaning forward, I stretched out my hand. "Do you agree?"

He shifted his gaze to my hand, back to my face. He opened his mouth, closed it before he said anything. After a moment, he slid his hand over mine. "I really am sorry, Neva."

I shook my head as I squeezed his hand. "I am, too." Then drew my hand back, settled back against the seat.

I had no idea why I was so upset by their actions. It wasn't like I didn't understand betrayal and how I was always on the loser's side of the equation. Wishful thinking and busted dreams, I guess.

Thankful for the dark lighting in the car, I allowed the tears to slide down my cheeks.

We rode in silence the rest of the way back. Nothing but the sound of the road under the tires and the occasional tick, tick, tick of the turn signal. It was almost soothing.

By the time we made it back to the city, I had my emotions back under control. The tears dried on my cheeks as I worked through several possible contingencies. The biggest one was what to do if I had, in fact, been burned by my boss.

I had a secondary lab in one of my bolt holes, but it wasn't nearly as good as the one at home. But if I had been burned, staying in my family's home could spell a lot of issues for me. First and foremost, a cleanup team knowing exactly where I was.

And what the hell was I supposed to do about the school? About Jorgenssen? I couldn't exactly traipse around undercover knowing that my every move was being tracked by people who wanted to kill me. And that would screw up any possibility of me getting inside Jorgenssen's organization and figuring out what I needed to know.

We pulled into a garage as I struggled to come up with any good answers. The bright lights of the shop pierced my eyes as a thumping bass beat through the floor. Seemed Subterra was rocking and rolling tonight.

For the shortest second, I yearned. But I shook it off. No more playing for fun here.

Someone blew out a low whistle as we all got out of the car.

"What the fuck happened to Keys?" Dopey asked as he wiped his black, greasy hands with a red towel. The hood of another vehicle stood open like a gaping mouth beside him.

Rome looked at me over the car's roof, something close to broken in his eyes. But he sighed, stiffened his spine, shook back his shoulders. "She beat the shit out of me for spying on her in her home, in her bed." He turned around to face the rest of his men.

I fought to not let my jaw drop in astonishment.

He blurted it right out there, knowing full well what the three men who were in the car did to him. Not only did he just state it, he stayed still, his body braced for whatever his other brothers wanted to dish out.

Iggy came up first, his anger almost white-hot as he punched Rome in the stomach, then rammed Rome's face into his knee when he buckled over from the first blow. "I

fucking told you not to play with it. You promised me. Us."
He lifted his elbow, bringing it down on Rome's spine.

Rome tumbled to the floor with a heavy groan.

Banshee darted in next. His heavy booted foot kicked
Rome in the belly. He hit Rome so hard his fallen body
smacked into the wheel of Beck's car.

With an anger colder than anything I'd ever seen
before, Det walked over. He leaned down, grabbed Rome
by his hair. "You looking at me, boss?"

Rome's head moved the slightest degree.

"Good." Det pulled his hand back and almost punched
his fist through Rome's skull. "Don't ever lie to us again."

No one moved in to help. No one moved in to stop it.
Not even me.

Because in that moment, Rome wasn't their leader
anymore.

He was just some guy they needed to break.

And I realized in that moment he did it to preserve their
relationships. Their trust, their bonds. He came clean and
accepted their punishment as penance.

Another kind of anger lit inside my chest. An anger that
had scabbed over long ago. An anger I didn't have a handle
on.

As Dopey lined up to take a turn at his brother and
friend, I stepped into the middle of them. Deflecting
Dopey's swing cost me, and more than just physically, but I
would never tell anyone that.

I didn't raise my voice. Didn't have to.

"Back. The fuck. Up."

I shifted low into a stance, steady, unyielding. I let
them do the math—how much damage I'd already done,
how much I'd still be willing to do.

He loomed over me. "Step aside, Snow. You don't
belong here. Not in this."

I accepted the blow, knowing it was nothing but the
truth. But I didn't back down, and I didn't step aside. "I
said, back the fuck up. I'm tired of you fuckers not listening
to me."

Squirrel came over. He didn't stand in front of me, but
he lent his size to my cause. "Back up, Critter. Listen to her
before your ego gets you put down."

Dopey's mouth fell open in shock, then he snapped it
closed with a look of pure hatred aimed at me. "Tell me
why I shouldn't kill her right now? All of this"—he waved
his hand around the shop—"is directly tied to her. What

301

she's done to this family." He slapped a hand to his chest. "To *our* family."

"And we all agreed to invite her in so we could get her help, or don't you remember that part?" Beck said softly. "You could have spoken up when we made the deal, you didn't. Because you know as well as the rest of us, we can't break the Sisterhood without her. We've lost more brothers than we can count and now you want to kick her to the side because Rome broke a promise to us?" He shook his head, his red hair a blaze of fire under the bright lights. "She's going to handle it. Rome agreed."

Dopey shot daggers at me as he stared down into my face. "I don't care. She doesn't get to stand in the way of us and how we do things. She's an outsider, someone we can use, but she's going to leave at some point. It's us. Only us."

I rose to my full height once again. "And that's why I won't let you beat him anymore. Because I will be leaving at some point. If you're still pissed at him, beat the shit out of him then. Outside of a broken promise to you all, he's hurt me more. I showed him the error of his ways. These guys did, too, when they found out. But I won't stand around and watch you beat on your brother, your friend, your chosen leader." I shook my head. "Not when he won't defend himself out of love for you, because of the relationships he's trying to fix by not defending himself. Families don't do that to each other."

Dopey leaned down. "What do you know about family?"

One side of my mouth lifted. "I know what the shitty ones do. You want to be part of that kind of family, by all means, beat him to death. Kill him for breaking a promise." I stepped aside, waving a hand for Dopey to attack.

The man stood still, his chest heaving as he glared down at Rome.

I nodded, felt my heart rate drop back down into a more normal rhythm. I wasn't quite sure what was going on, but I knew I couldn't allow them to kill Rome. "Palmer," I said softly, drawing Dopey's attention back to me.

He blinked for a second as I used his real name. Then he glared at me, his head lowered as if he was about to rush me. "What?"

"Do you need to hit him for breaking his promise to you?" I couldn't say I understood the need for physical violence over something so small, so mundane as a broken promise, but I also wasn't a part of this family.

Dopey was right, I wasn't part of their crew, their brotherhood, their family. In the grand scheme of things, I was nothing more than a means to an end.

Dopey dipped his chin.

I stepped out of his way.

Dopey eyed me for a moment, a look of calculation in his eyes. He stepped forward, then squatted down until he was even with Rome's face. He studied the fallen man for a long moment. "Don't ever lie to me again, Keys."

Rome nodded again. "I'm sorry." The word was drenched in pain and covered in blood as he spat out a glob of the stuff on a hacking cough.

Dopey heaved a sigh. He reached out, poked Rome's swollen eye with a stiff finger. "Stop being a shit." He stood up and backed away, his arms crossed over his chest. He gave me a nod.

I quickly swallowed around the hoot of laughter. None of these men were in the mood for my skewed sense of humor right now.

But I saw their game. And if that's how they wanted to deal with things, then I was more than willing to show them I could be a team player. "Now that we've got all of that cleared up, line up, you motherfuckers."

Dopey backed up his eyes wide with fear. "Why the fuck would we do that?"

My smile was a little evil. "Because Rome told me what you all planned to do to my house. You beat the shit out of him for breaking a promise, I figure I get to beat the shit out of all of you for breaking my trust before we even started working together. I've already ripped through Rome. It's everyone else's turn." I shifted to look Dopey right in the eye. "That's how you guys settle things, right?"

He backed up some more, his hands in the air. "You stay away from me, you psycho. Don't come anywhere near me."

Iggy walked around his brother, planting himself in front of me. He lifted his chin, his arms out to his sides. He had traces of sorrow in his gaze, but that didn't stop him from meeting my eyes. "Yes, Snow. That is how we settle things. I'll take my punishment."

I lifted one hand, set my fingernails into his chest, and pushed until he winced, careful not to break the skin.

303

"Don't ever make plans for or about me without me in attendance. Do you understand me?"

He nodded. "I'm sorry."

I reached up, tapped a hand to his cheek a little harder than necessary. "Thank you."

He blinked down at me for a long time. "That's it?" He shifted his gaze between me and Rome for a couple seconds.

Nodding, I sighed. "Rome had it coming, in more ways than one. And Dopey is right, I'm not part of this family. I settle things my own way, ways that don't leave me down a man in case things get bad." I shrugged. "Can't say your way isn't effective, but I won't help you guys hurt each other just to make amends. Nor will I hurt you for the same reasons."

Dopey snorted loudly. "Tell that to Rome."

I smiled. "Like I said, Rome had it coming. Let's leave it at that unless you want to get down and dirty, Dopey."

At the edges of my vision, I saw Happy, Squirrel, and Beck all shake their heads at their brother.

Dopey eventually took their advice. "No. I'm good."

Chapter 30

Rome

Breathing hurt. Existing hurt. My ribs felt like they were crushed under a steel beam, my spine one wrong move from snapping. But none of it compared to the quiet fucking annihilation in Neva's voice.

I almost wish they kept hitting me. At least then, I wouldn't have to sit in this shame. At least, then, the worst of the pain would be on the outside.

She made us sound like careless psychos out to get our pound of flesh for the slightest offense. She wasn't wrong, but I didn't really enjoy hearing it.

"If you're all done trying to beat the shit out of each other, I suggest we do some planning so I can help you, then leave. No reason for you to put up with my shit any longer than you have to, right?" She shrugged as if it didn't matter to her one way or the other.

It might have been the concussion or the blood in my ears, but I thought I heard an ache in her voice. She sounded almost sad. Whatever it was, it certainly didn't match the fuck-it-all attitude she just showed.

"Did you have time to look through our dossiers?" Iggy asked as Squirrel and Gigs helped me to my feet.

"No. I was interrupted by threats of bombs in my home."

I leaned against the car, the metal a refreshing wash of cool at my back. "But you're still going to work with us?" I gritted out through clenched teeth.

Holy fuck, I hurt. And I heard the plaintive tone of voice when I asked the question. Which meant she definitely did, damn it.

She turned to look at me. Nodded. "I'll still read them, but I planned on joining up anyway. Especially after you told me you stabbed Brantley."

My moment of relief at the first part of her answer got sliced in fucking half when I winced as something else I hadn't told my brothers made its way out into the light.

"For fuck's sake, Keys!" It came in stereo as the guys made it into a chorus of bitchiness.

"I'm sorry." I bit back the rest of the words that wanted to tumble out of my mouth. Nothing but excuses and platitudes. I did what I had because I couldn't stop myself at that moment. I was more than paying for that right now. "I swear none of this will ever happen again."

Neva raised a single brow. "Seems I should have let them beat you to death. It might have been easier for you. Anything else you want to share with the class?" She folded her hands at her waist like she was taking one of her kindergartners to task.

Talk about humiliating.

I grimaced at her, then shook my head. My behavior in my office while I watched her masturbate blazed through my mind again. Fuck. I nodded. Blew out a breath.

"Which is it?" Squirrel demanded.

I heaved a sigh. "I'll tell Snow first. If she doesn't kill me, she can decide if she wants me to share it." I prayed she would just kill me, honestly. She wasn't wrong about it being the easy way out at this point.

She raised her brows. "Well? Spit it out." She waved her hand at me to spill it out for the entire group to hear.

I shook my head. "I'll whisper it to you. If you want them to know, then you tell me to tell them. But I won't abuse your trust again." I held my breath.

Please, for the love of all that's holy, please don't make me say it out loud, I begged her silently.

Her gaze darkened as she studied me.

I was getting sick and fucking tired of being evaluated and judged. And for all of the judgements to come back as lacking. Yes, yes, I knew I earned it. But that didn't mean it didn't suck to withstand it.

As I waited for her to decide, I held my hand to my stomach against the blow Iggy delivered. The man had fists like fucking Hulk. How he was so fast and smooth on a keyboard without destroying the whole thing every time was a mystery.

Neva finally made her way to my side. She rose up on her toes and leaned forward. "Tell me."

Heat rushed my cheeks, but I didn't back down. It was a damn bitter pill, but she needed to know. And I needed to tell her. Especially with how I watched her without her knowing. Turnabouts and all that fair shit.

Why the fuck was I so stupid about this woman?

The scent of her hair distracted me for a moment, but I blew the dark brown curtain away from my face. "I watched you while you were in bed this morning."

She nodded, easing back to look into my face. Confusion decorated her beautiful features. "You told me that already."

I blew out a breath, gritted my teeth. Damn it. She was really going to make me say it.

"What I didn't tell you—" My mouth dried up. My tongue stuck to the roof of it, words rotting before they could escape.

Neva blinked, waiting.

My body screamed at me to stop, to shut the fuck up, to find some other way to make amends.

But there wasn't another way.

"...I did, too."

The vulgar words, the explicit words which would have been sexy as fuck to admit in almost any other scenario crowded the back of my throat.

She gazed up at me with a frown pinching her brows. "You did what, too?"

I forced myself not to look away as I willed her to understand.

Please, fuck, don't make me explain it. I was doing my absolute best to keep from thinking about her luscious body on that camera and now she wanted me to spell it out for her in graphic detail?

It eluded her for a couple moments, but I saw the instant it dawned on her.

I could have wept with joy.

Fuck.

She didn't move. Didn't breathe. Didn't even fucking blink. Then, after what felt like a fucking eternity, her pupils expanded like ink spreading through water. Her breath hitched in her throat as she swiped her tongue over her lower lip, leaving behind a quick wash of moisture. Her green gaze slid down my damaged body, back up to my face. Then one of her dark brows rose in question.

I nodded. My breath still stuck in my chest, and I braced for another blow. She might actually kill me this time.

Neva stood there, staring at me. I was pretty sure she wasn't even blinking. Maybe not even breathing. Then she shook herself, and leaned close once again. "Anything else to confess, Prince Charming?"

The whispered bite she put into the moniker shredded my honor. But I just shook my head, dizzy with relief that she didn't launch another attack. "We good?"

She cocked her head to the side. "Maybe. I'm not sure yet. But you can keep that one to yourself." Even as she spoke the words, she looked a little puzzled.

But she shook it off and turned back to the group. "Nothing of consequence. I'm going to read the dossiers tonight. I figure I owe you all for helping me with Lawrence, so I already planned to join up for our little jaunt through Poison Town. Even before Rome went rogue on Brantley."

Collectively, the guys all exhaled and relaxed. We really did need her and her expertise.

I came this close to ruining everything. Every single fucking thing. Whatever I felt for this woman would have to get stuffed down deep, locked away, buried. I couldn't allow myself to screw this up.

"Thank you, Snow," Iggy said. "I swear to you, we're on the up and up. Outside of being dishonorably discharged, we're clear as new glass."

Her brows quirked as she snorted softly. "What the hell did you do to get dishonorably discharged from the Navy?"

"We trusted the wrong people to do the right thing when it would have made the most difference," Dopey said, the words dropping like a bomb. "We don't make promises lightly. Nor do we easily accept the breaking of them." His tone still held anger, both old and new.

Neva nodded slowly. "I'll remember that and apologize for getting in your way, then. It won't happen again." She opened her mouth, but shut it before she said anything else, then dipped her chin.

We stood in silence for a long moment.

"Snow might be burned. Iggy, can you check your bitch to see if that's true?" Squirrel said, stepping in the awkwardness with his usual don't-give-a-shit attitude.

"How do you think you were burned?" Iggy asked even as he nodded. "I'll need to use the big system. My tablet isn't equipped for that."

"Then let's go to the bat cave," I said.

"Do I need to stay out here?" Neva asked.

I shook my head, but checked with my guys. "What do you want to do?"

"If she's joining up, then she should know what kind of systems we use. I vote she comes along," Iggy offered before he turned on his heel and walked off.

Everyone else nodded.

Everyone except Critter.

He stared at her, an odd light in his eyes. "That's it? You're not going to share what else Keys did to you?"

Neva shook her head. "No. Is that a problem?"

Dopey looked a little bloodthirsty still. Bloodthirsty and disappointed at her answer, the dipshit. "You're not going to beat more shit out of him?"

Neva snickered. "I hope he didn't shit himself the first time. Ew."

Dopey rolled his eyes. "You know what I mean."

Neva sighed, all humor dissolving. "Do you think I should hurt him for the last thing he confessed?"

Dopey nodded. "Yes. It gets it out in the open and resolved. One single action."

"That's how it works for all of you?" She looked at each man carefully, studying their expressions and nods of affirmation. "And if I told you the plans I have for him will also address and resolve this latest confession?"

"Will we get to witness it?" Dopey asked.

Neva shook her head. "No. It was against me alone."

Dopey pouted for a moment. "How will we know whatever beef between you has been cooked if we don't witness it?"

"He promised in the car, in front of witnesses. Will you take their word for it?"

"Did you do it to him in the car?"

She shook her head again. "No, it will happen in the future when things aren't so tense or critical. But if he

309

reneges, I'll tell the boys who were witnesses. Will that suffice?"

"Are you going to hold it over his head and drag it out like a regular girl?"

She laughed as she shook her head once more. "You're the one who keeps making comments about me not being normal, Dopey. Do you think I'll act like a regular girl in getting my restitution?"

He studied her for another long moment, then he shook his head. "No, I guess not."

"Trust me, what I have planned for him is going to be running through his head almost constantly. I think that will add enough drama to the whole thing to really let his lesson sink in."

Damn it. Now that she mentioned it, I was definitely going to be focusing on all the ways this tiny woman could hurt me. Fuck.

"What're you gonna do to him?" Dopey asked.

"Give him something to drink."

Dopey's eyes widened as he fell back a step. He looked at me, shock alive on his face. "You agreed to that? Even before confessing whatever this last thing was?"

I nodded. "I deserve it. And since she hasn't killed me yet, I figure I'm safe since I won't be acting like a selfish asshole moving forward."

Dopey turned back to Neva. "One of them witnesses him drink it, at least."

"I volunteer as tribute." Squirrel thrust his hand in the air. "Me, pix. Pick me. Please. Please. Please." He jumped up and down like a toddler asking for a cookie.

"Squirrel can stand as witness to the drinking. No one else will get to witness the outcome. I promise I won't kill him." She turned back to me, some kind of expression on her face I couldn't really put a name to.

Whatever it was, I was equally terrified and intrigued.

She turned back to Dopey. "Will that satisfy you?"

Dopey nodded. "An eye for an eye, Snow. That's how we settle things. So don't ever stake what you can't afford to lose."

She smiled. "Acknowledged and understood, Critter. Thank you for telling me."

He narrowed his eyes at her, but nodded and walked off before he said anything else.

I hissed out a sigh of relief. Thank fuck.

Out of all of us, I knew Dopey struggled the most with betrayal and keeping our words. He'd been burned too many times in the past not to keep his shit straight and honest. He bordered on brutally honest, usually to a fault. And got himself into a lot of trouble to uphold that line he set for himself.

Beck and Happy came over, and helped hold me up between them. At this point, I wasn't really sure I could walk very far without meeting the ground face-first. The guys' beating I could have weathered. But not with it being the icing on the top of the absolute thrashing Neva dished out earlier.

"I'll take him to the infirmary. I need to check everything over again to make sure nothing's going to get infected," Happy said.

"I can come to help out," Neva offered.

Everything in my body literally pulled away in fear of her hands on my body again. "I'm good with just Happy, Snow. But thanks." I couldn't help the whimpering. Right then, I didn't even care.

She snickered softly, but didn't push it. "Squirrel, lead the way, lover."

"Come on, sugar mama. I'll take you right to the treasure at the end of my rainbow." They veered off to the left as we headed to the right at the next hallway branch.

Damn it. Why the fuck did she have to rub it in? She was fucking mine!

I bit back the jealousy at their easy relationship, at the intimacy they shared. It should have been me, but I screwed it up. I was determined to earn her back, but fuck if it didn't burn in my belly that I'd travelled so far off-point with her thus far.

"What the hell is the matter with you, Keys?" Beck asked softly as we entered the small med room Gigs demanded when we renovated the warehouse holding our businesses. "I've never seen you like this. Ever."

They both helped me up onto a thinly lined hospital bed. Laying flat on the three-inch mattress felt like heaven. Fuck nuggets, that felt good. I blew out a low breath of relief as I tried to get my thoughts in order.

But I shook my head when nothing came to mind. "I can barely make sense of it in my head, Schnauze. I have no idea why I react to her the way I do. It almost got me killed and almost destroyed us, and I'll never let that happen."

311

I sealed the promise on my heart, on my fucking soul. I couldn't destroy us, certainly not my brothers and family. I'd serve up my head on a platter before I broke them any more than I already did.

"I knew you were struggling, but not this much," Beck responded. "You're close to feral and psychotic. Not a great combination…especially if you're really wanting her in your bed."

"Unless she's into that combo. But from everything I've seen, you're less than dog shit to her right now," Gigs said as he started cutting away my clothes.

I clenched my fists, the deep ache in them reminding me how I used the van as a punching bag earlier tonight. I truly have lost my damn mind. "Yeah, pretty sure dog shit would be a climb up, honestly."

"Then you better start taking this shit seriously. Start talking it out, because you keep letting that shit simmer and stew, you're not going to be climbing the ladder. You'll probably fall down into the depths of some kind of mental health crisis." Beck helped ease me up onto my side so they could pull the clothing away from my back and out from under my ass.

He gave a low whistle when he saw me in all my glory. "Snow did all of this?" He flicked his gaze from mine to Gigs's.

Gigs nodded, that slightly psycho smile on his face. "She was a vision, man. Smooth, sexy as fuck, she struck like silent lightning. At one point, I'm pretty sure he couldn't do anything but protect himself, even if he wanted to fight back."

He snorted after praising her, the knowledge that he and Squirrel would have held me still for her to pay her respects for my behavior was a clear and easy sign. Not that I would have ever doubted Gigs being one to dish out attitude modifications for being disrespectful.

They helped me lay flat again so Gigs could get to work checking all of my various wounds. Luckily, whatever Gigs did to my dick out in the airfield was still holding up, so he didn't have to manhandle my manhandle.

I snorted mentally at my own joke; Squirrel would have been so proud. I had a sneaking suspicion Neva would have laughed at it, too. Maybe if I made her laugh, she would let me back in. At least let me in closer.

Yeah. That could work. It couldn't hurt.

"See?" Beck shoved his finger in my face.

I blinked back into the room around me.

"That. That, right there. You're thinking about her again. You're laid out, almost incapacitated by the damage she inflicted, and you've got a look in your eye that says you want to go out and find her so she can give you some more. And, bro, it ain't loving she's got on her mind. What the fuck is wrong with you?"

I shook my head, trying to blink away whatever he saw. Made sure my mouth wasn't smiling or anything puppy love like that. I hadn't had the warm and tinglies for any woman in my entire life. The sloe-eyed ingénue never held any appeal for me before. And Neva was anything but a sweet, innocent little princess who needed some big strong man to save her.

I had the lasting marks on my body as proof left by the woman herself.

"Does she remind you of someone? Anyone?" Beck dug deeper.

"Not that I can recall." I heaved a sigh. "Look, the only thing I can tell you is that something about her pulls this stupid asshole out of me. Like I *need* to be there for her. Protect her. Annihilate anyone who tries to get between us."

I flopped my hand in frustration. "I don't fucking know. What I do know is that I realize my behavior has been fucking crazy. Even in my own head, I can't make sense of it. What comes out of my mouth, this shit I keep acting out…" I shook my head. "I don't know, man. I really, honestly don't know."

Lifting my gaze to meet those of my brothers was almost harder than standing still for their beatings. But I forced myself to do it. Forced myself to let them see the confusion, the fear, the driving, pulsing need to be there for a literal stranger. Clearly, I couldn't handle it on my own, so I might as well ask for help from two of the men I called my brothers.

Beck turned to Gigs. "Could it be something chemical? We all agree he's batshit crazy right now. By his own admission, he doesn't understand it either. Could it be pheromones or something like that?"

Gigs opened his mouth—then shut it. His smirk flickered, then died. I watched the exact second he realized this might not just be me.

Might not just be my problem.

He swallowed hard. "I don't know."

No one spoke. No one moved.

313

A beat passed.

Then another.

Beck's voice came out quiet. Too quiet, even for him. "What if it wasn't just you?"

The thought hit like a fucking bomb.

For the first time all night, I felt actual, physical terror.

Could it really be something outside my control? Since meeting Neva, hell, since seeing her on the camera feed in Subterra, I felt the first instant of peace. Maybe there was something wrong with me, something altered or broken which could explain my reaction to her. The fact I was praying for something to be wrong also didn't escape my notice.

Both men turned back to me.

"Do you need to fuck her? Like an obsession you can't quite kick until you've tasted her?"

I blinked at the string of words that just came from Gigs's mouth. My own mouth worked open and closed as I tried to reconcile the words with the man speaking. "Did you really just ask me that?"

Beck looked almost as stupefied as I did.

Gigs nodded. "Yes. If we're going to start looking at biological, chemical, or physiological reasons you could be experiencing aberrant behavior, we need to be examining any mental health reasons as well." He raised a finger. "And yes, I want to kick my own ass for even talking about her like that, but we need some damn answers." He waved his hand at my injured body. "Obviously."

I ran the idea through my head. And just like before, it brought out some kind of beast that lived inside me. Even just the thought of getting her under me had me needing to get up and go search her out, to claim her, to hide her away.

Fuck. Note to self, thinking too hard about her made things worse.

I shook my head. "No. That way leads to nothing other than increased obsession and more feral thoughts."

Blanking my mind, I focused on something—anything—to help me settle back down. A brief image of holding a huge-ass flap of skin in place on Squirrel's thigh after a particularly brutal fall back came to my mental rescue. When I was able to blow out a low breath without desire clawing at me from the inside, I blinked up at my brothers.

"Is there a way to look at neurotransmitters? Brain chemistry, something like that?"

Gigs studied me for a moment. "You've thought of something."

I nodded. "Is there?"

He dipped his chin. "We'll need to bring in a neurologist if you want full-scale answers. The best I can do for you is tell if something isn't firing correctly." He wiped the back of his wrist over his mouth. "What did you think of?"

Great, another too-exposing answer. Why not, right? I gritted my teeth for a moment.

Fuck, this was embarrassing. "It wasn't a thought. It was a compulsion. I didn't just want to chase her down—I needed to. The same fucking way I need to breathe or fucking live. It sat in my chest like a second heartbeat, pounding, thudding, driving me to find her, to claim her, to rip out the world that kept us apart. I couldn't just ignore it."

I shook my head. "Anyway, I had to purposely cast my mind to fucking field surgery back in the Pit to get my head back where it belonged. It shouldn't have been that hard. It shouldn't have taken that much effort. Something is wrong with me."

Both men nodded, grim acceptance on their faces.

Gigs heaved a sigh. "Let me get your blood drawn."

Beck stayed him with a hand on his shoulder. "Draw all of ours. If something happened to Keys, it might have happened to all of us."

That thought wasn't just a bomb. It was a fucking detonation, sending shockwaves through each of us.

Because if this wasn't just me?

If this was something in my blood?

In all of us?

Then we weren't just compromised.

We were already fucking doomed.

315

Chapter 31
Neva

Blinking in the low light of the aptly named Bat Cave, I fought to keep my mouth from hanging open. "Where the hell did you guys get all of this?" If they were astounded by my lab, I was amazed at theirs.

"Iggy," everyone answered at the same time.

The man himself smiled, gave a two-finger salute. "I've got a thing for tech."

"Yeah, you want to fuck it more than any woman alive," Dopey piped up.

Iggy shrugged, but didn't deny it. "We've all got our kinks."

Everyone laughed.

"How many servers do you have?" I asked, trying to see beyond the darkened glass wall filling the far section of his space.

Iggy shrugged again. "Enough."

I nodded and sat back in my chair. I knew when I wasn't welcome. "So...how are you going to tell me if I got burned?"

"Like this. Lights, fifty percent." The room darkened and a soft light bathed the area directly in front of the tech

317

guy. Iggy lifted his hands to some kind of holo keyboard. His fingers floated in a rapid dance over the faint blue keys.

As I watched, the center of the massive table glowed that same eerie azure before it snapped into hi-res pictures that wavered ever so slightly at the edges in front of each person. My brows winged up as I recognized the system he was tapping into.

"You can hack the CIA's mainframe and database?"

No one answered. No one even chuckled.

Okay, first rule of Bat Cave, we don't speak about Bat Cave. Noted.

Sitting back, I waited for him to finish his wizardry. He maneuvered faster in the system as an outsider than I did with dedicated access. Whistling mentally, I was glad he wasn't an active opponent of the United States of America; he could do a ton of damage with the system he put together.

By the time the pictures and windows finally stopped shifting on the screen, I was a little motion sick, but I pushed it away. There was my employee file; Agent Aniera de Witte, with my picture sitting just under my name.

I blinked, then frowned. "Why are you looking at my legend?" Not that I minded the detour, but we were trying to find my native data, not my fake sleeve for the current job.

Iggy's brow furrowed as he almost stabbed at his projected keyboard. We were all quiet as the admitted Tech God Supremo worked his magic. After a long couple of minutes with nothing changing on the screen, he turned to me.

"This is all that's available. Even in the black files. Your native documents are no longer being held on the server either. I can't find them anywhere. I can't even find the cache of the files from when we pulled your information a couple days ago."

He went silent as he started pulling up other governmental databases I was sure he shouldn't be able to access. Some of them supposedly only the president could open. But since he was trying to do me a solid, I sat there with my mouth shut.

I really needed to read those dossiers. These men were much more than they originally seemed. Not that I wouldn't join up with them, but they certainly operated at a much higher level than I thought in the beginning.

"Light, seventy-five percent," Iggy called out, then he turned to me. "Do you have any other names, legends, aliases? I can't find anything except for Aneira de Witte in any database. And according to a broad, fast run, not even financial documents are currently carrying the name Neva Bylur."

My brow furrowed. "Seriously?"

Even if I was burned, I should still be in the system. They would need to keep tabs on me, make sure they could track me. They couldn't do anything if I didn't exist. "Birth records for Neva Kendrick?"

"I got no results for any name with Neva, including alternate spellings. What other aliases do you have?" Iggy lifted his hands, his fingers poised over the keyboard.

My brain blanked for a long time. There should be *something* still around, something of me that stood as testament to having been born, being alive.

Then my brain fractured.

Not just erased—erased completely. No trace. No cache. No digital fingerprint.

I didn't exist.

My lungs locked, my pulse hammering in my ears as my vision fuzzed at the edges. The chair beneath me wasn't solid anymore. I was…floating. Drifting. Like my body understood something my brain didn't.

Because if I wasn't in the system…then maybe I'd never been there at all. Maybe I wasn't real.

A terrifying slew of moments in my life slid through my mind at that thought. Reinforcing it. Etching it into my soul.

A warm hand engulfed my arm, snapping me back.

"Pix? You good?" Squirrel. His voice was too careful, too soft. Like he knew what just happened.

I nodded, pulling my arm away from Squirrel's touch. "Yeah." I cleared my throat. "Yeah, I'm good." Shaking my head, I looked at Iggy again. "Sorry. What did you ask?"

He repeated his question.

I gave a crooked smile, swallowing back the messy mix of fear and sorrow. "Please don't expose them. If Neva is gone, then they're all I have left. Literally."

"I'll keep them safe, Snow." The look he gave me was the slightest hint insulted, but mostly full of compassion.

"Do you want my legends or my aliases?" I caught myself from wrenching my fingers together into painful knots.

Iggy's brows winged up even as he shook his head. "Whatever you want to share. If we can piece all of them together, we might be able to find Neva."

We might be able to find Neva...the words ran on repeat in my head.

With the knowledge that my birth name was actually gone, I felt...lost. Adrift. Like I didn't quite belong anywhere in this world.

I hadn't had firm ties with anyone for a very long time, but at least I had my name. Some kind of identity. Something to acknowledge my presence in this world.

"Neva, Neva, Neva." I whispered my name over and over again, my fingernails digging into my legs. I was still here, still alive. Still someone.

Shoving it all away, I called myself an idiot. No one but you cares about that, Lark. Keep your shit together.

Clearing my throat again, I began, "We'll start with legends first, then. Nix Whitley, Eira Bela, Carole Douglas, Viola Whitaker, Elurra Gavino, Lehloa Fintan, Kiona Vanora."

The guys just sat there and looked at me with stunned expressions until I felt like ants were running both under and over my skin. I forced myself to hold up under their gazes.

"I'll need spellings on some of those," Iggy finally said.

I gave him what he needed to go searching for the records.

"Good. Aliases."

I blew out a breath as the terror swamped me. He was asking me to just hand over the last vestiges of my digital life, and in this day and age, it might as well have been my actual life. "Seriously, you could do a lot of damage if you screw those up. They're my last resort kinda options."

Squirrel tapped his giant shoulder to mine. "You don't have to share them, pix. But if Iggy says he might be able to piece Neva back together from them, I would give them to him. I promise you, right here, right now, you'll never come to harm by us. If you help us take down the Sisterhood, I'll personally guarantee your safety until I die."

I stared up into his eyes for a long time. If I was going to die from finding the maker of the poison I was tracking, then I might as well give this to them. In the grand scheme of things, it would be nothing more than another stepping stone to finally finding my mother's killer.

Nodding, I said, "Blake Leski, Kali Veduva, Sable Anka, Melaina Carmal."

Dopey started chuckling after a long beat of silence. "Seriously? Your aliases are all variations on Black Widow?"

I felt my cheeks heat. "I had to do something to keep them all straight in my head." Flipping him off, I focused on Iggy again. "Need any spellings?"

He nodded.

Once I was done spelling things out for him, we waited for him to work his magic again. By the time he sat back, he was shaking his head. "I'm sorry, Snow. All of your legends are gone. I found two of your aliases. I locked and copied them into our server system so they can't disappear completely, but you're down to Blake Leski and Kali Veduva."

My heart froze in my chest at the knowledge. Someone had been working to erase me for a very long time. "Graham Mortengart. That's my boss at the CIA. See what you can find on him."

Iggy did his dance with the computer. Mortengart's face soon popped up on the screen.

As I studied the full dossier on my boss, I noticed Iggy jerk. "He's got the same marker on his file I found on yours as Neva Bylur."

He walked around to my side of the table and pointed at a small set of symbols and letters near the bottom of the page. "I've never seen anything like that except in your file. Since I didn't know what it was, I didn't want to dig too much further into your data. Do you know what it is?"

I shook my head. "I've never seen it either. Can you click on it? Does it take you anywhere?"

He hovered his finger over the string of characters on the picture in front of my seat, and something popped up on the screen. His eyes widened as he moved back to his main station. "That didn't happen on yours originally."

Everyone waited in silence as he did whatever tech geniuses did when presented with new information. Finally, he called out, "Critter, is that any language you've ever seen?"

Their linguist shook his head. "It looks like a combination of characters from at least four languages, but not put together correctly. I couldn't even tell you what the individual characters say because they're out of context as they sit." He pulled his phone up and snapped a picture of the screen sitting in front of him. "I'll start running it. See what I find."

"So...are you going to click it?" I asked.

Iggy shook his head. "Like I told you before, we're mole hunting. I'm not clicking on anything that's foreign. I can't tell you where it goes or what it does, so I'm not doing anything with it."

"Do you have a laptop I could use? I could connect to my portal, see if it shows up on his. See if my stuff is still there from an internal perspective."

Iggy nodded and turned for a tall, slim cupboard. "This is wiped, so it's completely clean. I've also got it set up with a VPN, so it's as good as it's going to get for an unregistered user."

The guys passed the laptop down to me. "Thanks."

Opening the device, I waited for it to bo—damn, that was fast—then blinked at the waiting desktop. Shrugging it aside, I clicked for the browser. Navigating to the right place, I input my credentials and waited for the system to clear me.

ERROR. UNREGISTERED USER. YOU DO NOT HAVE ACCESS TO THIS SITE.

"Well, damn it. I guess I have been burned." I slumped back in my chair, my chest so tight it felt like I struggled to get air into my lungs. Everything swirled and bounced around inside me, but one thing was very clear.

"We need to go get everything we can from my house. Now." The words tumbled from my lips as I fought through the horror of another betrayal. All the years I gave to the Agency, and this is how they treated me? For something I didn't even do?

"What do you need to get most of the stuff from your lab?" Det asked. "We've got a utility truck. Can we get it in there?"

I huffed a laugh. "It won't matter unless you also happen to have thousand-pound dollies, suspension systems, ramps, and high voltage meters."

I wanted to cry, but I pushed back the sorrow. Whoever ruined my life was going to pay. And pay with their lives. My mother designed that lab herself. Slowly adding to it until the day some monster took her from me. To know it was going to be ripped out and abandoned killed some part of me.

"We've got that. Anything else?" Det asked. "I'm in command while we're waiting for Keys to get back on his feet. You'll probably also want to grab some of your personal stuff. We're all too big for you to wear our clothes." His mouth quirked up at the corner. "Especially our shoes."

I smiled, but it didn't last very long. Nodding, I pushed my chair back. "Looks like we're taking another field trip."

"I'll stay here with Critter, see what we can come up with," Iggy said.

Det, Squirrel, and Banshee all rose to their feet. "We'll go scoop up Beck if he's free." Det led the way through the doors, back out into the too bright hallway.

Walking through the offices when I was actually invited to do so made me smile for an altogether different reason. From the very beginning, Rome knocked me off balance. Made me show my hand before I was ready. Now here I was, part of his team for the next little while.

Winding through the maze of hallways, we finally made it to the infirmary. On the floor plans I memorized a couple months ago, it showed up as a massive storage closet. I could see the shape of it in my mind, as if I were still looking at that architect's blueprint.

Stepping through the door, my brows furrowed when I saw Happy drawing blood from Beck. All other thoughts disappeared.

"Is everything okay?" I asked as I slid through the group of guys with me. "You're hurt? Sick?"

All three men shook their heads.

"Just a precaution, Snow. All good," Beck answered.

I looked at Rome and tried to ferret out any details they were trying to keep from me. When he stared at me with heat in his eyes, I fought not to roll mine. Seems he hadn't learned his lesson very well.

"Keys, eyes up here," Happy said as he moved to Rome's far side.

Rome fought against the command, but finally obeyed.

Confusion must have been clear on my face when Beck finally looked at me. "We have a hypothesis. Not a good one, not one that even makes a lot of sense, but it is a hypothesis."

I nodded, glad someone was going to share. "Okay." I crossed my arms and waited.

Beck started talking about pheromones, neurotransmitters, foreign chemicals, all kinds of stuff that sounded more sci-fi than actual medicine or science. But

323

when neither Happy nor Rome interrupted to correct him or call it a joke, I had to guess they were serious.

"So you're going to run blood panels to see if there are any changes in your systems?"

Happy and Beck nodded as they looked at me.

Rome was still staring up at Happy as if the man held the secrets of the universe in his mouth.

"And Rome is some kind of rabid animal when it comes to me and no one, including him, knows why or even understands what's going on with his reaction to me?"

All three men nodded this time.

"Thank fuck," Det whispered.

I jolted, looked up at him. "You want this to be real?'

He nodded, scraping a hand down his face. "Keys is unbreakable. Steady, almost pathologically controlled to the point of having a steel pike up his ass about most things."

"Asshole," the man himself called. "Not that you're wrong, but it's still a bitch move to point it out like that."

Det rolled his eyes. "If it's something that's happened to him, I'll sleep better at night." He shrugged. "We all will."

Looking at every single man in this brotherhood nod along told me a lot more about their family structure than anything I witnessed up to this point. And it also boded better for Rome…if we could figure out what was going on.

Unless he was just some kind of closet fuckwit who didn't understand boundaries. Then he was on his own.

"Do you have the ability to run blood panels here?" I asked, although a quick look around the room told me they didn't. "Never mind."

Det filled them in on what we were planning. "Beck, are you free? The more help we can get moving shit, the faster and safer it will be."

That tripped a thought in my head. "Oh crap. I shut down the security system. And the internet routers from the second floor up. We have no way of knowing what we're walking into."

All the men turned to me, even Rome.

Varying expressions settled on each face, but the most prevalent was strained acceptance. I had a feeling they looked like this a lot while still in the Teams. The knowledge that things were going to suck, but that they still had to go kill some shit.

"Doesn't matter. We've got to get your stuff out and anything else you think will be helpful from your lab. Then we can set you up here with something until you tell us what you need. We can outfit the rest of it," Det said. "If you're going to be helping us, it will be safer for you to do your work here."

I shook my head as problem after problem with that whole idea ran through my mind. Far and away, the worst of the problems was Oskar Jorgenssen. He knew my home address. Or, at least, I assumed he did.

Wait.

"What are the odds Jorgenssen is behind this?" I asked the room. I had too much flying around in my head to think straight, so I might as well start acting like I was part of a team. What better opportunity?

"I don't know, pix. He's all kinds of happy for you to be helping his daughter. Do you think he would screw up any chance he has for you to help him? Or not hurt his daughter if it came out that he did do this?"

The doubt on Squirrel's face settled something inside of me.

"Besides, he thinks I'm your man, so you moving in here or into my place would make more sense. Especially if he's old school."

A guttural sound ripped from Rome's throat—low, ragged, animal.

I barely had time to process it before he turned his back to his, staring at the far wall like his life depended on it. His hands flexed. Relaxed. Flexed again. Every muscle in his body locked tight like he was fighting something physical, something alive inside him.

"You've got to leave." His voice was wrecked, jagged like broken glass. "If you're going to talk about her moving in with him…I need you to fucking leave."

Squirrel stiffened.

Even Det took a cautious step back.

For the first time, I saw some of that control they all touted. Maybe there was something to this whole chemical thing.

"I won't be moving into Squirrel's place. I also won't move in here. That puts all of you out, and I still have to be able to move around when and where I want. Even if I come up with some kind of cover for not being at school, I can't just ditch it."

Another string of problems blared through my brain like a parade. Shit. "What if I'm burned at the school, too?"

Issue after issue, problem after problem. I had no solid answers, no real information, and no great guesses that could lead to anything that allowed me to keep the work I already completed.

"I'll go check with Iggy on that part really fast," Det said as he ran off. "Stay here," he yelled back.

"If not here and not with Squirrel, where are you going to go? You really can't go back to your house. Not until all of this, whatever it is, is over," Beck said softly. "We can protect you, Snow. No worries on that score."

I shook my head. They didn't understand why I needed my own space, and I wasn't going to take the time or emotional capital I still held to try to explain it to them. "I've got a couple bolt holes around here. No way for anyone to connect them to me." I snorted.

Thanks to some very smart ancestors, I had my pick of no fewer than six holes within a three-mile run, which said nothing about the ones across the river. Or even the rest of the world. I would have to check the local listings to make sure they were vacant, but any of them would do.

Hell, at least three of them were in this very neighborhood. My great-great grandpa loved the docks near Red Hook, and he bought every single piece of real estate he could. Honestly, the guys might have bought their building from the trust. Who knew?

"Do any of them have space for your lab equipment or will that still need to be housed here?" Beck asked.

That was the single wrench in my works. The only other lab space I had was more than thirty minutes away in a space which was leased long-term as a medical processing facility before it went out of business due to bad management. They ended up leaving all of their equipment and the banks never came to repossess it. Boon for me, sucked for them.

"Are you guys housing any of the poison you need assayed here?" I asked. It would be easier to have everything here. Or at least within walking distance.

I knew at least one of the empty dock properties could be outfitted pretty quickly. And it offered expansive space, so I could technically hole up there without any risk from anything I might be testing.

Det ran back in. "You're burned at the school. Iggy hacked your principal's system, found the notice of your resignation, sent by you personally. Seems your aging parents need you to come back due to an emergency of some kind."

"They're not burning you," Rome murmured, still not looking at me. HIs voice was low. Flat. Final. Like he was reading a death sentence.

My blood ran ice cold.

"They're caging you."

The words dropped like stones in my gut.

"They're closing off every exit, sealing up every crack. Cutting you off from your job, your money, your past—unitl you have nowhere left to run but back to them."

I sucked in a sharp breath as something my mom always used to joke about slammed through my mine. That if the cancer hadn't gotten her, she wouldn't have died from guns and threats, but from paperwork and vanishing records.

I looked at Rome's back, my mouth dry. "How long do you think until they cut off the last door?"

This wasn't a burn. They were trying to corral me. Shoving all the air that wanted to get caught in my chest out through my mouth, I tried to think in straight lines.

"Okay, school's burned. Which is better for those children to not be around me. I'm burned at the agency, no longer have any access to any of my files or …" My voice trailed off.

Shoving a hand down my shirt and into my bra, I felt the first flicker of hope.

"Uh…pix…whatcha doing?" Squirrel asked.

My fingers closed around the small, body-warm, plastic devices, my pulse rocketing.

I pulled the thumb drives free, holding them like they were trophies. The fucking proof that I still existed. "They took my name." My voice shook, but I let it. "They took my job. My school. My fucking identity."

I looked at Rome, at every single one of them, then back down at the small devices in my palm.

I curled my fingers around them like a promise.

"But they didn't take Neva."

I smiled, sharp and vicious. Opening my palm, I showed them the two small devices. "We'll have to work out how to deal with Jorgenssen, but then? Then I'm going to watch them burn."

Chapter 32

Rome

Listening to the group of them leave for Neva's home to get her stuff and lab equipment, I blew out a long breath. I tried to stifle the thoughts and rage that were gradually filling my body.

She was going to be in a van. In close proximity with all of them. They were going to be in her home with her, alone. Able to touch her skin, smell her sunshine and spice. Hell, they would get to experience her sass.

The room snapped sideways—no, folded in on itself. My stomach dropped like I'd stepped from a helo, and then—

I was standing.

No transition. No shift of muscles, no effort. Just one blink and I was somewhere else. Moving. Breathing too hard.

Ready to fight.

Anyone who kept me from her.

"What the fuck do you think you're doing?" Gigs asked as he jumped in front of me, his brows lowered in confusion. Then his expression cleared into surprise before being chased away by anger. "Are you seriously trying to go after her right now?"

My breath heaved in my chest, but my mind was blank. No thoughts, no plans, no memory of standing. Just a torturous need to go find her, consume her, absorb her into my very essence.

Gigs's voice barely registered through the pulse in my ears.

My brain cleared as he gripped my dick in a hard fist and squeezed until my eyes crossed. Bile rushed up my throat and I fought to breathe around the pain.

"Go sit your ass back down. And if you make me touch your dick again, you won't have to worry about having it for fun play times. I'll cut it off and leave it on *my* shelf." He wiped his hand on his shirt like he'd touched something slimy.

"Fuck." I breathed out the word, limping backward. Every single inch of me felt nothing but bone-crushing pain. Which didn't make any sense. "How did I get up from the table?" The words came out too slow, too detached. Like I wasn't really in my own body anymore.

He shook his head as he pulled the rails up to keep me caged in. "I have no damn idea, but I think you might be onto something with this whole outside influence idea. You can barely walk, but you cleared that bed like you have fucking wings or springs in your ass." He stared down at me. "Do I need to handcuff you?"

I glared at him, then gave the suggestion true consideration.

Blowing out a breath, I nodded. Couldn't hurt at this point. "I can't guarantee I won't try it again. At least it will offer up some resistance."

Gigs stared at me harder, like he could look inside my brain and see what was actually wrong. "We've got to get this figured out, Keys. You're almost useless."

There was no trace of humor or even a hint of bite to his words. He simply stated facts, however hard they were to hear.

I winced. "Get the cuffs. And we need to identify a good lab or neurologist. Pathologist. Someone who can help with doing these workups."

"Snow is a pathologist," he offered slowly. "Question is, will you be able to keep your cool long enough for her to try to help you?" He swallowed hard. "Or us."

I lifted my gaze to him, tried to read his expression for what he wasn't saying. "You're scared, too."

He flinched the tiniest bit, licked his lips.

Gigs shifted a look over his shoulder for a quick second before he looked at me again, then lowered his voice. "Do you remember, probably three years now, around a year before we got kicked out? They asked for volunteers for some kind of tracking program. We wouldn't have to wear any devices, nothing that would show on any foreign scans. Hell, they promised we would effectively become invisible."

My mind cleared to crystal with his words. I remembered exactly what he was talking about, as if it happened yesterday.

"We got it a couple weeks before going after the cartel in Columbia. It's when we found another Sis—" I stared up at him as my mind exploded. "The Sisterhood attack. It was the first time we were able to link their strikes."

He nodded, scraping a hand down his face. "What if there was something in that injectable?"

My face scrunched up as I tried to sort through the many pieces of information floating around in my head. "Like what?"

He threw his hands up in the air. "I don't know, Keys." He spun a circle, huffing out a big breath, his blue eyes as wide as his arm span. "They told us before we left on the mission that our bodies couldn't handle the RF emissions or some shit."

Tapping a fist to his temple, he shook his head. "I can't remember exactly what they said, but it was along those lines."

Horror and rage ate through my veins as some of the pieces fell together. "There was a breakdown in the compound they injected into us. It didn't mix with some of the vaccinations we got for being where they put us. It worked a grand total of eight days, then we all felt like shit. Puking, literally shitting ourselves into dehydration. Call Iggy and Critter. Get them down here. We need to all talk together."

When Gigs shook his head as his shoulders relaxed, I realized he'd been more than worried about this. He was terrified. "It will be easier to take you in the gurney down there. And for fuck's sake, cover up. Your dick isn't that special."

I snorted as I pulled the sheet over my lower body. "Hey, you're the one getting handsy."

He snapped his teeth at me as he slammed the gurney into the doorjamb before he got the rolling bed angled correctly. "Fuck. Sorry. And keep this shit up, next time, I'll let Snow deal with your shit. How 'bout that?"

I cringed and tried to hide. Legit whimpered at the fucking idea. I cupped my dick in my hands and tried to breathe through the nightmares.

"Yeah. Keep it up, numbnuts. I'll do more than sic Snow on you. I'll tell her all your weak spots, then sit back and enjoy the show." His laugh trailed down the hall like ghostly fingers of doom coming to get me.

We finally made it to the Bat Cave.

Iggy and Critter were hard at work at different stations, each mumbling to himself as he fought with whatever he saw on his machine.

Gigs rammed the gurney into a second doorjamb as he tried to get me into the room. "Fuck, we should have made these halls and doors bigger."

"Or not bring hospital beds to the tech depot," Critter drawled softly as he glanced over at us. "What are you doing here? And why is Keys cuffed to the railing?"

Iggy looked up from his computer at that. He sat there in stunned silence as he flicked his gaze up and down the length of my body and the aforementioned bed. "What Critter said."

Gigs gave them a rundown of what we were thinking.

Before he could finish digging through the injection story again, Iggy was up at the main computer. Inventive curses colored the air as he dug into a familiar system we all hated. Department of the Navy. When he didn't pull up anything and shove it to individual screens, I assumed he didn't find anything of value yet.

Turning to Critter, I studied him. He looked equal parts sick, furious, and quizzical. I understood the first two. The third was a bit of a mystery.

"You good?" I asked softly, not wanting to disturb Iggy or his process. The man filtered more information than an entire floor of data crunchers.

Critter nodded, then immediately shook his head. He turned to look at me. Horror rode his piercing blue eyes. "If they gave us something that could possibly have lasting implications or caused whatever the hell is going on with you and Snow..." his voice trailed off. He shook his head again.

Yeah. The whole idea made me feel violated in ways I didn't think were possible, either. Especially this late in the game. I knew the government was more interested in money, international standing, and power than anything else, but to purposely screw us over like this?

I thought the mission we'd devoted ourselves to was noble, at least. That the people we trusted with our lives on the daily were on the up and up. To find out they might have fucked us over like this in some kind of secret…whatever the fuck this was?

"FUCK!" Iggy shouted. He spun a tight circle, threw one of his hulk punches at the wall. A hole cratered open under the blow, plumes of sheetrock dust shifting through the air before it settled again.

My heart sank as my belly twisted. "What? What did they do to us?"

Iggy shook his head. "I can't find it. Anything. Just like Snow, all of our fucking records are gone."

My brow furrowed, my brain stalled at the answer I definitely wasn't expecting. "What?"

Iggy gave a rushed report of what they found for Neva, or rather, what they hadn't found. "That's one reason they left immediately to go get her stuff and hopefully clear out the lab." He paced another tight circle and landed a second blow to the wall.

I winced, but said nothing. He, better than all of us, knew how to patch walls. Although, we should probably think about something other than sheetrock for walls if we were going to keep getting shitty news.

"Well, when she gets back, make sure to remind her to give you the thumb drives she had in her bra," Gigs said. "She was all kinds of excited and terrifying when she promised to kill them and watch them burn."

Critter snorted. "She's fucking crazy, man."

She was, and it was a thing of sheer, stunning, terrible beauty.

Crap, I couldn't think about her too hard. I shook my head. "You still have our original files, right?" I asked Iggy.

He nodded. "Yeah. A few hundred copies of each one are stored around the web, drop servers, and black boxes. We've got hard and digital copies. So we're good there."

"Then why are you so butthurt about our files being erased?" Critter asked.

I sighed and rolled my eyes. Neva might really be onto something calling him Dopey.

"Because it means we've been made." Our tech guy just stared at him.

Dopey dipped his chin as if he knew that. "Yeah, but we were planning on that happening, though. So why are you upset about it now? Just the fact that it actually happened, or is it something related to what we could've been doped up with?"

Huh. I hadn't thought of that. There might still be hope for him.

I turned to Iggy for that answer as well.

Iggy heaved a sigh. "A few reasons, actually. One, none of my alarms tripped telling me were made. Two, do we assume this is somehow in connection with Snow, or did someone finally get around to deleting our entire collection of native data from the US government's system? Three, I had backdoors programmed into those files so I could continue to access certain systems without a lot of trouble. As long as those files remained on the servers where they were hosted, we had open access. That's gone." He spun and slammed his fingers through the holo keyboard.

I might know why he changed to a holo keyboard.

Shifting to look at the screens that popped up in front of each of us, I studied the picture on the screen. No fewer than eight government databases blinked with red text and warnings of the consequences of accessing secured sites.

"Shit."

Iggy nodded. "Like I said."

"Technically, you said fuck. But yeah, that too." Critter blew out a breath. "So we're out with no recourse? No way to move forward against the Sisterhood?"

Iggy plopped down into a chair, the wheels sending him off for a short ride over the cement floor. He rubbed at his eyes with both hands. "Not out, out. But it's going to take time to get access to some of those databases again. And they aren't cheap or easy."

"Are they absolutely essential?" I asked.

Iggy scooted his way back to his usual position at the big table. "They certainly make things easier to verify and double-check."

"But not 'we'll die if we don't have them' essential." A curl of relief slid through me.

He shook his head. "No." He sounded like he lost an entire harem of girlfriends. Honestly, I thought he might be about to cry, he looked so sad.

"Can you run our files and see if there's any mention of the tracking program or the creators and all that jazz?" Gigs asked as he shuffled around the hospital bed and took a seat at the table. "I'm sorry we lost access, but we did come down here to ask about something specific."

Iggy shook himself, nodded. "Yeah, sorry." He stood up and resumed asserting his digital dominance. "You said a couple years ago? Before we got the boot?"

Gigs and I both nodded.

"Yup," Gigs then answered since Iggy was too busy to look at us. He turned to Critter. "What do you remember about that experiment?"

Critter shook his head. "Nothing, really. Just another failed biohack they were super pumped about. Other than having recurring nightmares about the shits that lasted for what felt like forever, I haven't given it another thought. Especially since it didn't amount to anything."

He tipped his head to the side as he snorted. "You guys remember when Squirrel tried to get through that dead zone in training? They lit him up like a fucking Christmas tree before he made it a couple steps. He just about threw a table through the ballistic glass where the geeks were all huddled."

"How long after the injection did he fail the training?" Gigs asked. He pulled his phone from his pocket, went searching for his notes app, and opened a new note.

Critter shrugged. "I don't know, man. We were all close to dead in the infirmary for roughly a week. So I guess a couple days after that." He shook his head. "It was weird, though. I felt better after that week. And it was more than not just shitting my pants, anymore. I felt fucking awesome. I repped and maxed out in the gym for two weeks. New personal records across the board." Running a hand over his arm in appreciation, he tipped his head to the side. "Didn't you guys?"

Casting my mind back to that time of my life, I tried to bring up anything other than the horrific gastrointestinal issues. I guess they were more traumatizing than what I originally thought, because they were really the only part of that whole mess I remembered. Other than the disappointment of the failed biohack we could have used to our advantage a hundred times over out in the field.

Next to me, Gigs nodded and said, "Yeah. I didn't rep or max out, mainly because I didn't want them trying to up my routines or give me another stress test and end up shitting all over their equipment. But I do remember a lady sometime around then. I went for hours. Literal hours and didn't feel any strain, exhaustion, nothing. Just felt like I

335

could keep going, maybe for days. She tapped out, which is what stopped me."

They both turned to me, eyebrows raised.

I shook my head, shrugged. "I remember feeling good, but that's about it. Probably happy I was no longer destroying the bathroom every fifteen minutes."

"You were lucky if you got fifteen-minute breaks," Critter mumbled.

"I've got the records. Of course, most of them are redacted, but they're there," Iggy interrupted. "I don't remember anything particularly special about that time either. Just the overwhelming relief of not feeling like wet trash for time unending. I didn't go hard at the gym or have a lady to help me out with anything. But I do remember the training event, though."

He tipped his head to the side. "And really the only reason that sticks out in my brain is because I had to help cool Squirrel down. He was like a fucking rage machine. When you said he almost put that table through the ballistic glass, you weren't kidding. His pupils were pinpricks. If I didn't know him so well, I would have thought he was tweaking."

My brows lifted. "I don't remember that at all."

Iggy shook his head. "No, it was me, Critter, Squirrel, and Schnauze. The rest of you were off doing something else." He closed his eyes for a moment, tapped a couple fingers against his forehead. "I wanna say they were going to try to pit us against each other in some kind of trial run? New gear, new biohack." He thumped his head a little harder with a loose fist. "What the hell was it?"

I pushed my mind back, trying to think through those years. Having come out the other side, it felt more like soup in my brain. Everything weaved and flowed together, without any particular beginning or end points, just a bunch of hell, day in, day out. Nothing but doctors, nurses, a never-ending stream of techs in our faces.

Something tickled the edge of my brain.

"Wait." I tried to dig out whatever it was. It sat there, niggling and wiggling, like a mite trying to burrow deeper into my memory. I just had to catch it, draw it out. "Iggy, say that again."

He repeated himself, adding a few more details. "We were going to meet somewhere in the middle of an unknown compound. Helo drop, hike in. It got tossed bec—"

336

"Because Squirrel threatened one of the techs. They knocked us down, then wanted to do more tests." I opened my eyes and met the gaze of my guys. "They put us all together in a barracks off site and wouldn't let us go home, even though we already got the green light."

Gigs nodded, his eyes wide. "Yeah, yeah, yeah. Instead of immediately sending us out to Columbia, they made us wait for two weeks while we ran more tests and drills."

"Oh, fuck. That's right. Squirrel went from tweaking to almost useless," Critter added. "We couldn't get him out of bed. He could barely stand upright longer than five minutes without crashing down."

The full picture finally emerged in my head. "They came in after we failed to keep Squirrel on his feet for the third day in a row. They injected us with something else. Told us it would flush out our systems, that the original tracking tech was wrecking us."

Iggy dug through the records again. "I don't show any secondary injection records for any of us. But I remember it happening as well."

"Yeah, me too," Critter offered.

We all looked at Gigs. He nodded. "I remember praying it didn't kill us by making us shit ourselves to death. That's no way for a SEAL to die."

I turned to Iggy. "Did all of us get the same initial injection, according to the records?"

He nodded before he doubled back to his information. "Yeah, I'm pretty sure, but I'll check again. You really think they could have dosed us with something other than just the tracking hardware they told us about?"

Something else dinged in my brain. "Shit."

They all turned to look at me.

I shook my head. "Give me a second; we need confirmation, not just me making shit up because we're all freaking out." I licked my lips, felt my heart rate kick up a notch in my chest. "Iggy, when did we find the first SRD attack?"

I felt each gaze land as if it were a physical weight on my skin. I shook them off and kept looking at Iggy. "The date, man. Give me the date."

Iggy slowly turned back to his computer. His fingers were no less quick over the keys, but each phantom press of the holo keyboard felt like a drumbeat to my funeral dirge. "We reported the first SRD attack in February of 2020."

The room got smaller, trapping us in with the truth that would do anything but set us free.

"Three months later, they tag us for an experimental tracking program." I let the words sink in.

Watched them ripple through my brothers.

"Then we were sent into an SRD site," Happy added.

Iggy's jaw locked. "And the next one, and the next one. The fucking one after that."

"And every fucking time we got pulled back out, someone else died...but never us." Critter's voice was tight, clipped.

"We weren't just in the right place at the right time. We were put there." The words were barely more than air.

"We got tasked for the biohack, got fucked over with it, then went out in-field, and found the second SRD strike site. But we weren't taken seriously," Critter said through clenched teeth, his voice heavy with pulsing anger.

"And every time a job we were put out on came back with some kind of tie to SRD, we were hushed. But we still got assigned to every single attack. No other Team Three came back with reports of SRD," Iggy replied. "We were the only ones."

Gigs sucked in a noisy breath through his nose. "We were targeted. Over and above what we thought before, we were fucking targeted. They gave us something, claimed it didn't work, but then put us on point for every damn call out for suspected SRD involvement. Whatever they dosed us with..." He shook his head, his words choked off.

The beat of silence was heavy in the room as fury and horrific amazement settled on our shoulders.

He clenched his hands, then banged them against the table with a heavy thud. "Whatever they dosed us with must have been some kind of control or antigen, immunotherapy, something. We're the only ones who got that close to the carnage left behind and not died from it. Our specific team. Anyone who went with us, or the doctors who came in to help, they all lost people. We lost how many support members to this shit?"

"Seventeen," Iggy said softly. "Seventeen brothers and sisters in arms to this fucking nightmare. That's not including civilian and medical personnel from outside the Navy."

"They didn't just use us," I said, the words tasting like poison. "They tracked us. Watched us rot. Measured our

338

fucking survival rate. And when we didn't die fast enough, they sent us back."

The weight in the room shifted.

"They dosed us, then sent us into death zones. Just us. No other teams. And when SRD's poison didn't touch us— they kept sending us back. Again and again."

Critter's jaw flexed. "We were the test subjects. The civilians, the medical teams—they wer the fucking control group."

No one moved. No one spoke. The horror settled into our bones.

They sent us into SRD's carnage like fucking lab rats. And we were too good at surviving.

"It makes the most sense. Beyond the shit we ran into personally with SRD, we're literally the only team who hasn't lost someone," I said. "And fuck me, but we should have. The number of times we found an active SRD site and none of us got sick? None of us even got so much as a blistered toe when those bodies are riddled with—" I cut off the words.

We were all too familiar with what SRD's victims looked like.

"The minute the guys get back with Snow, we need to hunker down and run those tests. As many as we can think of," Iggy said, his voice vibrating with emotion. "As many as possible and as quickly as we can."

We all nodded.

"Iggy, do you have any footage on file from her lab? See if there's anything we can get ordered, put it on rush delivery, if necessary. I don't think they'll be able to get everything out of there, so we need to be prepared to get everything and have it done here. Especially with her skillset, we can't afford to lose her," I said.

I waited a beat, but knew I had to speak the words resting on my tongue.

"If I lose it," I swallowed around the gravel in my throat, "take me out."

I let the words hang, but I already knew. This was a ticking bomb. Maybe a day. Maybe a week.

Maybe tonight.

"I mean it. If I try to get to her, if I start acting like some feral piece of shit—stop me. No hesitation. No second chances."

No one laughed. No one even smiled. They knew what I was saying.

Hell, begging.

Critter's voice was quiet, like a silent blade through the air. "And if she's the one to take you out?"

I forced a smile that didn't feel like mine. "Then at least I went out under her hands."

"We'll take you out, Keys. No worries on that score," Critter promised. "But if she comes after me for trying it, I'm out. One of the others can suffer her wrath." He shuddered.

I snorted as the other two laughed.

He wasn't wrong.

Did it make me a sick fucker that I hoped she tried to hurt anyone who came after me?

Chapter 33

Neva

"I've got everything I need; where are we at with the suspension system?" I asked as I ran back down the stairs with a couple duffel bags. Tossing them on the floor, I stood with Det near the service door at the back of my family home.

"Squirrel and Banshee got the pieces covered in as much foam and cushions as they could manage. They're working to get things strung up across the back of the truck right now. What other pieces do you need that you can't replace quickly?"

"As long as I have the GC-Mass Spec, the High-Performance Liquid Chromatograph, and the PCR Machine, everything else can be replaced within two days. Including all the chemicals and reagents. Don't worry about anything else right now."

Saying the words made pieces of my heart rip off and fall away, but I promised myself when all of this was done, I was going to come back and put my mom's lab back together. It was all I had left of her, and I wasn't going to lose her legacy. Not like this.

"We didn't find the gold boxes, Snow. I'm sorry," Det said softly.

I sighed, shook my head. "We knew it was a long shot. I have the data on my computers, so as long as Iggy clears those, we should have at least a baseline idea of what was going on. Not to mention my notes and everything else I stashed in the hidden closet."

Det smiled down at me, his features bathed in shadows. "That was quite a collection you had in there. Get the rest of what you needed?"

I nodded, tapping my foot to the duffel bags at my feet. "Yeah, and I can hold them in my lap if they won't fit in the back." I managed to distribute my advanced plant kits among the three bags and still fit most of my clothes, toiletries, and other stuff for daily living.

"You'll probably end up holding them. The others are going to be in the back until we get all of this shit back to the shop. They'll be able to watch and hold the suspended items to make sure everything arrives safely." Det crossed his arms, then looked up to monitor the work of his team. He nodded to himself as we stood there.

I fought not to watch them manhandle the ridiculously delicate equipment. I knew going in we would need to have a technician come out and recalibrate everything—which reminded me, I needed to call Iggy and see if he could find someone to get on that.

Pulling my phone from my pocket, I held the button to turn it back on.

Det grabbed it from my hands, quickly smashed it down on the pavement, then crunched on it a couple times with his boots. "Not until we get you a new one. Use mine until we get you squared away." He held out his phone. "All their names and numbers are programmed already."

I glared up at him. "You didn't need to kill mine."

He bared his teeth at me in a feral grin. "Nah, I didn't. But it made me feel better to do so. You've caused a lot of problems for my family, Snow. That's not to say I'm not grateful for the help you're going to give us, but I'm still pissed about all of it. Taking it out on your phone was the easier option." He smiled wider. "Not to mention safer."

I snorted a laugh. "Never let it be said you don't think things through, Smartie."

He rolled his eyes. "That's not one of the Dwarfs' names, Snow."

"Yeah, but except for Dopey, Happy, and Bashful, none of the rest of you really fit any of the Disney names. So I'm handing out new ones."

Det studied me for a moment. "Banshee isn't going to appreciate being called Bashful."

My mouth fell open. "How did you know I nicknamed *him* that?"

Det rolled his eyes. "Oh, please. The way he blushes and fades into the woodwork around you? Of course, you're naming him Bashful. Not that he is, but you're not exactly one of the brothers yet. Once you get to know him better, you'll change his name."

I narrowed my eyes at him. "You're kinda bossy, you know that? Not quite as bossy as Rome—because I've yet to meet a man who is—but you're rising up to second place."

He shrugged. "Change my name then. I'm smart, but we all are. At least be a little more original than that."

Squirrel chose that moment to hop down from the truck. "If I get a vote, I'm claiming Hotsy Totsy for my name." He pumped his thick dark brows up and down as he sent me air kisses.

I rolled my eyes. "Sure thing, Hotsy."

He thrust both fists into the air and gave a low hoot of victory. "Hear that motherfuckers? I'm Hotsy Fucking Totsy."

Beck and Banshee jumped down from the back of the truck, giving Squirrel a wide berth as they came and joined us on the sidewalk by the service door.

"What's he going on about?" Beck asked.

Det explained while Squirrel did another victory lap.

"He does know that's not exactly a badge of honor, right?" Banshee asked, his face screwed up in confusion. "A hotsy-totsy is mostly an idiot who only survives on her body. At least that's how I understand the term."

Squirrel came around and grabbed his brother in a loose headlock. "And? What's your point, *Bashful*? Least I'm not out here running scared of the delectable Snow."

When he gave Banshee a noogie that made my head hurt in sympathy, Banshee's cheeks darkened in the low light. "I'm not bashful." He glared at me from his restrained position under Squirrel's arm.

I shrugged. "Sorry." Leaning down, I hooked my hands into the handles of my duffels and hoisted up the full bags so I could throw them in the front cabin of the full box truck.

Squirrel let Banshee go and quickly leapt forward to grab my bags. "I've got those for you, pix."

Beck reached out and grabbed Banshee's shoulder before the other man could topple to the ground after Squirrel essentially dropped him. "Easy, Hotsy. We need Bashful alive and well, not splattered on the street."

Bashful glared at his buddy. "I'm not fucking bashful, Schnauze." He turned, glared at me again. "Change it, Snow. Change my name, right now."

I laughed a little. "Well, Det is officially Bossy. What do you want to be called?"

The guys all shifted their gazes from me to Bossy, then back to me, and burst into laughter.

Squirrel came over, gathered me up into his arms. "He really is bossy. That's a good one, pix." He nuzzled his face into my neck, gave a deep sniff.

Rolling my eyes, I pushed him away. "Why are you sniffing me again? You know how weird that is, right?"

As he eased back, the look on his face had me raising a brow.

He looked like he was blissed out, high on life. I didn't see the hunger I saw from Rome when he got close to me, but more like Squirrel was finally home. As if I represented something more than just a random woman momentarily invading his life.

He heaved a sigh. "I don't know, Snow. Every time I get close enough to smell you, it hits me right in my feels." He put his gigantic hands against his chest, looking at me with puppy eyes. "Like being back at my Memaw's house when she gave me a hug and the biggest plate of cookies you've ever seen. And they're all for me."

I turned to look at the other guys and saw the same confusion and wariness on their faces. "You know that's not normal, though, right?"

Squirrel just shrugged. "Don't care. I loved my Memaw more than anyone in the world. You bring her to mind, and the memory doesn't hurt like it usually does."

"We really need to get that testing done," Beck whispered.

I nodded. "He sniffed me at the school, too. That's why Jorgenssen thinks we're together."

"What does she smell like, Hotsy?" Banshee asked.

Squirrel shook his head. "The past and cookies."

Beck leaned down and sniffed at my hair. When he leaned back, he shook his head. "Just smells like girl shampoo to me."

Banshee and Det came over and gave me sniffs, as well. They gave similar answers to Beck's.

"So why are Squirrel and Keys up in arms over you?" Banshee asked. "One like a lover, the other more like a brother?"

Shrugging, I admitted, "I have no idea, guys. I can honestly say this, or anything even remotely resembling anything like this, has never happened to me before. Usually, people can't stand me, and since I hate people, it works out. Only since meeting you guys has anything unusual started happening."

A long string of cars slid by on the street, jerking all of us back to the purpose of the evening. We were being hunted by trained agents intent on who knew what. Standing around on the street outside of my last known location wasn't exactly the smartest move we could be making.

"Get up in there, take your positions," Det ordered.

"Roger that, Bossy," Squirrel teased as he jumped up into the truck.

Beck and Banshee snickered as they followed the larger man.

Det just glared at me.

I shrugged. "You said to call you something other than Smartie. Guess Bossy is here to stay." I moved to the passenger side of the truck and climbed in.

The rolling slam of the rear door was my only answer.

Bossy got into the truck beside me, then waited for someone from inside the truck to knock three times before he put the large vehicle into motion. We pulled out and slid into traffic. "Are you going to make things easier or harder for me to keep my family safe, Neva?"

His tone was low, but I didn't doubt the promise of violence in it.

"It's not my intention to make anything harder for anyone. I just want to get to the end of this particular rainbow and move on with my life." I shifted to look out the window, watching the familiar neighborhood slide by in the dark.

"What is this rainbow for you?"

I shook my head. "Don't worry about it. Nothing that involves you guys."

I couldn't exactly say that I fully planned to be dead by the time I found the pot of gold at the end of it. Not that it would be anything but the gleaming pile of lies I'd been told my entire life.

"If it's nothing and doesn't involve us, why are you hooking up with us? That's what I can't figure out. You say you joined up because we helped you with Brantley and Lawrence. If you've been with the Agency for as long as you have, then you wouldn't be this trusting. Not with a group of literal strangers. What you're saying and your actions aren't stacking up to the same answer."

I turned to face him and saw him watching the traffic and road.

He was skilled as a driver; barely a bump could be felt as we drove with the delicate equipment in the back. If we were lucky, we'd be able to get a technician out soon and get the machinery recalibrated quickly.

"Answer me, please," he said. He turned to look at me for a moment before he went back to studying and attacking the road to give us the smoothest ride possible.

I shook my head. "Why does it matter to you?"

He snorted. "This is the only family I have left. I'll protect them until the day I die. That's why it matters to me."

I smiled, the curve of my mouth tinged with sadness. The only person I knew who loved me like that was my mother—in her own special way. "For the same reason. I'm avenging someone taken from me."

We slid to a gentle halt at a stoplight. He turned to look at me in the brighter light of the streetlamps at the corner. "Avenging."

I nodded. "Yes. Righting a wrong."

"Your mother."

I bumped a shoulder in the air, nodded again. "Yes. But does it matter who I'm avenging?"

He shook his head. "Not at all. Who are you looking at to bring down?"

I blew out a breath. This man asked some very direct questions. I could understand why and how he got to be the second-in-command of this particular group of men. "I don't know."

The light turned green, but he didn't put the truck back into motion. "You're searching for answers just like we are."

Nodding, I curled my arms around my belly and stared out the front window. "I have been for the last couple of years."

A chorus of horns blared to life around us and Det finally eased off the brakes, allowing the truck to glide into drive again. "Why now? And why the long way around?"

I shook my head. "I'm done sharing, Bossy."

He reached across the bench seat, but I scooted away before he could put his hand on me.

"Will the information hurt my brothers or impede my ability to keep them safe?" His hand fell to the seat in a clenched fist.

I shook my head again. "No. Not that I know of."

And it shouldn't. For as long as I could remember, I knew my mother died from cancer. It wasn't until a few years ago that I began to realize there was someone stalking her. That what and who she was as a person was the reason she was dead. And that someone was using the world as a stage to perfect the very poison someone used to kill her.

"Will you tell me as soon as you think it could?" His question was quiet, and I had a feeling this man didn't ask for a lot from anyone.

Turning to look at him in the shifting light, I studied his profile. The clenching of his jaw muscles, the white knuckles of his fingers around the steering wheel…this was a man accustomed to having as much information as possible. The fact some unknown entity might have some information he didn't must be driving him crazy.

Since I wasn't actually a monster, I blew out a steady breath. "Yes, Bossy. I'll tell you if that ever changes."

He relaxed the slightest degree, but didn't turn to look at me. All he did was dip his chin and continue driving in that focused way of his. I wondered if this is what he looked like while diffusing bombs.

By the time we pulled into the brightly lit garage, I felt like I'd aged a decade. Too many thoughts not spoken. Too many memories of promises sealed on my heart. And far too many things to worry about.

I slid down from the front passenger seat as the garage door sank closed. When it hit the cement with a soft thump, the back door of the truck rolled up. Someone jumped out and hit the bolt near the bottom of the garage door, locking it into the floor.

"All locked up and ready for bed," Squirrel said as he came around the end of the truck. "Wanna cuddle, Snow?" He opened his arms wide, a look of nostalgia on his face.

"For fuck's sake, Squirrel. She's not a cuddler," Critter sniped as he came into the garage. "And Rome will still try to beat your ass if you attempt it."

"Too fucking right," the man's voice filtered from everywhere and nowhere, echoing through the garage.

Critter snorted. "He's in Ops. We need to have a chat. I drew the short straw. Follow me." He spun on his heel and walked away.

Squirrel came over and curled his arm around my shoulders. "Let's go, pix. That mean asshole can't do anything to me out here."

"I'm watching you, shithead. Keep touching her and see what happe—" the voice went quiet.

Squirrel and the guys with me chuckled.

"Sounds like Iggy cut the feed," Beck explained. "And don't provoke him, Hotsy. We need him coherent, not a bowl of whatever fucked up soup his brain is whenever she's around."

Squirrel heaved a sigh and scooted away a couple inches. "Fine. But I'll get my cuddles one of these days, pix. Don't think I won't." He pouted like a grumpy teenager, but he didn't try to touch me again.

Considering I was this close to trying to scoop the mountain sized man into my arms, I just dipped my chin and followed the rest of the group. Maybe if I didn't focus on the warm and fuzzy feelings I also got around Squirrel, I could successfully ignore the hot and bothered feelings I got around Rome.

We finally made it back to Ops. Which was apparently also the Bat Cave. And Tech Depot. And Iggy's Gloryhole. Plus a couple of other names I wasn't willing to remember.

I blinked when I saw Rome. Strapped down. Not just handcuffed, but restrained like a psych ward patient. His wrists and ankles pinned to the gurney, his chest belted for good measure.

At least this time he was fully clothed.

Small mercies.

I cleared my throat. "Uh...seems a little kinky for a group meeting."

All the guys except Rome chuckled.

"It's for all of our protection. Once Iggy got the alert the truck was moving back home, we had to lock him down so he wouldn't try to run out and meet you. And by you, I mean specifically you, Snow. He was more than willing to let everyone else die, by his hand, if they touched you."

Happy rolled his eyes as he leaned back in his chair. "Hence the extra cuffs."

My brows winged up. "Extra?"

Happy nodded, gave us a quick report of what happened right when we left.

Everyone turned and gaped at Rome, who was too busy examining the far wall to look at any of us.

"He promised to look at the wall or I would blindfold him," Happy added.

My mouth fell open. "Things have gotten that bad since we left?"

Rome snarled low in his throat as he started to turn his head.

Happy slapped him, forcing his head back. "It's gotten worse since." The resident psycho didn't even sound exasperated anymore. Just resigned. Like he already accepted Rome was a lost cause.

"Since we tracked you back here, he's been…" Happy trailed off, looking at the others for help.

Iggy's voice was quiet. "He stopped talking."

"Yeah," Critter added. "Like completely. Just sat there, staring at the monitors, like some kind of demon predator waiting for the van to roll in. Barely even blinking."

"When I finally restrained him, he let me." Happy's voice was grim. "Didn't fight. didn't even look at me. Just whispered your name under his breath like a fucking chant."

The room went deathly silent.

I sat down as far away from Rome as possible, then waved for the group who stayed here to share said intel. Sitting in the farthest corner of the room, I studied Rome as the team worked to remember specific things from their history in the Teams. Each of them added to the story until a clearer picture came together.

"So you were all injected with some kind of tracking program, but no one knows for sure what it was supposed to do?" I asked, my brain almost folding in on itself as I tried to follow along.

They all nodded.

"What kind of biohack would do that? Unless they reached some kind of leap into technology so advanced as to be alien, there's nothing that could even begin to offer that kind of cloaking." I shifted to look at each one. "Right?"

Iggy cleared his throat. "Some of the things contractors come up with are pretty advanced, Snow. Who were we to say this wasn't a viable option?"

"Uh…common sense? How would an injected compound of any creation be able to hide your heat signatures? If anything, it would have made you more visible to tracking equipment. An RF sweep would have exposed you immediately. Especially out in the middle of nowhere." The sheer idiocy of what they were claiming the biohack supposedly accomplished was giving me a migraine.

"Well, when you put it like that, we all sound stupid as fuck. At the time, it made sense," Dopey sneered.

I turned to Bossy. "You thought it was a good idea, Mr. Bossy and Needs All the Information?"

He dipped his chin, a resigned look on his face. "We were desperate for something to change, Snow. Everywhere we went, we were getting tagged. All of our missions FUBAR before they even began."

Grinding my teeth together, I fought not to scream at them all. I counted to ten before I could breathe easily.

I exhaled sharply, the kind I usually only released when dealing with bratty kindergarteners. "For fuck's sake." I met each of their gazes one by one. "You didn't get tagged. You got baited."

Silence.

"They didn't screw up your missions. They put you exactly where they wanted you. and when you started questioning it, they fed you a shiny little biohack lie and watched you line up for the needle like good little soldiers."

Horror sat on each face.

f they didn't come up with the right answer, I wasn't sure I could trust them to help me think through my own issue enough to be even remotely helpful.

They all just sat there, grumpy and gloomy looks on their faces.

"We were set up even then," Rome finally answered. "The tracking program was a direct fantasy of the shit they put us through. Something that would make it easier for us to willingly submit to the supposed testing."

At least one of them understood.

I nodded. "You weren't set up. You were groomed."

Another silence.

The sound of flesh smashing wood filled the room like a mini bomb. Iggy swore. "FUCK!

"What?" I asked when no one else bothered.

Iggy looked at me like he saw a ghost.

"Snow…what if it worked?"

Chapter 34
Rome

Dread, rage, and humiliation pulsed through my veins. We walked into that testing like kids walking into a stranger's van for the promises of candy. The fact it was Neva who pointed it out made the shame eat through me like acid.

Especially having her point it out so quickly.

We weren't stupid men. In fact, we were highly intelligent, trained, and adaptable. But it seemed we were too deeply entrenched in our thoughts, behaviors, and understanding of what the situation entailed to actually see things correctly.

"Fuck."

Turning to look at the guys in the room, I was careful not to search her out. The same look I probably had on my face sat on each of theirs. The horror of what we allowed to happen, what we eagerly brought upon ourselves under the guise of being able to do our jobs better.

They played us like puppets.

"You said you found the first possibility of this Sisterhood group a couple months before they asked for volunteers for the program?" Neva asked.

I nodded, clenched my fingers into fists. "Yeah."

"Who is this group? I've never heard of them. Especially not as some kind of poison dealers or creators; and I know most of them around the world."

Iggy, already at his computer station, pulled up the information and sent it to everyone's screen. We could have recited the whole dossier by heart at this point.

"What the fuck are you playing at?" Neva spat.

Turning my head as far as I could to find her in the darkened room, I saw her wrenched back in her seat as if a snake sat coiled and ready to lunge for her from the desk.

When I checked her screen from the reverse side, I blinked. Saw nothing out of the ordinary. "What do you mean, dewdrop?"

She stabbed a finger at the picture of Solana Nicollier. "Why do you have her picture?"

"She's the leader of the Sisterhood," Beck answered. "She's who we've been tracking."

Neva shook her head. "There's no possible way that's who you're tracking. When was this picture taken?" She glared at each of us as she made her way through the ranks of my men to shoot eye daggers at Iggy. "Are you fucking with me right now?"

He shook his head. "Why the hell would we do that, Snow? That is Solana Nicollier. Age fifty-five, leader of the Sis—"

Neva slammed her hand down on the desk. "That's my mother!" The bite of her voice echoed through the glass enclosed room. "Why do you have a picture of my dead mother on your screen? Tell me. Right now, or I swear to the gods, I won't hesitate to kill all of you" The faintest sob broke through her tone, but she didn't waver or bend as she demanded answers.

"I swear on all that's holy, dewdrop, we know that woman on the screen as Solana Nicollier," I said softly. "Gigs, get me free." My words were less than a whisper.

He got to his feet and let me loose. Levering myself up from the gurney, I hissed out the pain, then moved around the big table toward her.

She tracked me around the room like she was about to attack.

"Neva, I swear to you." I held my hands out in front of me as I approached.

Please, fuck, don't let her launch herself at me. My body couldn't handle any more damage. Although, some stupid, reckless, neurotic part of me wished she would touch me in any way possible.

But even I knew that thought was crazy. Nothing about her screamed soft and delicate right now. She was stone cold and rock-hard. Capable of inflicting more abuse.

I also couldn't stay away. Not right now, but certainly not from her. Especially when it looked like her world had cracked open at her feet.

She stopped me before I could take another step.

"Stay right there, Charming. Start talking. Give me timestamps, give me all the data you have." She held herself stiffly, locked away her personality as if we might somehow infect her in some way.

Iggy gave her the rundown of information. "Solana Nicollier, fifty-five, French national. Five-four, born to Yvette Lataille and Garron Bazin. She's been the head of the Sisterhood of the Rising Dawn since its inception. She's the only leader we've been able to identify."

Neva shoved her hand into her pocket and brought out the thumb drives from earlier. "Grab a still from the file marked Lilla. Run her against your female." She tossed one of the devices down the table toward Iggy. "How long have you been aware of her?" Her tone was frigid, but her fingers dug into the armrests. Her nails close to ripping through the fabric as she fought to hold herself together.

The guys got it down to the man and we all waited for him to do what Dewdrop demanded.

"First attack we could attribute to them was five years ago. A hit out in some deserted village no one knows the name of. Killed over twenty in a single strike."

I could feel her vibrating a few feet in front of me. Whatever we found, I prayed like I never had before that she was wrong. And then prayed even harder that we were wrong about this. Hell, in this instant, it was neck and neck between praying for us to be wrong about SRD or wrong about getting dosed with something to make me crave this woman.

I couldn't be responsible for her world crashing down around her. Not right now. Fuck, not ever. But definitely not right now. We just got her onto our team so she could help us.

And not a single part of that mattered as long as I could save her from this hurt.

My arms literally ached to pull her against me, but I held myself off. She wasn't in the mood, and I really couldn't suffer any more damage.

"How did you get called out? Aren't you a bioterror team?" She glared at me like it was my personal responsibility for being tasked with answering the call.

Iggy finally got the information loaded and brought up a picture from the file Neva instructed. He ran facial recognition on the two images. As the task bar slid closer to one hundred percent and the markers on each face matched over every feature, I knew my prayers were in vain.

"Ninety-seven-point-six percent match," Iggy said softly.

Neva collapsed back into her chair, her features a rictus of pain.

A high-pitched keening noise came from her throat as she stared at the screen in horror. Her long dark hair slid back and forth over her shoulders as she shook her head, her mouth gaping. Twin tears glistened in her eyes as she studied the pictures.

She shifted her tortured gaze to mine, everything in them seemed to reach for me with her spirit.

"Out. Everyone get out," I muttered as I drew closer to her.

Shoving the pain out of my head and ignoring it as it washed through my body, I focused on her. Pulling her into my arms, I curled around her until I felt the trembling in her smaller frame. Without turning around to see them go, I knew the moment we were alone.

She wilted against me, her sobs buffeted against my chest as screams ripped through her throat. Her nails sank into my flesh, and I welcomed the pain. I couldn't do anything but hold her as the betrayal sliced her into shreds. It felt as if each emotion ripped through me as well, and I fought to hold both of us together through sheer force of will.

With my bruised and battered arms, I held her to me as tightly as possible. She didn't squirm or struggle. No, it seemed like she tried to get closer. Tried to hide inside my skin with me.

We sat there for time unending, just trying to survive the storm that quaked through her.

Us.

I wasn't moving without her attached to me in some way. From this moment on, there would be nothing keeping me from having this woman in my life for the rest of my days. With her luscious form on my lap, I shoved my face into the space between her neck and shoulder, inhaled her sunshine and spice scent as I formulated and discarded plans.

Nothing I thought of could fix this. No plan, no strategy, no revenge grand enough to put her world back together.

She wasn't just broken—she was shattered.

I knew, in that instant, I would never let her feel this way again. Not while I was breathing. Not while my body could still move.

I would drag Solana from the fucking grave if I had to. Find her. Rip her from the walls she hid behind. Bring her to her knees in front of my woman.

And if she didn't give Neva the answers necessary to settle her heart? If she even attempted to shatter Neva like this again?

I'll tear her apart. Dust would have more composition by the time I was finished.

I'd carve every fucking secret from her bones.

Because Neva was mine. And nothing in this world had the right to take her apart but me.

Her green eyes were wounded and hollow as she looked up at me from inches away. "My mother's alive."

I dipped my chin. "We'll find her, dewdrop. I promise you that."

She shook her head. "You don't understand." She tried to ease back, tried to put distance between us.

"You're not going anywhere. Say what you have to say, but you're doing it while I hold you."

She couldn't even work up a decent glare to throw at me, and I felt fury slice through my guts.

"I've been searching for her killer. That's why I'm going after Jorgenssen. That's why I put myself on this case with Brantley. She's supposed to be dead so I can avenge her." More tears slid down her pale cheeks as heartbreak darkened her eyes some more.

My brow furrowed. "Your mother died when you were young, right?"

She nodded, then wiped her hands over her cheeks, dashing the tears away, the movements rough and angry. "Yeah. When I was twelve." She swallowed, the sound loud in the space between us. "Why would she fake her death? Why would she leave me alone with them? She knew what

357

they were like, what they all were like, and she left me with them?" She shook her head, disbelief wrenching her features. "She wouldn't have done that. Not willingly."

I bit my tongue to keep the words back. The words that wouldn't do her any good right now. The words that could break the rest of her spirit. I couldn't bring myself to do it, so I just held her in helpless fury.

"Could the pictures you have be wrong?" The words were barely more than breath, but I understood them.

I gritted my teeth. "Dewdrop…"

She put her finger over my lips, pleaded with me silently.

Her finger was damp and before I could stop to think it through, I opened my lips and swiped my tongue over that moisture. The salty taste of her tears hit me like a fucking semi truck. The flavor of her sank into my body, into my fucking DNA, and rewrote itself around her.

Opening my mouth more, I sucked until her finger popped between my lips and I got my first taste of her flesh. I groaned as my dick, my aching, almost broken dick, went hard against her ass as she sat across my lap.

Her eyes widened before her lids lowered and her gaze went to smoke. Instead of pushing me away, instead of pulling her hand from my mouth, she slid a second finger between my lips.

Fuck. I needed more of her. More of all of her. I didn't care that my body was in shambles, I needed her.

I *needed* her.

And I needed her right here. Right now.

The door behind us smacked into the wall as the guys rushed back in, most of them yelling at me to step back, to get away from her. Threats and promises that meant nothing while I was holding her against me.

"Don't even try it, Charming," Squirrel bit out. "It's bad enough watching you maul her, but I'd be damned if you do it in front of me."

A chorus of groans rang out through my guys, but I was still struggling to clear my head of her. She felt so fucking good in my arms, on my body. The weight of her was a sultry blanket across my lap and chest.

Without thought, I tightened my abused abs, shoving my dick more firmly against her plush ass. A moan filtered from my throat as I thrust my face into her fragrant hair, and my eyes closed as I inhaled.

Fuck, I had to have her.

Agonized craving clawed at me from the inside.

She rubbed her tits against my chest, as a low whimpering sound came from her. "Rome."

My name on her lips brought to mind watching her in her bed, the way the toy fucked this body that belonged to me. I pulled back so I could see her beautiful face.

Her nails sank into my pecs as she huddled closer, green eyes dark with lust and demand. She shifted on my lap, her legs parting to make room for my hips between them. Her heated core settled against my dick like a dream.

Shudders wracked my body as I fought not to go off from the feeling of being wrapped up in her scent and her weight. "Dewdrop." The pet name fell like a prayer from my lips.

Just as I was going under for the last time, a hard arm came around from behind and hooked an elbow under my chin, drawing my upper body away from her. As I watched, a set of arms yanked her from her perch on my lap and against the body of one of my brothers.

My vision went crimson. "Let her go, Markus." More hands came around me, locking me to the chair that had become my prison.

Squirrel just stared at me, my death written in his dark eyes. "Don't ever touch her again." He backed away.

"Don't talk about me like I'm not here, Hotsy," Neva said in a hoarse whisper. She reached down and gripped his crotch, fingers locked in a cruel hold I knew all too well.

Squirrel's breath hitched, but he didn't let her go. Didn't make a single move to stop her—he waited. Daring her to go further.

Like the fucker was waiting for her to squeeze harder.

The muscles around his eyes flinched, but he still didn't move.

"Keep waiting, Markus. You think I won't. You think I can't break you?" Her voice was all silk and steel, sharp enough to cut. "Try me."

Squirrel grinned. "Maybe I want you to. Keep thinking those kinds of thoughts, pix," he whispered, voice low, deadly, "I'll give you what you need."

She froze. And for a single split second, I saw something in her gaze.

Not hate.

Not disgust.

A flicker of heat.

359

"Damn it, not him, too," Gigs grumbled. "We can't fight both of them." Out of the corner of my vision, I watched him rush up to my side. A filled syringe in his grip.

Without a warning, he plunged the needle into my arm and hit the depressor.

Just as the world went wavy around me, Gigs got Schnauze over to help him wrestle Neva from Squirrel's grip. Gigs gave the big man the same liquid treatment I got, and Dewdrop fell into Beck's waiting arms.

"Get them both to the ground. Now. We can't afford concussions."

It was the last thing I heard before the world went black.

**

Blinking the obsidian out of my gaze and mind, I felt the world spin a couple times. When I didn't toss my cookies, I looked to either side to try to figure out where I was. With the cold seeping into my back, and the familiar lighting in the ceiling, I was going to go with the knowledge I was laid out flat on my back in the Bat Cave.

"He's back," Gigs called, his face upside down from my vantage point as he peered down at me. "How you feeling, boss?" A psychopath's taunting tone in his voice.

I glared at him. "What the hell did you give me?"

"Just a little chemical nap. You were about to go apeshit with her and since Squirrel joined the Crazy Party, I had to put you down fast. Don't worry, Squirrel is still down. She's safe."

An image of a beautiful face wavered at the edges of my memory, but I couldn't trace it through the shimmering of the world right now. Nodding, because that's what he seemed to need, I just laid there for a little longer.

Two other faces appeared in my vision. Det and Schnauze. They looked concerned and relieved.

My brain kicked at me for some reason, but I couldn't figure that one out either. So I left it alone, too. Something was very wrong, but under the weight of the chemicals, I couldn't really be bothered to care too much.

As I contemplated my existence, I realized I was fucking tired; felt like I haven't slept in weeks. Since we weren't in the Teams any longer, I knew I should have been more rested. But right now, I felt like I could sleep for a year and still need some down time.

"What day is it?" My throat rasped around the words.

"Friday. We have a big day planned, so don't think you'll get to laze the day away sleeping, you asshole," Gigs answered, with that psycho's grin on his face as he continued to peer down at me.

My brows furrowed as confusion swept through me again. "It's Friday?"

He nodded, so did Det and Schnauze.

"Which Friday?"

"The one after Thursday," Squirrel deadpanned from a little farther away. "Idiot. Friday is always after Thursday."

Using all of my strength, I managed to raise my arm and flip him off. Wincing when my arm smashed back down into the hard floor beneath me, I felt my mind clear a little.

Huh.

Lifting my arm, I let it crash back down to the floor again. Yup, a smidge clearer. By the time I washed enough pain through my system to come fully back to the world around me, furious rage ate through my veins with every beat of my heart.

Forcing myself into a seated position, I glared at my brothers. Dewdrop was nowhere to be found. "Where is she?"

"Safe. Which means she's not here where you two are going to fight over her like a fucking bone," Det said, his tone hard, unflinching.

"Did you touch her? Did you put your hands on my girl?" Shoving my way to my feet, I bobbed and weaved as I tried to keep steady while I approached him. The room kept tilting this way and that, but I managed to put my face into his. "Did you touch her?"

He rolled his brown eyes and shoved me back with a hand in my face. "Not how you mean. But she's safe and as soon as the technician comes by to calibrate the equipment we got set up for her, we'll start getting some answers about your demented shit. Now sit the fuck down before you fall down."

Since it was either fall to my ass or stumble back into a chair, I chose the better part of ego and managed to land in the closest chair. "What the fuck happened?"

Gigs gave me the shortest debrief in the history of information downloads. By the time he was done, Squirrel managed to get into a seat a couple spots down the length of the table.

We glared at each other like we were in kindergarten and just got held back from recess for fighting.

I flipped him off, then glared when he returned the gesture.

"Fuck," Gigs whined. "I'm glad she got the draws while they were both out. This is going to be brutal."

I shifted my gaze to him. "What draw? She was here? Did she touch me?" I sifted my hands over my body as if I could detect her warmth, her light. "Bring her back. Let her touch me again." I fisted my hands and knocked them to the tabletop.

"Yeah, bring her back, but get him out of here. He's going to try to hurt her." Squirrel sent me a death glare. "Snow is a lady, you fucking monster. Don't think I'll let you break her heart or her body. You have to go through me to even smell her." He stabbed his thumb into his chest, promises floating in his gaze.

"We might need that contingency she mentioned," Schnauze said.

Whipping my head around to study him, I asked, "What contingency?"

He shook his head and backed up to confer with Iggy.

Our resident tech lord nodded and started jabbing at his holo keyboard again. When the screen in front of me shifted to video, I cleared my mind.

There she was. Bent over my side, her long dark hair cascading over my face and belly as she did something at my arm.

Lifting my hand, I ran my fingers over my other arm, feeling the bandage in the crease of my elbow. "She drew blood."

The men around me nodded.

I snarled low in my throat as I watched Dewdrop go to Squirrel's side and do the same thing. "I'm going to kill you, Lowman. Filet you like a fish. Stop touching my woman."

"Face it, Charming. You're not enough for her."

I snarled, my entire body coiled to launch at him.

"Hey, she came to me, asshole. Not the other way around. If you were a better man, she wouldn't have needed to."

I heard the smirk in his voice, then saw it spread over his face in my head. "But don't worry. I'll take care of *my* girl. The way you can't."

Shifting to launch myself at him, I got maybe two inches before I was restrained and yanked back down into my seat. When I saw Squirrel receive the same treatment, I blew out a low breath.

"Fuck. It got worse." With my arms trapped against my body, I couldn't even rub my hands over my face. "Damn it."

"Yeah. She's putting together a little cocktail that will take both of you out of commission for tonight's festivities. You'll have a bad case of the stomach flu so she can get her business done with Jorgenssen without you both acting like fucking idiots." Gigs stood back, his arms crossed over his chest. "And I'll personally pour it down both of your throats if you try to give her a hard time about it."

I shook my head, trying to shove the anger out and think through the volatile mix of emotions swirling around inside me. But the only thing I could focus on was her. I swear I could smell her perfume, feel the heat of her body, and taste the slightest tinge of salt on my tongue from licking her tears away.

That's when the bomb went off in my head. "I licked her finger."

"Yeah, we all saw that part," Gigs said, shaking his head.

"She had tears on her finger. I tasted her tears." I looked up at him, trying to get him to understand. "It was my first real taste of her. My first sample of her. She's inside me."

I tried to describe the feeling when I took her essence inside me the first time. I knew I kissed her before, knew I memorized her flavor, but this was different. This was…I didn't have the words. Everything inside me changed, everything shifted to make her the center of my entire universe.

"You think that's why you went off the deep end?" Gigs let his arms fall to his sides as he studied me.

I shrugged, still trying to sort things through in my head. "It's the only thing that makes sense. I even made you guys promise to take me out if I threatened to ruin anything before she got back with the rest of the team. I was clearer headed then, right?"

He nodded.

From across the room, I saw Iggy and Critter nod as well.

"So something about her chemistry is making yours go absolutely ape shit," Gigs mused softly. He was quiet for a long time before he spun to Iggy. "Call your contact, tell him he can double the fee if he's here in the next half hour and can get our system up and running by noon."

Iggy gaped at our medic, but only nodded as he picked up the phone.

Gigs turned back to me, then shifted to look at Squirrel. "We don't have an answer for what happened to Squirrel. Unless he's been licking her when no one knows about it, he's only ever touched her skin, flirted with her, and pissed you off."

He heaved a sigh. "We're all going to get run for testing. She already drew your vials, so you're in the clear. You have two options and two options only. Option One: let me sedate you until her showdown with Jorgenssen is done. Option Two: let her dose you with her concoction and pray she doesn't kill you."

He looked at Squirrel. "Those are your only options, too, big guy. Which one are you choosing?"

"I, for one, choose death," Squirrel said, glaring daggers at me. "Give me Snow's mix. Best man standing gets the girl."

I rolled my eyes. "Give me the same, but only because I don't think I'd forgive you for putting me completely out of commission when she's about to be in danger."

The door swung open and there she was.

Cool. Collected. My fucking annihilation in yoga pants and a sweatshirt.

Neva stepped through, holding two cups resting on a tray like a queen bestowing judgement. Like she hadn't just shattered our world and left us to crawl through the wreckage.

"Wonderful. Let's get to drinking, shall we, boys?"

No hesitation. No explanation. No room for arguments.

I started to rise, not even realizing I was moving until the weight of hands pushed me back down. And fuck me, for just a second—a sliver of time—I was lost to the instinct to kneel before her.

Chapter 35

Neva

I fought against the pull of need in my belly as I walked into the room. Both men drew me in like I was a fish with a hook in the mouth.

And to say I was more than a little surprised and kinda freaked out by how my body now saw Squirrel as some kind of sexual option would be a massive understatement. There had been thought, no emotion. Just a simple knowledge that I would climb that man like a fucking tree and consume every part of him.

Something in my chest tightened. My stomach clenched, and my pulse skipped ahead like my body was bracing for something.

I swallowed. Again. My throat was dry, like I was overheating from the inside out. A sharp, heavy pulse beat between my legs—wrong, wrong, wrong. This wasn't real. It couldn't be real. I refused to let it be real.

But that pull in my belly? That sick, intoxicating weight pressing lower?

It *was* real.

And I fucking hated it.

When Beck got me out of the room after Happy put the boys down, I fought with myself not to run back in and keep them safe. Right then, they only needed to be away from me to be safer. They didn't need me thrusting myself back into their midst. So, instead of beating myself up about something none of us understood at the moment, I went to my notes and journals.

In a completely different section of the building. It wasn't until I was in the room farthest away from the Bat Cave that I felt like I could actually think without desire pressing down on my shoulders.

As soon as I settled on some kind of weird roller chair, I opened my mother's journals. Within those pages, I found my peace, just like always. Knowledge, facts, science all of it calmed me. And I needed the solace and centering more than usual.

Today was Friday and I had to meet with Jorgenssen. I just had to pray I would get to sleep at some point before that asshole showed up. Being at the top of my game was more imperative now than before. Especially if my mother was still alive.

Shoving all the conflicting emotions about that very idea out of my head, I focused on the plant information written on the pages in front of me. I—we all—needed to have both Rome and Squirrel out of commission for completely plausible reasons to excuse them not showing up tonight. No matter if I didn't have the backing of the CIA anymore, I still needed the information the Swede could provide me.

Skimming my finger down the familiar facts I'd memorized a long time ago, I allowed my mind to drift as I came up with a specialized blend for the two men currently driving me batshit crazy. I needed them out, but not dead. Sick, but not fighting for their lives. Luckily, my plants had many gifts to give a talented creator, and I was nothing if not inventive.

A little bit of castor bean, some rhododendron, a wisp of buttercup, a sprinkle of soapwart and English ivy, with a hint of nightshade. They would have tummy troubles like Satan himself was trying to take up residence in their intestines, but they would come out the other end just fine.

I snickered to myself. It wasn't the only thing going to come out the other end.

Rome's arrogant face popping into my mind had me flipping to a different section of the plant bible I held. For all the hassles he put me through since I met the annoying man, I was going to give him a little something extra to make sure he remembered me for the rest of his life.

With a couple crumbles of some fly agaric mushroom, I would make their trip through hell bright and memorable. Who knew, maybe the hallucinations and delusions would give them some insight into their own crazy.

Feeling calmer and more ready to face the rest of these problems, I got everything brewed up and put into the containers necessary. The med bay served as a temporary base of operations the guys were able to help me with. We would use the infirmary until I could get one of the bolt holes established. I think the one just down the block was going to give us all the best chance of meeting our mission objectives.

"Let's get to drinking, shall we, boys?" I asked as I moved farther into the room. Carefully keeping my gaze trained on their foreheads, I made my way to their sides.

Well, I started to, anyway. Happy and Iggy intercepted me, and each took a glass from the tray I held.

"This way we don't have to listen to them bitch and complain about which asshole you served first," Happy said softly.

I bit back the chuckle. He probably wasn't wrong, so I just stood there and waited for the two idiots to drink what I gave them.

"Does this count as your secret drink to get me back, dewdrop?" Rome asked.

I snorted, setting the tray on the table, I crossed my arms. "Not even close, Charming. Drink up."

Squirrel raised his glass in a toast and then shot the whole thing down his throat in a single swallow. His eyes bugged out for a second as hacking coughs shook through his chest. But he settled down once again in short order. "Pussy." He glared at Rome.

Rome rolled his eyes and poured his own drink down the hatch. He managed to hold back the coughing I could see shaking his chest, but it was by the thinnest of margins.

"Don't either of you want to know what you just drank? What is it going to do to you?" I asked.

Dopey walked in behind me, snorted. "You already gave it to them? Damn, I wanted to watch the show."

I smirked. "Oh believe me, you'll still get to see it." I glanced at the digital clock on the wall. "Give it about fifteen, maybe twenty minutes, and you'll see the opening credits."

Both Rome and Squirrel gave me terrified looks before they washed their expressions clean.

Dopey took a spot at the table, his fingers intertwined as he sat there, avid interest on his face. "Oh man, I can't fucking wait." Honestly, he looked like he wanted some popcorn or Milk Duds as he waited for the show to start.

"What's gonna happen to me, pix? Tell Hotsy what you did to him. Come whisper it in my ear." Squirrel waved me over with one of his huge paws. "Give me cuddles while you destroy my body with your wicked ways."

Rome slammed a hand down on the table, glared at his brother. "She's not fucking yours, Squirrel. And what the fuck kind of nickname is Hotsy?"

Squirrel didn't even bother to glance in Rome's direction. "I'm her Hotsy Totsy, she's my little Cinnamon Roll. Aren't you, baby? Just warm and gooey and sweet with some of that spice I want to lap up with my tongue." He made a low growling sound in his throat that had my mouth watering and my pussy going tight.

Before I knew what I was doing, I stepped toward him.

Dopey grabbed my wrist, stopping my forward motion. "What the fuck are you doing, Snow? You're not going over there. You just poisoned both of them, you psycho."

I bit my lip as I fought with myself not to wrench Dopey's fingers off my skin. It burned where he touched me. Made me want to cut his fingers off and use them as flavor sticks in my next concoction.

He let me go, practically shoving me away. "Leave my fingers alone, you crazy witch." He pushed back from me, his eyes wide in horror.

Oops. Guess that thought got away from my brain/mouth filter. My bad.

"Snow, honey. Are you feeling the need to go to Rome or Markus?" Beck asked softly as he came up on my other side. He approached slowly, his entire demeanor calm and neutral.

My chin dipped before I could control myself. The words spilled out of my mouth like a geyser shooting water into the sky. "It feels like some kind of weight in my belly. Like I can feel a string connecting me to both of them."

I rubbed my hands over my abdomen, guilt and shame washing through me. I was stronger than this. Stronger than whatever happened to these men. I didn't cave, didn't waver. Didn't succumb to the nonsense that these giant protectors fell victim to.

368

"Is it easier to ignore when you can't see them?" Beck asked.

I nodded, then spun on my heel without another word. I had to get away. Had to get far, far away, so they didn't drag me down with them.

Didn't make me need them. Didn't make me yearn and then rip it all away like I knew they would. Everyone did. I was the person always left behind.

They had each other. Once we got everything figured out, they would still have their family, and I would be alone.

Again.

Just like always.

Shoving my shoulders back, I lifted my chin. It was better for me to be alone. Better not to rely on anyone, need anyone. Just me. Just me and my plants.

Walking farther down the hall, I blew out a breath as the pull of them continued to lessen the more distance I put between us. I heaved a sigh. Thank fuck.

"Hey Snow, we've got a guy here at the front office. He says he's going to calibrate your machines. You ready for him?" Banshee's voice came over the intercom in the hallway.

Immediately, I brightened. "Yes, Whispers, I'm on my way."

He scoffed, but didn't demand I change his Dwarf name again, so I was going to go with it until he got bitchy about it. "Come on up. I'll have Iggy and Gigs meet you here." The line clicked closed, leaving me alone in the hallways once again.

Switching directions, I headed to the front of the big, renovated building. The more I thought about it, the more I was sure the guys bought this building from the trust. At least, it wouldn't surprise me. I'd have to look through the acquisitions and sales paperwork at some point when I had some downtime.

Stepping into the main office, I saw Happy and Iggy chatting with Whispers and an unknown male in a blue polo shirt, khaki pants, and brown shoes on his feet. Somewhere in his fifties, he had the beginnings of graying hair, a full beard, cheeks that reminded me of Santa Claus, and a bag of equipment dragging his shoulder down under the weight of it.

"Hi, I'm Aniera de Witte," I said, approaching the small group.

369

The calibration tech turned to me, something flashing in his eyes before I could fully comprehend it. "Ms. de Witte, nice to meet you." He stuck his hand out, a curl of tension falling in the room with the motion.

I studied him for a long moment. Something was off, but I couldn't put my finger on it. I shoved my hands behind my back. "Sorry, I haven't had a chance to wash my hands after fiddling with some plants. You don't want to itch for days, so it's better if we don't touch."

He chuckled and withdrew his hand. "That's for sure. Nothing like poison ivy to ruin the good date I have planned for later." He shifted to look at each guy. "Where's the equipment?"

Iggy stepped in front of me, almost shielding me with his body. "This way." He waved his hand out and waited for the guy to move past him.

"I'm so sorry, I didn't catch your name," I said to the technician.

"Harvard Long, Ms. de Witte. I'm with MedPro Scientific and Tools." He returned to his small talk chat with Iggy as they preceded us down the hall.

Happy came up beside me. "What's the deal?"

I shook my head, kept my voice low. "Something is off about him, but I can't tell you what. How are the guys feeling?"

Happy chuckled for a moment, the ghostly curl of a sociopath's humor was a welcome sensation down my spine. "Looking pretty green around the gills. I got them headed to the bunk area with buckets for both ends. What did you give them?"

I bumped my shoulder in the air, felt my mouth stretch up in a smirk. "Oh, you know. The easy, peasy stuff. They'll puke, run fevers, see and hear horrors that aren't there, probably shit the bed. The normal stomach flu stuff if Jorgenssen needs verification of illness for tonight."

Happy's chuckle took on new life when he stared down at me with his mouth hanging open. "Damn, girl. Remind me not to piss you off."

Looking up into his face, I smiled, "Happy, don't piss me off."

He laughed again, putting his arm around my shoulders, and moved both of us to follow Iggy and Harvard Long.

When Beck came up behind us in the hallway, his added calm presence made it easier for me to push the odd sensation from the technician away.

Once we arrived in the med bay, I gave the space another hard look. This wasn't going to work. Not long-term. Especially not if they were going to need me to run all of the tests for whatever was impacting Squirrel and Rome.

And me. I couldn't forget that part.

Slowing down so Happy would stop beside me, I waited for him to look down at me. His blond brows rose in question.

"One of my bolt holes is across the street and up a block. Do you think we could somehow get the tech there and out again without him knowing? Or without having to kill him for finding out?"

Shock and confusion swept through his gaze, but he didn't pepper me with questions. He studied me for a long moment before he nodded.

Stepping forward, he said, "Mr. Long, if I could have you come over here and look at this for me. We've been having some issues with our refrigeration unit, and I wanted to make sure it was still cooling things the way it should."

Whatever alert he gave his brothers in that statement had them closing ranks around the technician. Within moments, Whispers and Beck had Harvard's arms stretched out between them and Happy sliding a new syringe needle into the man's neck.

He went limp, spread between them like a pig on a spit.

"Why did we just drug the guy coming to help us?" Iggy asked.

I stepped forward. "We can't set up shop here, not with everything I'm going to need to do all the testing, especially running it on everyone here. Including me," I gritted out. "I told Happy one of my bolt holes is less than a five-minute walk from here. If we can get Mr. Long and the machine to the new building for him to calibrate it there, it would be better. And if we can get him to do it without knowing where he really is, that would be even better."

They all stared at me as if I were, in fact, crazy. But they obviously weren't as familiar with clandestine games as I was. Sure, they were black ops, but that didn't mean they played the game the same way.

"Load him into the truck. We'll all go so at least some of you know where I'll be. We can meet up after the

371

shitshow with Jorgenssen is over tonight." I waved for them to hurry back out the door.

"You couldn't have told us this before we dragged him all the way down here?" Happy grumbled as they heaved the guy up to the last gurney.

"Sorry, he gave me weird vibes in the office, and I didn't think it all the way through until I saw all of us standing in here. There's just not enough room. And if we can keep everything together, it will be better in terms of results, testing, and possible inoculation creation."

All four men turned to me, a skewed sense of hope on their faces.

"You think you can create some kind of cure?" Happy asked.

I shrugged. "Considering what you guys told me about you possibly already carrying it in your systems, I don't know why I wouldn't be able to duplicate it. We'll have to wait for test results and everything else to come back on it, though."

With that happy statement, I spun on my heel and made my way back through the building. Bypassing the front office, I headed for the garage.

As we got into the big truck, Happy's phone rang.

Damn, I still needed one of those to replace the one Bossy broke.

"Yeah? I'll tell you when we get back. Make sure to keep an eye on Charming and Hotsy," he said, shooting me a wink. "Dopey, you'll be fine. And I'll make sure Snow doesn't put you in her sights. Just don't screw anything up." He hung up and tossed the phone onto the dash. "Dopey is scared of you."

I shrugged as I hooked the seatbelt. "Not my fault he's a baby."

He laughed as he waited for the garage doors to open. He backed out and followed my directions. The building I was claiming was literally over one block and up two. After I got the bay doors open and Happy pulled the truck through, they got out into the huge open warehouse space.

Iggy stepped down from the back of the truck and gave a low whistle. "We looked at this building for Subterra and Locke. The company wanted too much for it." He turned to look at me, one dark brow raised.

I shrugged. "I'm the sole survivor of the trust. Which means I can use any of the properties however I want as long as they're empty. After we get Mr. Long awake and the equipment placed, will you be able to hook up a system for me?"

Iggy nodded, smiled. "It would be my pleasure. Any budget I need to worry about? Or system specs you want in particular?" He sounded like I gave him a blank check and full consent with the woman of his dreams.

"Can I get a server room like the Bat Cave has?"

He spun a quick circle to turn back to me. "You want a server farm? Why?"

I shrugged. I honestly had no idea why, but he made it look really cool and super useful in the Bat Cave. "Help with computing, chemical analyses, assays. Whatever you think would work for a fully equipped genetics and biology lab, that's what I want. I figure we'll have to build everything from the ground up, especially going against whoever is out there gunning for us right now."

I jerked my chin at the truck. "The only reason I brought that equipment from the lab is because I didn't think we wanted to wait anywhere from a couple weeks to a few months to get started on the testing we need. Certainly not since the new hypothesis came up."

All four men nodded at me.

"Yeah, Snow. We can get you set up. I'll come back tonight while you're working with Jorgenssen, make sure we can get you secure and safe inside the building for the night. Moving forward, we'll make this place airtight," Iggy offered.

I smiled. "Thanks. For now, the first floor is going to be the main hub. Come along to the back and I'll show you where we're going to put the lab equipment. I'll call and get the power turned on while we wait for Mr. Long to rejoin the land of the living, if I can borrow one of your phones."

Within a couple hours, we had the heavy load electricity running and the biggest machines put back together. Mr. Long didn't bitch too much about having been knocked out, but I thought that was more to the hefty bonus Iggy passed him than any moral outrage. Happy put Mr. Long back under the swing of the chemical nap and then Beck dropped the man off at his truck.

With the extra time on our hands, the guys helped me get the main floor swept and dusted. Even going so far as to bring some of the equipment from their building to get things going faster. I had a better idea of what I would need to make this place into a fully functioning lab, including a home for myself, by the time we were finished.

A bathroom on the second floor could be changed to accommodate a shower without too much fuss, so that's where my housing would be for a while. It wouldn't be anything near the plush and inviting furniture of my family home, but it would do well enough until we could figure out what was really going on.

"With Squirrel and Keys out of commission, how are you planning to approach Jorgenssen tonight?" Happy asked as we got the borrowed cleaning equipment loaded back into the truck.

I shook my head. I still didn't have any good answers in that corner, and I needed to get them figured out. Stalling now, especially considering everything I went through to get to this fucking point of the op, wasn't an option. But Jorgenssen was expecting to meet with me, Squirrel, and Rome.

"I'll tell him they're both down with the stomach flu. Give him proof that they're out for the night." I heaved a sigh. "And pray it works? I guess," I offered, then shook my head. "I have no idea. Any suggestions?" I looked up at all of them gathered around with me.

"I think the bigger question might be what are you *not* willing to do to get where you need to be?" Beck asked as Iggy pulled down the truck's loading door and locked it.

I tipped my head to the side. "What do you mean? We're meeting at Subterra for a meeting. We're going to talk."

Beck gave me a look I couldn't quite interpret. "You're going to have a business meeting at sex club. What else do you think this asshole might want to see as proof that you're not working against him, Snow?"

My brain exploded at the question. Mouth falling open even as I shook my head. "I'm not fucking anyone! Especially not with him watching me." I felt rage eat through me at the very idea. "I don't care what he thinks he's getting, all he's getting is a conversation."

"And if it means you don't get the information you want?" Beck asked, his tone neutral and calm.

I was beginning to really hate that tone of voice from him.

"You really think he's going to want proof that I'm a member of Subterra? More than just being there and chatting with him?"

How was this even a possibility? Honestly, the more I thought about it, the madder I became. I narrowed my eyes at the guys. "Would you be expecting to watch someone fuck if they were coming to meet you for a meeting at a sex club?"

All of them nodded.

"If the purpose of having the meeting there was to show that you're not part of the government or anything else, hell yes. And that's not just me being an asshole. Unless he can rip through your mind and find the real answers he wants, he has no other way of knowing, or getting any guarantees, that you're who you say you are. This is a method of mutually guaranteed destruction. One of the lesser versions of it, really," Whispers said. "It's just sex."

Just sex. Like it was so easy to just jump into bed with someone and trust them not to kill you. Sure. We all lived in fairy tales.

I rolled my eyes. Even with the partners I found at the sex clubs, I didn't approach to negotiate terms until I ran each one of them through every program I could access. And with the infrequency with which I went to Subterra before having it axed as a venue for myself, I was able to vet most of the patrons the first week. Certainly, the larger portion of them within two weeks.

Another thought dawned on me. "And I already put both Squirrel and Rome down." I rubbed my hands over my face.

"For what it's worth, I think that was the best idea. We have no way of knowing what those two will do when they're fully functional. You've seen for yourself how volatile Keys is around you. If Squirrel moved from seeing you as some kind of Memaw stand-in to now wanting in your pants…" Happy trailed off. "That's not a fight I want to witness."

The other guys nodded in agreement.

"But if Jorgenssen comes and is expecting me to have sex with someone, who am I supposed to choose?" I looked at each one of them. "Draw straws? The least appalled by me? The person who wants to kill me the least?" My head tipped to the side. "Dopey is definitely out."

They all burst into laughter, nodding again.

"Snow, honey, you're not appalling in the least. And none of us want to kill you." Beck smiled. "Well, probably Dopey does, but he's already out." He swallowed. "Any of us would be more than willing and eager to be your partner for the evening."

A big glaring red sign flashed in my head. "And if it turns out that something inside me is interacting with something inside all of you? Which of you is willing to turn rabid like Rome and Squirrel?"

That set them back on their heels and made them think things through a little harder and longer than they seemed to before I mentioned the possibility.

"From what we can tell, it happens the more one of us touches you. Or you touch us. At least skin to skin," Happy began.

As a group, we all agreed.

"Of those of us here, I've touched you the most. First, when I helped you in your home when you got sprayed with the box poison. That was skin to skin. Do you feel anything toward me like what you feel for Squirrel or Rome?" He held his hand out, the palm broad and steady in the space between us.

I felt my belly lurch as my eyes widened. "You want to test it now?"

I shoved my hands behind my back, trying not to run screaming from the room. This was such complete and utter shit. My life could not possibly be dissolving around me like this.

"We might need to test it with just a small, controlled group. We certainly can't with Rome or Squirrel anywhere around. If Happy gets too…happy then we'll know we'll have to find a volunteer from Subterra's rosters. But whatever happens, I guaran-fucking-tee you will be as safe as we can make you," Beck promised.

The men gave me long looks, agreement and promises written on each face.

My breath backed up in my lungs as I shifted to look at Happy again. "You're sure you want to test this?"

He nodded. "Baby, this is one of the better things I'm happy to do if it means you'll be safe."

Fuck. Fuck. Fuck.

"Okay, how do we test it? I need parameters, boundaries, measurable data." I scrubbed my hand up and down my thighs. "And don't snicker at me like that. I'll light you all on fire. I don't like touching people, certainly don't just jump into bed with them. And you're asking to potentially get us even more deeply entwined than any of us understand."

The looks of humor on each face made my cheeks heat, but they really didn't understand how I felt about people.

You would think when I told others I hated people, they would listen. But it never worked that way.

"Well, first, you might want to grab my hand. That's the least invasive measure we can all agree on for right now," Happy said, wiggling his fingers at me.

I glared at him, but stepped forward and slid my palm over his.

It was warm, slightly rough, and felt huge around my smaller hand. My heart slammed against my chest as we stood there in tense silence. My senses were all hyperalert. Fuck, what if this didn't work?

Hell, what if it proved something?

Iggy coughed, startling me so badly I jumped a fucking foot in the air.

The guys all laughed as I turned to glare at him. "Not funny."

He raised his hand, his thumb and index finger about an inch apart. "Kinda funny."

I looked back at Happy, scanning his face for the telltale flicker of something.

A change.

A reaction.

...All I saw was nothing.

But he still wore that happy psycho grin with placid blue eyes. "Anything?"

He shook his head. "You?"

I shook mine, already exhaling in relief. "Nothing."

"Want to try a hug?" he asked softly.

I opened my mouth to say no—but my tongue felt heavy. My breath stuttered, heat rolling down my spine in a slow, paralyzing wave.

I shook my head, but said, "Yeah, I guess." It sounded like I was heading to my beheading.

Happy laughed. "I'm not sure if I should be insulted that you look and sound like that at the thought of touching me, Snow. Good thing my sense of self is more secure than that."

Grimacing, I shrugged. "Sorry. Sorry. It's not you." Great, Neva, make the man feel less appetizing than roadkill, why don't you?

His hands slid over my back and the heat this man pumped off had me thinking I'd stepped into a blazing fireplace. Holy aconite, he was hot. His hands slid down my arms, touching the skin of my arms where my sleeves didn't protect me

377

Well, damn, he smelled good, too. Why couldn't any of these men smell bad? Or at least not good enough to lick like a popsicle.

A shiver ran through me. He was so warm. How? How was he this warm? Curling my hands over his hips and around to his back, I slid them under the hem of his t-shirt, trying to get to more of that warmth. I sighed when my skin smoothed along his bare waist.

"Uh, peaches?" Happy murmured, the sound of his voice was a rumble under my cheek.

"Hmm?" I felt so relaxed. It was odd. Almost peaceful. Downright soothing. I snuggled my face against his lower chest and heaved a sigh. "You feel really good."

Shit.

Shit.

Fuck.

Nope, I was fine. I was fine. I just needed to—

A slow, agonizing hunger bloomed under my ribs.

Tipping my head back, I saw that the blue of his eyes was slowly being eclipsed by the black of his pupils. Hunger lashed his features as his fingers dug into my hips. The perfect counterpoint to the blissful tranquility I found in the heat of his body.

Not Rome. Not Squirrel.

Happy.

As I stared up at him, I realized the guys behind us were yelling amongst themselves. Hard hands gripped my shirt, trying to tug me away from Happy's big, warm body. I snarled as I hung onto the man in front of me. "Get away from me."

"Snow, you're both falling under. You've got to step back," Beck demanded, urgency slicing through his tone like an arctic breeze against my bare skin.

With those words, I crashed back into my own body.

Shoving Happy away, I staggered—drunkenly—toward the edge of the room. My hands shook. My vision blurred. I tripped over my own feet, nausea rising so violently I could barely choke down a scream.

I wanted him.

Needed him like oxygen.

I gagged, horror ripping through me as the bile and something thicker shot up my throat and splattered against the floor. The taste of it—bitter, burning, chemical—had my stomach rolling, another violent heave wrenching my body forward.

No.

No, no, no.

I wasn't like them. I wasn't. I could fight this.

Couldn't I?

"FUCK!" I barely got the word out before another round of sickness forced me to my knees.

Chapter 36
Neva

"Neva, sweetheart?" Beck called softly as he came over to me.

I shook my head, shoving a hand at him to get him to stop. With my throat burning, my belly aching, and the pressure in my head, I felt like I was about to shatter into a million pieces.

What the fuck was wrong with me? With all of us?

My life was controlled, rigid as much as possible, and stable, damn it. Stable as a fucking marble floor. But here I was trying to work with the first group of people I actually thought could be helpful and I couldn't fucking reach out because something was wrong with me.

Insulation and isolation were my life's mantra. No one got hurt except me, no one was put in danger except me. Just me, because when I died, it wouldn't hurt anyone else. If any of these men lost one of their brothers, they would be in so much pain.

"Snow, honey, I'm better. I swear to you, I'm better. I'm not foaming at the mouth, or trying to kill Beck for standing that close to you," Happy said, his voice raised.

Looking over through the curtain of my hair, I saw that Iggy and Whispers were standing between Happy and Beck, their arms up as if to be ready to catch him if he tried to do an end run around them.

Happy stepped back as he lifted his arms out to his sides. "I'm fine, I promise."

Beck stepped forward, cutting the other man off from my sight. "How are you?" He bent down, getting eye level with me. "It doesn't matter how he is, not right now. How are you, sweetheart?" I saw the aching pain in his eyes, and heard the faintest whiff of agony in his voice.

I squeezed my eyes shut, shook my head. "This can't be happening, Breezy."

He chuckled. "Breezy?"

I peeked at him through slitted lids. "Yeah, Breezy. You're so calm, easy breezy." I smiled fully. "Beautiful, Cover Girl."

His nose wrinkled. "I'll stick with breezy." He straightened to his full height. "How are you feeling?"

Heaving a sigh, I stood up. Rubbing a hand over my belly, I winced. "Could be better. But I'm not dying, so I should stop acting like a baby about it. We don't need a Dopey Jr. in the group."

He laughed, his blue eyes twinkling. "That we don't. You good to come over and chat?" He tipped his head toward the group.

My spine stiffened and my chest caught, but I shook it off and nodded. "Yeah. I guess."

Walking a wide circle around him, I moved to rejoin the group. Casting my gaze over Happy, I studied him. He didn't seem any worse for wear. Maybe even a little more energetic.

Iggy and Whispers moved to the side, so we all stood in a loose circle. Each of us studying the others.

"So we know any physical contact—skin to skin specifically—isn't a great idea," Iggy said softly.

I nodded, pulled my arms around my midsection. "It seems that way." Struggling to separate myself from the whole thing, I thought about the science of it. "But I don't understand how that's even possible. Let's take the injected foreign body to its most logical conclusion."

The guys nodded, waiting for me to keep going.

I licked my lips. "Think of it as targeted DNA hacking." I forced my voice to remain steady. "Whoever created it needed my DNA—blood, sweat, tears, something organic."

That should have been the hard part. The creepy part.

382

But it wasn't.

"Except…that's not enough." I gnawed on my lower lip, my pulse climbing. "Even if they got the sample years ago, that's just a blueprint. To create a reaction this…volatile? It means the compound had to be evolving inside me."

Silence. Heavy, crushing silence.

Whispers cleared his throat. "You mean…it's been alive?"

I shrugged, unwilling to examine that answer too hard right now. My brain literally couldn't process the information I just presented.

"So, we're looking at close to five years," Iggy supplied.

I nodded. "It's easy enough to keep biological samples secured and stored. What doesn't make sense is how or why those samples were used to create an answering and inflamed response in you guys. And how would I have been dosed with the same thing to have me respond in similar ways back to you?"

"As far as I know, I would have to be dosed with each of your DNA for me to carry the same response markers. But unless they chose a different path for each of your samples, then my body would potentially dispose of all of them because they would be vying for the same receptors." I rubbed my forehead as the confusion threatened to twist my brain into noodles.

"You're saying that if you received samples from all of us—each created and modified in the same way—they would've been in competition for the limited number of receptor sites in your body. Essentially, survival of the fittest?" Iggy clarified.

I raised my head, nodded. "Yeah. I can't create new receptors for whatever you were given. And I haven't been dosed with anything except the poison that got shoved in my face a couple days ago."

"Would that have been enough to hit you at the molecular level?" Happy asked.

I shrugged, feeling like the world was weighing me down with all the answers I didn't have. "I don't know, simply because I didn't have a lot of time to test it. My focus was looking for ingredients, not particulate DNA matter. And whoever cleaned out the lab before we got there took the only samples I had."

"Is it better to assume that's what happened, or do we need to keep our options open?" Whispers asked.

I looked at him, confusion pulling my brows down. "What do you mean?"

"I can ask my Twists, see if anything like this has been used before. Really, any information they can find on it. But I can't exactly send them off on a wild goose chase for anything that is an aerosolized poison."

My brain blanked as I tried to understand what he was talking about. "Twists?"

Whispers smiled. "Like Oliver Twist, the group of street urchins in the gang who picked pockets and heard information to report back to Fagin."

My lips quirked. "So you're Fagin in this instance. I'm not sure that's a great character reference."

His smile widened. "Oh, they're treated better than any of the orphans. Believe me. They like working with me."

The rest of the guys nodded.

"You're going to send your Twists on an information gathering campaign to see what you can find about all of this."

Whispers nodded. "But I need some kind of way to whittle down the information, otherwise we'll get too many hits and be drowning in it."

Which brought us back to the main problem. "Okay, so what do you guys think? Do we assume the gold box poisons were the delivery system for my responses to you or something altogether different?" I had no idea and right now, I didn't want to be the only one responsible for making that determination.

They studied each other, the walls, the floors. Basically, they looked everywhere but at me as they came to whatever decisions they made.

"Let them look for the gold box poison as the delivery system. If we get a bunch of nothing, then we can widen it back out. But that should be a relatively easy answer to find out. That will help us winnow things down on our end, too," Breezy offered.

Whispers nodded and stepped back from the group, his phone out of his pocket. "Be right back."

Happy checked his watch. Then again, like he didn't quite believe what he saw. "Snow," he said, voice too calm. It grated over my nerves like electrified steel. "You've got ninety minutes before Jorgenssen is expecting you at Subterra."

My guts iced over. Ninety-minutes. Not just to prepare, but to plan, to control every possible outcome, and ensure I wasn't waltzing right into a trap with a fucking smile on my face.

And instead, I was standing here, debating who the hell I could even touch. Like a high schooler at a fucking Sadie Hawkins dance.

Fuck. "I refuse to bring someone else into this. Some innocent who doesn't understand the danger." I shook my head. "But we need to move. Now."

"I was thinking the same thing," Breezy said as the other guys nodded. "Now that Happy is out of the mix, we're down to me, Iggy, Whispers, and Bossy."

"I can't if I'm going to be here putting together the initial system. And I'll need help," Iggy said. He gave me a sad look. "And not for nothing, Snow. But you're fine as hell, so I am sad about it."

I just stood there and blinked at him. Did he really just say that? To me? "Uh…thanks?" I hadn't meant to make it a question, but here we were. Social disgrace, thy name is Neva.

They all chuckled.

"I'll keep Happy with me, since he's been triggered. And Whispers, since he knows the systems better than anyone other than me." Iggy pulled the other two men away and they stepped off to discuss the building and the system they were going to install. I was trying not to find the lie in Iggy's words when he sounded more excited about installing a security system than he had about getting up close and personal with me.

"And, as much as I hate to admit it, I'll be running point between the two ops," Det said. "I can't tell you how much I hate that fact right now, Snow." He wandered off to join the tech crew.

With Breezy the only guy still standing there like a sacrifice, I studied him. "You sure you want to do this?"

His smile was bright. "You don't really know me. And in the grand scheme of things, I don't know you. But we seem to share some common characteristics. The primary one being I don't like to be touched either. Now, one of the great things about the kind of sex I like to have is that I can keep both of us safe from skin-to-skin contact—for the most part—while still putting on a good show." He eyed me closely for a long minute. "Are you capable of putting on a good show?"

For the first time since they brought this whole fucking notion to my head, I felt a wave of relief. I nodded so hard and fast, my head tried to come off of my neck. "Yes!" The exclamation practically leapt from my mouth.

I cleared my throat as my cheeks burned and said in a more modulated, adult tone, "Yes, I can put on a good show."

He smiled. "Good. Then we'll negotiate before Jorgenssen gets here, so we'll know what we can and can't do. He'll get no input in the matter because fucking no one gets to tell me how to be with a lady. And as my partner, your wants and needs are higher than his ever will be."

I felt like he'd just given me a cosmic hug. "Thank you, Beck."

He dipped his chin. "Thank you for trusting me."

I just smiled at him. "Are we going to negotiate now or do you need some time to prepare or game face it or whatever?"

He tipped his head back as he laughed. "Snow, you're one in a million." When lowered his head again. "Which will make you more comfortable?"

My cheeks heated again. "I'd prefer now, but that's just me. Leaving things a mystery isn't really something I'm good at. And has definitely gotten people around me killed for poor planning. Since none of you are going to die because of me, I would like to get things settled now."

All traces of humor left his features as he studied me again. He opened his mouth, but closed it again without saying anything for a long time.

When he opened it again, he said, "Well, let's jump in. Are you into any particular power dynamic or just enjoy sex?"

I blinked at the question, but couldn't find fault in his delivery. He was straightforward and open, which is what I asked for. Not sure the cut and dry approach was something I prepared for, but, oh well. "Power dynamic. I'm sexually submissive."

He nodded, smiled. "Good. I'm a Dom. More of a master, but for a single scene, we'll go with Dom. Hard limits?"

I listed them off. "Hard degradation, blood play or anything that can draw blood, dollification/bimbofication, suspension, gyno play, suffocation, trampling/hitting/kicking, watersports."

386

He dipped his chin. "Those are on my list as well. I'll add nothing anal on or for me, no other men, fire play, scarification, bastinado, or anything that leaves marks longer than twenty-four hours." He pumped his brows a couple times. "I like a clean canvas every time so I can leave new marks."

I chuckled, nodded. "I should add no other women for me. Not a fan of the lady taco." I felt my face screw up in disgust. "I don't like my own vajene, I certainly don't like others'."

He smiled at my answer. "Are you okay with anal?"

I nodded. "Assuming it's not going to rip me in two, sure. Probably need a bit of training or lots of patience. I haven't had it in a while." No one seemed trustworthy enough for me to offer my ass up in terms of play in a very long time. Not that he needed to know that.

"That's fine. We can take it off the table for tonight, no need to push more boundaries than we need to, especially just for Jorgenssen's benefit." He crossed his arms. "Anything else you don't want to do if he's watching?"

My belly twisted as heat rushed my face. Well, hell. Why did he have to put it like that?

"That brought an answer to your mind. Are you going to share it with me?" His chuckle was a little darker.

I glared at him, but it didn't phase him at all. He just continued to stare at me with quiet expectation.

Heaving a sigh, I figured he would need to know the real answer since I was trusting him to keep me safe through this whole ordeal.

I licked my lips, opened my mouth. When no sound came out, I snapped my jaw shut. Spinning a tight circle, I tried to ramp myself up.

Come on, Neva. Just say it. Just spit it out, we're negotiating a scene. Just like any other partner you've been with. Easy breezy.

My lips quirked. He was Breezy. Officially now. Surely he could handle it.

Walking back to him, I lifted my head to face him head on. "Not saying you will, because I've yet to meet a guy who can, but please don't make me orgasm."

His mouth fell open as his arms dropped to his sides. "Don't make you come?"

I nodded and felt heat invade my entire body.

As I watched, he seemed to give my previous statement a longer, harder thought. He raised a single finger. "You're saying no man has ever made you orgasm. Is that correct?"

I nodded again. "I just don't really want that to happen right now, especially if it's for a job. Please, Breezy. Please?"

His jaw went slack. "You're the first, and only, woman I've ever met who is negotiating with me to not make you come." He squeezed his eyes shut, rubbed a hand down his face. When he opened his eyes again, he was back to being calm and neutral. "That's really what you want?"

I nodded. "I can fake it really well." I snorted. "Like, Oscar worthy performance. None of my partners have ever felt bad about themselves. I promise I'll make you feel like a king."

His back stiffened and a look of insult twisted his features. "Just the fact you said that makes me want to hunt down all of your previous partners and beat them to death with their own dicks. There is no way you can fake it and make me feel like a king, Snow. Not in this or any other lifetime."

The first bubble of laughter escaped as I realized the absurdity of this particular conversation. I lifted my hands to cover my mouth, my eyes wide. Please, please, please don't let him think I'm laughing at him.

But then more laughter sprang out of me, so it didn't matter that I had my hands almost completely inside my mouth to hold back the noise. My eyes started to water as my belly ached trying to hold it all in.

He rolled his blue eyes, sighed. "Let it out before you hurt yourself, sweetheart."

Huge guffaws and snorts pumped out of me like I was a noise machine set on eleven out of ten. I barely maintained my upright posture as I watched the other guys come over and ask Breezy what was so funny. That made me laugh harder. I put my hands between my legs, on the verge of peeing my pants, I was laughing so hard.

"She asked me not to make her come." Breezy still sounded insulted by the idea and that's when I lost the battle.

I fell to the ground, my legs going boneless. I bit my cheek until I tasted blood as my eyes started to burn. Shoving the heels of my palms into my eyes, I shook my head. Shit, no, no, no. Don't cry.

Do not fucking cry.

Curling up in a ball, I held my knees against my chest. Please just let it keep being laughter.

But the ache in my throat made me a liar. I felt the control I had on my body slipping, ripping to shreds even as I struggled to cling to it.

In the end, I focused on keeping a hold of my bladder, and just let all of the pent-up pressure melt away. My chest hurt, my throat burned, my legs cramped. At one point, Whispers leaned down next to me, sorrow in his eyes.

That just made it all worse.

Shoving my face into my knees, I tried to hold myself together. To wait out the storm.

It didn't feel like it would end.

Not the shaking. Not the shame. Not the heat licking at the edges of my thoughts telling me to—no. No. I wasn't thinking about that.

But I could still feel the warmth of Happy's skin against mine. The way my body just…gave in. Like it was waiting for it. Fucking primed for it.

And that?

That was fucking horrifying.

The poison wasn't inside me.

I *was* the poison.

By the time I stretched out on the cement floor, I felt like I'd been scraped clean on the inside and weighed less than a feather. Four men stood in a circle above me, each giving me looks that made my belly churn with acid. But I just smiled up at them all.

"Thank you, Breezy."

Three of them laughed as the man in question nodded. "Sure, Snow."

"Breezy?" Iggy asked.

"Easy, breezy, beautiful, Cover Girl," I said softly.

"Shoulda gone for Cover Girl, Snow. I think it suits him better," Whispers said softly.

Breezy flipped them all off as he crouched down beside me. "Feeling better?"

I nodded, pulling myself to sit up. "Yeah. Thanks." Enough of the crazy show, you stupid bitch. You're making everything harder on them and they're just trying to help you, I yelled at myself mentally.

Happy bent down, his hand out. "Consider this a timed test. Iggy, get your stopwatch."

See? Perfect. Knowledge acquisition. Facts. We did need more information, and since the rest of my night was with Breezy, this should be easy enough to manage. Sliding my hand over Happy's, I let him pull me up to my feet.

He immediately let me go and stepped back, pointing a finger at Iggy. "Time?"

"Eight point two seconds. Snow, how do you feel?"

All four men watched me.

Doing an internal check to see if I had an overwhelming urge to get closer to Happy, I waited for a second to give it my full attention. When nothing felt abnormal, I shook my head. "Nothing. You, Happy?"

He wiggled his hand in the air slightly. "Kinda. But that could just be nerves because while I really like you, Snow, I don't really want to get addicted to you." His smile was a little sad, but I fully understood what he meant.

"Are you feeling a ravenous need to protect her, to clobber any of us, want to shoot us in the face, or hack our legs off and beat us to death with them?" Whispers asked.

I blinked at the normally quiet man. He was...interesting when he wasn't being bashful.

Happy shook his head. "No, none of that." He turned to look at me. "Just Snow being pretty like usual. That's about it. But I don't have a driving need to hide her away, either."

I smiled, relief washing through me. "Good. That's good." I nodded. "That's great, actually. So we're clear under ten seconds of touching once whatever this is has been triggered."

They all nodded.

"Or at least less than ten seconds with someone who hasn't already developed an emotional tie to you," Breezy amended.

My nose wrinkled. Damn it. He was right. "We'll definitely need to measure oxytocin levels."

"Can you do that with the equipment you have here or with what you're going to order?" Iggy asked as we all moved back to the truck as if by silent agreement.

"I can get the most basic analyses done with the GC-Mass Spec. Outside of that, we're going to be ordering shit like crazy. I'll give you a list. First and foremost, though, we're going to need a full team to get cleanroom, sterility, and security systems setup. We'll also need soundproofing and RF nets."

"Snow, I think I might love you." Iggy said, as his lids lowered halfway, his breathing was deep and a little harsh, his fingers clenched and relaxed at his sides. "What kind of budget again?"

"Get whatever we need, don't worry about the cost. I've got a couple of offshore accounts you can use. Will you be in charge of getting everything and running logistics?"

He made a low groaning noise before he cut it off. "Fuck, yes. Give me your list and I'll get started tonight while I go through our inventory. Happy, Banshee, you're both with me."

I smiled, glad I could make at least someone happy in all of this. "That leaves me with Breezy, Bossy, and Dopey." I looked at the guys. "Does that work for everyone? Should Charming and Hotsy be fine by themselves?"

They all nodded.

Iggy snickered. "They'll be baby bitches about it all, but they'll get over it. And as much as Dopey whines, he's a good guy to have at our backs. He can be the go-between for me and you through this whole thing. We'll get you patched in with our comms so you can stay up to date on everything."

I smiled. "He could also be useful in getting inventory. We might need to buy from overseas to get everything as quickly as possible."

Breezy rocked back on his heels. "How long are you thinking for a full system setup?"

I did some mental math, prayed really hard, and said, "If we're lucky, we're looking at a minimum of two weeks. Assuming we'll have to wait for at least some of the bigger pieces, we're looking at a month."

"So we need to keep you away from Charming and Hotsy for a month?" Whispers asked, his brows high.

I shrugged. "Or keep us all in hazmat suits, reducing the possibility of pheromone or biochemical spread."

The guys chuckled. "That would be interesting to watch unfold," Iggy said, his nose already stuck in his phone. "I've got enough inventory to get the whole place rigged tonight, assuming I get to keep Whispers and Happy. As soon as the meeting with Jorgenssen is finished, if everyone can come back here, we'll get the rest of it done."

"I've got a couple suppliers for more, if you need them," I added.

He nodded. "I'll take all of it. Go get showered, changed, make voice notes while you're doing whatever it is you're going to do. Send me the notes, I'll get started."

"While you're working on that, do you have any antidotes or remedies for Charming and Hotsy? If we can give it to them after Jorgenssen verifies they're out, we could have them working with Iggy and the install crew," Breezy said.

I dipped my chin. "Yeah. We'll need to get some stuff from the store, but that should be easy enough."

"Send me that list as well," Iggy said.

We all got back in the truck and headed down the street to their building. It was going to be a long night.

Chapter 37

Rome

Rolling to the side again, I dry heaved until it felt like my stomach was trying to evacuate my body through my mouth. My throat was raw, my hands shook like I had some kind of palsy, while the sheets I laid on were drenched in sweat and other things I didn't want to think too hard about.

"She's evil, Keys. Fucking evil," Squirrel's words fell off as he puked again.

I nodded as much as I could. "Don't make her mad at us. Please, whatever god is still out there, don't let her get mad at us again."

The entire bunk room smelled like sick. The dim lighting did nothing but add to the grim misery of it. Even with a fan blowing directly on each of us, all I could smell was bile, shit, and sweat.

It was torture.

The door swung open, blinding me with the bright light of whoever stood just inside the door. The fast switch in lighting had my brain twitching and horrors rising through my consciousness again. I flinched back from the phantom hands that reached for me. "Get the fuck back."

I swatted at them, but was pretty sure my hands didn't even lift fully from the bed. Low murmuring came through my ears, but I couldn't make out any words.

Still battling the nightmares in my mind, I didn't bother with whoever had invaded our sick bay. For whatever reason, I kept seeing Dewdrop riding Squirrel like he was a horse. He somehow had a dick on his back, so he was fucking her while running at the same time.

Every time Dewdrop squirted, it would run down the flanks of the black hair of Squirrel's horse. His sides were painted in green and gold, the colors of her eyes when she was angry. She would laugh and giggle, give me a little finger wave, then go back to fucking Squirrel's back dick.

The door slid shut again and my mind washed clean one more time. "Thank fuck."

"Horse dick?" Squirrel whispered.

I groaned my answer.

"At least you get to have dreams of her. All I've got is my hand that keeps fucking me, even when I tell it not to. It sprouts more hands and fingers. I've been molested by my own fucking body."

I hissed out a pained laugh. Mine was definitely the better of the two options. Probably said more about our particular neuroses than anything else, but at this point I was fine with that. "Just means she's mine, Raper Hand."

The door swung open again and this time I actually recognized the person. "Happy. Happy, you came to save us."

He snickered as he shut the door behind himself. "Well, I come bearing gifts from Snow. Does that count?"

I reared back so hard, I smashed my skull into the cinderblock wall. "I'm not taking anything that demon woman makes. She's already killing us slowly. Does she want to hurry it along now?" What did I ever do to her to make her hate me this much?

"You blew past her boundaries like they weren't there, treated her like trash, spied on her, and then made her feel guilty for it, you asshat. That's what you did to her," Happy answered.

My brows furrowed. I didn't remember asking that question out loud.

"You've been talking the whole fucking time, Keys. We've had you on camera. Neither of you will shut up for longer than it takes to groan or puke. You even talk while you're shitting yourselves. It's creepy."

I shrugged, then felt the world tip sideways again as my belly revolted. I moaned as I reached for the edge of the bed. The bucket was probably full at this point, probably splashing up and hitting me in the face.

Oh gods, kill me now.

"No. Drink this, take these supplements, and you'll be feeling brand new," Happy said, shoving a mug of something warm into my hand. "Fine, maybe not brand new, but at least good enough you can help keep Snow safe. You want her safe, right?"

I dragged my head up and down in the affirmative. I needed her to be safe. It was well beyond *want* at this point.

"Good. Then drink up. Once you're done with that, you're going to drink the electrolyte waters I put on the floor by your buckets. All of them. Go find Dopey in Ops when you can walk again."

He pulled the door shut softly behind himself and for that I could have kissed him. Loud noises did nothing but trigger some ridiculously scary nightmares from the past that I thought were forgotten. But no, Dewdrop brought those back with her witch's brew, too.

In the bed across the room, I heard Squirrel slurping back whatever Happy brought us. He groaned and sounded like he was about to chuck again, but he managed to keep it all down.

Since he wasn't dead yet, I followed suit and drank the brew. It did little to soothe my throat, but at least it didn't get my stomach roiling again. After I managed to keep it down for about ten minutes, I attempted the small cup of capsules Snow insisted on.

Within about thirty minutes I almost felt normal. I blinked as the room around me flashed into vivid detail. Pale sterile walls greeted me, but at least there were no hidden horrors or terrors etched on them like before.

Reaching down, I grabbed the electrolyte water. Taking timid sips, I managed to kill two of the four bottles delivered. As my body moved along the path of healing, I fought not to get sick from the scents overflowing the room.

"Fuck, it's rank in here."

Squirrel nodded, his fingers pinching his nose closed with one hand as he drank from the water bottle with the other. He lowered the bottle, keeping his nostrils blocked. "We're going to have to torch it to get the smell out." He finished the bottle and managed to get to his feet. Stretching himself out to his full height, he heaved a huge sigh. "Damn, that feels good."

Getting up from the bed, I grabbed my remaining two water bottles. "Let's get out of here and see where everyone's at."

Walking for the door, I paused when Squirrel shook his head. "I'm showering before I go anywhere. I'm going to puke just from sniffing myself." He cupped his hand over his mouth as his chest bucked again.

He wasn't wrong.

"Let's shower then. Locker rooms will work. You got an extra set of clothes?"

He nodded, already going through the door.

Slamming it shut behind me, I made a mental note to put up a hazardous material sign. We might actually need to firebomb it.

Feeling like I aged fifty years in the sick bay, washing up in the shower felt like heaven. By the time I felt clean, I was down a couple layers of skin, but that was nothing. I pulled on the clean gym clothes and swiped the towel over my hair before picking up another water bottle.

Cracking the lid on it, I tipped it back and chugged it down. "Whew. I never knew electrolyte water could taste this good."

Squirrel groaned next to me as we made our way to the Bat Cave. "I hate grape flavored anything, but this is next level shit. I want to swim in it right now."

Chuckling at the mental image, we walked into Ops and I rocked to a fucking halt. "What the hell is going on?" The empty bottle fell from my fingers as I saw Dewdrop on a screen, decked out in club gear that made me feel like the top of my head was about to pop off. The shiny PVC barely covered the essentials.

Dopey turned from a secondary screen and sliced a finger over his throat. He answered whoever was on his phone in rapid Arabic, nodding as he did something on a notepad by his station.

"Is our Snow in Subterra right now?" Squirrel asked softly, horror drenching his tone. "Wearing that collection of straps and buckles?"

I nodded, unable to look away from the picture on screen.

We were watching live security footage from one of the private rooms. Dewdrop stood there looking sexy as hell, with a sheer black robe covering her body. It played hide and seek with her skin as she nodded or shook her head to whatever Jorgenssen was saying.

When she glared up at him, her fisted hands slapping down to her hips, I almost had a heart attack. Her tits. Her tits were about to come out of the barely there cups and that monster was going to see them.

Plopping into the seat in front of me, I clenched my hand around the last bottle of electrolyte water to keep from rushing out there and killing him.

"Wadaea, shukran," Dopey said before he tossed his phone on the table. "Keep your mouths shut. She's on our comms link."

He hit a series of buttons, not waiting for us to answer. As her voice tripped through the room, I felt another attack on my belly. But this time it wasn't horror. No, this time, it was nothing but sin and sex.

"Oskar, you called the meeting here. We've discussed what we came to discuss, you didn't want to play ball. Feel free to leave," she said. I heard the threat in her tone, but apparently the Swede wasn't too familiar with her sweet promises of death.

"Ms. de Witte. Surely you can't believe that all I came for was discussion."

She stepped back by the smallest margin. "Actually, yes. I do. I made no promises outside of the discussion. What you assumed and what will happen are completely different things."

Jorgenssen leaned forward, his lips so close to her skin he could probably scent her sunshine. "I am not so foolish as to believe in the naïve answers of women. We are holding this meeting here so I can be assured of your dedication to helping my daughter."

"You have my assurances. Take it or leave it." Neva glared up at him.

He laughed, the sound like sandpaper on my nerves. "Do not be so simpleminded, Aniera. You will enjoy your time here tonight, as will I. We will not leave until things have been fully settled between us."

She drew back, disgust on her face. "I'm not fucking you. Your daughter isn't that important to me. If you don't want my help, I'm more than happy to leave." She moved to step past him.

He caught her arm.

I shot out of my chair until I saw Schnauzer move in from the darkened section of the room. "Take your hand off her or I'll do it for you and send it to your men in a gold-lined box." His low voice didn't detract from the threat.

In fact, it made it a little more sinister.

Jorgenssen removed his hand, but didn't back away. "You will help my daughter. And tonight I will watch you fuck whomever you want, and if you try to betray me, I'll release not only the footage of your personal life to your superiors, but I'll make sure the footage is also sent to your aging parents as part of your final goodbye. Your personal and professional lives will be owned by me, Ms. de Witte. Make no mistake on that score."

She stood there, her body visibly vibrating with rage even through the camera feed.

For a split second, just one, her fingers curled so tightly, her nails dug into her skin. That was all. A flicker of something real, something raw.

Then it was gone, swallowed by the smirk curling at the edges of her lips.

I also prayed for Jorgenssen to get out of there without losing any body parts.

Almost. Except he'd threatened her, so I was more than willing to help remove anything Dewdrop wanted to dispose of from this asshole.

Neva pushed up into his face, laughed a hard chuckle. "You and what army are going to force me to do anything I don't want to do, Oskar?" She crossed her arms, raising her brows high in question. "You don't have anything on me yet. Other than the fact I'm in this place, dressed within club rules, you have nothing to hold over my head."

He looked a little stymied by that for a moment, but then shook his head. "I'll kill your parents."

She shrugged. "They're monsters, anyway. Kill them."

My brows furrowed at the hard tone. That didn't sound like playacting. I knew her real grandparents were standing as her fake parents under her Aniera de Witte legend. Did she really dislike her grandparents that much? Her mention of the terrible Uncle Lawrence flashed through my head again. Maybe they weren't great.

I made a mental note to get Iggy to do some more digging.

Jorgenssen tipped his head as he glared at her. "You haven't left yet, and you claim my daughter doesn't mean anything to you. What do you want if you're so willing to continue to bargain with me?"

I saw the light of victory fill her eyes for a heartbeat. "I wasn't just stringing Brantley along because he was an asshole. He had certain access I needed. Access you robbed me of. Get me that, and I'll gladly give you the leverage you want to ensure my compliance."

Jorgenssen backed away, a thoughtful look on his face. "You were using your fake boyfriend for access to his professional networks."

She nodded. "Yes. You know my specialty. I've been looking for someone specific high up in the American agencies. When you killed that asshole, you removed my only avenue of reaching them."

It was a careful twist on what she truly needed. I could see it both working and falling apart around her in equal measure. If he questioned too carefully or thoroughly, she would be dead before she got a chance to use any of the information he gave her.

"And what information do you need?" he asked, his arms crossed.

She shook her head. "I'm not that dumb, Oskar. We come to an agreement, with both of us having damning information on the other, or we stop here, and I'll go my own way. It will take me longer and cost me more money to cultivate the contacts I need, but I can easily do it without you. Can you say the same for your daughter's condition?" She raised a brow as she threw down the gauntlet.

He steamed and fumed silently as he glared at her. I could almost see him weighing her words, sincerity, and his own desperation for his daughter as she trapped him in a single conversation.

Jorgenssen paced away from Neva. He joined the men he had standing at the door, where they held a short conversation in Swedish. Dopey snickered as he listened, but he didn't offer any translations so everyone else in the room could stay in character.

The Swede finally rejoined Neva and Beck. "I need some idea of what this information is. I can't guarantee I have what you seek if I don't know what you want."

It was reasonable. Somewhat.

She stared up at him for a long moment. Tapping her fingers on her crossed her arms, I saw her play the consternation to perfection. Stuck between a rock and a hard place, she made sure to look just uncomfortable enough to let it seem like nerves leaking through her control. "I need to find someone who commissioned a designer poison." Her lips pursed and relaxed as soon as she said it, signaling fear and disgust with herself.

Jorgenssen's smile was oily. "And if I can hand you this information without a need for wasting any more of your time…what will you give me?"

She jolted for just an instant. But she did it so hard that Beck came up and stood directly behind her, his body against hers as if in support. "You can do that?"

Jorgenssen shrugged a single shoulder. "Perhaps. But I have not heard the price for this information you seek. What are you willing to give me?"

Neva licked her lips, her fingers wrenching on each other. "Wh-wh-what do you want?"

"My daughter healed. And a favor sometime in the future."

"That's it?"

Jorgenssen shook his head.

She practically wilted in disappointment. "What else?"

"Again, we came here for a reason, Ms. de Witte. You are pleasing enough to look at. I find myself curious to watch you in such intimate acts. So you will still give me the show I want, I will record it, and upon you successfully healing my daughter and completion of future favors, I will return the footage back to you." He gave a smile that made me want to reach through the camera and tear his face off.

She nibbled her bottom lip, her toe now tapping out a rapid rhythm on the floor. "One favor to be completed within two years' time. Your daughter healed. In return, I get the information you have. Verified. If it's not verified as accurate, no deal. In exchange tonight, you get to perv on me while this guy here rattles my bones, and I'll post the information of your daughter's illness in a failsafe black server that will go live if anything happens to me." She jerked her thumb behind her.

"The fuck he's gonna touch her," Squirrel spit out, his thumping fist bashing against the table like thunder.

On screen, Neva winced the slightest bit. Her shoulders stiffened for a fraction of an instant before settling back down. She didn't give herself away by anything other than that small action.

Dopey glared at Squirrel and sliced his finger over his throat again slowly.

Squirrel pushed up out of the chair and stomped from the room.

Dopey gave me a long stare, one dark brow raised.

400

I shook my head, fisting my fingers around the arms of the chair. No fucking way was I leaving. I had to know where he touched her. How he touched her. So I could erase it from her mind later. Replace every touch, every look, every breath from her memory and give her only me in return.

"You will not post anything about my daughter, or I will walk away right now. She will not be made a target in any of this." Jorgenssen spit out the words through clenched teeth.

Neva laughed softly. "I already have. You see, I had to have leverage on you as well. Otherwise, you're getting what you want with me having no assurances that you keep your word. I'm not so naïve or simpleminded to believe the word of someone like you."

His face darkened in anger, but he held himself very still. "If a single byte of data leaks on her, I will do everything in my power to destroy you and anyone you hold dear."

"If you can get me the information I need and want, I'll never do anything to harm your daughter. You can even have an extra favor from me to show my appreciation. It's not like you offered any such gifts in return for my participation in tonight's events. You're one up, Oskar. Take the win." She crossed her arms, waited him out.

He finally stepped back, his expression going cold. "Did you have this planned all along? Me to kill your fake boyfriend so you could hold me over the barrel?"

She shook her head. "No. It took me a very long time to gain Brantley's trust. But I'm neither stupid nor arrogant enough to believe I'll be successful in any of my endeavors without hard work, luck, and taking advantage of things when they happen. Do not think to cross me, Mr. Jorgenssen. We will have a very successful relationship if we both hold to the terms outlined tonight." She stuck her hand out.

"And if the information I have doesn't satisfy the terms of your request? What then?" He ignored her outstretched hand.

"Then you will dig. And if you fail, you won't just lose your leverage—you'll lose your entire reputation."

She took a step closer, her voice dropping into something dark, something almost gentle. "Because if you fail me, Oskar, I will make sure every major player in your world knows where and how you're weak."

401

Jorgenssen's face stayed still, but his knuckles whitened. "And does that include hurting my daughter?"

She shook her head, lowered her hand. "Again, Mr. Jorgenssen, your daughter will never come to harm from me. I will do everything in my power to help her. Unless you backstab me or fail to uphold your end of the bargain, me potentially releasing the information of her illness lies in direct proportion to you bringing me good data within the one-month timeframe."

"If the information you seek can't be obtained within this thirty-day time period? Will you neglect my daughter if she's not yet fully healed?"

Neva shook her head again. "No. She is my leverage for you to participate. I will not endanger that leverage. But if after the time limit ends and you have done nothing to satisfy the terms on your end, I will make it known far and wide that you are weak through her. Whatever happens at that time will be your fault. However, if you've made earnest attempts to find me what I need, then I will gladly continue working to help Ada." She stuck her hand out again. "Do we have a deal?"

Chapter 38
Neva

My breath backed up in my throat as I waited for Jorgenssen to shake on the deal. After talking it through with Breezy some more, we came up with the story I just gave the Swede to explain everything. From using Brantley to coercing Jorgenssen's participation for what I really needed from him.

Putting it out there in black and white made things much easier from a clandestine perspective. No gray areas, no wiggle room. Everyone gets something they need. The perfect deal.

Jorgenssen put his hand in mine. "I will watch you fuck this man from inside this room."

Breezy snorted. "No. You won't. Neither will your men. How I fuck a woman isn't up for discussion. That's *my* rule."

The heat of Breezy at my back had been what kept me plugging along with the game. The show, as he called it. At least to the degree I achieved. If I was all alone, I probably would have caved a little sooner just to get this guy out of my life.

I tipped my head to the side at the audacity of the guy standing across from me. "Looks like you and Tweedles

Dumb and Dee over there will be waiting outside." I released a long silent sigh of relief.

Thank fuck. I was fairly certain I wouldn't have been able to put on that good of a show if they'd remained inside the room.

Jorgenssen squeezed my hand unnecessarily hard. "Do not talk down to me, Ms. de Witte. I'm not like that toad Brantley for you to disrespect."

I pulled my hand away, glared up at him. "The same to you, Mr. Jorgenssen. Treat me with respect and I'll provide the same to you. You disrespected my partner, you earned my response. Learn from the lesson." I pointed at the door. "Now leave, if you want your sex video."

I buried the shock that accompanied my statement. Stinging tree and spindle, had that actually just come out of my mouth? Without laughter or hysteria? I would have been impressed if I wasn't stunned and a little repulsed by my own words.

Jorgenssen waited a beat longer than necessary, but he turned and pushed his men out the door. Within moments, they were standing at the window of the adjoining room. They all stood there like statues. Glaring, grumpy statues.

Breezy's laugh ruffled the hair at the top of my head. "Damn, Snow."

I turned toward him, keeping my expression neutral until I looked up at him. The smile almost broke my face. "Oh gods. I can't believe I just did that."

He snorted. "That's the least impressive thing you've done in here tonight. Believe me." He studied me for a moment. "You ready for the next part of the show?"

I nodded and said, "No. But here we are. Are you ready?"

His smile was dirty as his crystalline blue eyes twinkled. "Ready to give you so much pleasure you don't orgasm? Sure, Snow. More than ready. We're going to test my skills to the limit here. I hope you know that."

I burst into laughter. "Thanks again."

His expression lost the edge of lust as he nodded down at me. "Anything to keep you safe." Leaning down, he pressed a kiss to my forehead. "That's it for skin-on-skin. You ready?"

I nodded, unable to do anything more than move my head. The number of times I've negotiated a scene with the expectation of orgasm was high. The one time I negotiated for myself to not orgasm…one. And, of course, this was the one time I was worried I might not get what I want.

Girl brains are dumb.

"You might want to look like you're not heading to your own funeral, Snow," Breezy said as he pulled on black nitrile gloves.

Hurrying to rearrange my face, I looked up at him with what I hoped was a convincing smile.

From his laugh, I had to assume I failed.

"Close, but no cigar." Once his hands were covered by the sterile black gloves, he put his palms on my shoulders. "You tell me when you're ready. Nothing starts or stops unless you want it to."

I sighed. "Don't be nice, Breezy."

He chuckled again. "I'm not going to be an asshole. You'll have to take me as I am."

Gathering up all my courage, I lifted my head and smiled at him. "Yes. I'm ready."

We already discussed how all of this was going to go. It was more like a mission brief than a scene negotiation by the time it was all said and done. The amount of attention he expended for a single scene made me curious about what kind of long-term partner he was.

I knew every single detail of what to expect. But I also knew this was nothing like anything I've ever done before. Not for a job, not for personal reasons. Everything was getting caught and trapped in my head.

"I'm going to lower the lights," Breezy said. Walking around me, he went to the door. Hitting the button to lock it, he then turned down the dimmer for the lights.

With the lower lighting, I felt like I could actually breathe normally again. I leaned against the padded bench, inhaling and exhaling slowly so I could bring myself back under some semblance of control.

Breezy moved in front of me again. His hands back on my shoulders. "Better, sweetheart. Lift your arms when you're ready for me to take off this joke of a robe."

I stifled the smile as I raised my arms. "Sexy is what I was going for. Not a joke."

He snorted softly. "You definitely got the sexy part right. Does nothing but make a man want to rip it into tiny shreds and then tie you up with whatever's left. The joke is on us, sweetcheeks. Believe me on that score."

I blinked up at him, amazed at the honesty in his voice. "You're not just saying that?"

He shook his head. "Why would I lie about something like that?"

I shrugged. "Trying to say what a girl wants to hear?"

He laughed again, the sound lower in his chest. "Another point where you don't know me very well. I don't say things I don't mean. I don't have the time or patience for it. Really, that shared trait is one of the things I admire most about you."

He lifted me up to the bench with nothing but his hands around my waist. He waited for me to look directly at him, green gaze to blue. "You're gorgeous, sweets. Even for just one night, I'll enjoy treating you like you're mine."

With nothing else to say or do but nod, that's what I offered.

He smiled and helped me get situated on the bench. With the main part of it supporting my belly, chest, and hips, he got me buckled down at my wrists and ankles. He already told me he was a spanko, and the activity would also allow us to keep skin-to-skin contact to a minimum.

"Comfortable?" he asked as he backed away, his gloved hand sliding down my side to my mostly bare ass.

I wiggled under his touch. "Yeah." It was rare I allowed a partner to lock me down. Too many horrors raced through my brain for it ever to be something I just ran toward with a stranger.

While Breezy wasn't quite a stranger, he wasn't exactly my boyfriend either. So here we were, putting on a show for some voyeuristic idiot who thought he had me over a barrel.

"Sure you don't want anything in your pretty pussy?"

That particular part of my anatomy absolutely wanted something, but being an exhibitionist really wasn't part of my kink list. I was doing this for a job and no other reason. "You read them and do what you think is necessary. We need to sell this."

"They're looking a little bored, honestly. Jorgenssen is on the verge of being pissed. I say let him be pissed, but I don't know how he'll react later down the line if we don't give him something to get hard about."

I chuckled as I turned my face toward the side where Breezy stood. I couldn't see the windows from my new vantage point, but it didn't mean they couldn't see me. "Maybe put one in, just don't turn it on."

Breezy groaned. "You're killing me here, Snow. How about I edge you? Make not coming part of the fun instead of the requirement." He walked toward my head, crouched down so he was eye level with me. "Then at least you wouldn't have to fake it."

I rolled my eyes. "All men say that, Breezy. None of you are actually good at sex."

He sneered and leaned back for a moment. "How about this, then? I edge you until you're a squirming, screaming mess, then I drop you flat like all these men you keep mentioning. If, by some miracle"—he rolled his eyes—"you do get off, I'll help you tell men they have no idea what they're doing. I'll take out a fucking billboard."

Narrowing my eyes at him, I studied him from a couple inches away. "You'd really take out a billboard espousing how men suck at sex and that's it just women feeling bad for them that their egos don't implode?"

He laughed right in my face. "Sure, Snow. I'll let you write it, then I'll paste it up by hand." He went quiet. "Do we have a deal?"

"So you do your best to actually get me off, edge me until I'm out of my head. Drop me flat and make me whine like a baby. If you do get me off, you're going to put up a billboard saying men are trash in bed." I outlined the deal.

He nodded. "It doesn't sound right when you put it like that, but yeah. Deal?"

"If I do whine like a baby, what do I have to do?"

He blinks. "This is the weirdest conversation I've ever had with a woman. And that includes our talk earlier today. If you do get close and I drop you like a hot rock, you have to put up a sign saying Breezy is amazing in bed and send all your friends to me."

I giggled. "I don't have any friends."

He rolled his eyes. "Then write my accomplishments on a Facebook post, Tiktok video, X post, damn, scrawl it in the bathroom stall, something. Hell, write a fucking poem about how great I am."

I laughed again. "Deal, Breezy. I'll write you a glowing recommendation if you can truly do what you're saying you can do." I settled in. This might actually be fun.

He glared at me for a second. "You've thought of something else."

I shrugged. "Maybe I have, maybe I haven't. But chop, chop, Breezy. Get to edging me. Let's give Swede and Co a good show."

He leaned forward without putting his skin to mine. "Deal, Snow. Get ready to have your world rocked. Anything you want to change about your limit list?"

I snickered. "Nope. Fair game as long as it's not on my hard list."

"Safe words?"

"Traffic light system."

"Good girl. Then I'm definitely filling this pretty pussy with something, sweetheart." He rose to his full height, his dick right in my face.

For just a moment, my mouth watered. Then my brain went back to her normal state of disinterest. Maybe I needed to start drafting a billboard ad about men being shitty at sex. Settling in to get mentally drafting, I jolted slightly when Breezy drizzled some warmed lube over my asshole, then massaged it into my pussy.

I fought my body to keep from squirming.

From his dark chuckle, apparently I wasn't very successful. "Something wrong, sweetheart?" he asked, humor dripping from his tone.

"Not at all. Thanks for the moisturizer. She's been pretty dry lately." I buried my smile into the fake leather.

He grumbled but went back to what he was doing. Next thing I knew, my thong was pushed to the side, he spread my pussy wide, and slid a toy inside me.

My eyes popped wide as I blew out a breath at the rapid invasion. "Skyflower, Breezy."

He chuckled softly, but didn't answer with anything else.

As I felt him hooking something stiff and hard around my thighs, I lifted my head. He was not putting me in a harness. Shifting my head as far to the side as I could to see him, he just pumped his brows at me while he secured another cold strap down against my thigh.

"Good?" he asked.

I nodded, narrowing my eyes at him.

He spanked a hard hand to my left ass cheek. "Good."

I yelped under the blow, feeling the blood rush to the spot. Buckthorn, that was…interesting. Maybe all of my negotiations in the past were trash. Could that be the problem? I wasn't willing to let down my guard enough to enjoy myself?

Relaxing back down onto the bench, I shook my head mentally. Nah. I was free-spirited. Member of numerous sex clubs, I knew how to get my freak on. It was definitely the men's problems for not knowing what to do with me once they had me for the night.

"Focus on my voice, Snow," Breezy said.

I nodded.

"I'm going to massage your ass. Your cheeks are amazing, big enough to grab." He put action to words and grabbed a double handful. When he dropped my flesh, he slapped both hands down on me hard. "And the sound…" He groaned. "Fuck, Snow."

Over and over, he told me exactly what he was going to do. And then he did it. No question, no hesitation. When he turned on the toy in my pussy, I felt my eyes widen. Damn, that was bigger than I thought it was.

"Good girl, Snow. Let it move up and down inside that gorgeous fucking pussy. I know it's not the menu for tonight, but I would have loved to taste you. Get your juice all over my face. Down my throat, covering my beard." He growled low in his chest. "Something about a woman enjoying my mouth on her will remain one of my singular favorite activities."

The heat of him faded for a moment. But then I felt the rough texture of his pants against the soles of my feet once again. "I'm gonna fuck you using this toy, Snow. And you're not going to be able to do anything about it."

My eyes widened as I fought against the restraints.

His laugh was dark and hard as I felt him grip the base of the toy. "Just like that, princess. Fight me. Fight to get free. I'm going to own your body, steal your mind." He pulled the toy until it was almost completely free of my flesh before he twisted it on a hard thrust deep inside me.

My back arched as he stole my breath. Fuck, fuck, fuck. Waves of heat washed through me, setting me on fire. How the hell had he done that?

He fucked me hard and fast with the toy until I felt my breath start to back up in my throat. No! No, he couldn't be this close to getting me off already. It wasn't fair. Not like this.

When he shoved the toy back inside me, he landed a blow to my right ass cheek that sparkled bright, zinging pain through my mind and soul.

Fuck. My entire body vibrated with the need to come. So fucking close. "Please, Beck. Oh fuck, please?"

His laugh made me clench my teeth. That was the last begging he would get out of me. Damn him!

"No, Snow. I don't think you've earned it yet. Do you?" He didn't let me answer before he unleashed another assault on my body in the best way possible. "Are you really begging a man to get you off? You dirty little slut.

Begging and whining already." He made little tsk, tsk, tsk noises as he continued to fuck me into oblivion.

Just as I was about to tip over the edge, he pulled the toy out and left me there. Heaving breath, body wrenching itself inside out, and my mind splintered.

"NO!!" I bumped and wiggled, scooted and flexed, but nothing would give me back the friction that would send me over the edge.

His laugh filled the room. "Yes, Snow. You see, it seems you need some education on what real men are. Not the boys you can boss around or walk all over. But a man who does what he promises." He danced his fingertips over my ass, pinching and twisting as he went.

I tried to get away, but the damn straps didn't have any leeway. Not a single hint of stretch to help me avoid him.

He spanked me hard. "Stop moving."

My body immediately stilled under the bark of his command.

He groaned. "Fuck, Snow. You listen so fucking well." He skimmed his hand down my flank. "And damn, the colors you turn." He moaned deep in his chest.

Before I could process what was happening, I felt him slide his cheek over my ass. "Breezy, no skin."

"I have to, Snow. Fuck, I have to. I'm so fucking sorry, but I have to touch you." No longer did he sound like my regular calm and collected Beck Maddox. Now he sounded like he was drugged.

"Beck, stop." I struggled to get free. "Stop, Beck. Please fucking stop. No!" I fought against the straps that had been a comfortable cage just moments ago. Now they were steel bars keeping me where I didn't want to be.

"Fuck, fuck, fuck, fuck." He dragged his tongue up through my pussy, the sound of his groan thrumming through me.

"Red, Beck. Red!"

To the side, a door burst open, the sound of wood splintering before something heavy smashed against the wall.

"BECK! Stop touching her. She said for you to stop." Rome's voice thundered into the room. "It's bad enough I had to share her, now you're going to rape her when she changed her mind?"

My eyes widened as Rome crashed into the other man. Since Beck was still crouched between my spread legs, I got tumbled to the side as well, and the fingers on my right hand got smashed between the bench and cement floor.

My scream filled the air as I watched Squirrel rush into the room. "Squirrel, honey, get the Swede and his guys. Get them. We can't let them leave."

It took him a minute of squeezing his eyes closed and pinching his nose shut, but he finally nodded and raced for the far side of the room. From the sound, he ripped the door off its hinges and took out all three watchers with some kind of tranq gun.

Beck and Rome were still fighting each other in the corner of the room. Nothing but grunts and groans and the sounds of flesh hitting flesh.

Squirrel came back in, stepping over the fallen bench. He looked down at me, horror and anguish on his face. He lowered his hand from his face. "Snow, baby."

"Get me up, Squirrel. Please get me up. We have to get them out of here." He reached out, grabbing my arm and petted me a little.

"No! Don't touch my skin." Once again, I tried to skid back away from his touch. Away from making whatever this was any harder for any of us.

But as soon as he touched me, his eyes darkened. "Pix." He lifted me up, bench and all, and brought me face-to-face with him. "Fuck, sunshine. You smell so good."

"Get your hands off her, Squirrel. I'll beat you to death," Rome shouted.

"I'll help him. She's mine!" Beck yelled.

"Hotsy, baby, let me go, please. Let me go and I'll make it so good for you. Only you. You're the one I choose." Holy fuck, what was I saying? I shook my head, it didn't matter as long as he got me free.

He got me free of the harness before he hit the straps for the table, his eyes fierce as his chest worked hard under his shuddering breaths. "Fuck yeah. You hear that, assholes, she chooses me." He steadied me before I could fall over, drawing me into his bigger frame.

With his shirt on, only parts of his skin touched mine. Enough that I could push through the feeling of him pulling me closer, drawing me into him so that nothing else mattered. But I was able to step away, give him a smile. "Thanks, Hotsy."

Then I turned and dashed from the room, pulling what remained of the door shut behind me, and locked it from the outside.

411

Chapter 39

Rome

The moment the door slammed shut, I felt the drain of her absence. I quickly pulled the punch angled down at Beck's face. He was stretched out under me, his hands and arms up guarding his head. I leaned back, my still bruised body aching more than it had while forcing myself to watch Beck touch my woman.

"What the fuck?" Beck asked as he lowered his arms. "What the fuck just happened?"

"You assaulted Pix, you asshole. I'm going to rip your limbs off and then beat you to death with them." Squirrel shoved me to the side like I had no more substance than a dead leaf in the breeze.

Crashing into the wall and the small section of cupboards, I struggled to get my feet stable under me. I knew Beck would never have done what he did had he been in his right mind.

Hell, none of us would have. But I also knew, firsthand, what it felt like to be gripped under the spell Dewdrop wove over us. Sure, she didn't know that she did, but here we were, anyway.

"Get up here, you prick. You bastard. She begged you to let her go. To stop touching her and you didn't. You licked her pussy after she told you to stop." Squirrel pulled his fist back and let it fly into Beck's face over and over and over.

I might have gotten to my feet a little slower, enjoying the way Squirrel beat the shit out of Beck, but I eventually stepped in. I want the points for stepping in between them.

"Squirrel, look at him. He's got it as bad, if not worse, than us. Let him up. Let him go." I grabbed one of Squirrel's arms and physically held back his next attack on our brother.

Squirrel shook his head like a dog coming out of water. He let Beck's shirt drop from his fist as he turned away, then threw the spanking bench through the window as he screamed.

"What the fuck is happening to us?" His arms fell to his sides, his head bent, shoulders drooping. "Why can't we protect one small woman from ourselves?" He turned back to me, and I felt gutted by the look in his eyes.

We were protectors, by nature, by training, by blood. We prided ourselves on it and our ability to do it well. We were failing over and over again with this woman. And I had a feeling she was the one for whom we most needed to get it right.

Beck groaned as he rolled to his side. "I swear, I wasn't going to touch her. We negotiated and made plans. I even put the fucking gloves on so I wouldn't accidentally touch her skin with mine. It should have worked." He got to his feet, swayed a little as he held his head in both hands. "Fuck, Squirrel. You jarred my brain loose."

"Good. You sick fuck. I can still hear her begging you to stop touching her. Be glad you're not dead right now." Squirrel spun and put his fist through the wall.

Beck straightened like someone shoved a steel spike up his ass. "She begged me to stop."

The horror in his face and voice soothed the rest of the heat in my body and soul. None of us were abusers. Sure, we liked to cause pain within certain parameters, but not out and out assault. We didn't do it for shits, giggles, or orgasms. And we mostly killed anyone who did it to any woman in our vicinity.

Beck spun a small circle. "Where is she? Where is she? I have to apologize. I have to tell her I'm sorry. So fucking sorry." His eyes were wild as he lifted his gaze back to mine. "I have to tell her. Have to make her understand."

Sighing, I reached out and patted his shoulder. "We all do. And we need some fucking answers. We'll find her. You'll get to explain."

"With all of us there, you bastard. All of us will witness it." Squirrel shoved his finger in Beck's bruised face. "And you'll stand still if she wants to get her pound of flesh from your body."

Beck nodded immediately. "Of course. She can chain me to the cross if she wants."

My brows winged up at his admission. Beck wasn't one to dabble on the submissive side of any pairing. But he voluntarily offered up strapping himself down to make amends?

"Squirrel." I waited for our biggest brother to turn to me.

He kept glaring at Beck.

"Squirrel, look at me."

He finally turned, anger still riding his features. "What did he just say to us?"

Squirrel shook his head.

"Beck, say it again."

Beck repeated his words slowly. We both waited for Squirrel to finally let them trickle through his awareness. When Squirrel finally heard them, he seemed to deflate like an old balloon. "Good." He wiped a hand over his mouth. "Good. That's better. That's the Beck I know."

"I swear to both of you, I didn't plan for whatever just fucking happened in here. Neither of us even thought it was possible. After the skin test with Happy, we thought we were safe."

Squirrel and I both turned to face him slowly.

I licked my lips. "Skin test with Happy?" I felt the rage building inside my chest again.

Beck nodded, backed up, his hands outstretched.

"Yeah, the skin test," Dewdrop's voice rang over the intercom system. "We didn't want a repeat of what happened with you two idiots, so we did a skin test. Touching Happy for a couple minutes triggered both of us, so we decided as a group to use Beck since he'd never touched me before. Even in passing. At least not skin to skin. So crawl out of his ass about it."

I breathed through the anger, the fury, the sorrow. Everyone was touching her, trying to claim her, and she was fucking mine. MINE!

"Did you agree to what happened in here before you told him to stop?" I kept my gaze on Beck, holding my breath to keep from launching myself at him.

"Yes." I swear I could hear Neva rolling her eyes through the intercom. "Now, truss up the turkeys, and get your asses out of there. I have a hypothesis about why this didn't work." The line went dead again.

Beck blew out a breath. "Oh thank fuck. I wasn't looking forward to dying today." He turned on his heel and made his way to the watcher's room. Within moments, he was back out with one of the guys over his shoulder in a fireman's carry.

Making my way into the smaller room, I shoved the spanking bench off the other two. I grabbed Jorgenssen's collar and hauled him up over my shoulder. Almost stumbling over the arm of the last guy, I finally made my way out into the main room and followed Beck out through the hallway.

"Get the last one, Squirrel. And hurry. We need to get back to Snow."

Striding through the halls back to the smaller area we could use for holding cells, I tried to clear my mind. Obviously, something was very wrong. With us individually, and as a team. Something was also wrong with Dewdrop. Whenever we interacted, someone went over the line.

If what Schnauzer said was true and he hadn't touched her skin except for the super short kiss he pressed to her forehead, then whatever was inside us didn't actually require skin-to-skin contact to initiate. We just had to be around each other.

Was that a thing? Could just being in the same room with her activate whatever they did to us? Gods, I prayed not. There was no way to avoid her for the rest of my life. I didn't want to avoid her, didn't want to lose her.

Adjusting the weight of the Swede on my shoulder, I tried to reason through it. Even before I knew her, before I touched her or talked to her, I saw her. And I'd been intrigued. Interested.

Granted, that interest skyrocketed to exponential heights in a very short time. But when I thought of never seeing her or getting to talk to her again, part of me felt lost. Broken. Dead. Was it just a function of what someone programmed me to feel, or was it her and wanting to know her as a person without the influence?

Turning the last corner, I tossed Jorgenssen down on the cot next to the other guy. I was out of time to ponder it all. We needed real answers, not some kind of whimsical trip down fantasy lane. Bypassing Squirrel with the last bad guy in the hallway, I aimed for Ops.

I came to a halt and blinked at what I saw. Neva was decked out in a hazmat suit with rebreather equipment. Head to toe, she was covered and obscured from view.

"Uh…did we have an alien invasion I wasn't made aware of?"

She rolled her eyes and stabbed a gloved finger at the other side of the table from where she sat. "No. But you're all sitting over there."

By the time the rest of the guys came in, we were all smashed on the far side of the table. I, for one, wasn't really interested in being that close to my brothers. Especially when they kept breathing all over me.

"Now that you're all here, I'll tell you my idea as a group."

"I was doing important stuff, Snow. Some of us were trying to keep you safe, remember?"

Beck growled low under his breath. "Shut the fuck up, Iggy. It was an accident."

Iggy's brow furrowed as he looked at the guy practically in his lap. "What was an accident?"

"Not important right now. What is important is that I think I have an idea about how they're getting you triggered by me." Neva's voice was a little robotic through the suit, but she didn't let that stop her.

I waved for her to go on. "And…what is it?"

"I think whoever screwed with you used my chemical makeup to be your triggers. We're talking viral payloads, biohacking pheromones, gene editing. Heavy, deep sciencey shit. Take Charming. He was around me longest, touched my skin, held me against his body. The longer he did, or more often he did, the worse the symptoms became. Same with Hotsy." She pointed at both of us.

We all nodded. She wasn't wrong, and having some kind of idea as to why was making me settle down at least a little bit. "Go on."

She nodded. "We did the skin test with Happy. Got positive results. We moved to Beck. Except for the forehead kiss, we haven't had any physical contact. At least not skin-to-skin."

"Then why the fuck did he lick your pussy after he promised not to? After you told him to stop touching you?" Squirrel demanded.

Happy launched himself over the group and caught Beck in a chokehold. "You did what to her?"

"Happy, stop! He didn't know. None of us did. Hell, we still don't. This is just best guesses right now." She slammed her hands down on the table. "LET HIM GO!"

Happy just gave her a psycho's smile. "He knows the rules. Did he even apologize?"

Neva's mouth opened and closed, but no sound emerged.

Happy shook his head, then tightened his grip on Beck's neck.

Neva sighed and pulled a tranq gun from the seat and slapped it down on the table. "Let him go, Happy. He didn't know what was happening."

Happy shook his head again. "He'll apologize first. He'll apolog—"

"I'm SORRY!" Beck beat at Happy's arms, trying to dislodge the other man's grip, but the tortured sorrow in his gaze was all for Snow. "I'm so fucking sorry, Snow. It will never happen again. I'll hang your billboard and do anything else to show you're right. I'm sorry." The last words came out as a whisper. Although I wasn't sure if it was due to Happy's grip or the emotion clogging Beck's voice.

"I won't tell you again, Happy. Let him go." Dewdrop picked up the dart gun and aimed it at our medic. "You're forgiven, Beck. No harm, no foul. No worries." Tears glimmered in her eyes. "You would have won the bet, so that's something, huh?"

Beck snorted, the sound wet, but he managed to nod around Happy's arm. "I won't hold you to it. If that happened to me, then it happened to you. You told us you feel it, too. Not quite the same bu—"

"Excuse the fuck out of me." I held up a hand. "What did you just say?"

Dewdrop cast her gaze to mine, and I saw the guilt riding her pretty face. "I feel a similar pull to you that you feel to me. Not the same, like Breezy said, but enough that I can identify it."

"To me, too, right, Snow? To me, too?" Squirrel pleaded.

418

Her features softened. "Yes, honey, to you, too. Even to Happy, although right now I want to put him down like a lame dog."

Happy finally let Beck go after he whispered something in the other man's ear. Happy just nodded and smiled. "All good in my hood, sweetcheeks." He blew her a kiss.

Squirrel snarled low under his breath.

"That's why you're in the hazmat suit," I said, trying to get us all back on track.

Dewdrop nodded. "If Beck got activated with nothing but my pheromones leaking into the air after a single forehead kiss, then we need to be thinking beyond only skin-to-skin transmission. It has to be chemically based, some kind of genetic manipulation they did to you that triggers when my chemical markers are around for you to encounter."

She let the knowledge just sit in the air like a bomb. After a long moment of silence, she nodded. "I'm thinking, at the very least, we're looking at oxytocin, dopamine, testosterone, and cortisol for chemicals. We're also going to be looking at amygdala functioning, endocrine system, amounts of those chemicals in cerebrospinal fluid and blood." She blew out a breath, her hair dancing around in the cage of her helmet. "Something is wrong. With all of us. And someone did it to us intentionally."

"The Sisterhood of the Rising Dawn," I said softly.

She turned to look at me, pained acceptance in her pretty emerald eyes. "I'm guessing, yeah. If my mother is really the leader of that group, then it would make the most sense. At least in terms of using me as the activator. I have no idea why you guys were chosen."

"Why do you just assume it's your mom and that she would do something like this to you?" Dopey asked softly.

Neva's laugh was hard, brittle. "The first lesson my mom ever taught me was not to trust anyone. If there's a mark in the room and you can't identify him or her, it's you."

Dopey let out a low whistle.

Dewdrop nodded. "Yeah, great childhood."

"But you still want to avenge her?" Beck waved a hand. "Or at least you did when you thought someone murdered her."

Dewdrop nodded again. "She was hard, but she was my mom. Better than her parents, better than any of her relatives." She shivered slightly.

"What about your dad?" I asked.

She shook her head. "I don't know who he is. Mom never talked about him. Only ever called him the Sperm Donor when I badgered her enough to break her down."

"And she was all you had left," I added.

Neva's smile broke my heart. "She was. Or at least, I thought so for a lot of years. But turns out good ol' mom still had to teach me a lesson on trusting people, I guess. I'll make sure I learn it this time. I'm just sorry you guys are caught in the crossfire."

"If it wasn't us, it probably would have been someone else, pix. At least we want to help you," Squirrel offered.

She smiled, dipped her chin. "Yeah, that's true." She straightened her spine. "I'll try to be fast about coming up with the science and cures. Get out of your hair, and systems, as quickly as possible." The smile she blessed us with made mannequins look lively.

"In addition to the testing, we also still have to help you get a cure for Jorgenssen's daughter. Not to mention the people who sent you the gold box poisons. Or the ones who threatened to blow up your home," Iggy said.

Neva seemed to wilt right in front of me. "Yeah. Lots of fun over the next couple of weeks." She winced. "I'm really sorry, guys. I think I can handle all of it on my own, other than getting your samples. You guys don't need to worry about me. You have lives to live, businesses to run. I'll be fine." She tried for a bright smile. A reassuring smile. But it didn't land. Not for me anyway. I saw through her mask.

"Yeah, that shit wouldn't have worked before, it sure as shit isn't going to work now, Snow. You're still my girl. I'm still protecting you," Squirrel said with a snort. "And you can't run me off anymore." He gave her a huge, predatory smile.

"Me either. Because you're mine," I said, elbowing Squirrel in the chest.

He snorted again, shoving me to the side. "Please, Charming. Get in line. She claimed me in the room. She's mine. She said her piece, learn to live with the disappointment."

420

"Well, I still don't want to kiss or cuddle you, but I won't say no to helping you either," Dopey added. "If you've got baddies you need to get dead, then I'll help."

Tears shimmered in her eyes again. "Aww, Dopey. You're so sweet."

He made a disgusted face and backed away from the table. "Don't get it twisted, sister. I'm doing this to kill shit. Not make you all gooey." He stabbed a finger in her direction. "I like killing shit."

We all nodded. He really did.

Dewdrop waved that away. "Oh please, Dopey. You know you love me."

He snorted. "Yeah. Love to hate you. You keep those activator fingers and chemicals to yourself. I'm not getting close to you without a full hazmat from here on out."

"Just a little hug? Please, Dopey. Please, make my life complete and give me just a little squinch." She thrust her arms wide and started around the end of the table. "Just a tiny, little baby one. I'll make it really good for you."

He jumped up from his chair, darted over the top of the table, and landed on the far end. "No, you witch. Stay there. Boys, get your girl." He waved at all of us. "Go. Go get her before she gets herself hurt."

Squirrel, Beck, and I all scooted our chairs back to give her a clear path.

"No, you traitors!" Dopey pounced up onto the table again. "I hate you all. Every single one of you."

Dewdrop darted around to his end of the table, trying to climb up on top of it.

He caught her with a gentle foot to the top of her helmet, laughter rising from him. "Stop it, crazy woman. I don't love you. I barely tolerate you. Now keep your creepy fingers to yourself."

She grabbed his foot, made yummy grumble noises when she brought his ankle to her masked face. "Just for that, I'm going to lick you some time. Make you want me."

This time, his kick wasn't so gentle. Thankfully for him, she landed in a chair that slammed back into the wall.

"Don't ever say that again," he glared at her. "I'll cut your tongue out."

We all stood up and snarled at him.

His shoulders slumped. "Damn it."

Neva cackled like the witch he kept calling her. "Oh, please, Dopey. Get over it. I'm not actually going to lick you. I don't want whatever diseases you're carrying." She crossed her arms, lifted her nose.

Dopey turned back to her, a sly smile on his face. "What are your thoughts on being shared, little flower? Or are you going to torture them all and only pick one?"

Her mouth dropped open as she looked at all of us over his shoulder. Her throat worked, but no sound came out.

My brows winged up. That wasn't a scenario I thought of entertaining.

But it might just be what saved my brothers and me.

About the Author

Cadyn James writes the kind of stories that sink their teeth into you and don't let go. Blending dark romantic suspense, psychological warfare, and dangerously addictive tension, she crafts characters who don't just battle each other—they break, reshape, and consume one another.

With a background in trauma therapy and the BDSM community, Cadyn brings raw authenticity to the power dynamics and emotional depth in her books. Her stories push boundaries, toe the line between obsession and devotion, and prove that love is never simple—especially when survival is at stake.

When she's not writing, you'll find her researching poisons, designing her own book covers, or deep-diving into the science of attraction and manipulation—all in the name of storytelling, of course.

www.ingramcontent.com/pod-product-compliance
Lightning Source LLC
Chambersburg PA
CBHW072336020726